THE WIZARD'S BANE

THE WIZARD'S BANE
BANE

BITTERGATE: DRAGON REVOLUTION BOOK TWO

Michael J. Allen

Delirious Scribbles Ink

BOOKS BY MICHAEL J ALLEN

Blood Phoenix:
1. Ashes of Raging Water
2. Ruled by Tainted Blood
3. Vengeful are the Drowned
4. Rise of the Exiled Lady
5. Razing the Last Bastion

Scion (Original):
1. Scion of Conquered Earth
2. Stolen Lives
3. Hijacked
4. Unchained

Bittergate:
1. Murder in Wizard's Wood
2. The Wizard's Bane
3. Forge of War
4. Scythe of Illusions

Guns of Underhill:
1. Fey West

Dumpstermancer:
1. Discarded
2. Duplicity

Delirious Scribbles:
(Short Stories)

- Wyrm's Warning
- Scraping Bottom
- Criminal Justice
- Dreams of Treasure
- Desperate
- The Bottom Line

COMING SOON:

Binarai Online:
1. Storm Refuge
2. Rogue Planet
3. Power Break

Wayman Chronicles:
1. Crossways

Guns of Underhill:
2. Mettle Kingdom

Dumpstermancer:
3. Decoy

Scion Rising (Remaster)

COPYRIGHT

This is a work of fiction. Names, characters, places, and incidents are a product of the author's imagination or are used fictitiously. Locales and public names are sometimes used for atmospheric purposes. Any resemblance to actual people—living, dead or in between, businesses, companies, events, institutions, or locales is completely coincidental.

Delirious Scribbles Ink, Inc.
4519 Woodruff Road
Suite 4, #108
Columbus, Georgia 31904
www.deliriousscribblesink.com

Interior Layout ©2024 Delirious Scribbles Ink
Author Photo by Jim Cawthorne, Camera 1
Cover Design ©2024 Delirious Scribbles Ink
Cover Image by ©2024 Andrea Fodor

ISBN 978-1-944357-27-6 (hc 1st ed)
ISBN 978-1-944357-50-4 (hc 2nd ed)
ISBN 978-1-944357-26-9 (intl. tr. pbk. 1st ed)
ISBN 978-1-944357-49-8 (intl. tr. pbk. 2nd ed)
ISBN 978-1-944357-28-3 (ebook)
ISBN 978-1-944357–83-2 (large print)

Printed in the United States of America
10 9 8 7 6 5 4 3 2 1
The Wizard's Bane / Michael J. Allen. — 2nd ed.

My sincerest thanks to Mercedes and Larry for inspiration and encouragement, to Mercedes and Andre for giving Drake bad ideas, and always for B, B & J.

DELIRIOUS SCRIBBLES READERS GROUP

Like free stories?

How about curated deals for Science Fiction and Fantasy books?

Get your first benefit—a FREE story sent right to you—by becoming a member of the Delirious Scribbles Readers Group.

Begin your journey, just scan this image with your phone camera!

CONTENT ADVISORY

In order to provide my readers the best possible experience as well as be responsive to reader requests, I've created a reader-curated content advisory on my website. If you are sensitive to certain kinds of fictional representations, please check this book's listings before reading.

I hope you enjoy this story…

— MICHAEL J ALLEN

To visit the advisory, just scan this image with your phone camera.

PROLOGUE

Stillbirth

A chestnut centaur mare lay on her side beside a tranquil pond anything but at peace. Her breath wheezed in fits and starts. Her eyes squeezed tight with pain despite a healing aura clinging to her like a sheen of sweat.

Two other centaur, both dressed in silver robes declaring them Shaman of the Path, bent over the laboring woman. On one side the bay roan's hands stroked the aura, swelling it where her fingertips brushed.

"You're almost done, Feilahdi U'Noa. Another push or two and it's all over," Midall E'Cru soothed.

Feilahdi U'Noa nodded behind clenched teeth, bore down and pushed.

Midall E'Cru caught the new foal. She blinked away the itch in her eyes.

"How is she?" Feilahdi U'Noa asked. "Why isn't she crying?"

"Patience," the other shaman wiped Feilahdi U'Noa's brow.

Midall E'Cru closed her eyes. Magic spread into the newborn foal, searching her for injury. She felt it circuit through the frail chestnut body. She met the searching gaze of the other shaman with a slight shake of her head.

Feilahdi U'Noa caught the gesture and wailed. "No!"

The other shaman pushed her down gently. "Midall E'Cru is very talented. She will do what she can."

Midall E'Cru sniffed. "There is nothing I can do. She is stillborn."

"But I felt her move," Feilahdi U'Noa cried.

A horn sounded in the distance. Both shaman ignored it at first, but its insistent fanfare drew their eyes to the Mythela'Raemyn. Atop the ziggurat-style pyramid, a large centaur in moon-silver armor blew the horn once more. He glowed a brilliant silver that made the sunlit valley seem otherwise in twilight.

A soft rustle drew Midall E'Cru's attention back around. Silver light glistened on the foal's coat. She shifted, trying to rise only to fall again. Overlarge silver eyes blinked against the new light.

"Thank the Creator," Feilahdi U'Noa sobbed.

Midall E'Cru peered into the newborn filly's too alert eyes.

Terror filled the eyes, pursued by pain then replaced by sorrow. The filly keened, a moan of anguish foreign to a newborn foal. She folded around herself on the ground, eyes closing.

1

DIA DE LO MUERTO MAGO

A cream-colored lounge chair hovered atop an open grave under a clear, blue late autumn sky. The scent of fresh cut marigolds floated in a soft breeze. A voluptuous woman lay beneath the warm rays, bronze skin shining and honey-brown hair fanned out like a halo. Her tiny white bikini hid as little flesh as possible. She'd have forgone the top, but going topless had produced disastrous distraction to her new apprentice.

Mauve raised her head, glancing around for the boy.

Around her the cemetery buzzed with activity, families cleaning graves, preparing altars and arranging offerings for the evening's festivities. Happy chatter and sung prayers overlaid the graveyard's usual hush. Despite the bustle, none of it encroached on her sunbathing island. Around them, frowning spirits stared forlorn at their activities.

A scowling bandito reached spectral hands toward a young woman.

"No." Mauve's sultry voice cracked like a whip. Every dead head shot up her direction, but no living soul seemed to hear. "Hands off the living."

The bandito narrowed his eyes and snatched a long knife from its belt.

"Don't sass me, Juan." She raised a warning finger his direction and scanned the crowd. "Kane?! Where is that boy?"

An adolescent boy slunk out of the crowd. Tiny for twelve and rail thin, black swathed his pale skin from his boots to a padre's hat he'd lifted from a preacher's tomb. He didn't look at her directly, though she could tell by the pinking of his cheeks when he snuck a glance her direction.

Stuffed cheeks garbled his words. "Yes, Mistress?"

"You're supposed to be minding the dead, not stealing candied pumpkin from the altars," Mauve said.

"I'm hungry," he said to her feet. "It's not like the dead can eat it."

"They eat its spirit...forget it. Stop stealing candy and deal with Juan."

Kane glanced toward the bandito. "Again?"

Juan sneered at him. An exaggerated sigh shifted Kane's slumped shoulders. He stomped toward the bandito, flexing his fingers. Juan retreated.

"Stand right there," Kane whined. "I'm not chasing you again."

Juan darted for cover.

"Stop," a whisper of command invaded his whine. "Damn it, Juan, *stop.*"

The specter froze.

Kane pointed to his shirt. Grimacing skulls and tormented spectral faces covered his black t-shirt. "In."

"No," Juan said.

Kane stomped across the intervening distance. Juan slashed his knife across Kane's face. The blow dislodged his black, ring spectacles and left a white line on already white skin. He thrust both hands into the specter, hooking fingers into claws. "*In!*"

Juan screamed as Kane balled up his spectral body and shoved into the shirt. His cries joined other spirits crying out for release in the moment when Juan's spirit rippled the imprisonment spell's barrier plane.

Kane cradled his cheek and mumbled his way through a dozen curses. He looked up to see a little girl gaping at him. "Mind your own—"

"Kane," Mauve snapped.

Kane shot her a dirty look, forced a smile onto his face and dug a piece candied pumpkin out of his pocket. He offered it to the little girl. Her expression grew more shocked. He dusted it off and offered it again. "Here?"

"Mama!"

Kane watched her flee to a position behind her mother's skirts.

Mauve rose, drawing his quickly retreating gaze. She swept hands down her body, replacing the white bikini with a curve-hugging silk dress. "It's safe to look now, darling."

Kane glanced up at her. Wide eyes shot back to the ground. "M-mistress, your...um, I can see...um..."

"Pay attention to your spell. You've got two about to escape your shoulder."

She shook her head, using his distraction to conjure underwear beneath her attire. *How long must I coddle this awkwardness?*

A girl screamed, then another. More screams rent the air, and people fled toward them. Mauve craned to see what sent them into flight, expecting a ghoul or some other dead malcontent causing trouble to spite those celebrating life around it. Several dozen mounted figures galloped toward them.

"This isn't the old west, boys," Mauve said. "If you're going to come around scaring people and stealing candy at least act like you live in this century."

"Mistress?"

The concern in his voice felt sharper than normal. She looked again, noticing the double image of glamour hiding a band of heavily armed centaur. Movement flashed in her peripheral vision. A faun landed a gigantic leap just behind her. Another landed on the other side followed by two other before her. The four—half bare-chested teenage girl and half doe—circled her in a flouncing skip. Each had hair of shoulder-length curls matching the soft coat that clothed their lower half. Softest flax colored two fauns' hair. The third shone honey-brown to match Mauve's own. Brindled hair covered the fourth's head and legs—the color of sand with clumps of honey brown. Reed pipes bounced between breasts too-ample for their short, lithe frames.

The first curtseyed, introducing herself in a high alto. "Jiji, Sorceress."

A girlish bosom-jiggling laugh accompanied the second's curtsey. "Kiki."

Kane's red face shot to the ground.

Mauve slapped him upside his head, sending his hat flying. "Eyes up."

"But they're *naked*," Kane said.

Centaurs fanned out around them.

"I don't care if they're writhing around in an orgy, never look away from danger," Mauve said.

"But—"

The third cupped her bosom toward Kane, addressing him in a husky contralto. "Do you think Lili's breasts are dangerous little man?"

Kane responded with incoherent stammers.

The last faun curtseyed, her voice a sweet soprano. "Mimi, Lady Mauve."

"Quiet," the black mare said. "Mauve Cortez, I, Glent Se'Lailos, second elder of Wizard's Bane place you both under arrest for crimes against the Fey. Surrender or face summary execution."

Mauve laughed. "You're not High Tribe, even then I don't answer to Fey."

"Kill them," Glent Se'Lailos said.

The fauns' skip turned into a complicated dance, each raising their reed pipes. Grasses and flowers sprung up in a ring they wore into the grave dirt, the path laced with a braid of auras.

Mauve shoved Kane behind her, though she couldn't truly protect him from all angles. "Stay down and out of the way, Kane."

Despite superior numbers, the centaur held fire while the four fauns wove around her. Jedediah might've tried to reason with them, but Mauve lived by the simple creed of doing unto others before they get a chance to do unto you. She reached out to the dead filled cemetery and felt her reach blocked at the dancing circle. She altered her reach, but the thoughts commanding her power waded through a rising fog.

Mauve cursed. "Cover your ears, boy."

"I've heard that kind of language before," Kane said.

"Block out the music, child."

The four faun stopped, extending hands as if commanding them to stay. A different colored magic pulsed in each upraised palms. Mauve's thoughts took a split second to catch up before four energy bolts streaked toward them.

Mauve drove Kane to the ground just ahead of the coursing magic. The scent of ozone filled the air, accompanied by freshly turned soil, new rain and singed hair. Mauve pushed herself up, brushing dirt from her gown.

"You girls are talented," Mauve said, "but you know what all of those elements share in common? Death."

She threw her hands forward, a fan of light-sucking violet power knocking two fauns from their feet. She reached downward before they could recover and sent her will into the grave soil.

"There's a reason I have to watch this place on the Day of the Dead." Mauve lifted her hands as if dragging an enormous weight from the earth. "They've buried a lot of really bad boys here."

Skeletal hands thrust from the ground around them, sending up a shower of dirt as the fleshless undead crawled from their graves. Ghouls clawed up in their wake, wild-eyed monsters wearing the tattered remains of their former clothes and shredded flesh from their last victims caught in jagged piranha teeth. One ghoul lashed out at the honey brown faun, Jiji, hamstringing her. It brought back a bloodied claw to its mouth, licking it clean with a two-foot tongue.

The centaur opened fire.

The first volley tore through the rising skeletons, shattering skulls and splintering bone if only by sheer volume. Mauve threw a scythe of flame around the circle's interior, gutting the second volley and forcing the fauns back.

Kane rushed past a ghoul, snatching up two jagged femurs and slashed at the downed Jiji. A blast of electricity slammed into him, driving him back but not before he added another pair of jagged cuts.

"Stay down so I can protect you, boy," Mauve gestured at the ghouls.

As a man, ghouls each snatched up a fallen skeleton spine. The attached ribs vibrated, shifting together and unfolding into skeletal shields which thickened without respect to the amount of bone consumed. Bones jiggled across the ground, assembling into jagged spears and presenting themselves to the ghouls.

Mauve pirouetted on the spot, hands waving like a conductor pulling a hundred puppet strings.

A shard of stone lanced up from beneath her feet. She side-stepped, feinting forward and jogging right as two others followed the first. Lili rushed to Jiji's side, setting a rippling blue aura over the wounds already stinking of rot.

"The fauns have failed, first flank charge," Glent Se'Lailos said.

"We have not." A deep melody exited Mimi's pipes ahead of rumbling earth.

Lightning slashed out from Kiki's hands, blackening rib-bone shields and filling the air with static.

Arrows lead the charge, followed close by a dozen centaurs with lances tipped with serrated blades. The ghouls positioned spear butts on the ground, receiving the charge like pikeman. Against normal horseman, it would've proven deadly, but centaur differed from men atop simple steeds. They jogged to the side of the spears, cutting them in angles, leaping their tips and making a path for their brothers. Three still fell to the spears, writhing and screaming as the ghouls discarded defense to fall upon them with eternal hunger.

Kane stood at Mauve's back, hands outstretched. His voice cracked halfway through his shout. "Kill them for your freedom."

The collective, imprisoned dead flooded out of his shirt in a mad horde. In moments a wedge of centaur disappeared under the wave of ravening spirits.

"Jiji!" Kiki shrieked.

Mauve ripped the souls from dying centaur and forced them

back into their former bodies regardless of their condition. Her centaur soldiers waded into their former comrades with twice their earlier ferocity.

Jiji wobbled to her feet beside Kane. "Here, sister."

Kane stared, an odd expression on his face.

Kiki fought her way forward, throwing a wave of ice shards at Kane. "Get away from her, monster boy."

Mauve appeared over the boy in a moment, two shield bearing ghouls rushing to protect their flank.

Jiji extended her arms toward Kiki. "I thought you were hurt."

"No, you got...how are you're standing," Kiki said.

Jiji's smile grew piranha teeth. Jiji's entire body seemed to slither in a thousand directions at once. Her hands thrust out, gouging a chunk of flesh from Kiki's gut and shoving it into her mouth. Mimi and Lili appeared at her side, blasting the ghoul backward with stone and wind.

Mauve lent Kane heat stolen from an animated centaur, tapping the last lingering life as she made it her slave.

Despite her seizure of the centaur dead, her defense crumbled under their onslaught. She taxed her energies to their limits. The number of dead within the fauns' warded circle dwindled. Without the boy to protect she might have a chance, but as long as he remained, she suffered a disadvantage.

Kane stirred as the heat finally won out over the ice spell. Mauve grabbed the boy and shoved him into the arms of her newest convert. "Take him to Jedediah. Warn Jed, boy, tell him what's happened."

"But Mistress—"

"Do as you're told." She shoved all the energy she could into the centaur corpse. "You'll have to sustain him when he starts to crumble. You can do it."

"M-mistress you're—"

"Sexy as hell and just as mad, now get going."

Mauve slapped the centaur's rump, feeling stupid for unnecessarily encouraging it to bolt. Kane disappeared through the press, his mount's face, buying enough confusion for him to win clear.

Mauve turned back to the centaur. She scooped up a pair of bones, pushing energy into them to reshape them into short, sharp blades.

She twirled her bone swords. "Okay, mules, Mama's ready to mamba..."

Ghouls and dead centaur flourished their weapons.

The centaur swarmed her.

2

———

SEARCHING

Jordan drove up the tree-lined, gravel drive to the farm. The wrecked farmhouse drew her eyes through sunlit gaps. Her eyes itched, and her gut writhed. Lanea had been murdered the last time she'd been there. Her hand went reflexively to the long gone welt where the very same sniper had shot her in the forehead. She'd woken from that ordeal to find Jedediah pacing and gibbering, his eyes wild and terrifying.

He'd paused only long enough to verify her wellbeing before telling her he needed to go back to Sanctuary Hole to check something.

He said not to worry, that he'd be back. I haven't seen hide nor hair of him for two months since.

She pulled the car to a stop in the circular drive. The old antebellum farmhouse was a wreck. Cars and trucks previously encased in a miniaturization spell stuck out of the rubble at odd angles. Clothes covered the surrounding area—exploded from the extra-dimensional closet spell she still hadn't learned.

Need it too with the tiny closet I've got back at Weems.

A dark shaped rushed her the moment she climbed out of the car. She reached into her core, summoning the deep rumble of an earth tremor and pushing the magic against her skin as armor.

13

She stretched for her staff, bringing to mind the rough texture of the heavy piece of petrified wood. She envisioned the two runes formed slowly by her practice under Mama Yamai. The first cut a sigil across the wood with a red like cooling magma. Gold edged the second, glassy as obsidian.

It leapt from earth to her hands as she braced for the attack.

It took her a moment to recognize the dirty brown wolf growling at her as Nip. The mudpuppy had grown considerably during Jedediah's trial, almost half the size of his mother Sarah who brought up the rear with her hackles raised and teeth bared.

"Guys, it's me, Jordan."

Nip's ears twitched forward, and his tail wagged. Sarah's stance eased, but she remained on guard. Nip trotted up to Jordan.

"Hey, boy. I've missed you." She ruffled his ears, but her eyes stayed on Sarah. Jordan set her staff on the ground. "It's okay, Sarah. You know me."

Sarah let Jordan approach and stroke her coat. She licked Jordan's face once, but only eased marginally. Jordan scanned the area with Sarah, her palms itching while Nip took the opportunity to attack her face with kisses.

The creek of a greenhouse door drew all eyes. A tiny ball of adorable mud wobbled out followed by a few littermates. Sarah growled. The pups cowered, all but one scurrying back into the greenhouse before the door could close. The first one sat down, cocked its head with ears pressed tight and whined.

Sarah's growl grew more menacing. Her hackles rose once more.

Before Jordan told Sarah that she'd never intentionally hurt one of the pups, a shadow sprang out of nowhere, pouncing on it. Nip and Sarah bolted across the intervening distance with rumbling snarls. The shadowcat gripped the animal in her teeth and gave a growl of its own.

Sarah and Nip slowed, stalking the dark Fey.

Jordan stood. "Release that pup."

The shadowcat glared at her. It dragged the pup toward the greenhouse corner. Its grip started the puppy yelping.

Jordan narrowed her eyes and summoned her staff right beneath the cat. The six-foot geyser of petrified wood sent the cat sky born and out of its protective shadows. Jordan sprinted toward it, rumble solidifying her fist.

Sarah reached it first.

Shadow and mud whirled in a tornado of blood, dirt and smoke. Nip snatched up its sibling and barreled through the greenhouse door. The cat sank its teeth into Sarah's throat. Jordan snatched up her staff and cracked it across the cat's head, ripping its teeth from Sarah in a spray of oil-like blood.

The cat landed just inside the building's shadow and growled at Jordan.

Jordan stomped toward the cat, sucking Earth's strength into her body. "I don't think so. This is Jedediah's land, and you'll leave Sarah and her pups be, or I'll carpet their den with your skin."

The cat bristled, spitting challenge as a reply.

Nip hit it from behind, exiting the other greenhouse entrance shaped like a bulldog. His charge drove the cat toward Jordan and into the sunlight. It whirled toward Nip and shadow, but petrified wood slammed into its hind quarters. The cat tumbled end over end, rolling to a stop with one back leg unnaturally bent.

"Get."

The shadowcat limped into the nearest shade and vanished.

Jordan knelt next to Sarah. The mud puppy growled at her. Nip slid his wolfish body between them, barring teeth and nosed her away from Sarah.

"Okay, okay." She raised hands in surrender. "I'm just trying to help."

Jordan crossed to the greenhouse entrance, intent to check on the brave little pup. Sarah's growl brought her up short.

What is going on out here? You know what, I've got bigger fish to fry.

Jordan turned back to the farmhouse and sighed. "Where do I even start?"

She made her way around Jedediah's smashed work shed to the farm machinery kept on the property for appearance's sake. She climbed onto a beefy looking tractor and turned the key. It rumbled to life.

I'll be gorramed.

She drove the tractor to the farmhouse and backed it up next to the nearest protruding car. Foraging the ruins of Jedediah's shed turned up some heavy chains. Jordan strengthened her limbs and lugged it out to the tractor. Despite unfamiliarity with the farm vehicle, she pulled one car after another out of the house's ruin, parking them in a line on the nearest fallow field. When the chain proved too short to reach any more cars, she started dragging chunks of wall out of the way.

She stopped and dug a sports drink out of the cooler in her back seat. Jordan drank half its contents, lower it for a breath to find a cross between a Ken doll and a star-nosed mole glaring through spectacles at her.

"Can I help you?" Jordan asked.

"Got any more of that?" the old brownie asked.

She offered him the bottle.

He wrinkled his nose. "Without wizard spit in it."

Jordan chuckled, shook her head and dug another from the cooler. The brownie took it without a word of thanks. He drank deeply, stopping to wipe some from his greying facial fur.

"Is there anything else, or can I get back to work?" Jordan asked.

"Sure, sure, just one thing. What're you trying to accomplish dragging that trash around the property?"

"I'm trying to find something that will enable me to locate Jedediah."

He nodded, sipped some sports drink and nodded some more. "He wasn't in there when the dragon crushed it."

"I know that."

"Then why look in there?"

"I don't know where else to look. If I did, do you think I'd be out here sweating my ass off?"

The brownie shrugged. "Normals don't make sense on their best days."

"I'm not a normal, and you know it."

"You're just about as bad, digging through that rubble instead of checking the other properties."

"He's not at the Weems house," Jordan said. "He's not answering his cell phone, and I have no idea how to even get to Sanctuary Hole."

"Might be something in there." He inclined his head toward the farmhouse.

"You just said I was wasting my time."

It shambled off with a belch. "Maybe not. Maybe there are more working portals underneath all that ruin."

Jordan's memory flashed back to the library at Sanctuary Hole. Amidst the eclectic collections of books, curios and Madlibs, there'd been a floor to ceiling window scrolling through scenes. She'd thought it ornamental until Jedediah had stopped it and stepped through into the farmhouse den. She'd intended to dig her way into the room and find a way back to that library. It'd never occurred to her that every one of those other scenes might each be real places.

"Wait. I've given you a drink, and we share earth affinity—"

He chuckled. "If you say so."

"Are there other portals here on the farm?"

"Oh, one or two."

Her pulse surged. "Where?"

"They're around," a malicious grin curled his whiskers. "Just chilling out."

He shambled away heading in the direction of the boneyard.

"Thanks. You've been a load of help." She marched toward the tractor. *Crotchety old bastard must've gotten along like gangbusters with Jedediah. Load of useless, cryptic bullsh—*

Her eyes flitted back to the retreating brownie. Beyond, a graveyard of old appliances, toilets and wrecked cars spread out in all their redneck splendor. She'd once accused Jedediah of alphabetizing his junk. When she'd offered to take the doors off of all the refrigerators for safety sake, he'd flatly refused her.

Telling me taking them off would put people in real danger.

She followed the brownie deep into the boneyard. Small Fey of various shapes peeked at her from within toilets and washing machines. They weren't the pixies, sprites or fairies she'd seen so often. Most seemed bizarre cousins—exotic butterflies, birds or small animals crossed with the more common Fey she knew. She had no idea why they lived in cast off junk rather than forest communities like other Fey. Even the most fleeting glance reinforced by her earlier encounter told her one thing—they were terrified.

They need Jedediah back as much as I do, maybe more.

He'd left her a limitless debit card, a car and the comfort and safety of the Weems house. Mama Yamai's training during Jedediah's long incarceration had equipped her to take care of herself, even if she still had trouble with external magic. Jordan had lived the easy life, troubled only with her stomach, boredom and loneliness. After all the years in foster care wishing she was on her own, she found solitude the worst curse.

Even that had been solved in a way. Billie Jo, timid as a mouse approaching a shadowcat, appeared at the doorway a week into the school year with a truant officer in tow. Lanea had removed Jordan from the system, but Jordan never thought to ask if that meant the whole system or just the foster system.

Going to school got Billie Jo's guard dog off her case. It also gave her something to do—run on the cross-country team.

At least after a passable forgery of Jedediah's signature.

She'd had to put up with extra sessions with the school counselor thanks to Billie Jo. The woman was still freaked out by the revelation of Jedediah's magic. Her continued paranoia exposed itself by making excuses to keep Jordan under as much *normal* adult oversight as possible.

Another good reason to track down Jedediah. The counselor wants to meet with him, and I can't make excuses forever.

Jordan approached the nearest refrigerator. She raised her magic's rumble to her eyes, seeing a thick shroud of sorcery surrounding the appliance before her. Strings of power spiderwebbed out of the boneyard in all directions while thick roots sank deep into the earth beneath her.

Her gut knotted.

She'd never seen anything so intricate. It could be some sort of portal system. *Or it could be an elaborate prison holding God knows what and if I open the door I may let something I can't stop out to rampage through the city—not that there's a lot of rampaging available in this little backwater.* She chuckled. *Hardly worth an effort, let alone a full rampage.*

She steeled her will. She grasped the door handle. Icy metal sank dull teeth into her sweating palm. She inhaled and threw open the door.

The old Frigidaire gaped empty.

Jordan cursed, wiping her brow. *I'd have taken the monster over nothing.*

She turned back toward the tractor and marched away. She'd gotten her hopes up that his junk held doors that might lead her to Jedediah. She stepped around a fridge door lying bent on the ground and tried to figure out what new lie she'd tell the counselor when the weekend ended.

Jordan stopped in her tracks.

She turned back to the broken door, scanning the nearby refrigerators until she found the one and only one in the entire boneyard that didn't have its door in place. A dark wooden door stood in the back of the small appliance's depths. She approached it. New refrigerators were huge compared to this old thing. She didn't even recognize the brand—Kelvinator.

She lowered her head into its depths and smelled the heady perfume of fabric softener. She reached an arm inside. She pulled it out, feeling stupid but not entirely unjustified. As she did so, her view shifted to one side, and the wooden door vanished.

What the hell?

Jordan leaned sideways, and the door reappeared. She leaned away. It vanished. A laugh bubbled from her. *It's the Last Starfighter. You can only see it if you look dead on.*

She ducked down not sure how she'd fit through the small opening and eased her head inside. A moment later she was bent over in a linen closet, trying to scrape the taste of mint and orange juice off onto her teeth. She pushed the door open to find herself back at Weems.

"Oh my God, magic is *so* cool sometimes!"

She turned back to the towels. She couldn't see the boneyard, but Jedediah'd disappeared down this very hallway on her first full day in his care. She closed her eyes and walked into the shelves.

She collided with them, bumping her head.

She blinked. *Why didn't it work?*

She backed up, in case she was too far inside the spell. She tried again with her arms outstretched, but all she felt were fluffy towels. She searched the door frame for a mark, a stud, anything that might open the portal back to the farm.

Nothing. She cursed. *How am I going to get the car back now?*

She stepped into the closet, sure she had to be missing something. She moved every towel. She tried to shift every shelf. She ran her hands along the back wall, the side wall, nothing. Finally, she noticed a screw head sticking out of the drywall just above the door frame. She touched it.

Vertigo assailed her. She tripped backward falling under the bright afternoon sky surrounded by boneyard. She made a disgusted face and licked her hands to dislodge the horrid taste once more. She hurried to the other fridge she'd opened and bobbed her head back and forth until a small, lamp-lit garden came into view.

Finally, now I can find Jedediah.

Jordan stepped through without bothering to duck.

The air on the other side was cool but drier than Georgia in evening. Bamboo, rocks and flowers flanked the small wooden structure from which she'd emerged. A stone path wound to a wooden bridge arching over a pond.

"Jedediah?"

Movement drew her eye to a shifting wall out of some Samurai movie. An old Asian man appeared in the opening, gibbering at her in a language she didn't immediately recognize. A wife or daughter appeared, looking at her with an expression mixing excitement and confusion. She called into the house until a younger copy appeared.

"You are Magi Jordan?" the girl asked.

"Uh, my name is Jordan."

The girl bowed, and her elders followed suit. "We are honored to welcome you to your home for the first time."

"My home? How do you know me?" Jordan asked. "Where am I?"

"Yes, all the Master's children are known to us. I am Jiang Wen. This is my mother Jiang Liu and grandfather Jiang Hong Wu. We, the Master Magi's caretakers, welcome you to the People's Republic of China."

"Holy shit. Please tell me Jedediah is here."

Jiang Wen's face closed down, but it might as well have shoved spikes into Jordan. *He's not here, but there are other refrigerators to search. He's got to be somewhere.*

Drake skulked out of the woods to where Jordan had been dragging debris from the farmhouse. Glamour kept her from seeing him. He couldn't face her or Jedediah. He couldn't face how they'd treat him if they knew he'd lost Lanea's killer. Fleet Hoof had offered Drake discreet refuge after Marc O'Steele escaped him. They'd taught Drake their ways, entertained him with plays and stories, even brought him fresh game instead of cooked meat—though never Cherry Coke—in hopes of lifting his despondency.

He'd expected Jedediah to find him eventually, but in the meantime, he plotted and planned his revenge. The *Namhaid* leader had taken Lanea from him before he could kindle enough inner fire to tell her how he'd felt.

He dug into the farmhouse rubble, careful not to break anything. He'd practiced his shapeshifting to near exclusion for months but didn't trust Jedediah's precious possessions to clumsy fingers. He found the clocks first, lurking in the bent oak frame and shattered piles of leaded glass. His breath caught in his throat. None of the nineteen hand-crafted clocks moved.

He searched them one by one, their dread-invoking silence

reanimating his last meal. It slithered within his stomach. He carefully excavated each of the ornamentally carved timepieces used to store Jedediah's life.

Drake laid a clock decorated with gay colors, horses, a baseball glove and bat on the front steps. He added one carved with a horse and buggy parked before a church. Sixteen more joined the first. He set the very last clock onto the stair, its perfectly detailed sails and rigging intact despite its utter silence.

None of them ticked. None of them tocked.

Jedediah's dead. My Master's gone. I failed him, failed Lanea and now I'm all alone. Tears cut paths down uncleaned scales, blurring his view of the time pieces. He shook them away. *No. I won't believe it. Nothing can kill Jedediah, nothing. He's just not using the years he stored in his clocks. Surely he wouldn't have risked death to save his very last days. There had to have been some days beyond. There had to be. Someone must know.*

Drake didn't understand the magic which stored Jedediah's life anywhere near as well as Lanea had. Thoughts of her hurt like no wound he'd ever taken, even worse than what Muler'd done to him.

He pushed the pain away, digging through the rubble and removing Jedediah's mantle pictures one by one until he found photos of Lanea. Each one he touched felt like Dragonsteel in his chest. He couldn't get full breath no matter how much he filled his lungs.

He needed to find Marc. To find the normal, he had to master himself and his magic. The ache weakened him too much to return to practice. He set the last picture with the clocks and dug into the rubble, burrowing through wreckage in pursuit of a scent which balmed his pain. Lanea's scent—sweet and spicy like cinnamon from yesterday's baking—lingered faintly after so much time, fading much as her light had from his life. Drake shimmied through the wreckage of her door and onto her bedding without regard to the ceiling collapsed atop it by his mother's tantrum. With minor effort, aeromancy heightened his sense of smell. Drake caressed Lanea's scent from her blankets, curling up in the pleasure of her presence and settling into impossible dreams of romance with the dead half-elf.

Billie Jo smoothed out her Sunday dress. She fidgeted, adjusting her position in the otherwise comfortable seat across from an empty leather chair. Mason slouched in the chair next to her, ganglier than ever.

The young man announced in that morning's services as her new pastor entered, closed the door and took the high backed seat with a smile. "Thank you for staying after services to meet with me."

"Why can't we continue our sessions with Pastor Landry?" she said.

Pastor Fulton smiled a young man's smile, though something in his eyes felt wiser than his apparent years. "Miss Bartlett, Joseph—Pastor Landry—feels my extensive counseling experience would be of better service to you and Mason."

Mason glanced up from his fingernails. A sudden mischievous grin crossed his face as he leapt to his feet and extended a hand. "I'm Mason."

What's gotten into him?

Pastor Fulton shook the hand. "Simon Fulton, pleasure to meet you."

Mason frowned at their joined hand, releasing his grip and dropping back into the chair with a sigh.

"Sit up straight, Mason." Billie Jo forced a laugh. "Adolescent boys."

"Quite," Pastor Fulton said. "Why have you been meeting with Joseph?"

"Mason is demon possessed—maybe devil possessed—I'm not sure, but we need to get him an exorcism."

Mason rolled his eyes.

"I see. What makes you think he's possessed?" Pastor Fulton asked.

Billie Jo considered him. *Why do I have to go through this again? It was bad enough with Pastor Landry whose known me almost a decade. Why would he make me rehash it?*

"Miss Bartlett, everything you tell me is in strictest confidence."

"Mason and I were exposed to witchcraft. I was dating—well, he ended up being a warlock and a murderer."

"Jedediah was acquitted, Mom. Besides, he's a wizard, not a warlock."

"Whatever," Billie Jo forged on. "Somehow even though he's Saved, Mason ended up infected with this demon, and now he can perform witchcraft."

Pastor Fulton chuckled. "I'm not sure that's how it works."

"I don't know how it works, maybe he invited it in by eating something—"

"Maybe it was the evil tuna," Mason grumbled under his breath.

She sighed. "Point is, he needs an exorcism whether or not you believe me."

Pastor Fulton rose, rounding the desk to sit on the nearer edge. He took Billie Jo's hands in his and peered into her eyes. "Calm down. No one here thinks you're lying. I just don't think things are as simple as you suggest."

"The Bible says in Exodus, 'Thou shalt not suffer a witch to live,' and in Leviticus, it says, 'A man also or woman that hath a familiar spirit, or that is a wizard, shall surely be put to death,'" Billie Jo said.

"I can't argue with your memory of Bible verse. Shall we round up the congregation and stone young Mason here?"

"This isn't a joke, Pastor. Magic is witchcraft. Witchcraft is evil, and I want that evil out of my son asap." Billie Jo asked. "Can't you help us?"

Pastor Fulton turned to Mason. "Didn't you take Jesus into your heart?"

Mason rolled his eyes, letting out his answer in an exasperated sigh. "Yes."

"You're Saved? No question?" Pastor Fulton asked.

"None." Mason folded his arms. "I'm not possessed, and I'm *not* evil."

"Of course, you aren't." Pastor Fulton chuckled.

Her voice rose an octave. "That's it? He says he's okay, and we're done?"

Pastor Fulton returned his attention to her. His gaze pierced hers and for a moment she felt as if he weighed her soul. A shiver shot through her. She looked away. He steepled his fingers. "What makes you think your son is involved in witchcraft? Is he reading books on the subject? Wearing occult jewelry? Playing Dungeons and Dragons?"

"He can do magic," Billie Jo said.

"Card tricks?"

Card tricks? Is he serious? Billie Jo ground her teeth. "I can't show you. I won't have him using magic, certainly not in church."

"I think God's house can withstand a demonstration if it helps us protect one of his children," Pastor Fulton said.

Mason's smile flickered to life.

"No," Billie Jo said.

Pastor Fulton rose once more, rounding their seats and laying a hand on each of their necks. He closed his eyes, lips moving in prayer. Warmth spread down his hand into her akin to the warmth she felt during worship services, but also too similar to Jedediah's touch. She leaned forward out of his grip.

"I feel no dark presence in either of you," Pastor Fulton said. "I do not believe any demon or devil possess this young man. I'm happy to pray intercession with you, but I don't think an exorcism is warranted."

"I've been praying intercession since Jed-the warlock dropped us into our home, but Mason still has magic. I know he's playing with it." Billie Jo shot Mason an accusing glare. "I punish him when I catch him. We need rid of it."

Pastor Fulton lifted hands in surrender and turned to Mason. "Son, show me whatever it is that terrifies your mother."

Dread launched her to her feet. "I forbid it. I'll not let him cavort with evil."

Mason rolled his eyes and twirled a finger in the air. Papers around the room fluttered from the desk in a swirling breeze. Pastor Fulton watched them, astonishment on his face.

Billie Jo reached out to backhand Mason but stopped mid-motion—her desire to stop him at war with her objections to corporal punishment. She turned to the Pastor only to find delight entering his expression. She slapped a hand on the desk. "Enough."

The breeze died. The few floating papers fell. Mason picked up the ones on his side and placed them back on the Pastor's desk. "Sorry."

"Now do you believe me?" Billie Jo asked.

"I always believed you," Pastor Fulton said. "Now, though, I know what you meant."

"So can we have an exorcism?" Billie Jo asked.

Pastor held up both hands. "Hold on. Let's not jump to hasty conclusions."

"Hasty? My son just did *witchcraft*. I want whatever it is plaguing him out."

"It's a wondrous gift, I'll say that, but I can't rightly say its magic," Pastor Fulton said. "It could be anything, a trick, telekinesis maybe, I don't know."

Her voice rose to hysterical levels. "It's a black curse, rotting the soul of my child, and I want it out."

Pastor Fulton's expression flickered. "Now see here, *Madame*. Your son is Saved. His soul resides in Jesus's hands and is in no danger of rotting—or are you suggesting your Savior is incapable of safeguarding those that he's made promises to protect?"

Billie Jo closed her eyes, slowly falling back into her seat. She gazed at Mason, her heart wrenching at his confused expression. She set a hand on Mason's shoulder, drawing his gaze back to herself. The words which slipped her lips fell leadened to the carpet. "I love my son, but it's magic…witchcraft. The Bible orders us to kill witches. I just want my little boy back."

"I'm pretty sure that was Old Testament. We live under grace now, not law." Pastor Fulton held up a hand to keep her from interrupting. "Let me do some research, and we can meet again next week to discuss this further.

"Mason, I'd appreciate it if you didn't experiment with whatever this is until we've had a chance to meet again. Will you do your mom and I that courtesy?"

Mason frowned at him, drawing out his response. "Sure."

Pastor Fulton smiled. "I'd like you to stop telling your son that he's possessed or evil until we can get to the root of this situation. Surely that's not too much to ask?"

Billie Jo pressed her lips together, keeping her frustration and terror in tenuous check. "No."

"Great." He clapped his hands together. "Then I'll do my homework and meet with you next Sunday after service. How's that sound?"

"Fine," Billie Jo said. *Maybe the Catholics will take me seriously.*

MISERY FOR ALL

Mason dismounted the school bus unsure of the vast campus before him. His middle school had suffered a grease fire that rendered it unusable. He and all his classmates had been temporarily transferred to the very same high school where—cringe—his mother taught chemistry.

The same school Jordan attends.

He glanced at a classmate, receiving a shrug a moment before a bubbly girl in a cheerleading outfit appeared in an eerie echo of Lanea's regular cheer. "Hiya, I'm Christa, student body VP, welcome to Northside."

Mason sniffed. He wiped the itch from his eyes.

"So I'm going to give y'all a short tour while they set up orientation in the gym," Christa said. "A lot of things work differently in high school, and while I know you're not really freshmen, we're just going to have to pretend, all right?"

Sullen, uncertain murmurs braced Mason on every side. Christa flashed them a bright smile and started off in a passable imitation of Tour Guide Barbie. Mason lurked toward the back of the crowd, but close enough to catch her running chatter without having to ask others what she said. Girls from sixth through eighth grade hung toward the front near Christa forming a towering wall between him and their guide.

The bell ending the first school period rang. He jumped with everyone else.

The open air spaces between class buildings filled with much bigger, much older students.

A large boy with Jedediah's frame and tan lines bowled him over. "Out of the way, runt."

Another giant, tall and lanky but definitely not farm material laughed from one side of the clumsy goon, echoed by another thin pretty boy on the opposite side. The two boys accompanying the farm boy shared the good looks Mason associated with useless, spoiled tools or his father. Mason mumbled an apology. A hand snatched him before he reached the relative safety of his tour group.

"Hold up," Jordan glowered at the three boys. "Say you're sorry."

The farm boy snorted. "We know he's sorry, but someone forgot a condom and was too poor to pop for an abortion."

"Guess your parents got better jobs, Roland, but you still owe Mason an apology," Jordan said.

"No they don't," Mason said. "It was probably my fault."

Jordan folded her arms. "Not from where I stood."

"Little young for you, isn't he?" Jimmy asked.

Edgar laughed. "She has to find boyfriends before they find out she a homeless bitch."

Mason watched Jordan's jaw tighten. If he didn't do something she was going to take out her temper on them and it would be his fault. "It's okay, Jordan, really. It was my fault."

"I think I like this kid," Roland said. "He licks boots real good. Your name Shine, kid?"

"No way, he doesn't look to have any kind of *killer* instinct," Edgar said.

"Not like, Faye," Jimmy said. "She's got a taste for young ones just like the old psycho that took her in."

Jordan's knuckled cracked as she tightened her fists.

Mason pushed himself between them and extended a hand. "Mason Bartlett. My mom teaches here."

The three laughed.

"Oh, you're Tartlett's runt, huh? Her boyfriend molest you too?" Edgar asked.

Jordan took a step forward.

"Mason? Why aren't you with your tour group?" Billie Jo asked.

Mason cringed. *Oh, God, she's going to completely embarrass me.*

Billie Jo turned her attention to Jordan and the three boys. "You need to get to class. The bell's about to ring."

"Saved by the bell," Jimmy mumbled.

"By mom-my," Edgar taunted as he knocked a shoulder into Mason headed toward class, bowling Mason to the ground. "Oops. Sowwy."

Roland looked down into Mason's eyes, a snide smile on the verge of peeking out.

"Class," Billie Jo said. "Now."

Great. Between Mom and Jordan, I'm going to get my ass kicked from here to graduation—assuming I graduate before those morons.

"Stay away from Mason, Faye, and get to class." Billie Jo snatched Mason's ear and dragged him through the dwindling crowds all the way to Christa and the other students from his middle school.

The tour ended with pep talks and class schedules. At lunch, no one—not even guys he thought were his friends—sat near him. He found a section of wall at the edge of the outdoor dining courtyard and hoped it wouldn't rain. He picked at the lunch his mother'd packed him.

Why did she have to humiliate me like that? It's bad enough being a teacher's kid, but doesn't she realize—or care—how embarrassing that was?

Jordan stepped out of the cafeteria and strode to a table on the outer edge of the covered area. Mason watched a moment, but when no one joined her, he gathered his stuff and hurried to the table.

"Can I eat with you?"

Jordan shrugged. "Damned if you do, damned if you don't."

Relief washed over him. "At least with you, I know someone."

"None of your middle school friends here?" Jordan asked.

"They're here, but after what Mom did—"

"Right." Jordan bit off half a baby carrot. "You're toxic waste. Welcome to high school."

Mason talked into his sandwich. "I heard about Lanea."

Jordan stiffened.

"I'm sorry. How's Jedediah taking it?"

She concentrated on her carrots, talking through her chewing. "I haven't seen him in months. Wouldn't even be here if your mother hadn't sicced the police on me."

"How's Drake?"

"Haven't seen him either. Wait, how did you hear about Lanea?"

Mason shrugged. "That little pink sprite that used to come around all the time trying to earn candy. She traded me the information for an M&M."

"Oh." Jordan ate.

He watched her. She didn't seem as sulky as she had the first time he'd met her. She'd cut her dark hair into a bob, but its tips were still dyed acid green. Her arms looked thicker, more muscular and he'd noticed earlier that she carried herself more like a badass.

She turned, meeting his stare. "What?"

It escaped him in a whisper. "Can you teach me?"

Her brows pushed together. "Teach you what?"

"Magic?" Mason leaned closer. "I've been trying to get better, but Mom thinks it's witchcraft, so I have to be careful. I can't really do almost anything. I hoped Jedediah or Drake could help, but if they're gone...."

"I'm earth, you're air, and besides magic works different from person to person—especially where opposing elements are concerned," Jordan said.

"See, I didn't even know *that*."

"Didn't Drake run you through the basics?"

"Yeah, in about twenty minutes before Jedediah teleported us back home." Mason took a bite of his bologna sandwich, unable to taste it and happy considering how much he hated bologna. "Isn't there *anything* you can teach me?"

Jordan fidgeted, studying her fingers for several heartbeats. "Maybe. La-I learned some XYZ's that might help you."

"You're the best." His grin faltered. "Only, could you not defend me anymore, please?"

"Those guys are bullies, Mason. I did you a favor."

He didn't argue. Learning more about magic was too important —critical considering the target she and his mom had painted on his back.

Mason trudged up the driveway, pushing his bike toward the garage with drooped shoulders. Billie Jo folded and unfolded her arms, watching him through the living room window. Mason had slipped off before she could stop him, disappearing into nearby Heath Lake Park sufficiently that several drive-bys hadn't located him—not that the roadway granted access to even half of the forested land around Heath Lake.

She heard the back screen door open and hurried into the kitchen to cut him off. He bent, head in the refrigerator.

"Get out of there. You'll spoil your dinner," Billie Jo said. "What have you been doing?"

"I went bike riding."

"Who were you with?

His expression darkened. "Nobody, thanks to you."

"What do you mean by that, young man?"

His eyes rose, an uncharacteristic passion in them. "You humiliated me today. None of my friends will even talk to me—inside or outside school."

"You have no business starting fights. You know how I feel about violence."

"I didn't start anything. Some guy knocked me over. I tried to apologize and get back to the tour, but Jordan butted in."

Oh, God, he sent Faye to recruit Mason into his coven. Billie Jo tightened her hands into fists. "What did she want?"

Mason folded his arms. "She was defending me—not that she didn't almost do as good a job of embarrassing me as you did."

"You will not speak to me like that, young man. I'm your mother. You'll treat me with respect. What's gotten into you?"

Mason glared. "Evil tuna?"

Her hand lashed out without giving her a chance to think. Mason hit the ground with incredible speed, managing to duck the sudden blow. He stared up at her, fear and anger bending his beautiful boyish features. *What just happened? Why did I—I promised myself I wouldn't repeat—I don't believe in beating children.*

"Go upstairs." She took a breath, trying to calm her voice. "Bring down all your power cords, then you're to do your homework and go to sleep."

"I'm hungry."

"Then you shouldn't have treated me like that."

"I'm not the one throwing punches," Mason said.

She pointed toward the stairs. "Go. You'd better not hold back any cords, and if you want them back, you'll stay away from Faye."

He stomped out of the room, raising the temper Billie Jo fought down. She'd wanted to find out what Faye had said to him, particularly when he'd joined her at lunch. She wasn't sure how the whole situation had gotten so off track. She looked down at her hand, turning it over as if it were something foreign to her.

Mason dumped an armful of cords onto the table and stomped away.

"What did you and Faye talk about at lunch? Why did she seek you out?"

"Why were you spying on me?" Mason said.

"What I do and don't do is none of your concern. Now, answer my questions."

"I joined *Jordan* because no one else would eat with me after what you did."

"Did she pass you a message from Jedediah? Is he trying to

recruit you?" Billie Jo licked her lips, moistening her suddenly dry mouth. "Does he want to teach you magic?"

He rolled his eyes. "She hasn't seen Jedediah since Lanea's murder."

An emptiness swallowed her anger like a shark leaping from the depths. "What happened to Lanea, and how do you know about it?"

He sighed. "That little pink sprite told me a *Namhaid* sniper killed her right after they released Jedediah."

Cold swooped in, filling her hollow chest. She fell backward onto one of the kitchen chairs. Lanea was dead, murdered by the mercenary organization that'd been discussed during the trial. She'd watched the whole thing, of course, torn by a hope he'd been innocent and a desire to see Jedediah and his witchcraft permanently imprisoned.

She'd seen nothing in the news about another *Namhaid* murder. *There wouldn't be, though. No one knew poor Lanea existed.* Temper bit her. *She brought it onto herself, cavorting with—a sprite told him?*

Billie Jo surged back to her feet. "What are you doing talking to fairies? Did you summon it? I will not have you summoning evil spirits into this house."

Incredulous disgust washed across Mason's face. "She showed up looking for candy. I traded an M&M for news—an old one from the back of my sock drawer."

"No more. Feed those little beasts, and we'll never rid ourselves of them."

Mason scoffed. "Whatever."

Her arm tensed, hand flattening for the slap. *I have to get ahold of myself. I'm not an abusive parent. It's lingering evil from hanging around Jedediah, that's all. I can get rid of it. I don't want to slap him. I just need to read my bible. That's what momma said whenever—what if Faye isn't evil? What if what's tainting her is my fault for bringing her to Jedediah's attention?*

"Faye told you she hadn't seen Jedediah in how long?" Billie Jo asked.

"He took her to Weems after the sniper shot them." Mason

shrugged. "Once he knew she was okay, he left to check something."

Them? "Wait a second? Who did the sniper shoot?"

Mason counted fingers. "Jedediah, Lanea, Paulie and Jordan."

"Paulie?"

"The fairy that kept playing pranks in your classroom," Mason said.

She tried to sort it out in her head. "A sniper shot Jedediah, Lanea and Faye?"

"Yes."

"Lanea died."

Mason exhaled heavily. "Yes."

"But the sniper missed Jedediah and Faye?"

"No," Mason's irritation filled his voice. "He hit them, but warding magic protected them."

"Then why didn't—never mind. It doesn't matter. Jedediah got Faye shot and then abandoned her, that would've been several months ago," Billie Jo frowned. "That's why she didn't show back up for school."

"So what?" Mason said.

"She's in danger because of him, and he just abandons her? You can't just leave a child to her own devices."

"She's probably still warded. Besides Jordan's tough and basically an adult anyway."

Faye was tough and independent, but it didn't matter. This was criminal level neglect, and Billie Jo had to do something. *If I get her away from him and back into foster care maybe we can still save her.*

"Go up to your room like I told you," Billie Jo fished out her phone. "I need to make a call."

Jordan stepped out of a South Carolina house much the same as the ruined farmhouse and back into Georgia early evening humidity. The last house she'd found hadn't had a current caretaker like some of the ones she explored, but it'd been alike enough that she'd taken the clocks some Fey had dug out of the ruin and all of the excavated photos there for protection against the elements.

She hadn't come out to move Jedediah's things, and the time it took used up time she'd intended to search the portals for a way to Jedediah.

Her palms prickled.

She cast her gaze side to side, searching for another shadowcat. None lurked in the twilight shade. Nip sidled up to her. His relaxed ears and wagging tail filled her with relief. She pushed the sudden tension away and returned to the farmhouse for another load. Just clear of the boneyard the farmhouse rubble shifted. A hulking, mottled figure burrowed through it, moving left then right under a beam heavy with attached roofing.

Jordan summoned her staff. She hardened her skin and pushed strength into her arms.

Drake slide into view, his maw wide in a yawn that displayed terrifying fangs and serrated teeth. He'd grown. His hide seemed a patchwork of dull brown and brighter, redder, overlapping leather scales. Compared to his former hide the newer scales seemed bigger, better defined like what she'd seen covering dragons in fantasy movies.

He backed into the rubble again, doing a cha-cha movement with his eyes closed.

"Drake!"

Drake's eyes snapped open and straight to her. Their locked gazes showed Jordan fear. *Why would he be afraid of me? Was he doing something embarrassing?*

She bound forward, dropping her staff on the run. "Are you okay? I was worried about you. Do you know where Jedediah is?"

Drake frowned. He opened his beak, shut it and finally shrugged —the unnatural motion plunging her into a slithering chill.

She mounted the rubble, trying to close the distance. As she did so, she noticed the mottled, patchwork quality of his hide was actually reddish new skin under halfway shredded old.

"Go away," his voice croaked, apparently rusty from disuse. He turned back into the rubble.

"Wait, please, I need your help."

Drake slid further into the ruin.

She grabbed his tail. Anger hotter than any fire slammed into her mind. An equally powerful and twice as slimy wall of some other emotion scurried to hide behind the heat.

I need you. Jordan shoved everything that'd happened at him in a rush, hoping to get it out before he ejected her. The slimy emotion pounced on her. Drake's guilt, insecurity, and self-loathing buffeted her in cyclic waves like a dragon eating its own tail.

He snarled, a poorly combined exclamation and roar. His teeth snapped toward where she held his tail. Jordan released him. He slithered into the rubble, shoving some so that it stole her balance. She landed awkwardly in the mess, his projected thoughts and emotions a writhing, wrestling alligator pit within her mind.

"I get it." She yelled. "Lanea died, and you feel guilty. How do you think I feel? The only sister I've ever known dead and me here even though we were both shot."

More of his inner turmoil resolved in her mind, helping her identify the shame beneath all she'd seen.

"I loved her too," Jordan said. "Not like you, but it doesn't hurt any less."

Drake snarled.

"We're family. We need each other. I need you. Mason does too." She tossed some rubble to one side and flopped onto the arm of Jedediah's Barcalounger. Her voice fell twice as far. "Without you we're alone—babies in a world we don't understand."

The rubble didn't move.

She hated to admit it, hated to show weakness to anyone, but she needed someone. *Maybe I need more than just someone. Maybe I need Jedediah and Drake and Mason...maybe even Billie Jo.* Tears tumbled to suicide position and leapt from her cheekbones. *I'd had a family, finally after so much time, and just as sudden as before I lost them.*

She had no idea how she'd ended up in Georgia's foster system instead of remaining in New Jersey. As she'd often lamented, she couldn't have gotten kicked out of every foster home in a whole state. She'd cursed the move to this too-politely, backstabbing culture where everyone had a smile and a funny accent and acted like they were your family even though most of them only wanted to use you in some fashion.

Treevoran's caress flashed through her thoughts. Her hands touched where his had. The warmth and hunger of his touch rekindled. Her palms itched. Jordan stood, summoned her staff and glared into twilight. "Treevoran?"

A growl rumbled from beneath the rubble.

Jordan stepped carefully onto the cleared porch, hands wringing the petrified wood beneath her fingers. "Is that you, you lying son of a mongrel?"

Drake inhaled, filling his nostrils with fading Lanea. His chest twinged, but Lanea's scent wasn't why he'd inhaled. A rich scent like heated iron Jedediah had occasionally forged washed over his scent receptors. A sour tang undercut it mixed with a whisper of habanero and soft odors of a female in heat. Drake resisted the urge to knead his talons while still on Lanea's bed. He burrowed out of the rubble with slow motions that would never be stealthy under the moving wreckage.

He poked his nose out, inhaling deeply once more. He scented elf and a faint pollen smell distinctive to elf glamour.

A growl rumbled his chest. Smoke filled his nostrils, blocking any attempt to sniff out Treevoran. He coaxed greater sensitivity with beak-tingling magic.

If it is him, he'll smell like roasted flesh soon enough.

He pushed further out of the farmhouse, doubling back to climb atop the tilted crown. A talon flattened the old owl weathervane. He filled his lungs, spread his wings wide and roared challenge.

Enhanced senses picked up a spicy bite beneath the sweet pollen, but it didn't match the odor of Treevoran's fear. He turned, mouth-shaped and snarled. "Reveal yourselves."

Jordan whirled toward him then followed his gaze.

Two elves parted curtains of glamour, stepping through their hems with a beauty that seemed to reflect moonlight although the moon herself yet slept. Long, flaxen hair shamed their silver-green silken garb.

Jordan pushed at some of her hair. Her scent soured.

"You were warned about crossing Master's land without leave," Drake said. "Have you any reason I shouldn't punish your disrespect? Thestle? Chalet?"

The slightly taller elf genuflected. "We heeded your warning, Elder Lordling, and came to your master's house for leave."

"Yet, Thestle and I found it ruined beneath lingering whispers of angered dragon. Have you supplanted the mortal farmer?" Chalet asked.

Drake's answering snarls drew the word into a menacing tremor. "No."

Thestle lowered his head to the ground. "Point us to your master, and we shall trouble your greatness no more."

"He's not here," Jordan said.

Both elf heads shot toward her. Chalet darkened. "We address you master, thrall. Be silent."

The heated iron scent intensified. "How'd you even get on the property?"

Chalet took four quick stepped to her, hand raised to strike.

"You'd dare hit my thrall?" Drake landed a leap atop Chalet, talons driving him to the ground.

Jordan shot Drake a dirty look.

Thestle surged to his feet. "Forgiveness, Elder Lord. There are many dangers on the road, and our weariness has robbed Chalet of sense."

Drake licked his beak, and Chalet blanched.

"I'm no one's thrall. I'm sister to Lanea." Cracks in Jordan's words vented the heat in her tone. "Daughter of Lirelaeli Ermyn'Phir."

And I've never tasted elf.

<Please, we sought only leave to cross these lands,> Chalet thought. *<We meant no offense to you or our newly met cousin.>*

If you want my leave then you should pay tribute. A grin grew menacingly across Drake's maw. *Cherry Coke, as much as your life's worth.*

<Yes, Lord, we'll fetch it.>

If it isn't enough... Drake revealed his teeth.

<Would my Lord let me up that Thestle and I might fetch his libation? >

"Return with tribute befitting your petition." Drake stepped off the elf, eyes fixed on Thestle. "Don't make me hunt you down for it."

"Wait," Jordan said. "How did you get past the barrier onto the property?"

Thestle smiled. "Through the gaps, cousin."

4

—

INTERVENTION

illie Jo pulled onto the farm drive, her heart thundering in her chest like an echo of the storm above her. Rain poured onto her windshield too hard for her wipers to vanquish. A front wheel hit a large rock, jerking the steering wheel beneath her sweaty grip. The new Sheriff's SUV led her and a pair of cruisers through the trees to the circular drive. Her breath caught in her throat. A tornado had leveled the farmhouse.

Or a bomb. Dear God, let Faye be all right.

The two cruisers pulled to a stop first, John Ransom and his younger brother Eddie all too familiar with Jedediah's property. She parked behind the Sheriff. John and Eddie eyed the place, hurrying to the SUV beneath plastic wrapped wide brimmed hats. They waited in the downpour for the Sheriff to finish his call and exit his vehicle.

Billie Jo grabbed her umbrella and joined them.

Newly elected Sheriff Dunford exited beneath the umbrella John held over him. He towered over John and his younger brother Eddie. He looked at neither, assessing the farmhouse with arms folded across a barrel chest beneath a mustache to make Yosemite Sam envious. "Another wild goose chase, Miss Bartlett?"

"There're only two places she might be," Billie Jo said. "Here or Weems."

"My time is valuable," Sheriff Dunford said. "We already wasted half the morning at the other house looking for this girl."

"She's been abandoned. We need to find her before…" Billie Jo turned to see a red sedan rumble up the drive.

❧

Angesa Cooper stopped her car behind a platinum minivan. Her gaze settled on the ruined farmhouse then turned toward him. She straightened the grey jacket over a nice blouse and smoothed the jacket's matching skirt. "Is this the right place, Agent Ridley?"

How is it you don't know? Ridley smiled. "Thank you, Angesa. Yes."

The woman next to him appeared more frazzled than the attractive mid-thirties bleach-blonde usually did. Like himself or his partner Ellouise, Angesa did her job because she cared, applying her ample—if currently uncertain—intelligence with the strict diligence of a Catholic schoolmarm.

She'd been Faye Jordan's caseworker, though even faced with a photograph couldn't recall the girl. A check of state records verified that Angesa hadn't filed any status reports on Miss Jordan since just before Jedediah Shine's arrest. The local office held no records at all.

Erased, just like her memory, but how? Why would someone delete local files but not those uploaded to the state databases?

Ridley shifted his gaze out the window.

On the opposite side of a police SUV, an attractive mid-thirties woman narrowed keen brown eyes framed by long chestnut hair and cinnamon freckles. Deep frowns creased her fair skin. Beside her, a bear of a man glowered toward the new arrivals. Dunford flicked an imperious hand, sending Deputy Ransom their direction. The overbearing man had won office by slander, insisting his corrupt, incompetent and dead predecessor had let Jedediah Shine run loose slaughtering children despite a subsequent acquittal.

If I'd believed that made him innocent, I'd never have been here to see... Ridley exited.

Eddie stopped short. "Agent Ridley?"

"Afternoon, Deputy, call me Benjamin. We're all law enforcement here."

Eddie shot a glance over his shoulder. "What are you doing here, sir?"

"I understand we've finally located the Jordan girl," Ridley said. "Bureau hates lose ends."

Dunford marched over to them, sizing up Ridley's wrinkled suit and bookish appearance. The disgust on his face almost made Ridley smile.

"Sheriff, Agent Ridley—the FBI agent handling the Shine case," John said.

A bellow perched on the Sheriff's lips, but Ridley stole the floor.

"Afternoon, Sheriff. I'm sure you're familiar with Angesa Cooper—Miss Jordan's caseworker," Ridley said.

"You're the agent who let Shine escape custody," Dunford snorted. "Local child services office said the girl had no case worker."

Ridley smiled. "They were mistaken."

"Look, Riddles, this is a local affair. We don't need your type interfering," Dunford gestured. "I have more than enough backup to keep one little girl from slipping out of my hands."

Ridley let his brows rise. Movement drew his attention toward the greenhouse where so many of his men had been slaughtered. Faye Jordan strode around it from the direction of the old bone-yard seemingly unconcerned about the rain soaking her. A blood-hound the size of a full-grown mastiff trotted along at her side. Anticipation freed butterflies into his stomach. A laugh died on her lips, and the young woman's expression hardened. The hound's hackles rose, and gooseflesh scurried across Ridley's arms.

The girl stormed up to Miss Bartlett and glowered down a nose at least a hand taller than Shine's former girlfriend. Glistening steel chopsticks crisscrossed a crown of stringy, soot-black hair and acid green highlights. Careless paint splotches, glue and blood red glitter nearly camouflaged the vicious, shadowy feline claws and fangs on the dark grey jeans. A so black as to be new T-shirt clung to her. It appeared tight enough to scandalize even if dry, displaying a blood dripping pentacle superimposed above the words, 'Djinn Storm,' written in jagged lightning.

Billie Jo Bartlett ripped her coat off and pressed it against Jordan's chest. "Faye, there are men present."

"What the hell are you doing here?" Jordan asked.

The dog curled its lip.

Bartlett stiffened, shying away from the beast. Ridley examined the animal closer. He circled the group a few feet either way, scrutinizing the animal. He knew something about the so-called dog wasn't right, but he couldn't seem to put a finger on the evidence he desired.

Bartlett's southern accent thickened in response to her discomfort. "We're here to ensure your safety, Faye."

"How many times have I told you not to call me that, *Billie Jo*? My name is Jordan Shine." A mischievous smile preceded a gesture to the dog. "Besides, do you *really* think I need a better guard?"

Blood drained from the older woman, leaving her freckles as the only islands of color.

"Quite an animal," Ridley said. "He's grown a lot since Jedediah's release. Bet if he wanted to catch something he could really fly."

Jordan's smile faltered. She put a hand on the animal as if to steady herself and it glanced into her eyes. She recovered her composure and narrowed her gaze at him. "What are you doing here, Agent?"

"You know who I am?"

"I saw you testify on television," Jordan said.

"I have a few questions we never got to ask you before the trial. Angesa agreed to let me ask—"

"Ask questions on your own time," Dunford grabbed Jordan's arm and steered her toward his SUV. "Get in the car, young lady."

The hound snarled.

Wet hair fought to lifted along Ridley's skin. "Sheriff, I strongly suggest you slowly remove your hand from the girl."

"I told you," Dunford glared. "This is my jurisdiction."

"Her...," Ridley licked his lips. "Dog doesn't like how you're treating her."

"He—uh, he might be right, Sheriff," Bartlett said.

Jordan yanked her slick arm out of his grip, finger marks still visible on her tanned skin. "I know my rights. I haven't done anything wrong, and I'm not going anywhere with any of you."

"Look, you spoiled, entitled brat, you're the property of child services, and we're taking you into custody for your own good whether you like it or not." The Sheriff reached for her again. The hound showed his teeth. Dunford clenched his jaw. "Deputies, get the animal restraints."

Ridley's heart and lungs went on holiday. He closed a hand on Bartlett's wrist and slowly drew her away.

"No, Drake," Fear and a restrained sob broke Jordan's voice. "Not again, okay? Please?"

"I told you to get the restraints," Dunford said.

Both deputies stood absolutely still, their pale limbs locked and their eyes fixed on the angry dog.

Bartlett wrenched herself from Ridley's grip and dug a crucifix from her neckline. She pushed it toward the dog. "Back beast, your evil has no power here. I rebuke you and your master."

The animal shared a confused look with Jordan.

"Have you lost your mind?" Jordan asked.

"You're going back into foster care." Bartlett sidled forward and grabbed Jordan. "We can't have you wandering around homeless and unsupervised."

"I'm doing nothing of the sort. I'm not in the system anymore." Jordan gestured at Angesa. "Ask her—if she can even remember."

"What are you talking about?" Bartlett said.

"I don't care." Dunford set a hand on his holster. "You boys either restrain that animal or I'll shoot it and fire you."

"Shoot Drake, and I'll beat you until I've broken every bone in your fat body." Jordan snarled.

Dunford darkened.

"Faye!"

"Frak you, Billie Jo," Jordan said. "Frak all of you."

Dunford tensed. "If this is an example of what Shine's upbringing is like, you should be glad to be rid of him."

Jordan shot Bartlett a glare that with more practice could've turned her to stone. "Jedediah is the greatest man in this country, maybe the world."

"A murdering bastard that abandoned you," Dunford said.

"Acquitted, and he didn't abandon me. He left me in Drake's care."

"He was only acquitted because of Joe Franklin's incompetence, assuming Shine didn't have the old fart in his pocket," Dunford said.

"Sheriff," Ridley said. "I'd like to hear more about what Miss Jordan knows regarding her records erasure."

"Agent," Dunford said. "We're taking this girl into custody, kenneling that animal as a danger to the public and you can go lose another high-security prisoner for all I care."

A light tingle prickled Ridley's fingertips.

Both greenhouse doors opened. A wolf-sized brown dog exited each, postures hostile. Jordan knelt, pushing fingers into the rain-soaked ground. The new dogs gentled, the smaller cocked its head before glancing at Drake.

Jordan's expression hardened into stubborn steel. "Move me yourself, if you can, you fat pig."

"Faye!" Bartlett said.

Dunford marched over to her. Reddish brown flashed in Ridley's peripheral vision. He tensed and reached for a weapon to repulse the gigantic hound's attack. The animal had vanished, not even leaving footprints in the muddy ground where it'd stood only a moment before.

Dunford muscled her toward the car but couldn't budge her. He twisted her arm behind her, it stopped half way unyielding as stone and depriving him leverage. He cursed and grabbed her low around her midsection and strained to pick her up.

A cruel smile played across Jordan's lips.

"You're not helping things, Jordan," Billie Jo cursed. "You have to go back into foster care."

"No, I'm not ever going back. That's why Jedediah had Lanea—"

"Lanea?" Ridley asked. "Is she who hacked the local child services office?"

"The farmhand from Joe Franklin's reports?" Dunford's narrowed eyes shifted from her to his two deputies.

John spoke up. "There was a migrant farm hand we still haven't been able to track down. Could that be who she's talking about?"

"Do you two incompetents have a last name, an address?"

An involuntary hiccup spoiled Jordan's sneer. "The *Namhaid* murdered her because you idiots spent all your time on Jedediah instead of catching the real assassins."

Bartlett's voice cracked too. "N-No one was m-murdered. If someone had been, there'd have been a police report, a body."

"I wouldn't expect *you* to believe in what you can't see—or what you do see for that matter." A snide tone filled Jordan's next words. "Besides, elves aren't in the Sheriff's jurisdiction."

"Elves?" Dunford scoffed. "Get animal control out here to clear the place, and get her a psychiatric exam before she's placed. God only know what kind of damage Shine did."

A muffled roar rumbled the ground beneath their feet. Jordan's teeth pinned a bottom lip. She moved around Dunford fast enough to catch him flatfooted. She opened the door and slipped into the back of his SUV. "Let's go already. Come on."

"We'll go when I say we go," Dunford said.

Ridley scrutinized her, glancing around once more for the strange hound. Her pleading gaze sent cold through his gut with icy razors. *Why're you trying to get us out of here? Did you witness what happened to my people? Was your Drake to blame?*

Ridley rolled the dog's name around his mind, adding it to other things he suspected about the animal. He'd have to talk to her later away from the Sheriff anyway. "Well, Sheriff, then I do have time to question her."

"Time's up, Agent." Dunford climbed into his car, driving off before Ridley could ask any questions. Jordan turned back toward him, mouthing, her thanks.

You're welcome, but for what? Ridley frowned. "Maybe we'd best all be going. Angesa, we should keep up with the Sheriff considering he's got your charge."

"Sheriff wants us to catch the dogs," Eddie said.

"They're on their owner's property. Unless you've got proof of his death, animal cruelty, or expired licenses, you'd best leave them be for now." Ridley slid into the red sedan. *Or for good.*

Miss Bartlett took a few fearful glances around and hurried to her minivan. Her unease cemented the knots in Ridley's gut. He didn't have the answers he came for, but he'd glimpsed another clue. Heat rose together with an unsettling tightening of his gut instincts as he scanned the farm yard for the vanished animal. His gaze settled on Eddie and John. *If you two don't stop dithering and make yourselves scarce, you'll end up shredded like Flute and the rest of my people.*

BROKEN

A silver, pentagonal table stood alone in the wreckage of Jedediah's ruined spell chamber. Four tokens hovered over its surface in a web of magic—each unique to the cherished soul the spell protected.

The wizard curled beneath its feet, a ragged, emaciated vagabond in ripped and bloodied clothes. Long, tangled hair silvered beyond any hint of paprika hid all but glimpses of eyes swollen shut with grief. Ratty knots otherwise obscured his face and a small fairy doll cradled in ancient, wrinkled hands.

Only the occasional wheeze or infrequent convulsion offered evidence of the tiny, unsurrendering spark of life left in Jedediah's frame.

EMOTIONAL DAMAGE

Drake exploded from beneath a fallow field with a roar. His breath rampaged in and out of his lungs in frightened sprints. He roared again, turning toward Nip and Sarah as they stepped just out of reach and dropped to their bellies.

He glared at them. *How dare you try to drown me in earth?*

An image of Jordan flickered across his mind's eye from the cowering pup. *<Sister two-legs. Sister two—>*

Drake snarled.

<Peace, Elder.> Sarah remembered into his mind—Drake and Jordan watching television side by side. *<Your sister commanded us to protect you.>*

From what?

An erupting volcano flickered into his thoughts. *<From you.>*

Nip projected a terrified Jordan watching Drake and a sludge hydra shredding federal agents. The fear the pup remembered slammed into the dragon's mind so hard he could almost taste its bite along his tongue.

The taste of it excited him, but the image of Jordan burned in an entirely different manner. The scent of the deputies lingered in the air, uneasy but not nearly afraid enough.

They took her. They'll pay.

<She left unchained.> Sarah countered, adding images of him skulking behind glamour and burrowing into the farmhouse. *<So you might wallow in peace.>*

Drake rounded on her, but she slipped into the ground before he reached her. He dug, shredding the earth with his talons. They bit only soil. He blew it from his nostrils and inhaled. The new litter's smell lingered inside the greenhouse, but he had no quarrel with them.

The deputies remained.

Drake bared his teeth. He'd taught them better—though Lanea'd erased the lesson from their minds. She wasn't there to save their sanity a second time. He shook out his wings, unwrapping them from where they'd seemed seamless parts of his sides. Static electricity crackled in the air as he released the illusion magic hiding his true draconic form. He'd pushed terror enough into their primitive brains to send them gibbering back to the trees of their ancestors.

<Great, Drake,> Lanea's voice froze his thoughts. *<I'm going to have to clean up your mess again before Da gets home.>*

The deputies bolted as memories of one of Drake's more selfish blunders brought Lanea back to his thoughts. Even cross with her hands planted on her hips, there'd been amusement in her voice...and affection.

Instead of baked cinnamon, the acrid scent of urine and biting fear left a bitter taste on his tongue. He let the deputies scurry away.

Drake gazed at the farmhouse. Her scent remained under the ruin, but the fear he'd forced into the deputies had left other scents that all but destroyed it.

Jordan was right. I'd have thrown a tantrum and ruined everything.

A vehicle pulled onto the drive, shifting the gravel as it returned. Drake pushed down a flash of anger and instead wrapped wings and glamour tight around his frame. He crossed the field to see why the deputies had come back.

Chalet knelt before a red Coca-Cola delivery truck, a bottle extended above his hands as an offering. Thestle played a flute behind him as two blank-faced delivery men unloaded flats of Cherry Coke.

"Our first tribute, Lord," Chalet said.

Drake sunk fangs into the bottle. Its bitter plastic taste disappeared as sweet fruit and cola washed the fled deputies from his mouth. Sugar tingled along his tongue as carbonation sizzled down his throat, delivering a euphoric rush of caffeine. He sucked it dry, rolling eyes into his head at the buzz before he spat the bottle at Chalet's feet.

Drake laid a wing atop the elf's head. *Fine, for now. Have them unload it in the boneyard. I'll show you where.*

Billie Jo wiped hot tears from her cheek. The long drive back to town stretched out in a blurry eternity. She'd made that drive countless times, a smile on her lips and a heady anticipation making her soul sing.

What had all been a dream now crashed down on her as a nightmare.

It'd started so well. She'd met Jedediah, an old fashioned—if perhaps too old fashioned—gentleman. He'd included Mason in their dates, treating her son as if he actually cared. Certain aspects of the relationship—mostly little things like his unwillingness to sleep with her—had left her suspicious. She'd felt as if there were little things he held back, but she'd dismissed them as idiosyncrasies intrinsic to a private man. He'd been everything she'd ever dreamed, romancing her in ways that felt like a Disney movie.

Beauty and the Beast.

There'd been the murder investigation, but Joe Franklin cleared him of any guilt. She'd convinced Jedediah to take the troubled girl in her class under his care and seen Faye go from a reclusive and angry potential drop out to a promising student. Mason had even started to act more mature, emulating Jedediah's example rather than his cheating father.

Then the FBI found all those graves. He insisted he was innocent, but he'd escaped federal custody—hardly the actions of an innocent man. After so many omissions, inconsistencies and falsehoods, it reminded her too much of Marcus and his cheating. She simply couldn't find it in her heart to believe him.

The agent had later testified about Jedediah's forceful abduction. They had it on camera, but that had been after she'd learned about the magic.

Billie Jo liked the idea of a fairy tale romance, but she'd never wanted it to include real fairies. Magic was evil—the kind of evil that had plagued her through childhood. It was the kind of evil her parents had tried to drive from her with verse, prayer and beatings.

A flash of the old night terrors forced her to pull off the road. She hadn't experienced one in years. Past horrors blinded her to the rainy day. Death and blood, fire and lightning appeared and vanished in flashes like an old movie. Corpses leered at her. Horrors filled places she'd never travelled. Childhood terrors thought long purged resurfaced. For a moment she felt imprisoned, caught in amber unable to breathe.

The night horror and its accompanying panic attack faded.

Billie Jo cried herself to hiccups. She pulled back onto Georgia 80 West and continued home. Rain lightened until her wipers squeaked against dry glass.

The day had gone nothing like she'd imagined. After Mason had told her Jedediah had abandoned Faye, she'd called Angesa Cooper. The woman didn't remember Billie Jo. She didn't remember Jedediah. She didn't remember Faye, not even after Billie Jo'd met her with pictures of the four of them together. Angesa had humored her long enough to show Billie Jo that no file existed in Angesa's filing cabinet or any other cabinet in the local office.

It'd been like a bad nightmare...another one.

Joe Franklin had been a good man, so she'd approached his replacement. The Sheriff hadn't cared about an unsupervised teenager, telling her through his secretary to call family services.

Billie Jo tried approaching Faye directly over the next week, but after telling her to stay away from Mason, the girl refused to talk to her. She'd returned to her emo dressing style. She didn't answer the

Weems house door even when Jedediah's Dodge Charger sat prominently in the driveway. Everything she said over the phone garnered only scorn or sulky, monosyllabic responses.

Faye hated her, but Billie Jo knew if she didn't find some way to reach Faye, she might drop out with only one year of high school to go—destroying her young life forever.

She'd eventually cornered Dunford in public. He'd been polite for the cameras but hadn't paid her much attention until she mentioned Jedediah's name. They met the next day. She coerced his help. They'd started at social services. Either Dunford had no patience for other branches of government or an agenda he didn't intend to see delayed. They drove to Jedediah's Weems house the next morning, found it empty and continued out to the farm.

All I'd wanted was to ensure she had someone to care for her and was safely away from Jedediah's evil before it permanently corrupted her soul.

Billie Jo exited J. R. Allen highway onto Moon Road. She turned her minivan onto Weems in the opposite direction as Jedediah's house, drove down the hill and into her neighborhood.

The fire-engine red Corvette blocking Billie Jo's driveway drove a lead fist into her gut. Mason talked animatedly with the all-too-attractive man in designer clothes leaning on its hood.

When did Mason grow to almost Marcus's height? Isn't he too young for a growth spurt?

She parked along the curb and took a moment to close her eyes and take a few deep breaths. *Haven't I been through enough today?*

She crossed the lawn. Her ex-husband shooed Mason, crushing the grin that'd dominated his expression. "You're looking good, babe."

She glared at the car. "Too broke to spend time with your son, huh?"

He smiled and snatched a large manila envelope from the covered convertible's seat. "Neither is going to be a problem anymore."

She rolled her eyes. "Oh my God, Marcus, what kind of get-rich scam are you involved in now?"

He handed her the envelope. "Photography. Take a look."

She opened the envelope with an aggravated sigh and pulled out a half inch stack of large, glossy photos. She flipped the first over, getting a second gut punch from the picnic pictures of Jedediah, Faye, Lanea, herself and Mason. She squashed a sudden surge of warmth, using it to heat her voice. "Why are you having me followed, Marcus?"

"They get juicier, keep flipping."

She flipped a few more photos, gasping when she flipped to bloody carnage. Elements of the picture designated it as a crime scene photo. More followed, some blood and gore, others filled with bones laid out in some woodland.

"Where did you get these?"

He shrugged. "I know a guy."

"You know a man who steals crime scene photos?"

He snorted. "Says the woman screwing a mass murderer."

"They never had sex," Mason said.

"Mom tell you that?" Marcus turned to her. "You lying to the boy?"

"No, I never slept with Jedediah."

"He was acquitted, Dad."

"Mason," Billie Jo said. "Go inside so I can talk to your father in private."

Mason sulked into the house.

"My sex life is none of your business," she said. "We're divorced."

"Sounds to me like he didn't want a used up old broad either," Marcus said.

Billie Jo's fists tightened, but she resisted the desire to hit her ex.

Marcus smiled. "Damn shame, that would've looked great on camera."

Billie Jo followed his glance to a woman with a large camera in a white sedan just down the block.

"She's *fantastic*," Marcus let the innuendo hang a moment before forging on. "She's got photos of the FBI watching your boyfriend's property. It also seems you've been trying to get Mason an exorcism?"

Hair along Billie Jo's neck bristled. Heat prickled her skin. "I'm not seeing Jedediah anymore, but either way my relationships are none of your business."

"My lawyer thinks we have enough for a judge to give me custody and make *you* pay child support," Marcus said.

A chill swept over her skin leaving gooseflesh in its wake, her accent thickened. "You wouldn't."

His brows rose. "Sounds like I've got your attention."

She tossed the pictures into his face. "You don't want Mason. You just want out of paying child support."

"A teenage boy needs his father."

"So show up for a ballgame," Billie Jo snapped.

"Mason will love living in Atlanta," Marcus said.

She balled her fists. "I won't let you take him."

He caressed her cheek. "I'm a good guy."

She slapped his hand away.

"We could come to an accommodation," Marcus said.

"I'm not sleeping with you."

Marcus snorted. "Thanks, I've got women with less mileage."

The slap almost sounded like thunder.

Marcus recovered, glancing down the street. The woman extended a thumbs up through her open window. "You really are a dumb bitch, aren't you? Why did I ever think you were good enough for me?"

Billie Jo's jaw clenched. Her fist tightened and struck.

He caught the blow. "Hit me again, and I won't need to offer you this."

"Offer what?"

He grabbed another envelope from the car and tossed it to her. "Sign it. Waive all child support, and I leave Mason right where he is."

It took several splutters to spit words past rising temper. "That's extortion."

"Just negotiation. You keep what you earn. I keep what I earn."

"He's your son too," she said.

Marcus shrugged.

"I couldn't take care of Mason on only my pay," she said.

"Surely you can earn a buck or two in your murderer's bed." He smirked.

Billie Jo hurled the papers into his face. "Take me to court."

❧

Bianca Norway scrutinized their surroundings as Flash turned their SUV onto Brickyard Road. A massive complex stretched far back off the roadway opposite a railroad line. Huge chunks of cement half the size of a Mini Cooper lined the property's edge, connected by three-inch thick metal cabling, Truck loading bays gaped open to the elements. Several sections of roof had collapsed inward. Smaller buildings huddled near the larger, brick façade's cracked and leaning outward.

Still can't decide what Zero sees in this place.

The hulking Samoan turned onto the property, heading directly toward one of the barrier stones without slowing. Bianca steeled herself, refusing to flinch even if they hit real rock. Her reputation had suffered enough over the intervening months. Compelled by a curse laid on her by the blasted farmer—a magic spell Zero claimed he couldn't remove—she'd unlocked the *Namhaid* U.S. cell's database to the feds. Many of the agents and mercenaries that remained at large had challenged her, and once again the curse compelled her to admit her complicity. She'd tried to mitigate the damage to her reputation by telling them about the magic which would not let her lie, but no one believed her claims.

She heard Flash sniff, catching a smirk on his lips as they passed through the illusion. Two semi-trailers ducked partway beneath the first several covered loading zones. Moving trucks from a dozen rental companies huddled near uncovered openings, newly installed retractable doors opened to accept their cargo.

Flash parked inside an empty bay that had once facilitated loading of brick shipments for who cared where. She exited, almost immediately surrounded by the bustle. A burnt scent still clung to the cavernous L-shaped facility. Brick, debris and collapsed ceiling cluttered the ground. They spilled over rail tracks, down into a wide depression and up again over another set of rails. Industrial lights so old they burned amber—when they burned at all—gave halfhearted efforts to light the place.

Thuggish mercenaries and rented dozers excavated the ruined industrial building. Imported contractors who'd never return to be buried wherever they'd originated laid tile and carpet over cleaned areas. They framed new bathrooms and kitchen facilities while still more walled off the rearmost end of the L-shaped warehouse where freight elevators had lowered finished bricks to a basement rail stop. Once the rails and exit tunnel were excavated and repaired, trains would move arms and manpower throughout North and South America.

They'd collected as many of their secure caches they could before the feds, bringing it to the unlikely location for catalog and dispersal. She disliked having so much incriminating evidence in a single location and hadn't resisted the compulsion to tell Zero so. Stout engineers had extended the freight elevator downward below the basement, and they'd seal off the ground floor access once all the equipment was situated below, but in the meantime only the illusion magic protected them from a Federal raid.

"Morning, One."

She bristled. There was no point in wearing a mask like the man addressing her. She'd tried at first, but it seemed a mask was a lie and the magic had stopped her breathing until she removed it.

"Nice to see you back, One," another smirking merc said.

They're taunting me. Heat filled her gut rather than her cheeks. "If I find proof you're disrespecting me, I'll gut you with my own hands."

A mumbled complaint caught her ears. "Must be her time of the month."

Bianca whirled around. "That's next week. Get to work."

She cursed inwardly at revealing her cycle. It wasn't embarrassing in and of itself, but that she blurted such things infuriated her. Bianca hurried to catch Flash in the sectioned off area. A solid brick wall parted to allow her entry to a new elevator somehow installed in the old brick without leaving the slightest indication of re-engineering.

It took her and Flash downward. She hadn't even watched which floor the behemoth enforcer had keyed. The elevator settled. Its lights darkened and scanners went to work on the pair. When they'd satisfactorily verified their identity and scanned them for weapons, the doors opened.

A hall the sterile white of a hospital stretched out before them. Bianca checked the elevator's button bank and found a new one with a red cross at the bottom of its controls. Flash strode forward without hesitation. He sneezed, rubbing his nose at the faint anti-septic scent clinging beneath new paint and tile.

He led her down the well-lit corridor past medical suites and patient rooms. They rounded one corner and eventually reached a dead end capped by a security door which made some bank vaults look puny.

"Zero having any more surprises built for us?" Bianca asked.

"I do not share Zero's secrets with those that can't keep their lips together."

A series of biometric checks slid the door into the walls. A surgical suite filled the space beyond, braced by rooms behind thick aquarium glass. Light leaked through the blinds closing off the one to her right. Flash entered the one on her left, his entrance trig-gering its dim lighting to full strength.

She followed him in, stopped by an overpowering reek of old blood.

Two intensive care beds filled the room, like but unlike anything she'd ever encountered. Some of the tech involved exceeded her experience. Silver framed crystals glowed along the bed's underside in eerie sync with a soft, steady beat came from a pulse monitor mixed in with the rest of the sensors, scanners and computers. A vaguely human shape, bloated and ill-defined over-flowed it—a fur covered version of insect cocoons in science fiction movies.

Flash took off his sports jacket and settled himself onto the other bed. He stripped off his shirt, revealing a series of hi-tech IV plugs in arms and torso. He plugged in color-coded lines, pressed a button on the control unit near his other hand and laid back. He tensed as the first fluids filled otherwise clean tubes, but a moment later his eyes eased closed, and he started to snore softly.

Fluids pushed along the tubes into a matching machine. A moment later the cocoon spasmed. The movement brought her attention to the tubes running into the bloated mass. It subsided just as the door behind her opened.

"Good afternoon, Bianca," Zero said.

"What in the bloody name of mad science are you doing down here?"

Zero chuckled. "Flash is helping me replace Gordon. It's inconvenient having only one ready enforcer."

"So what are you doing in there?" She pointed across the surgical suite.

"Allow me to show you."

Zero's willingness to show her what he'd hidden behind the thick blinds left her uneasy. He seldom seemed eager at the best of times to share information, but his boyish anticipation left her chilled to her core.

He stepped out of her way inside, gesturing to the larger but segmented room. "Behold your new enforcer."

Two glass cells dominated the far end of the room, each twice as thick as the glass separating the room from the surgical suite. The far cell contained a mother panda and the nearer her cub. Both appeared shrunken and wilted.

Zero moved to the mother panda. She reacted at once, her angry noises exited holes bored through the top of the glass walls. He picked up something like a cattle prod. He shoved it somehow straight through the glass and into the panda cub's side.

The cub's mews curdled and warped with torment. Its enraged mother threw herself at the glass. Zero continued the torture until Bianca thought the mother's fury might enable her to break through the wall. He withdrew the prod and touched a symbol etched into the mother's cell glass.

Otherwise invisible runes burned into view, lighting the room with the orange-red of angry coals. Glowing tendrils lashed out at mama panda. She convulsed. Her skin seemed to ignite. Her flesh ran like hairy melted wax. Bones broke audibly, and a reek of burning panda seeped through the holes in the glass

The baby panda threw itself at the adjoining wall, wailing in panic.

Zero left them in that state. He strolled to the other end and withdrew two buckets from a cooler. He passed Bianca without hurry, allowing her time to see thick blood in their recesses. Zero keyed the door and stepped inside mama panda's enclosure. He hurled the blood onto her one bucket at a time. After each, his hands conducted a silent symphony and the blood cocooned mama panda with lazy, fluid grace.

He exited the far cage and knelt next to the baby, shifting his words into a tone one might use with an infant. "Mama won't be in pain long, little one."

It glared at him, and Zero smirked.

"Hold onto that anger," Zero cooed. "It'll be of use to me soon."

He strode past Bianca, turning off the lights as he exited. Bianca stared dumbfounded at the convulsing mass. *My enforcer, he said. That's my enforcer.*

"Come along, Bianca. I need to hear your report."

Bianca hurried after him, but her eyes fell on the mass in the bed beside Flash and then the sleeping Samoan. *What were you before?*

Zero cleared his throat.

Bianca fell into step with him, trying to restrain the chill intent to chatter her teeth. "Um, right, according to our sources, Marc is hiding somewhere in the Far East at this point, but he's still alive. Shine hasn't been seen since Marc's attack. A report to the local Sheriff indicated he abandoned the foster girl several months ago, and she's been living unsupervised since."

"Who made that report?" Zero asked.

"The girlfriend."

"Of course, continue."

"The arrangements you've requested have been put in place around the girlfriend and her son."

"And the foster girl?"

"Yes, sir, though I don't understand why we're diverting resources this way," Bianca said. "Gone as long as he's been, he's probably dead—especially considering Marc is still alive."

"Possible, but I don't think so. I'll admit Marc's attack hit Shine harder than I'd anticipated, but that only makes it more important that we keep all of our pawns moving exactly the way we want them to move."

They took an elevator up a floor or two "I still disagree with opening up a nightclub on the property, especially as we recruit and collect more resources."

Zero led her past other training rooms to another doorless wall that nonetheless parted at their approach. A reek of vomit and liquor and death nearly forced her stomach to empty.

Zero gestured to bodies slumped in bottle-riddled piles around dim crystals which bobbed up and down nearly a yard in height. "The homeless we found camping on our new property are insufficient to power my crystals. A nightclub will allow us to leech life into them without drawing much notice."

"Even with manufactured junk piles to keep people in designated areas, there's a risk someone will stumble into the wrong place."

"Pity for them."

"We can't disappear everyone. Sooner or later we'll get rid of someone connected to someone else unwilling to let their disappearance go," Bianca rubbed her nose. "What are the crystals for, anyway?"

"You must learn magic. Have you arranged the meeting I requested?"

"A messenger was dispatched."

"You made it promise? Followed every detail of my instructions?"

Bianca sighed. "If you don't trust me to make a deal with some little Fey insect, why'd you have me do it?"

Zero smiled. "Is that a yes, Bianca, dear?"

Her temper flared. "Yes, I made the bargain *exactly* as instructed."

"Good. I was saddened to lose Marc, but your adaptability provides me a resource much more useful for the coming days. Besides, you're better in bed."

"Marc said the same th-thing about y-y..." Her throat closed up, choking the words before they could emerge. The burn of a prolonged shock started at her fingertips and shoved inward until it drove her next words from her lips. "You never...in my presence."

Zero's brows arched. "We might make an elf of you yet."

7

SPECIAL DELIVERY

Jordan sulked at the end of her bunk bed, waiting for their driver to finally get around to her. She had a cross-country competition, but unlike the others at the small halfway house, she was under house arrest. The house parents didn't intend to keep her from the competition, but the others got early rides to the mall or the movie theater while she had to wait until just before the race.

And he's late, probably ran out of gas or burgers.

Impatience ejected her from the bed. After several weeks of prison treatment, she had little patience left. She paced up and down between the two bunk bed triplets, stretched against the wall, and paced her cell once more.

Fat slob has made me late for practice twice this week.

One of her wardens passed the bedroom door. "Can you believe she'd say something like that?"

Jordan closed her eyes and shifted magic to enhance her hearing. She knew aeromancy worked better, but the difference seemed hardly worth the effort.

Her warden's husband answered too loud. "She was joking, she had to be."

"She wasn't, Duval. She didn't know I heard her, but to tell her husband they wanted Faye because…," The warden's voice changed to a higher tone. "Taking in the murder's cast off will one up all the members of my bridge club."

"Jodie, come on, who'd want to foster someone as some sort of trophy?"

"They aren't doing it for the money," Jodie said. "It doesn't matter. No matter how much trouble she is, there's no way I'm recommending she be placed with a family that wants her only to show her off."

"Maybe we should just stay neutral in this," Duval said.

"How can you say something like that?" Jodie asked.

"She hasn't exactly got people coming out of the woodwork," Duval said. "Maybe you misunderstood, everyone would probably be better off if we didn't reject a gift horse right out of the gate."

A man shouted in Jordan's ear, making her jump "Ready to go, kid?"

She glared at the driver, releasing the magic in her ears as she noted the fresh grease stain on his t-shirt. Heat and revulsion played tug-of-war for her gut.

I don't need a family. I already have one.

She checked the time on the radio. The slug of a driver seemed unable to move the van faster than a snail's pace. They pulled up to the school.

Jordan bristled. *What's she doing here?*

Billie Jo fretted at the school's entrance, visibly relaxing as the social services vehicle pulled in. She waved at someone Jordan couldn't see, and Angesa appeared from a covered hall leading to a women's bathroom.

Slobwick rose only half his fat ass out of the van. "You got her?"

"Yes, we've got her." Billie Jo said.

"Ms. Cooper?" he asked.

"Yes, she's in our care. You can go," Angesa said.

The door to the van's rear unlocked. Jordan slid it from her way and stormed past the two waiting women in a rush. "I'm late. Keep up or don't."

"You're going to do great, Faye," Billie Jo said.

For an instant, Jordan tensed to round on her, but she didn't have the time. She still needed a full stretch after the ride from downtown to Northside. She found her teammates doing little stretches to stay loose while they waited for their next event.

Jordan dropped onto the grass and started stretching in earnest. Someone blocked out her sunlight. She ignored them, angry enough to hurl fire at Billie Jo if she continued to mettle.

"Nice of you to join us, Miss Jordan," Miss Setter barked.

Jordan glanced up at her coach. "It wasn't my fault. If they let me drive, I'd have been on time."

"That's not your car, Faye," Billie Jo said.

Jordan tightened her fists.

Miss Setter moved between them, lifting the shadow from over Jordan in more ways than one. The large woman folded muscled arms beneath a regal expression. "We appreciate faculty support, Miss Bartlett, but Jordan needs to focus. This is an important race."

Billie Jo moved off toward the track field. Angesa lingered, required to keep Jordan in sight except during the race.

"Thanks," Jordan mumbled.

Miss Setter crouched down, forced to toss her golden ponytail back over one shoulder. "Relax, breathe, you need to give your best today."

"I always do," Jordan said, trying to hide the volcano in her chest.

Miss Setter smiled. "I don't think we've even *seen* your best yet. Come on, you're up in just a few minutes."

Miss Setter led Jordan off to the side of the track field where the cross-country path which began the long distance race started. She gave Angesa a nod, Jordan a pat on the shoulder and got out of the way.

"Good running, everyone."

Jordan's attention jerked toward the unknown black woman designated a race judge by her vest. She pressed her lips together and inclined her head at the judge. Her wardens' conversation kept encroaching on her thoughts and stoking the anger in her. They were going to give her over as some sort of caged animal for display because no one else wanted her. She wasn't good enough.

The starter pistol went off, but it took the dust cloud of the other runners to make her realize it.

I'll show them.

Jordan glanced at Miss Setter, the judge and nearby Angesa. She kicked off her shoes and ran after the pack. She reached into the earth beneath her feet and drew the rumble of Mother's magic up through her toes. Lanea'd taught her magic's XYZ's—just like Mason wanted from Jordan. Jedediah and later Mama Yamai had added to her instruction, helping her connect to magic's source and the elements around her with greater proficiency.

All three had referred to the Earth as Mother, though each from slightly different standpoints. Mother existed before the Dragon Springs, before magic's source had borne the Fey and ultimately Jordan herself. Both could be drawn on, but for a terramancer, Mother usually answered first.

The rumble rose through her, spreading into every cell in Jordan's body. She felt the strength and stamina of ever-present, ever-caring Mother. She endured even the damage done to her body—the world—by normals.

If she can, so can I.

Jordan poured strength into her lungs, her heart. Sweat poured off of her as she exerted herself beyond a typical run. She passed the nearest runner, then the next far faster than she'd have ever expected. The next two fell behind her, one calling out, "You can't keep up that pace forever."

I think I can. Jordan wiped sweat from her eyes. *Though Lanea would've done it without sweating buckets.*

Jordan's anger waned, not because she used the heat of it or because she no longer felt it. The joy of the run stole its significance. The pounding percussion of every stride, a wisp of breeze across her face, the scent of nature and sound of its little ones all combined to make her soul sing chorus.

She passed the others until none lay ahead.

A water station marked the turn off the path and onto the trail.

She grabbed two bottles and leapt into the wood. Mama Yamai—despite being nearly spherical—had taught her to run with the antelope.

I'd wanted to race a cheetah, but they always rolled on their backs around her and begged to have their bellies rubbed.

Jordan fell into the rhythm of the African steppe, a mile striding pace for crossing great grasslands. Roots and branches added zigs and zags to her course, but they didn't slow her. They were cousin, family to the terramancer. One tree had even saved her life when a half-melted centaur had cornered her.

Thirst rose with much the same anger she'd carried at the race's start. The hot, humid air had leached moisture from her every pore, and the two empty bottled waters had only sated her thirst for so long.

She stopped at creek side and bent to drink unfiltered water with who knew what swimming in it. She flexed her legs as she swallowed, keeping them warm. A chuckle bubbled the creek's surface when she remembered chastising Jedediah for drinking out of a hose. She heard one or two of the other runners pass her on the trail. Their breaths sounded ragged, and they pushed their pace to new levels.

Jordan drank her fill, stretched once more against a tree trunk to ensure her limbs didn't cramp and set back out to regain the lead. She passed them with little effort as their strength flagged only two-thirds of the way along the race. She grabbed only a single bottle at the next water station, sorry to feel cool earth replaced by hot pavement.

She pushed magic into her soles, hardening them against damage and picked up her pace. The last third of the race whipped by like landscape along a highway until she passed a set of paramedics headed the opposite direction.

I hope whoever is okay.

Running pushed her worries to one side only to ambush her at the finish line.

"Holy shit," Miss Setter's wide-eyed gaze stared at her stopwatch. The judge joined her, her bright grin bobbing back and forth as she shook her head. They comparing their watches in hushed whispers Jordan didn't bother to hear over her own racing pulse.

Jordan walked cool down circles and waited for the others to finish. Not all of them did. Three of the other front runners lost to runners typically last to cross the finish line. One of those that'd passed her had been taken away by the paramedics, making guilt twist around Jordan's banked anger.

Miss Setter approached her. "Are you okay?"

"Sure," Jordan bounced around with her hands folded behind her head. "Good run."

"Yeah, real good. Michelle didn't finish. Any chance you're up to another race?"

"Yeah, no problem."

"You're sure you're willing after such a long run?" Miss Setter asked. "Don't hurt yourself."

Jordan grinned. "I'm still warm. Which one, eight hundred?"

Miss Setter nodded. "You don't have to place."

"Michelle would've tried to win," Jordan said.

Setter glanced at her stopwatch. "I doubt Michelle planned to run that last race so fast. Hey, don't forget your shoes."

Jordan trotted over to the track, staying warm and loose until the eight hundred. She ran it hard, finishing first with a quarter track lead on the other girls. She did cool down stretches and grabbed a hot dog while waiting for the award ceremonies.

"Quite a day," the judge said.

Jordan mumbled her agreement around the mouthful of food.

"You're a hell of a runner. Ever think about competing professionally?"

Jordan narrowed her eyes and swallowed. "Who are you?"

"A sports agent, scout, nobody important." She extended a hand. "Marnie Hepp."

Jordan shook the extended hand, but no indication of magic interacted with her own. "You'll forgive me if I don't trust agents."

"Smarmy bunch?" Marnie asked.

"Last one I met turned out to be a murderer," Jordan said.

"I've heard of sharks in the business, but never one that actually killed the competition," Marnie said.

"So what do you want with me?"

"Do you realize you finished that race in just over two minutes or that you ran it in an almost perfect even split?"

"What are you talking about?" Jordan asked. "I just ran."

"No bullshit? You ran that eight hundred only a few seconds slower than the junior women's world record and no one's taught you race strategies?"

Jordan shrugged. "Run faster than everyone else."

"Brandy called me," Marnie said. "She told me she had a girl hiding what she could do. She wanted me to look you over. Here I am, and there you are."

"You didn't answer my question. What do you want with me?"

Marnie smirked. "How'd you like to try out for the Olympics?"

Jordan blinked at her, anger forgotten and mind racing. A strange hopeful excitement welled up inside her.

"We'll need to really see what you can do first, do some training, but I'm pretty sure I can get you into a team qualifier if you can consistently repeat what you did today."

The Olympics? Would that even be fair?

"It could mean sponsors, scholarships, the kinds of opportunities not usually available to someone in your situation," Marnie said.

"You have a problem with foster kids?" Jordan asked.

"Nah," Marnie said. "Not into self-loathing."

Jordan considered her. Marnie offered a chance at something normal, a path to something not draped in magic, war and death. The excitement returned, but guilt made it waver. *Jedediah's my family, Drake too—not that they're around. What do I even have to contribute to a magical war? I can't do magic outside myself. Maybe I should do this, trade running for a future. I don't even know if Jedediah's actually coming back.*

Marnie watched her.

Who says I can't have both? I love running. Run for Marnie and make

Jedediah proud when he returns. Hell, it's a lot better than wallowing around like Drake.

Zero reclined in crimson leather set atop thick pearl carpet. A buffet table extended from the jet's wall had been set with golden tureens, platters and plates. He folded his laptop and fetched a bowl of chili, adding a dollop of sour cream. Spices rose to his nose, beckoning hunger from wakefulness to bestial anticipation.

He stirred in the cream and raised a pinkish spoonful of meat, peppers and black beans. The recipe would've scandalized, containing beans where none supposedly belonged, but it remained one of his favorites—not to mention strategically appropriate for his meeting.

As if on cue, a mercenary poked his masked head into the plane. "Um, Faun party to see you, sir?"

"Allow them access without search."

"We already searched them, sir."

Zero rolled one hand, and the merc hurried back outside. *The man is irksome, but Flash shall return to service as soon as his new brother evolves.*

Three women in suit skirts proceeded a lumbering man in his early twenties. The scent of game and woodland swirled through the jet.

Zero set his bowl aside and rose, extending a hand to the woman dressed in mint. He raised her hand, brushing the back of it with his lips. "Miss Mimi, good to see you again. Thank you for coming."

He repeated the greeting with the woman dressed in powder blue followed by the third dressed in daffodil. He turned to the man, scenting fear, urine and a hint of charcoal. His brows rose. "Where is Miss Jiji?"

"Dead," Lili said.

"Pity," Zero said.

Kiki tensed, but her sisters restrained her with a hand on either arm.

"Who is the gentleman?" Zero asked.

"You asked us to bring you wizards," Lili said.

Zero tilted his head from side to side, pops crackling from his neck. "I asked you to bring me the necromancer."

"Velith'Seravin refused to release her," Kiki said.

"May I ask why?" Zero sat, pulling the bowl onto his lap. "Oh, forgive my manners. Would you care to eat? The chef prepared a positively divine venison chili."

The fauns tensed. Kiki's glamour flickered, offering glimpses of her true form.

"No?" Zero asked. "Hmm. Do you mind? I never tire of this recipe."

"Lady Mauve dispatched her apprentice to Jedediah, Master Remi," Mimi said. "VelSera believes her messenger will bring Jedediah to rescue her."

"That necromancer is enormously powerful. Keeping her as bait will only cost Wizard's Bane lives." Zero enjoyed a bite of chili, watching their expressions. "You'll convince him of this and deliver her to me."

"I don't think he can be convinced to let her go," Lili said. "He's certain she'll not recover from her injuries as long as he continues to torture her."

Zero took another bite.

"We brought you this one instead," Mimi said.

"I gift you magic," Zero said.

"You *loaned* us power," Kiki said.

He smiled. "I gifted you a loan of my personal power. I provide you the locations of wizards and dragonlings, even provide solutions to their wards and protections. However, when I ask for a small concession in return, you offer me swill instead of the fine wine I requested."

Kiki's glamour vanished, revealing her dark scowl. "If you don't like it, we'll take him back, and you can address this with VelSera."

Zero set his chili aside, folding hands into a steeple in his lap.

"You're a powerful aeromancer, particularly among your mostly powerless kind."

Mimi and Lili stepped shoulder to shoulder between Zero and Kiki. He dabbed his face, the napkin concealing his smirk. *Oh, no, little girls. I'll not add you to the soup just yet. Certainly not after offering a warning.*

"How was your sister killed?" Zero asked.

"A ghoul," Mimi said.

"It was the boy's fault," Kiki said.

Zero's brows rose. "An apprentice summoned a ghoul?"

"A horde of spirits," Mimi said. "They fouled the centaurs charge and interfered with Lili's attempt to heal her."

I must find this boy. Zero's lips quirked into a half smile. "Too bad he got away."

"We'll find him," Mimi said.

"You certainly should." Zero licked his lips. "I'd like to meet him."

"We're going to kill him," Kiki said. "Vengeance for our sister."

Zero considered her. The loss of their pyromantic sister served his own needs better than all but the loss of Kiki. Mimi and Lili remained easy pawns, but Jiji and Kiki had proven harder to control. He considered killing her or setting the loaned magic to backfire at an opportune moment. There might be other ways to her heart.

"Have you brought the teeth?" Zero asked.

Mimi stepped forward, drawing a satchel from beneath her glamour. He took the offered bag and dug a hand inside. A tooth still stained with blood and gum came out first. Its tingle vibrated his palm. He moved three more examining each with magic veiled over his eyes. Thin lines of power stretched out in the same direction, linking each tooth to its dragonling.

A smile grew across his face. "When you return with the boy or his master, the talismans will be prepared."

"I told you." Kiki spat. "We're going to kill him."

"Did I tell you not to do so?" Zero asked.

"Forgive me, Master Remi, but you promised us the talisman in exchange for us leading VelSera to your targets," Lili said.

Zero steepled his fingers. "Have you slain any of the Guardians?"

"We need the talisman to take on a Guardian," Mimi said.

"I see. You require payment in order to complete the services purchased," Zero said. "I think perhaps my support of Wizard's Bane was premature. I'll return your teeth. Brace yourselves while I reclaim my power."

"Don't your clients pay for assassination contracts part in advance?" Mimi asked. "You've got a fire kindred's tooth there. Keep it and loan us the promised talisman. We'll slay one of the Guardians."

"And bring me their apprentices," Zero said. "Alive, agreed?"

They inclined their heads and turned to leave.

"Hurry back. I look forward to you joining me for lunch," Zero said.

8

FALSE FACES

An old bearded man with too-thick glasses sat across a massive mahogany desk from Jordan, haloed by a dozen certificates attesting that Doctor Maurice Ottrisan had spent way too much time in school to know anything. He blinked again, bolstering Jordan's doubt that he could actually see her.

"Miss Jordan, I agreed to see you pro bono because you refused to speak to the child services assessor." He blew out a breath which ruffled his grey whiskers in a way that created a knot in Jordan's gut. "We hoped you'd be more inclined to cooperate in a private setting."

Jordan folded her arms and glared.

"Miss Jordan, Faye—"

"Don't call me that."

"But it's your—"

A deep growl brought him up short. His gaze shot back and forth until it finally fell upon a wolfish, deep-brown muzzle and marble teeth.

"How did that get in here?" Ottrisan snatched up a bronze bust of Freud.

Jordan leapt out of her chair, yanking it from his hand before he could do anything with it. "Leave him alone."

Nip shifted his glance to her, his tail wagging twice.

"You know this filthy creature?" Ottrisan said. "It's soiling my Persian rug."

Jordan ignored him. "You can't be here, Nip."

Nip cocked his head.

"I'll be fine, just go."

Nip's ears folded back against his head.

"Go," Jordan said.

Nip slunk backward. As it neared the brick wall, Jordan dropped the bust onto Ottrisan's desk with a crash. Nip slid through the wall before Ottrisan turned back his direction.

Jordan resumed her seat.

Ottrisan glared her general direction, taking time out to wipe his desk and the bust before taking his own chair. "The Sheriff's report indicates you claimed to have had your records deleted by an elf woman who was murdered by an international organization of killers."

Jordan opened her mouth, then closed it.

Ottrisan leaned in. "Do you have special powers?"

The blood drained from Jordan's face.

"Did Mister Shine indoctrinate you into some form of cult?" Ottrisan asked.

The blood rushed back three times as heated. Jordan leapt to her feet, slamming fists into his desk to the sounds of cracking wood. Before the tirade escaped her lips, three solid blows struck the outer door.

"I'm in session," Ottrisan said.

Agent Ridley entered and pushed his glasses up over warm brown eyes. "I realize that, Doctor Ottrisan, but this evaluation is no longer necessary."

Cold washed up Jordan from her feet like a razor-edged ice age. "What are you doing here, Agent?"

"What's this about?" Ottrisan asked. "They've ordered a full psychiatric workup on this girl."

"Unnecessary, as I said, may I call you Maurice?" Ridley said. "The FBI has provided social services an up-to-date evaluation."

Relief washed through her. "I'm free to go?"

Ridley smiled. "I'm here to take you to your new fosterage."

Jordan narrowed her eyes. *He wants something. Why won't people just leave me alone? I wasn't bothering anybody before Billie Jo interfered.*

They stepped out of the doctor's office and onto the sidewalk outside. Morning heat climbed toward its peak as noon approached. Jordan turned a scowl on him. "Why you and not Angesa?"

"Several reasons, but Angesa agreed to me delivering you. If you're uncomfortable with just me, we can pick her up."

"What's your angle?"

"There are good people in the world. I think your time on that farm has shown you that already."

"There are a lot of sick people too," Jordan said. "Your job should've taught you that, but if you think the farm and hence Jedediah taught me about good people, why are you still watching him?"

"Are you hungry? Can we discuss that over lunch before I take you to meet the Bridgeports? We can pick up Angesa if you want, or I can drop you with her no questions asked. Your choice."

He's got an angle, but something makes me want to trust him. Maybe if I play along, I'll learn something useful. Jordan glanced up from her fingers. "You trying to get me to incriminate Jedediah?"

"You're a minor, Jordan. Anything you tell me would be hearsay at best."

"I'm not telling you anything about Jedediah except that he's innocent, but I'll take a free lunch out. Prison food sucks."

"Considering your life experiences, that you trust him speaks volumes."

"Unless it's the naïve viewpoint of a stupid child."

Ridley laughed. "I don't think you fit that profile. I believe that you stopped being naïve a long time ago. The questions I want to ask aren't about Jedediah per se. Shall we pick up Angesa to represent your interests?"

"No. I'll trade you a bit of trust for some good food," Jordan said.

"How magnanimous of you."

"Besides, I can probably break every bone in your body if you try anything."

Ridley searched her eyes. Whatever he found grew a slow smile. His gaze continued, unwavering until the contact became too penetrating.

Jordan dropped her eyes.

Ridley escorted her to a Government Issue sedan without ever touching her. He opened the front door for her but always left an accessible escape path. She could've run at any point, but she wanted to hear the agent's questions.

"Is there really an FBI evaluation?" Jordan asked.

"Pardon?"

"You told the shrink you had a psychiatric evaluation on me, but I never talked to the FBI."

"Since you didn't answer any questions for us, nothing you said caused the examiner any concern," Ridley smirked. "Easiest path to a clean bill of health."

"Who signed off then?"

"I did," Ridley said. "I'm fully rated. Seeing people for who they are has always intrigued me. I studied psychology and sociology long before I went to college for criminal psychology."

They pulled into the long outdoor shopping center off Whittlesey—she never could remember its name. A series of turns deposited them between a bank and a deli.

"An entire government expense account and this is where you want to go?" Jordan asked. "I thought we were getting good food."

"They have an excellent Reuben," Ridley said

Jordan wrinkled her nose. "That's the one with sauerkraut, right?"

"Yes."

"Yuck."

"In any case, this lunch is on me, not the government," Ridley said.

"Why?" She narrowed her eyes.

"Jedediah's case threw me one curveball after another. If there's one thing that gets under my skin, it's not knowing the answers."

"So you really are a bookworm, bet they bullied the hell out of you in high school," Jordan smiled. "So if I don't tell you anything, it's really going to gnaw at you, isn't it?"

"You get lunch either way." Ridley exited the car and rounded the hood to open her door. She leapt out before he could. He smiled and headed inside. "If you don't want to talk I guess I'll just have to live with the idea there's no such thing as magic—despite you taking a bullet to the forehead and surviving."

Jordan stopped dead, annoying a mid-thirties woman in a land yacht. "What did you just say?"

Ridley smirked. He went inside and stood in line on the opposite side of the glass, striking up a conversation with someone next to him. She wasn't cuffed. She could bolt. He offered her every opportunity in the world to run.

Except I can't. She cursed. *Not after that hook he just tricked me into swallowing.*

She hurried after him and lowered her voice. "You saw Lanea die."

"And what happened in the pond," Ridley said.

Heat blossomed in Jordan's chest. "Did you even bother to chase down that murdering bastard?"

"Once I'd recovered." Ridley looked down. "The shooter eluded me."

"Then we're done talking." Her gaze shifted to the door. If she could reach the boneyard, she could hide a hundred places he'd never think to look. The ones with caretakers would have to feed her unless she somehow found a way to retrieve her confiscated debit card. Unfortunately, none of them knew where Jedediah had gone, and none claimed any knowledge of Sanctuary Hole's whereabouts—assuming Drake's suspicion of his location was correct.

And I can't just hop a flight to Africa without a passport and wander around calling out his name—particularly with the FBI hunting me. Her stomach grumbled treasons. She glanced at Ridley. *I need to stall anyway, why not do so eating the most expensive thing on the menu?*

To Jordan's irritation, Agent Ridley didn't balk when she did just that plus two desserts. He made only idle small talk as they ate, refilling her drink when it got low. He never treated her like a prisoner nor a child.

"So, good thing we got everybody away from Drake the other day," Ridley said. "He didn't manage to catch that shooter either, even airborne, but I bet he could have made short work of that ass Dunford."

She froze mid-chew. The cheesecake turned to earthworms in her mouth. A swooping sensation made her feel as if she'd dropped beneath the ground in an earthswim and the thousand knife edges of guilt made her wish she could.

The man feeding her had been chasing her the day Nip offered her earthworms to fill her empty stomach. Velith'Seravin had killed Nibble not long after. She'd never mourned the precious mudpuppy as she should have. She'd been too numb from the terror of Drake and Lanea's sludge hydra shredding all of those FBI agents.

Her gaze met Ridley's. *His agents.*

Tears gathered in the corners of her eyes. She couldn't breathe, just like during the attack. Guilt held her as surely as the dragon fear that had immobilized her—forced her to watch carnage that permanently swore her off slasher movies.

"Are you all right, Jordan?" Ridley asked.

Tears escaped her attempts to restrain them. Words poured from breathless lungs, shaking whispers powered by only sorrow and quaking gasps. "I-I'm sorry. I'm so s-sorry. I didn't m-mean for it to happen. I swear, I w-warned them, t-told them to l-leave me alone. I never wanted to h-hurt anyone. I r-ran, b-but they chased, and Drake...D-drake...he only w-wanted to protect m-me."

Ridley's expression tightened. "Perhaps we should discuss this in the car."

"Everything all right here?" A woman built by merging Daisy Duke and Maryanne from Gilligan's Island interposed herself between the agent and herself. "There's a woman over at delco looking for someone. You aren't waiting on an Angela by any chance?"

Ridley unfolded his wallet. "Everything is fine. I'm FBI. This isn't a date."

The woman ignored him. "Honey?"

"I'll be in the car." His voice sounded tight as he scribbled something on the back of a business card and set it down. "Call Angesa if you don't feel safe going to the Bridgeports with me."

Jordan sniffed, raising her eyes from the number to the deli manager. "He doesn't want to hurt me."

The other woman folded her arms. "They never *want* to hurt us, honey. There's always some excuse. Need me to call you a ride?"

The carnage flashed through her thoughts once more. A shiver gripped her, but Jordan shook her head. "Thanks, I'll be fine."

By the time Jordan slid into Ridley's car, his smile had reasserted itself. She watched him in sidelong silence, her chest threatening to explode. "I really am sorry about those people."

A tiny shift in his steering wheel grip signaled the only change in his emotions. She wished she'd paid more attention to scent magic and telltales.

"You're apologizing for Drake murdering those agents—*my* people."

"They wouldn't leave me alone," Jordan said. "I told them—"

His voice softened. "They were doing their job, trying to protect you."

"So was Drake."

A low heat crept into Ridley's voice. "He murdered them. I can see it upset you, and I'll believe that you had nothing to do with it, but that animal must be put down. It's the law."

"Your law," Jordan said.

"Everyone's law."

Jordan shook her head. "You don't understand. Your law, this country, they're interlopers here. You can't punish him."

"I must. Regardless of cultural differences, no one's above the law."

She whirled to him, heat balling her fists. She slammed one into the dash to a sound of breaking plastic. "Don't you get it? Drake *is* the law. No one's higher than his kind, and if you ignore that, he'll eat you for lunch, literally."

She pulled a bleeding fist from the caved-in dashboard.

"He eats people?"

She sighed. "He eats regular food. Steak, pizza, Cherry Coke, but he's an apex predator, Agent Ridley, and trust me you're not even in the foothills."

"As opposed to you?" Ridley asked.

"A little higher—maybe. Even Jedediah fears Drake's mother."

"What's the difference?"

She mumbled her answer at her lap. "Magic."

"Magic."

"You said you saw what happened in the pond. If not magic, how do you explain that?" Jordan asked.

"I can't. I might be able to blame drugs on Angesa's memory gaps, but I can't explain a full-scale assault on an armed convoy with no casualties. I can't explain a well-seasoned agent acting like a giddy rookie, charging into professionally held guns and slaughtering them all without a scratch."

"Magic."

"Then Muler and O'Steele didn't break Jedediah out of our custody. He tricked me into lying on the stand in his defense."

"Muler attacked your convoy. Jedediah's magic protected your people," Jordan said. "The *Namhaid* murdered Joe Franklin, those others."

"You witnessed this?" Ridley asked.

She shook her head.

"Then how do you know?"

Jordan raised her chin and met his gaze. "I know Jedediah. He's a grumpy bastard on the outside, but he's different. I've been through who knows how many foster families, caseworkers, cops...no one cared about me like Jedediah did from the first day." A lump filled her throat. "Even after how I acted."

"A soft spot for you doesn't mean he isn't a liar and a murderer."

She clenched her jaw to keep from screaming at him. As smart as Agent Ridley seemed, he just didn't...wouldn't understand. "If you attack Drake, you'll die. I'd rather that didn't happen."

"Where's Jedediah?"

She shrugged. "He said he'd be back."

"What makes you believe him?"

She shrugged one shoulder.

"Why would he let you be taken if he cares the way you say?"

"H-he doesn't know. He can't, or he'd c-come get me." A chuckle bubbled from her lips unbidden. "Unless he wants me to rescue myself."

"Why did you find that funny?" Ridley asked.

"He's like that. Always testing us, making us prove to ourselves what we can do." Jordan pled with her eyes. "Leave them alone, please?"

Ridley started the car. They drove in thoughtful silence, and Jordan found she couldn't help liking the FBI agent. Before Jedediah, she'd have pushed such instincts away sure in the belief that everyone wanted something and had an angle to get it. Her chest tightened, cinched so tight she could hardly breathe. *I miss him, Lanea too. I never thought having a real family could hurt so much.*

Ridley asked questions slowly. Her answers about the magical world proved clumsy. He asked deeper questions, and she found her knowledge of all but terramancy to be filled with gaps. She apologized for her rudimentary understanding and its many holes until even she tired of hearing the excuse. Ridley took it with grace. The set of his mouth, the cast of his eyes told her suspicion and disbelief ruled the gears behind his gaze.

She barely noticed as their drive took them from busy commercial areas to empty rural streets followed by small, newer communities. A turn took them into a heavily wooded drive she expected to regurgitate mobile homes and shanty-style trailers. Instead, secluded drives and spacious homes sprinkled the sides of manicured, well-kept roads.

The island of upper-class homes didn't matter. Somewhere beyond the trailers waited to offer another dismal country exile in a system where she'd be a ward to some southern redneck family doubling their income by fostering her.

The agent mobile pulled up to a huge, lavish house with perfectly tended lawns. A fountain big enough to swim in dominated the front yard. A BMW and a Mercedes, both brand new, sat in an open four car garage. The house's backyard stretched past several large outbuildings to wild woods.

"We're here," Ridley said.

Jordan gaped. "No way. You've got to have the wrong address."

Ridley reached behind the seat and presented her a file folder. "Mae and Louis Bridgeport, both forty-one, son Arthur, seventeen, foster daughter Crystal Potter, twelve."

"How big is this place?" Jordan whispered.

"Four thousand square feet, not counting a mother-in-law cottage on the back property," Ridley said.

Twin doors opened up beyond the ornately-railed porch. Their ovals of stained glass glinted a rainbow of afternoon sunlight as they disgorged a well-dressed couple. A tall, plump boy followed with an anticipatory expression, one hand dragging a mousy, cringing girl.

Holy June Cleaver. Moneyed. Well dressed. Well fed. Jordan's eyes settled on the brunette trying to fade into the woodwork. *Mostly anyway.* "What's their angle?"

Ridley answered the question she hadn't realized she'd spoken out loud. "Maybe they just like sharing their good fortune."

"Maybe they're serial killers," Jordan countered.

"They've fostered a half dozen orphans over the last ten years. I'm still waiting on some of the sealed files to complete my background check, but there were no fatalities. Your things were delivered this morning."

"Why're you doing a background check on these people if social services sent me here?" Jordan asked. "Why do you—right, I'm bait."

"You're not bait, Jordan." Ridley exited the car.

She hesitated, glancing at her clothes. *They're new, why do I feel out of place?*

Mae Bridgeport hurried down the drive, a pastel cotton dress fluttering in her rush. She hesitated at the sight of Ridley. Frown lines appeared on her forehead. She replaced them with a polite smile. "Can we help you?"

"I'm Agent Ridley, FBI."

The plump boy stepped back from Ridley, all but his ears losing color. Crystal took advantage of Arthur's distraction, slipping from his grasp. She backed against the house wall and nestled beside a pedestal planter supporting a fern a head taller than her.

Louis Bridgeport stepped leisurely forward, blocking Jordan's view of his son's curious reaction. "Is there something amiss, Agent?"

Jordan exited the car to get a better look. All eyes tracked to her. Arthur's expression brightened, his gaze sweeping up and down her. His approving grin spread a not-quite-even line across his face.

Mae's gaze swept up and down Jordan too, a flicker of genuine opinion declaring her less pleased with her new foster daughter. A bright smile flashed toward Ridley, travelled to Jordan and hardened into place as she bustled up and embraced her. "Faye, welcome to the family. We're so glad you're here. Everyone say hello to Faye."

No whisper of magic tingled across Jordan's skin, though gooseflesh slithered up and down her limbs. "Jordan. I'm not a big hugger."

"You just aren't used to it, but in this house you'll get used to being loved on." Mae tightened the embrace. "It's so nice to have another woman in the house. Crys, come down here and say hello to your new big sister."

Louis's handshake drew her from the hug, as dead of magical energy as his wife's. Before Jordan could address him, Arthur caught her up in a full body embrace. He whispered hot, breathy words into her ear. "So glad you're here, Faye. You're so beautiful."

"Jordan." She struggled to escape his grasp.

His grip tightened. "Faye."

She drew upon Mother and forced him away. "Jordan. I don't like being called Faye."

"Nonsense, Faye's a beautiful name," Mae said. "We're not calling you by your last name, that's so libertarian."

Crystal lingered toward the back of the group, eyes not meeting Jordan's.

Ridley cleared his throat.

"Oh, Agent Ridley, forgive me a mother's distraction. Was there a reason you brought her to us instead of that darling Ms. Cooper?" Mae asked.

His gaze swept each Bridgeport, eyes tightening. "Jordan is helping me with a few lingering queries."

"Do you have a judge's order to talk to her?" Mae asked.

"Ms. Cooper granted permission," Ridley said.

Mae shook her head. "That's all well and good, Agent, but I'm her guardian now. If we're in no danger, then I don't think you should bother Faye any more. We wouldn't want the child suffering, forced to relive the previous year's unfortunate nastiness."

"I don't mind," Jordan said.

"I do, Faye, dear." Mae's hard expression softened. "Thank the Agent for bringing you so he can leave."

Louis extended a hand. "Thank you, Agent, we'll take her from here."

Ridley frowned at them. He removed a business card from his suit jacket. "Here's my card, Jordan, in case you have any questions for me."

Jordan lowered her voice. "You already gave me one."

Mae snatched it from his hand. "Thank you, Agent. Good day."

"Good afternoon." Ridley smiled at Jordan, inclined his head at the Bridgeports and returned to his car. "Take care."

"Thank you for lunch." Jordan watched him drive away with her new foster family at her back. Her palms itched. Tension rose behind her to an almost physical press upon her back.

"Crystal!" Mae's voice cracked like a shot. "Get Faye inside. Get her changed into proper clothes. That chore list won't finish itself."

"Chore list?" Jordan asked.

"You two have to make this pigsty immaculate before tonight's party guests arrive," Mae said. "You'd better get to work if you don't want to be punished."

9

LITTLE LORD OF THE FLIES

D rake sunbathed in the boneyard just outside the portal to Weems—his wings fully extended. The maze of appliances, junkers and piled toilets kept him hidden from traffic along the sparsely travelled highway. The boneyard's inhabitants kept their heads down, their otherwise incessant chatter silent lest they displease him again.

It's good being Elder.

He crunched the last can of tribute, leaving him buzzed but forlorn with no one left to fetch more from the market. The larger bottles of Cherry Coke had gone before he realized it, his own junkyard of empty plastic collected in the backyard slope behind the Weems house.

Ianyss and her sister dryads would have a fit if I did that out here. A lazy chuckle bubbled from his drunken thoughts. *At least I'd have someone bigger than a brownie to fetch me more. I wonder where Jordan ended up... I could send her to the store.*

His mind wandered with thoughts of excitement, adventure. He recalled the trek to Mythela'Raemyn and their climb up the grand stair. At its foot, he'd had his first real thoughts regarding death. Not his death, of course, he'd live forever—aging and growing until he dwarfed buildings like his mother.

He shifted an eye to the farmhouse ruin, the home she'd crushed in a fit of temper. *Where am I ever going to get enough Cherry Coke when I'm that size?*

He knew from lessons about his kind—taught to him by Jedediah rather than his mother—that once dragons reached a few thousand years, some entered long sleeps. They'd embraced those torpors to make years pass faster, though he couldn't figure what goal they served. He imagined once more what it would be like to have Jedediah long gone, dead to old age. His chest ached.

Where are you master? Sanctuary Hole? How do I reach you?

In his early years of apprenticeship, he'd have given anything to be alone, have his own lair, be rid of Jedediah and master of his own destiny. Drake shook his head, but the buzz clung to him like cobwebs.

I haven't practiced in... Drake strained to remember how long it had been since Thestle and Chalet delivered their tribute—how long he'd wallowed in unlimited Cherry Coke intoxication. *Weeks? Is this what life is for a dragon—endless sunbathing? Why hasn't Jordan visited?*

Jedediah had told him another dragon claimed some of his kind took their own lives after ten or twenty thousand years. He'd thought the teller lied, pulling his master's leg. Staring at empty days stretched immediately before him, he had to wonder.

Another bee landed on his beak. He blew a nostril's worth of smoke at it, but rather than force it away, the bee settled atop his beak, buzzing and vibrating in languid but urgent tones—not that he had any idea what they were trying to say. He hadn't stolen honey in weeks. When he had, they'd harried him, buzzing tones which required no translation. They'd all but ignored him when Jedediah had been around. As the only air kindred on the farm, the thousand irritable insects bothered him incessantly.

I'll sneak out to the Britt David sports complex by night and raid their Coke machines.

The hives emptied their entire population in a vibrating uproar a moment before the far horizon lit with an explosion of light brilliant even in daylight.

Drake whirled to his talons. He gathered his focus, feeling the tingle of power akin to high wind along the tiny flight hairs on his scales. He aborted the shape change, discarded his glamour and stretched out his wings.

Why bother with magic when I can enjoy the wind for real?

He gathered wind beneath his wings as he bound forward thrice then into the sky. Winds caressed his scales. It ruffled the tiny, fine hairs, giving him extreme sensitivity to the constantly changing press of air. His scales would eventually lose them as he grew, but he might regenerate them with shaping magic—he liked their tickle.

Like how Lanea used to caress my frills.

Empty farmland turned to wild wood—both kept and maintained by Jedediah to protect the collective wild Fey kept safe within his borders. A flurry of lights beneath dappled shade shot underneath him.

Pixie races—always entertaining. I'll return once I've dealt with the border challenge.

The magical barrier only reacted to magical creatures. Jedediah had entrusted each Fey community with a talisman to allow their peoples to come or go as needed, so the intruder had to be unwanted—like Velith'Seravin.

I want him. He or his rogue centaurs will serve as a nice distraction, especially without Jedediah around to stop me from playing with my food.

The tiny sliver of Dragonsteel removed from Jordan flashed through his thoughts. Heat bubbled through the loosening seal on his flame lung, its warmth fighting chill fear of the magical metal invented to slay his kind.

Like iron to elves. I'll just have to hit them like a falcon diving out of the sun.

Drake fantasized about getting his talons on Velith'Seravin, ripping the arrogant centaur that had ordered his death while still a Fleet Hoof tribal elder. His rogues ambushed Jordan. They killed her mudpuppy Nibble and nearly killed her while he'd fended off an FBI incursion intent to imprison her. He imagined doing to rogue centaur what he'd done to the normals hunting his sister.

Blood scent filled his nostrils. Copper tang and spicy fear painted his tongue. His talons practically felt the flesh ripped limb from limb in their grasp.

I'll gorge on them, gnaw the marrow from their bones, make a nest of their hides and a throne of their skulls.

Woodland fell away to open fields as he neared the barrier. He circled higher on a rising thermal, eyeing the spot for a possible ambush before he got too close. A lone centaur lay oddly slumped against the barrier.

Stunned. Easy prey. Drake chuckled. *Must've slammed headfirst into the barrier.*

Drake checked the sun at his back, folded his wings and dove. Wind whistled through his frills. A pale white face peered up at him. Even through the wind whipping past him, Drake scented putrefied flesh and the acrid aroma of confused terror.

He flexed his claws in anticipation.

The centaur shrieked like a little girl.

Drake narrowed his gaze.

The centaur had a little girl tangled in its limbs, a pathetic attempt to use normals as protection. For a moment, Drake considered striking anyway—through the normal if need be. He wrenched himself out of the dive at the last moment, wings beating furiously and stirring up a hurricane of debris. He landed on all four talons, lip curled and teeth bared beneath his beak.

Fresh urine ran from the girl over her captor.

Drake's chuckle filled the air with menace.

"Dra-dra-dra."

He paused. His prey was long dead, splattered headlong into the barrier like a bug onto a windshield. Broken bones stuck out of the rotting meat at odd angles, already home to thousands of maggots.

"Dragon," Drake finished.

"It talks!" She shrieked.

Drake rolled his eyes. "Talk quick, girl."

She scowled. "I'm not a girl."

Drake snarled.

"Please don't eat me, not after all I've survived." The girl fell to her knees, groveling satisfactorily. "Call me a girl, it's okay, I'm a girl."

The reek of death intensified. "Talk."

Words spilled from the girl in a high-pitched, rapid-fire stream. "Mistress Mauve sent me. I'm her apprentice. Kane. I'm Kane. She sent me...here, somewhere here. I've got to find a wizard. My last surname's Batson, not that I'm a bat's son. Please don't eat me. My mistress is in trouble, centaurs...centaur, whatever the right plural is, they attacked us. I'm supposed to tell the wizard."

"Which wizard?" Drake asked.

Kane blinked. "How many do you have?"

Drake growled.

"Jed, she called him Jed." Kane squeaked. "We attended his trial."

"Master is unavailable at the moment," Drake said.

Kane mouthed the word master a few times.

"What was Mauve's message?" Drake asked.

Kane narrowed his eyes. "Why should I tell you?"

Drake raised onto his hind legs, spreading his wings.

"Wizard's Bane attacked, there were so many of them." Kane's rattled off the whole story faster than his first ramble. His last words fell from his lips with creeping dread. "She might be dead by now."

"Get your things and touch my side," Drake said.

"Why?"

"You want through the barrier or not?" Drake asked.

Kane touched Drake, causing the scales beneath the boy's fingers to crawl. The stench of death filled Drake's nostrils. They made it almost to the barrier when the boy gasped, releasing his hold. His body catapulted through the air back off the property.

Drake closed his eyes. *Don't yell. Don't laugh.*

He turned to find awe and horror mixed on Kane's face. Drake stepped back through the barrier and waited at its edge for the boy to recover. Kane returned to his side, fingers stretching but almost as unwilling to touch the dragon's scales as Drake was to have him touch them. Both stepped away from the other the moment they entered the property.

"Tell me again what happened. Slowly this time."

Drake made him repeat the story over and over, particularly what combat Kane could recall. It dulled Drake's awareness to the boy's reek, but having ridden a rotting corpse across half the continent had soaked the stench into every pore of the boy's body.

Drake led him to the pond. "Bathe."

"I need to see Jed," Kane balked.

"Master Jedediah is occupied." Drake lowered his voice. "Bathe."

Kane waded uncertainly into the water.

The water's surface broke, two mottled green and brown heads rose barring razor teeth and hissing. More heads joined the first two, disgust vibrating the long whiskers protruding from its faces. Kane gawked up at it, lost in the mesmerizing undulation of its necks and heads.

"Bathe," Drake repeated. "He *won't* harm you."

The sludge hydra's heads whipped toward Drake, a snarl on every lip. The snarls softened beneath tightening gazes. Lips concealed teeth and each head grudgingly inclined toward Drake before slipping back into the pond.

Kane shrunk down in the water and removed his shirt.

The hydra's weed-tangled body emerged. It shot Kane several disgusted glances, wrapped glamour around itself like a cloaking spell and trudged away across the nearest field.

The reeking boy removed the remainder of his clothes in fits and starts, spinning to check for observers several times before removing each item and letting them float.

If I had clothes for him, I'd destroy those horrid things. Would Mason's spares fit?

Kane bathed, putting his filthy clothes back on.

"No, stay there." Drake dug into the ruin, coming back with Jedediah's homemade lye soap, perfumed soap left behind by Billie Jo and three bottles of shampoo. "Use it."

"All of it?"

"Definitely," Drake shook his head. *What am I going to do with this kid and what am I going to do about Mauve and Wizard's Bane?*

Zero settled the last of his four power crystals into the abandoned warehouse rearmost on the Brickworks property. Their dim glow troubled him, but less so then how long he'd gone between rituals. Blood mixed with magical fire drew out concentric rings with elaborate glowing runes—some foreign to the original spell unearthed so long ago in Mythela'Raemyn's archives.

The wizard provided by the faun sisters knelt within its innermost circle. Silver cuffs anchored his arms and legs atop more writhing symbols of living shadow laid in the concrete beneath. A swirl of glowing energy haloed the prisoner like a dozen bright sprites dragging light through the dim air.

Zero circled the construct once more, checking every line and mark. He retreated from its edge and let his robe fall to the ground, exposing skin and scars to his captive, Flash and the otherwise empty room. He stepped into a shower of enchanted water, letting it quiet all magic within him save his own.

He paced the circle once more, took in a deep breath and stepped over the first lines of embedded gold.

"Zero, we have a—"

"Do not move," Flash whispered, soft gurgles escaping his grip around Bianca's throat. "Silence."

She fell silent.

Pressure redoubled against Zero's ears as he entered the second most inner ring. He turned his attention to the crystals beyond the ring, tapping each to feed the construct before beginning the weaving, widdershins dance around the brightest of the rune markings.

Wind swirled to life in his ring. It tousled his red hair and lifted his feet. Thick stone bands ripped from the concrete to his elevated waist's height. Watery rings rose too, the two suspending a waltz of stone and water rune shapes.

Silver cuffs drew the captive wizard upright and into the air. Dark tendrils writhed beneath him, and blazing light swirled above, forging the glowing inner sphere of light and shadow. The prisoner's silver restraints stretched his body within the milky, almost too small sphere.

Darker than my last supplicant, an immoral man cleansed for my purposes.

The fiery symbols Zero danced around rose last, shifting snakes of angry oranges and reds flitting around the innermost sphere. Stone and water spun in different directions, gyroscopic rings of the calmer elements containing the rising whirlpool of wind and its fiery eels.

"By light and dark, infernal and divine." Zero's dance sped up. The weaving path grew perilously closer to blood-fire serpents glowing brighter despite the light sucking tendrils folding around the inner sphere. "Four points around your life to bind."

The wizard's body snapped ramrod straight.

"Futures beckoned, pasts declined, surrendered now Dragons' gift delivered thine."

A blood-fire snake struck the sphere. The wizard screamed. Another hit and another. The air within Zero's ring became an oven. An attack broke through. The sphere burst like a bubble, light and dark magic imploding into a writhing tangle at the wizard's center.

Screams turned to shrieks.

The blood-fire lines gorged upon the prisoner until sated only to dart from the weaving tendrils and into Zero. Pain shot into Zero, needle after needle of blazing power. Magic and memory, dreams and destinies pummeled their way into him. His captor's screams collided with his own deep in Zero's consciousness. Past and prophecy hammered his brain, cracking the barriers of his sense of self.

Strike after strike, the half-expended power of a lifetime only a fraction the length of his own flooded Zero.

Within the sphere, the mage's body shrunk and aged, tightening into a wrinkled, withered shell. Infernal tendrils won their battle over divine, claiming his soul with nothing but crumbled remains left to float downward.

Zero fought his identity into a fortress, repelling the mire of mad image and illusion until his reality sharpened into focus by a single, triumphant will.

He collapsed the spell, returning to the ground before his strength failed him. Hands touched skin that slithered at their contact.

"He's bleeding," Bianca said somewhere far off.

Hands wrapped a robe around him, protecting feverish skin from the chill.

"That scar always bleeds," Flash said. "It will stop in a moment."

Drake lay on the hot sidewalk outside a local country store. Glamour made him resemble a hound dog leashed to the nearby no parking sign. Kane exited a few minutes later, glancing backward as he struggled to keep his feet under a half dozen twelve packs of Cherry Coke. The kid still stunk of death. Gnats and horse flies swarmed him almost the moment he emerged from the pond. He flinched each time one landed on him. He'd refused to move another step until Drake gave him enough time to cast a spell which smelled like citronella. The insects hadn't departed, but they no longer landed on him.

"No, sir, I'll be fine," Kane said. "I'm stronger than I look."

He tripped, spilling the twelve packs onto the ground, breaking open several of the boxes and—by the sound which reached Drake's ears—cracking several cans. He scrambled to collect them all with sidelong glances into the store. When he had them corralled, he went back inside for several doubled plastic bags, collected the loose cans and brought the load over to Drake.

"I still don't understand how these are going to help my mistress."

Drake pressed up against Kane with a cringe. *Potion ingredients.*

"How can you brew potions, you don't have any hands."

Dragons can mix potions in one of their spare stomachs, Drake lied.

"Oh," Kane said. "Makes sense I guess."

Drake nudged him. *Give me one.*

Kane glanced back at the store and offered a can. Drake barely pierced one of the cans, luxuriating in the heady sensation that fizzed across his tongue.

"How do you get the potion back out? Do you vomit it or," Horror filled the boy's expression. "You don't like…never mind, don't tell me."

The old man who ran the store stepped out with a scowl. "Don't give those to your dog, boy. It'll make him sick."

Kane looked from him to Drake and back. "Um, okay, mister."

The grocer harrumphed and returned inside.

"Can we get out of here?" Kane asked.

Drake trotted around the side of the store. He drew up his focus and shifted his wings into something resembling loose saddle bags. Kane loaded the purchase and struggled to keep up with Drake's cross-country lope.

As they walked, Drake considered his options between twelve-ounce doses of paradise. Drake could go after Mauve and Wizard's Bane alone, but he couldn't take the boy. Fleet Hoof would take the kid if Drake insisted, but they wouldn't join him in a rescue and assault on their former tribesman.

If they have the numbers the boy describes augmented by Dragonsteel, there may be no way for me to rescue Mauve alone—if only Lanea were still here to help. Drake bit into another Cherry Coke, willing the soft drink to burn down his throat and burn away the pain of her memory. *We need Master. I suppose I could stash the kid, maybe get Jordan to watch him while I fly to Africa.*

He drank another. Reaching Sanctuary Hole only solved one problem. If Jedediah had locked himself within his spell sanctuary, no one could get to him—no one alive at any rate.

He might open the door if I struck it hard enough.

His thoughts kept the slowly rising scent from his forethoughts until it overpowered his distraction. Pungence hung in the breeze, peppery and sweet with a tinge of burnt hair—like a half barbequed deer covered in dry rub combined with the scent of adolescents in heat he'd smelled at Jordan's school.

A copse of pine parted, revealing the odor's source. Three fauns blocked his path to the farmhouse. Magic pulsed in each of their hands.

"That's them." Kane reached downward. "They work for Wizard's Bane."

Drake bared his teeth.

The fauns lowered their hands.

A faun with a brindled coat stepped forward, lowering herself until her forehead touched the ground. "Elder Lordling, we greet you. Forgive a humble Fey, but we must ask if this child is either meal or slave."

Her sisters bowed beside her.

How do I answer that? Unsure, he fell back onto one of Jedediah's negotiation standbys, silence.

The first crawled closer. "I am Mimi, Lord. I crawl in obeisance to touch your talon that your thoughts might deign to command your lowly servant."

"What the shit?" Kane said.

The three fauns sucked in a breath.

Lili half rose. "Silence in the presence of your better."

Kane threw a thumb toward the Drake. "Him?"

Mimi reached out and touched Drake's talon tip. "Let us punish this boy, Lordling. He slew our sister, but worse he shows you no respect. We promise he'll endure great pain in punishment before we enact our own revenge."

Drake commanded wind to amplify his voice. "Sanctuary is granted him."

"No," Kiki wailed. "You can't."

"Quiet, sister." Mimi turned back to Drake. "Your generosity is as great as you are. We shall quit our claim while he lies within your care."

"Move from my path," Drake said.

The fauns scattered to either side.

Drake led Kane through the barrier without a backward glance. Their eyes pressed against his scales. He took a deep breath as the barrier washed their scrutiny from his skin. *No doubt watching the boy. As if things couldn't get any worse.*

"What was that all about?" Kane asked.

"If you're outside the barrier without me, you're dead," Drake said.

Kane exhaled. "Good thing you aren't going anywhere, right?"

Instead of answer, Drake crunched into another Cherry Coke. Its flavor offered no refreshment.

"Right?"

He walked on in silence. *Now we really need Jedediah.*

1 O

SHATTERED

Jedediah crawled across his spell chamber floor. Long hair fouled his movements, and shattered crystal dug into too-heavy limbs. He wheezed with mountainous effort. He managed another yard, arms shaking to hold up his weight. He struggled across another, too stubborn to lay down and die no matter how much he yearned for it.

They took her. My last child, the one I'd never intended. The one I failed to protect.

Spells not feet from where he crawled had warded her from harm. His beautiful, strong-willed daughter had invaded the room and removed herself from his protection.

She exempted herself from the spell to help me, and I didn't feel it. I let everything else blind me to her vulnerability. I failed my duty as father—again. Death stole another daughter, and I let it happen—again.

It hadn't been the mysterious *Namhaid* wizard or some arrogant centaur. It'd been a man. A normal killed his Lanea with a normal gun and a normal bullet meant for him.

Better that it had killed me instead.

Gnarled, bloody hands dragged him across the spell-treated marble and broken remnants of the power crystals that'd once bordered the room. His hand brushed a shard. It illuminated.

Energy arched into him, and the shard darkened. The power eased his breath for a single lungful. Another shard of air crystal surrendered its power, his body summoning the stored magic like dry soil absorbed rain.

Fewer energized crystals populated each trek across the floor. His tantrum left the crystals shattered throughout the room, forcing him to crawl further hunting those few which still retained energy to sustain him. Through wars and disasters, a small voice had driven him to survive. It drove his crawl, but Jedediah forced away its other screams.

Lanea was gone.

His family had been murdered. His farm had been smashed. He'd even been robbed of true justice. There was nothing and no one left. The little voice refused to accept it. It demanded he draw in all the magic in the room. It demanded he pull himself up by his boots. It demanded a meal, a bath and a cold vengeance delivered to those that took his precious daughter.

Jedediah shook his head. *Revenge is a fleeting meal. Its seduction would fuel me with darkness, filling my emptiness with more of itself... more of the darkness that nearly consumed me. Last time...last time my mad vengeance almost cost the whole world.*

More crystals gave their lives to restore his. They eased his breath. They soothed his aches.

Jedediah crawled back to the pedestal. He cradled the fairy doll he'd used to protect Lanea—an unintended daughter worth the world to an old, tired man.

His voice cracked, weaker than the last time he'd crawled the room. He cried on his little fairy doll and apologized—over and over until exhaustion either killed him or forced him to crawl once more.

Over his head, four spell tokens slipped through a flickering web of power to the pedestal's top—unheard and unnoticed as the magic flickered one last time and died.

11

PERVERTED MAGIC

Two cars cut Bianca off before she managed to pull into the teaming Brickyard Nightclub parking lot. People streamed in and out of the place, ignoring mercenaries directing traffic with quickly waning patience. One of the few cell members to have survived the purge gestured her into a VIP slot.

The automatic bay doors rested in a closed position. They'd be open on the other side, allowing patrons access to the closed off courtyard and its outdoor furniture.

She stalked across to the entrance, her plain attire earning her considerable scorn. She approached the entry without bothering with the line. A few jeers rose, changing to complaint as the bouncer opened the door for her.

Inside, the loading bays had been changed into a multilevel nightclub filled with swirling lights, thundrous sound and young adults pressed together having clothed sex without much rhythm.

She bulled her way along the edges, avoiding the press of bodies in the recessed area of floor serving as both dance floor and stumbling point for drunk party goers. Several bars had been constructed on the rails left in the floor, sliding up and down the facilities length and occasionally knocking over unobservant patrons.

I knew those things were a bad idea, but they're fun to watch.

The energy in the place all but made her skin thrum. She licked her lips and stepped through a door marked: Office. Behind it, the first section of closed off loading dock continued—much of it devoted to alcohol storage and spare furniture. She stepped through an illusion of empty warehouse space. A security door behind it led into a nest of mercenaries, weapons and surveillance. She walked between them on raised floor until she reached a guarded third door—this one thick enough to be battleship armor. She submitted to its biometrics in order to open the barrier separating the party from party favors—what Flash kept calling their stores of illegal weaponry.

The noise vanished with a heavy clunk and whirring locks. She closed her eyes, taking a deep breath. The thrum of life pressed against her skin despite the barriers. Her new awareness left her fidgety in large groups, but she mastered the sensation whenever it arose. After doors, elevators and checkpoints, she found herself outside the restricted sparring room.

Flash frowned at his doppelganger and the tall, muscular woman facing off with him. Her appearance crossed a fantasy barbarian with a Mongolian beauty. She was a head and a half shorter than his twin, but it didn't seem to offer him any real advantage. They fought one another with animal savagery Flash had been trying not to tame so much as to transform their wildness into the core of more advanced fighting technique.

Despite magic and focused lessons, neither grasped language much better than an obstinate four-year-old. Fighting they understood, handicapped by inattention to technique and tactics he kept trying to beat into their thick skulls.

Zero's fault. He's played them off one another since the moment they understood him.

Every spare moment—almost every time Flash turned around—they tried to kill the other, and Zero encouraged it. Creatures imbued with such size and strength but only restrained by a toddler's will offered recipe for disaster. They remained useless for operations until he could get them to think.

Were Gordon and I like this? Flash cleared his throat "Enough."

Both gave him half a glance before attacking the other. Mismatched rudiments of martial arts, wrestling and schoolyard brawling crept into their fight. Technique fell away too often, the fight devolving into savagery.

The door opened. Flash's thick arm shot across it to restrain Bianca from entry. "Falcor! Mo Sha! I said enough."

Bianca leaned against the frame. "Problem, Flash?"

"Nothing a good spanking wouldn't solve," Flash said.

She shrugged. "Spank them then."

An almost bestial smile filled his face. *Not a bad idea.*

Flash strode into their midst. He didn't yell. He didn't warn. Beside the curl of his lip, it was hard to tell that he wasn't merely upon a stroll. Fists struck out, two directions at once. He sprang left then right, driving one then the other to the floor in all but simultaneous beat downs. They stared up at him in childish confusion.

"I said enough."

Bianca clapped.

They jumped him together. Primal and powerful, they weren't experienced combatants, but they refused to back down. Flash hurt them, ending the fight in viciously short order.

"That's supposed to be my bodyguard," Bianca said.

"They'll heal."

"Zero wants them ready. They can't train in traction."

"They need to learn to follow orders and traction will give them time to develop their minds so they're more than two-legged pit bulls."

"He's right," Zero said. "Mo Sha and Gordon must learn to follow orders."

"Falcor," Flash growled.

Zero's eyebrow shot toward his dark hair. He tilted his head slightly and a flash of red reflected in his short locks. "Falcor?"

Flash strode toe to toe with Zero and pointed. "That isn't Gordon. Gordon is dead. You want your queer naming theme, then I name him Falcor."

"Head of the Birdmen—loud, boisterous, strong. I like it."

Flash turned away, his tone biting. "I'm so glad you approve."

Zero grabbed Flash from behind. Pain and torment shot through him, the gleaming power crystals around the room dimmed. Flash fought the pain. Reflections showed Zero's obscene malevolent pleasure and his own drained color. He shoved the pain into the little place where it faced off against his roaring core. Bianca's color paled too, an indication that she'd felt the pain attacking his nerves.

"Obedience is important," Zero whispered. "Respect much more so."

Zero threw Flash across the room recently cleaned of homeless and other trash. The Samoan hit the crumpled behemoths. He whirled back to face Zero, a look of pure savagery barely constrained within Flash's human body.

All three are just beasts forced into our shape.

"Take them down for medical care, Flash." Zero circled them, every bit a tiger waiting for the moment to pounce.

"I'm still not sure about the nightclub, but your crystals seem happy," Bianca said. "So what did you want?"

"Are you trying to distract me?" Zero asked.

She didn't fight it. "Yes. Killing them after so much effort is a waste of time and resources, not to mention my blood."

Zero smiled. "True."

"I'm here now why?"

"More lessons and new toys."

A hand went to her gut reflexively. Phantom pain ghosted over a lump in her stomach behind a scar Zero had made look like an appendix operation.

Zero produced a jeweler's box, opening it to display a pearl necklace with matching bracelets and anklet. "These store a minuscule amount of power."

He handed it over and opened a larger case. Two semi automatic pistols lay in its recesses. Strange swirls and jagged lines marked their exterior. Four objects which resembled pistol magazines lay in the black recesses. Silver framed not bullets, but crystals glowing with swirling energy. The last object in the felt looked like a pager, its LCD glowing much like the magazines.

"The pistols require lots of practice," Zero said. "Once mastered, however, they'll offer a far more flexible arsenal than any you've ever carried."

"The pager?" Bianca asked.

"Another battery of sorts. For emergencies." Zero set the case aside and placed a palm on her scar. "I trust you've gained more sensitivity by now?"

"If you mean the constant prickle on my skin, yes. How do I stop the itching and the gooseflesh?"

Zero smirked.

Bianca sighed. "I don't."

"I imagine removing the implant may lessen it, but either way you're going to need to learn not to ignore it so much as accustom yourself. The irritation is a product of its sensitivity to magical energies."

Bianca rubbed her arms. She gestured toward the crystals. "Well, down here my skin won't stop crawling."

"Crawling skin offers reassurance that you've energy enough." Zero led her to a glowing crystal framed in a charred black metal dotted by shifting reddish patches like magma struggling not to cool. "This is pyromantic energy. Considering your complete lack of magical sensitivity, I do not know if you'll develop an affinity. I intend to give you a better way to access this kind of magic in future, so I suggest you practice it most. It's also the easiest for most apprentices to use as an attack."

She smirked. "I can work with fire."

"Very well, each magic has its own sensation and sensations vary from person to person," Zero said. "Place your non-dominant hand on the crystal and try to imagine a mote of fire above your dominant palm."

Bianca set a hand on the crystal. The gooseflesh grew fangs, and her skin felt sunburnt in an instant. A headiness filled her. Reckless invincibility accompanied it—a sensation she hadn't felt so strongly since she'd beaten her father to death at fifteen.

"Channel it as I instructed."

Bianca pictured the small glowing coal of fire in her palm. Searing pain shot up her arm. She flipped the mote away, cradling burned flesh.

"I said above your palm, not in it. Do it again correctly this time."

"My hand needs treatment."

"Bianca, dear, I seriously doubt that'll be the last time you burn yourself playing with fire."

"I get it, but can't I learn to heal burns? You've mended other injuries."

Zero watched her in silence. "Pyromancy can be only used for healing in limited conditions. You'll have very limited access to those, and fire healing is an extremely delicate and dangerous working. For now, deal with the pain."

I'll deal with it, you filthy sadist, but only until I've got the upper hand.

Zero smiled. "Try again, my little scorpion."

Bianca burned herself twice more—though not so badly—before she managed to imagine the small coal sufficiently above her skin. "Now what?"

Zero flipped his hand. A target appeared in the room's center flitting here and there like a butterfly. "Will it to strike the target."

Bianca pointed her palm at the target, sighting between spread fingers. It shot across the room and impacted a wall not far from where Flash waited after his return. The target slid through the air unharmed.

"I said hit the target."

"I missed, okay? I'll have to calibrate my eye to hit with this," Bianca said.

"This is not a gun, Bianca. It only shoots straight if you tell it to."

§

Velith'Seravin approached a large tank once used for storing oil. The exterior, grey steel bore countless runes, circles and symbols, all gleaming even in the light of day. Centaur knelt around it in pairs, eyes closed and mouths spilling an endless litany that empowered the spell.

Movement caught his eye. A small herd of wild horses raced across the old oil field, steering clear of the glowing tank. He ascended a long shallow ramp wrapping around the tank's exterior, its support scaffolding not touching the tank except at the top where it bridged to an open platform.

Beneath him, the necromancer caught in Mexico hung in taught chains, her white bikini blackened by the sludge just beneath her feet. Sound thrummed out of the tank, the chants of shamanistic life spells amplified a dozen fold. Surrounded by life, she couldn't summon her greatest power. Bombarded by endless waves of sound, she couldn't concentrate—not even enough to sleep.

A dun-colored sorrel joined him on the platform. "We should kill her. Hell, we should've killed her when we captured her. She's powerful."

Velith'Seravin clasped his friend on his unmelted shoulder. *No, not friend, I can have no friends in the eyes of my people. If anything befell him, the wizard's trickery would get the credit, dealing a deadly blow to morale.*

"She sent her apprentice to Jedediah, SinDon. He will come for her, and we will kill him."

"Perhaps Sinesh Ena'Donishe is right," Mimi said. "Master Remi would take her off your hands, slaying her in a way to increase the power my sisters and I have sworn to your service."

"I'll not relinquish my bait. I want Shine." VelSera gestured. "She's my way to get him."

"You don't need me with those marks on your skin, mule. He'll come for you and waxworks there. Mark me, you'll feel him soon enough," Mauve said.

"I'm not afraid to die in service to my tribe," SinDon said.

Mauve laughed. "Honey, death's only going to start your troubles."

"Perhaps you should cover the marks—for morale sake," Mimi said. "Perhaps wear robes of position, you and your chief lieutenants."

"Robes of state—fit for a true leader," SinDon said.

12

MEDIEVAL FOSTERAGE

Jordan examined the reflected outfit Crystal had shoved into her hands. Patched and worn blue jeans replaced her customized but otherwise brand new Levis. 'Jesus is My Boyfriend' scrawled across a t-shirt of some god awful pink. Mae arrived half way through her changing, confiscated Jordan's Twin Djinn top and ordered her to exchange her underwear and bra—plain white cotton replacing black sateen as if it'd come from some kind of brothel.

One solid knock proceeded Arthur's entrance into the mother-in-law cottage bathroom. "Oops, you're still...oh. You're dressed. Mother wants you."

Jordan closed her eyes and counted to ten. *I can put up with it, just until I learn the ropes here or Jedediah rescues me.*

"Well?" Arthur asked.

She gave him a flat stare. "Well, what?"

"Mother is *waiting*."

Jordan forced a smile onto her lips. "Tell her I'll be right there."

"I'm to escort you."

His bulk blocked most of her exit. He wasn't fat exactly, but he wasn't skinny like Crystal. "Fine. Lead on."

"You first."

"You're in the way."

"Ladies first." He smiled. "You can squeeze by."

She held her breath and counted toward ten once more as she shimmied by him. He shifted toward the door before she was entirely clear, his hand brushing her rump.

Jordan whirled.

He held his hands up. "Whoops."

Jordan turned her back on him and stepped from the bathroom, muttering to herself. "I'm seriously starting to miss, Paulie."

Crystal stood next to the front door in similar jeans and religious t-shirt, her eyes on the ground. She looked up as Jordan entered, gaze flitting from Jordan to Arthur and back as if trying to read the situation.

"You were supposed to go ahead, squirt," Arthur said.

"I-I wanted to wait for Faye," Crystal said.

"Jordan," Jordan said.

"Mother says we're not to call you by your last name," Arthur said.

Jordan chuckled. "You will if you want me to answer."

Arthur yanked Jordan around. "That's not how we do th—"

Jordan's instinctive shove sent Arthur careening into a menagerie of boxes filling the cottage living area. He sprawled into a tangle of Thanksgiving and Saint Valentine's Day labeled boxes, other holidays tumbling around him.

Crystal stared opened mouthed.

Jordan crossed to him, offering her hand. "Sorry, but don't grab me again."

Mae appeared in the doorway. "What's taking so long? There're a thousand things to do before tonight's party. Arthur, what're you doing on the floor?"

"She shoved me," Arthur said.

"You grabbed me without warning," Jordan shot back.

"Faye, girls don't shove boys," Mae said.

"They do if the boys deserve it," Jordan said. "It's Jordan, not Faye."

"Not in *my* house it isn't. You will not shove in *my* house either."

Jordan folded her arms. "Technically this is the mother-in-law cottage, not your house."

Crystal gasped.

Mae's teeth ground. She marched across the intervening distance, grabbed a handful of Jordan's hair and dragged her face down to Mae's height. "You'll do as you're told in *my* house or there will be punishments."

Jordan opened her mouth to argue, but terror filled Crystal's face as she shook her head back and forth violently. Jordan held her tongue.

"Better. They said you might be a bit wild. We'll fix that soon enough."

Mae marched them to the main house without releasing Jordan's hair. The angle made it difficult, but Jordan took in what she could. Expensive furniture, art and an unreasonably high number of knick knacks populated every room.

Mae released Jordan's hair. "You'll start here in the formal dining room. Scrub the floor, baseboards and the walls, clean the windows, dust the china cabinets, their contents and then start in on polishing the silver—"

"That silver?" Jordan pointed.

"Yes."

"Trying to blind your guests?" Jordan asked. "It's already clean."

"When that's all complete, clean the sitting room, foyer and formal living room," Mae said. "My hairdresser will be here in an hour to fix your hair."

"My hair is fine," Jordan said.

"Not for *my* house it isn't," Mae said. "Crystal will show you where to get the cleaning supplies, and Arthur will give you direction when you need it."

Mae waited suitable time for Jordan's reply. "Do you understand, Faye?"

"Sure."

"Yes, *Mistress*," Mae said.

Jordan's brows shot upward. "Mistress? What do you think you are some kind of witch?"

Crystal gasped.

Mae grabbed another knot of hair. She struck Jordan's bent face with a resounding crack. "There will be no talk of Satanism in *my* house. Mistress is the appropriate title for an affluent woman and head of a household."

Jordan took a long, slow breath to keep from breaking the woman's arm. She reached into herself and moved the answering rumble to armor her skin. "What do you expect me to call Mister Bridgeport, Master?"

"Hardly." Mae scoffed. "Get to work."

Jordan addressed the floor once the other woman disappeared. "When I see Jedediah, I'm going to kick him in his overall-covered ass."

Lanea's advice regarding magic and chores tempted Jordan, but she didn't think giving Mae reason to add more tasks or expect faster service played in Crystal's or her own favor. They scrubbed every floor, baseboard and wall in the house. They polished every silver utensil, lugged supplies around and slaved under the watchful eye of Mae or Arthur.

Drake led Kane deeper into the property in search of Jedediah's magic hut. Dull tasting Cherry Coke weighed down wings shaped to carry it.

Might taste better if I could chill it in the Weems fridge instead of having to cart it with me while I hide stinky somewhere within the property line.

It took most of the afternoon to find it. Under normal circumstance, finding a hut shouldn't have been a problem, except that this one got up and walked away whenever stretching its chicken legs suited it. He squeezed himself through the door, not remembering it quite so narrow.

Kane wandered the cavern, poking bottles and beakers at random, rippling their colorful liquids. "What is this place?"

"Master's alchemy shack," Drake said. "You should be safe inside until I can return for you."

"Where are you going?" Kane asked.

"First to fetch another of Master's apprentices. She'll look after you while I journey to seek him."

"You can't leave me alone here. They'll find me."

"They can't enter the property." Drake forced a laugh, trying not to let Thestle's chilling words about gaps show on his expression.

"They're sorceresses. They'll find a way, send rats or something to eat me."

"I think even rats would balk at biting into someone who reeks like you."

Kane glared and straightened his hat.

"Stay here and don't wander off. You don't want to lose the shack."

"I think I can find my way back now that we're here."

"Unless the shack wanders off," Drake said.

"It what? What if it leaves the property while I'm inside? Can it do that? Won't that take me outside the barrier?"

"It shouldn't. Besides, the shack only moves the entrance, not the cavern."

"Wait, so where is the cavern? Is it inside the barrier? One of the fauns is a terramancer. She could earthswim—"

"Do you ever shut up?" Drake snarled. "The cavern is safe. The hut won't leave the property, not after the stern talking to Master gave it last time."

"Stern—what good is lecturing a hut going to do?"

Drake glared. "You don't know Master's stern words. Stay. Put."

Jordan occupied a cheap folding chair set atop a drop cloth in a spacious but empty upstairs bedroom. Chemical odors and burnt hair choked the room. A handful of acid green locks lay in Jordan's cupped hands, casualties of Mae's stylist. The hairdresser pulled a towel from her hair, throwing it to the floor beside two sets of broken shears.

Mae appeared in the doorway, wearing an upscale June Cleaver dress. "Aren't you done yet, Paul?"

"It won't dye or cut." He gestured at several empty bottles. "She's cursed."

Jordan stifled a giggle.

"You cut some of it, you just need sharper scissors," Mae said.

"Won't work. Ask Billie Jo, my hair's protected by Satan."

"Cursed," Paul said.

"Not in *my* house." Mae thundered across the room and slammed a hand into Jordan's face. She snatched it back and cradled it against her stomach.

Jordan quirked an eyebrow. "Corporal punishment is illegal, you know that, right? I'll have to call Ridley if you don't—"

"Sparing the rod is exactly what's made you such a willful child," Mae said.

"Yup," Jordan said. "You should get to know Billie Jo."

"Can you fix her hair or not?" Mae asked.

He gestured helplessly at hours' worth of detritus. "I might have a wig."

"Fine, just get her ready. I need her dressed before the guests arrive."

Paul's wig refused to stay in place, finally forcing him to braid it in a way that hid his pins and allowed a graceful retreat with money in hand. Arthur took over, dragging Jordan to a girlie bedroom that reminded her of Esme's. Crystal squeaked and darted behind a dressing screen.

Jordan glowered. "You need to learn to knock before entering somewhere a woman is changing."

"Oops." Arthur grinned.

"Get out," Jordan said.

"I'm to keep my eye on you," Arthur said.

"I'm not changing with you in the room," Jordan said.

"Please, Faye, no more trouble," Crystal whispered from behind the screen.

Arthur folded his arms beneath a smug expression.

Jordan mimicked his pose. "Out and I'll change."

"Nope."

Jordan leaned in close enough that only he could hear her. "How're you going to keep an eye on me if I blind you, fat boy?"

"I'm not scared of girls."

Jordan's smile forced him back a step. He recovered quickly, snatching the hem of her shirt. "I'll dress you then."

Jordan's hand tightened around his like a vice, first forcing the shirt to stay down and then tightening around his fingers. Color fled from his cheeks to purple his fingers.

"Let go or I break them," Jordan said.

"You can't. You wouldn't."

"Can and will," Jordan said.

"I'll tell mother."

Jordan tightened her grip. "She can drive you to the hospital."

"Okay, okay, stop," Arthur said.

Jordan released him. "Get out."

He fled, and she locked the door behind him. Crystal peeked around the screen. Her body trembled. "She's going to punish us so bad. I don't want to go in the root cellar. I can't. Not again."

"What are you talking about?" Jordan asked.

Crystal's pitch rose. She wrapped her arms around her stomach. She gasped over and over as if she couldn't breathe. She collapsed to the floor in tears. Her head shook back and forth, mouthing words that wouldn't come out without air to fuel them.

Jordan wrapped her arms around Crystal. She drew off some of the magic hardening her skin and pushed Mother's calm toward the younger girl. She fought the rumble, trying and once more failing to extend the magic beyond her skin. She rocked Crystal. "It's going to be all right. I'll protect you."

Crystal's head shook back and forth, eyes squeezed so tight Jordan had no idea how the tears slipped out.

They placed ironed, folded linen napkin on a table laden with good foods. Mae slapped her hand away from a tasty bite, ordering all of it—even the food still unserved in the kitchen—remain untouched before and during the party.

The party lasted three hours. It ranged throughout the furnished areas until the house's seams burst with important guests impressed by the Bridgeport's wealth and charity.

Men in expensive suits dirtied the ceilings with rare cigars from Louis's humidor. They hung on Mister Bridgeport's boisterous but humble words as he declared the scriptural basis for the good will which opened their home to the wayward and troubled Jordan

Mae held court in the sitting room. Crystal and poor, disadvantaged Jordan sat to either side—perfect, silent dolls on display.

Arthur cloistered with other adolescents, whispers boasting behind innuendo and piled plates of expensive food. Leers removed the borrowed dress Jordan mustn't soil.

The cleaning started with the last guest's departure. Mae supervised the removal of even the faintest trace of the party. Rich foods disappeared untouched into padlocked refrigerators despite Jordan's rumbling stomach. When the work was at last done, and she was too tired to eat in any case, Mae set a kitchen table with a bowl of ramen noodles, a few near-turned broccoli florets and a hardboiled egg to share.

Jordan helped Crystal trudge out to the mother-in-law cottage, exhausted from a long day and keeping up her magical armor against surprise Mae assaults. She half carried Crystal up the stair and to one of two portable cots. She examined the sparse little bedroom. A closet and dresser offered refuge to the hand-me-down clothing from countless foster girls—well worn, patched, and mended by the girls forced to wear them.

"Faye?"

"Jordan," Jordan said.

"Missus Bridgeport said I wasn't to call you that," Crystal said.

Jordan bristled. "What do you want?"

"Would you sleep with your cot next to mine?" Crystal said. "Eve used to."

"What happened to Eve?" Jordan asked.

"She ran away."

"Smart girl," Jordan said.

Crystal's voice sounded on the verge of shattering. "You're not going to leave me, are you? Please?"

"Why?"

"Please?"

"Not tonight." Jordan dragged her cot over.

One heavy knock hit the door.

Crystal cringed and yanked her blanket up.

"Who is it?" Jordan asked.

"Drake."

Jordan bolted upright. "Drake?"

"Who's Drake?" Crystal whispered.

"My, uh, brother," Jordan said.

"Did they place him separately?"

"No, he's big enough to be on his own," Jordan said.

"Why don't you live with him?" she asked.

"I did until they forced me back into the system," Jordan said.

Crystal sighed. "It must be so nice not being in the system."

"Stay here, I'll be right back."

Jordan squeezed out the door, keeping it mostly shut in case Drake wasn't glamoured. His bloodhound appearance released her held breath. "Where in the gorram hell have you been?"

"Busy," Drake said. "So has Wizard's Bane."

Drake told her about the fauns and Kane as they exited the cottage.

"What're you going to do?" Jordan asked.

"Go find help," Drake said. "I'll need you to watch out for Kane."

Another one? Why me? I'm barely taking care of myself. I can't protect the whole world. She folded her arms, adding the last in Mae's frigid tone. "I'm kind of busy here. Chores don't do themselves."

"I can't take him to see my mother," Drake said. "She'll eat him."

"Couldn't you stop her?"

Drake snorted, flame shooting out of the dog's nose.

"How am I supposed to watch him?" Jordan asked.

"Can you hide him here?" Drake asked.

"I doubt it."

"Fine, I'll take care of him," Drake said.

"Have you seen Jedediah yet?" Jordan asked.

"If I knew how to get to him, would I go to Mother for help?" Drake said.

Jordan shook her head. "Somehow I doubt it."

A door shut in the direction of the main house.

"You'd better go," Jordan said. "Be careful, Drake."

"You'll be all right?" Drake asked.

"I'll manage."

Drake slipped into shadow a full minute before Arthur crept out of it.

"Still up I see," Arthur said.

"Yup," Jordan said.

"Did I hear you talking to someone?" Arthur asked.

"Did you?"

"Yeah."

"What do you want?"

"You're much prettier than Eve," Arthur said. "Stronger too."

Jordan showed her teeth. "You have no idea."

"You have a boyfriend?"

"No, keep breaking their hands when they get grabby."

Arthur frowned down at his hands.

A low growl escaped the darkness. Magic-adjusted eyes revealed Nip's wolfish outline snarling feet from Arthur's squinting face.

"What was that?" Arthur said.

"That means it's time for you to go to bed. Good night, Arthur."

Arthur looked at her uncertainly then scanned the darkness once more. He headed back to the main house.

Jordan dropped to her knees, stroking the mudpuppy. "I can protect myself, you know. You follow Drake here?"

Nip pressed himself against her and wagged his tail. *<Hunted sister two-legs. Tracked pack scent from farm. Protect pack mate.>*

"Great, now I'm going to have to clean these."

Nip's tail stopped and his ears pressed back. *<Sister two-legs mad?>*

"Not really." She ruffled his ears. "Stick around, boy, but out of sight, okay?"

Nip wagged his tail. *<Play now? Run? Chase pixies?>*

"Not tonight. Guard the house for us, all right?" Jordan yawned, returned to her cot and—comforted by Nip's protection—slipped into a deep sleep.

⁂

Midall E'Cru knelt next to a moonlight dappled pond. Sleep resisted her. Even in a deep meditative state, it eluded her until dawn's rays approached. She was troubled. Myn'Glent ah Elirymn —miraculously recovered stillborn foal—troubled her. It wasn't that the child proved more willful than other fillies her age, quite the opposite. Myn'Glent seldom made any noise at all if left to her own devices. She just watched everything with too-serious eyes.

She's grown more rapidly than others her age too but fractionally.

Myn'Glent had undergone Testing, particularly considering her miraculous recovery. The filly who smiled infrequently and laughed too little housed considerable power. Feilahdi U'Noa, the girl's mother, pronounced her daughter as the next Elder Shamaness of *Lah'Phriel.*

I can't even disagree, assuming she survives the strange things that happen around her.

MidCru gazed into the depths of the pond.

Naiads slept within, all but invisible in the moonlit water. The valley hadn't hosted Naiads before, but within days of Myn'Glent's birth, every pond hosted the flighty, playful Fey. They delighted, even bickered with one another for the right to groom Myn'Glent's gradually silvering coat at water's edge.

The changing coat color troubled MidCru too.

Initial coats did change color as did a baby's hair, but the speed and degree of change didn't seem normal. Myn'Glent had been born chestnut, but every day her hair turned more silver with only the slightest sheen of scarlet to mark its previous color.

The too serious eyes didn't change color, but occasionally they glowed. It unsettled the other fillies and none too few of the mares. MidCru shivered, wrapping arms across her chest. As if heralded by MidCru's worries, Feilahdi U'Noa rushed into sight.

"Shaman, come quickly," Feilahdi U'Noa said. "Myn'Glent's having some sort of nightmare."

"Then wake her."

"She won't wake," Feilahdi U'Noa swallowed. "And she's glowing."

MidCru rushed to FeiNoa's preferred glade. Long willow branches shifted like silent wind chimes in the evening breeze. A soft blue luminance escaped it with moans and half-spoken words. She pushed through. Cold sucked the air from her lungs. She knelt next to the girl.

Myn'Glent's limbs jerked and spasmed. Fury contorted babyish features that shouldn't have known such extremes.

MidCru jerked her hand away. Ice sheathed her fingers.

"FeiNoa, Set a fire just beyond the willow."

"How will you move her?" FeiNoa asked. "I couldn't touch her."

MidCru scowled.

FeiNoa rushed way.

MidCru focused, letting the spirit of *Lah'Phriel* fill her. Silver lit her arms. She reached down to cradle Myn'Glent only to jerk back when Myn'Glent blue aura lashed out at her.

"Easy, little one, I'm here to help you."

Myn'Glent mumbled something inaudible. Her head shook.

MidCru rushed to the nearest pond and stomped a hoof into their waters. "Awake, the child needs you."

A dozen of the short, water fairies poured out of the pond, not bothering to ask for directions. Their cerulean skin flashed silver in snatched moonbeams. Countless cilia crowned their heads like anemone hats of lightest pink, lavender and white. Squat legs, full hips and over developed bosoms turned their hurried sashay into a waddle.

MidCru ran after them.

Compared to the diminutive versions of their larger water nymph cousins, Myn'Glent was a pony surrounded by toddlers. They reached out to touch her. MidCru opened her mouth to give warning, but the glow didn't bite them. With gentleness belied by their tiny razor claws, they lifted Myn'Glent and carried her toward their pond like pallbearers to a Viking funeral.

"Stop them," Feilahdi U'Noa cried. "They must bring her to the fire."

MidCru raised a hand to shush the woman.

The naiads rested Myn'Glent on the water's edge—torso on the bank and lower body in the water. Naiads stroked her hair. The girl quieted. She placed a thumb into her mouth and slept peacefully.

One by one the little water Fey slipped under the water. MidCru knelt next to the last. "Thank you."

The naiad screeched something MidCru couldn't understand and disappeared behind her sisters.

13

LEFT BEHIND

rake stared at the open and unfortunately empty field. A few of Jedediah's more choice curses rolled around his mind.

Great, now I have to track down a bird-brained hut and a kid seriously in need of a deodorant factory.

He raised his beak, extended his tongue and funneled the air across sensory cells in the roof of his mouth. Bitter rot clogged his nostrils—foul upon his tongue. Alchemy and a uniquely Kane pungency accented aromas of chicken crap, boiled cabbage, and sausage. Combining aeromancy, his nose and Jedediah's lessons made his scent-tracking superior to any bloodhound.

Flying would be faster but tracking against that much wind more difficult. I need speed nearer the trail.

Drake settled onto the ground, reaching within to his inner echo of the far away Dragon Springs. Flight hairs along his scales tingled and rose. A scent of ozone and a prickle of static electricity haloed his body. Little sparks danced beneath his scales, arching through muscle and sinew. He ignored the tickle of slithering skin, focusing on the cheetah shape Jedediah required he practice.

His talons compressed, squeezing into paws several sizes too small. Limbs lengthened. Muscles slimmed to leaner, more concentrated shapes. Drake stretched his new limbs, a lithe cheetah triple the size of his biggest cousins. Practicing forms of every kind since Lanea's death provided him a better understanding and greater precision, but mass could only be compacted so far.

Unless I find some way to shift it into an extra-dimensional pocket. Explains why the hut and refrigerator doors are getting tight.

He imagined Kane's response to seeing a huge reddish-brown cat racing up his wake. His grin widened with pleasure. He bound forward along the trail, tail stretched out and shifting to maintain his balance. He remained on the ground but still flew across the property. The press of wind on his face delighted and exhilarated him despite the stench of its breath. Grassland and woods came and went. He followed the magical Scandinavian hut's long meandering course.

I've never tracked its movements day to day, but it's like its running from something. Maybe Kane's reek.

Drake dashed through a copse of oak and hickory, sending a cloud of tittering fairies into the air like tossed leaves. High pitched rebukes died, and the little Fey bid him greetings while bowing into one another midair. A shift in air warned him of a brownie enclave. He veered around it, avoiding the long-winded Fey and their lengthy tributes.

Won't even have any Cherry Coke.

The observances of his status entertained when it suited. Drake, Elder Fey and Lord of all save his dragon kin, had relished the groveling. He enjoyed using the circumstances of his birth to force lesser Fey to bow and scrape, bring gifts and perform favors. His status bought him lodging among Fleet Hoof and the adulation of all their centaur.

Not all, not Velith'Seravin.

Heat prickled his pelt. Fire bubbled tiny belches from his flame lung, and his movements sped up. Velith'Seravin reminded Drake of Stormfall. Selfish and spoiled they'd attacked Jedediah. They'd treated Jedediah as lesser, in his mother's case a meal saved for later only so long as Jedediah fostered him.

Jedediah had more than taught him. He'd taken Drake into his family, treated him no better or worse than even his own daughter. The teacher his mother had injured and tormented had even risked his own skin to arrange for an angry insolent dragonling to meet his Sire.

I never even thanked him, and Mother treats him like kine—destroyed his home.

How many times had he overheard her or other dragons tell some wizard his life's only value to her kind was in teaching fosterlings to use their power? How many times had they crooned about coercing talented kine into governess duty to raise their offspring out from under talon?

Drake burst out of a treeline to find a gaggle of young elves and younger centaur competing in some sort of hunting game. A fair-haired elf in biker attire waved Drake down. "Hail, Lordling, come and make sport with us."

Laughter and invitations rained down onto Drake.

"He could play the part of prey," a particularly small, grey colt said.

Drake pulled up short, skidding to a stop in a shower of claw thrown soil.

Silence consumed the glade, even insects forgoing breath. The colt's older brother by color and expression slapped him upside his head. He bowed low, front hooves extended and body bent. "Forgive him, Elder Lord, my young brother speaks as a playful foal unaware of the insult in his words. If you will take no offense and lay no blame, I bid you peace in the name of my fathers."

Drake forced his hackles down and inclined his head. "I go in peace."

He rushed away, but not far enough away to miss the sound of another slap and the older brother's rebuke. "Great job, stupid, you almost got us all eaten."

The idle words clung to him, reminding Drake of every encounter he'd had with other Fey since being abandoned in Jedediah's care. The Fey considered dragons sacrosanct, quick to temper and quicker to eat offenders.

Lanea convinced some of them to give me a chance, breaking down barriers by befriending me. She introduced me around, charming them to include me in their games.

Hollowness extinguished the former heat in his chest. Lanea personified life, love and the best in the Fey. She'd understood as only another outcast could. She'd teased him, abused him, and treated him like an annoying little brother. He'd loved her for it—more than she'd loved him.

The hut came into sight roosted atop a bramble-crowned hillock. It'd passed out of the barrier at some point in its stroll only to nestle just within another island of Jedediah's protected lands. Drake searched right and left for any sign of the fauns. He caught neither sight nor scent of them.

"Kane!"

A pale oval face poked out the doorway. "Drake?"

Drake shot a small firebolt out one nostril. "Check before you open—"

It struck the hut. The shack sprang to its feet, gigantic chick legs shot out its bottom as if from thin air. It towered over him with indignant squawks blaring out of the flapping door and cast a malignant shade. One huge chicken foot stomped down.

Drake sprang out of the way with cheetah speed. He twisted midair, tail doing circles. Another foot came down. Drake leapt again, claws swiping one leg as he shot past.

"Stop that."

It squawked a monstrous challenge and redoubled it stomping. Drake bounded, twisted, and leapt. He barely stayed ahead of the thing. Black green smoke carried dark odors from the doors and windows. It chased him up, down and around the hill, stomp after stomp.

Drake sprinted clear, leaping into a tree. "Hey, I'm Elder Fey."

A diseased green energy beam lanced out the door at him. He leapt from the tree as the beam set it ablaze. Sickly flame wrapped the tree without burning it.

Drake gazed up at his recent escape to find the old elm glowering down at him. It snatched at him with creaking limbs, twigs and smaller branches snapping away as the dragonling circled its trunk just ahead.

A chicken foot stomped, catching but not pinning Drake's tail.

He emptied his flame lung at the animated tree. Flame blinded it from further attack, animation magic and fire battling. Drake sprinted around behind the shack and leapt up, claws sinking into the back thighs just beneath the hut.

"Knock it off, or I'm lighting your ass up," Drake said.

It slammed itself down into a sitting position, Drake barely springing clear at the last moment.

"All right, I'm sorry, I'm sorry!" Drake said. "I was just trying to frighten the boy, not attack you."

The hut tried one more stomp. It turned, flirting its rear wall in a vulgar gesture for a hut before climbing the hill and roosting once more.

Kane slammed open the door and marched toward Drake. "Where the hell have you been? There's no bathroom in there. The damned hut's been moving around all night. Do you know how hard that makes it to use a beaker…never mind, did you bring any food?"

Drake held his tongue. *So much for Elder Fey making me special.*

Kane went back into the hut for his hat. Hunger knifed him in the gut. It gurgled like an incontinent zombie. *Mistress never made me go so long without a meal. I bet even being a centaur prisoner would mean regular meals.*

The dragonling led him across empty fields, through vacant woods and over streams. He forced Drake to wait while he filled his stomach with water, but rather than make him feel better it just made for more pee stops. They walked an eternity. The horrible beast back in its scale-protected dragon shape charged through wood, bramble and thicket without a second thought, sending branches and thorns snapping back into Kane's teeth.

We're being watched too. I feel it.

The ruined farmhouse came into view at long last, though what good it'd do for his stomach he could hardly imagine. Drake turned aside to a vast boneyard filled with refrigerators even his mistress couldn't resurrect. Something about the arrangement felt off as if the haphazard maze had a logic he couldn't quite puzzle out.

"I thought we were getting something to eat."

A pack of small muddy brown dogs peeked out at him from beneath a series of greenhouses. Another poked its head out of the ground, probably lying in a trench dug in the cool earth.

Constant hunger ate at him, made worse by unbearable heat. Mexico felt hot, but nothing compared to slogging through heat that soaked his clothes and sucked sweat out of him. He longed for the pond beyond the greenhouses.

Drake stopped in front of an old refrigerator. "Wait here thirty minutes, then open the door and step through."

Kane blinked.

"Understand?" Drake asked.

Kane smiled, nodded a few times and then shook his head. "Are you out of you scaly brain? It's a refrigerator! At best, I'll get locked inside and suffocate."

"Then animate yourself," Drake said. "Obey, or you're on your own."

"Why can't we just go to the store?" Kane asked.

"I haven't got any more money," Drake said.

"You spent it *all* on Cherry Coke?"

Drake smiled. "Food is easy enough to get."

"I can do the homeless boy routine I saw a gardener's son pull. It's truer for me than him right now. Surely someone around here would feed me."

"More likely, the fauns will eat you alive"

"Fauns are cannibals?"

"Focus, boy. Leave my side outside this property, and you'll be dead."

"I'm going to *starve* to death."

The beast had the gall to roll its eyes before it threw itself clumsily into the sky and flew away.

Kane kicked a broken appliance handle. "Good riddance."

The boneyard's puzzle held his attention a few moments before the pond's cool waters called him again. His stomach gurgled. He glared at the refrigerator, snatching it open out of desperate habit. The dented door resisted at first, its hinges bent. He fought it, hoping its resistance meant the dragon had set him waiting feet from secret caches of something tasty just to prove itself superior. It came open with a metallic moan and revealed a tomb empty of food.

"Stupid. Of course it's empty. It's not even plugged in." Kane turned toward the pond. A single small pup sat awkwardly on its rump and cocked a head at him. Kane shook his head. A shimmer within the open appliance caught his eye. A double take showed it empty.

Great, I'm so hungry I'm hallucinating.

The pup wandered up to him, stubby little tail wagging.

"What do you want? Food? Some sort of treat?" Kane asked. "I'm so broke I can't afford dirt."

The pup scooped up a mouthful of dirt, set it on Kane's shoes and wagged up at him.

"Great, now I've got dirt." Kane cast a longing glance toward the pond. "Wonder if there are fish in there. Hey, dog, can you catch—where'd you go?"

Its yip echoed oddly, a tail disappearing into the refrigerator.

Kane blinked. He reached in an arm. It didn't disappear. It came back when he drew it out. He titled his head to one side, summoning magic over his eyes. He'd barely started the spell when the fridge's interior resolved into a dark two-foot passage ending in a slightly opened wooden door and a brown puppy shaking its head and licking the carpet.

Kane stepped into the passage. The taste of orange juice and mint toothpaste assaulted his taste buds. Cold bumps prickled across his skin as icy air conditioning assaulted him. He tried to scrape the taste off on his teeth.

"Maybe I should lick the carpet too." Kane called out. "Hello?"

Kane wandered up the hall until his jaw dropped. A living room furnished with the latest in home theater and gaming toys sparkled before him. A carnival-style popcorn cart and a full soda pop fountain stood along one wall. He rushed forward, grabbing a handful of no doubt stale popcorn and shoved it into his mouth. It was fresh, even still slightly warm. He lifted his other hand from the side of the cart so he could shove another handful mouthward when the tingling he hadn't noticed vanished.

"Magic. An enchanted popcorn cart? How cool is that?"

The little puppy stumbled into the room whining. Kane glanced at her. He approached, but before he could close the distance, she flopped onto her haunches and howled a low mournful keen.

He stroked her head.

<Sistwo. Sis—>

Kane jerked his hand away, blood running from his face and mouth drying up. He rushed over to the fountain, took off his hat and ducked his head under one of the taps for a drink. His head triggered several at once, but he didn't care. Sweet citrusy goodness poured into his mouth while other flavors washed the dirt and heat from his head and hair.

"You're making a mess," Drake said.

Kane jerked upright, knocking his head into the taps, losing his balance and sprawling to the floor.

"And I told you to wait so I could make sure it was safe here," Drake said.

"Safe? It's heaven!"

Drake huffed, smoke shooting out his nostrils. "Get some towels out of the linen closet and clean that up while I check things."

"Don't you have any Mexicans around here?"

"For what?"

"To clean, duh."

Drake pointed a serrated talon. "Go!"

"But isn't that the way back to that wrecked house?" Kane asked.

"Only if you trigger it from this side."

Kane headed back down the hall and grabbed a towel. He couldn't see the farm or the open refrigerator, but he felt a strong current of magic within the closet's threshold. He set to cleaning up the soda soaking the carpet, wishing for his maid and barring that a tile floor that was easier to clean.

"I was afraid of that. This house isn't included in the barrier," Drake said.

"So?"

"No barrier, no safety," Drake said. "You'll be able to get food from here or order it delivered then go back to the farm. You can sleep in a junker."

"A junker? Why?" Kane said. "It's heaven here."

"Death."

"Boredom! How're they going to find me? I don't even know where I am."

"Magic?" Drake said. "You only travelled a few miles."

Kane frowned. The dragon had a point. *When is Mistress going to free me from this madness?*

"Get your food and go back. I'll send a babysitter," Drake said.

"I'm not a baby!"

"Someone has to keep an eye on you."

"No, they don't. I'm twelve."

"I can't just leave you on your own," Drake said.

Kane pointed two thumbs at himself, answering the irritating lizard in exaggerated tones. "Twelve, almost thirteen."

The dragon went quiet, almost thoughtful. It shrugged, a horrifying motion that made every bone in Kane's skeleton itch. "Fine. No babysitter. Grab food from the stores here. Take it back to the farm while I arrange some camping gear. Don't linger, and take her back to her mother."

"Fine, whatever, but like what if I want to watch a movie?" Kane asked.

"Leave a note at the farmhouse so we know where to find your corpse." Drake exited the double glass doors to the backyard and jumped into the air. Kane wasn't sure where he'd gone, but he was glad to see the annoying creature leave. He turned to the gaming system and rubbed his hands together.

"All right, my pretties, who wants to be my bitch first?"

14

DRAGON WRECKAGE

Drake rode the wind just above a layer of nimbostratus clouds raining all over the countryside beneath it. The wind jerked and juked, a combination of mixing temperatures and pressures more fun than your average rollercoaster. He could've flown above the mix, but couldn't resist the wild ride. County roads and rural highways crisscrossed farmland, unspoiled woods and country estates. The occasional interstate cut through seemingly empty land blurry through the downpour.

He made good time, eventually bending glamour around him to give him the appearance of a puffy cloud as the carpet of grey camouflage thinned. The sweet scent of renewed earth and fresh water invigorated him despite the headwind. Someone should have noticed him, a grey-white cloud moving opposite the wind, but no exclamations of discovery reached his ears.

Drake's insides writhed like the tumultuous storm he'd left behind.

His mother chose to be difficult at the best of times. When the haughty elder dragon heard his request, he'd be forced to gorge on crow without even the luxury of a Cherry Coke to wash it down.

Don't think about it. It'll be here all too soon as is.

He let his steady wing beats lull him into a meditative trance.

Stomach grumbles broke his reverie as the sun outran him to the horizon, setting in the distance. He circled. Wild Fey lurked somewhere nearby but hid from him. The land beneath him belonged to Jedediah even a thousand miles from the farmhouse. Others guarded areas across the Mississippi River. Drake didn't want to deal with another wizard over a meal and night's sleep, so he searched east of the river.

Minimal patience won him a buck and one of its slower herd mates. Drake's attempt to grill it with his breath reduced the buck to charcoal. He bit into the smaller deer raw. The fresh meat and warm blood caressed his tongue, but might as well have been as burnt as the buck.

Maybe it'd be better slow-roasted with a spicy rub.

Stormfall would've scolded him had she known he let wizard troubles rob his meal of flavor. Kine were beneath him, never warranting even a moment's passing worry. She didn't know them like he did. Jedediah and Jordan, Lanea and even stinky Kane were good people, people worth knowing, better in their own way than many of the older dragons Drake had encountered. They cared for all Fey, protected and hid them with their short lives.

She'd have liked them—as a meal. She probably couldn't even remember her years of fosterage—if she'd ever been fostered at all.

The brush rustled, moving aside for a pair of very young centaur. The boy raised a bow at him. Drake tried not to snort. The resultant flicker of flame would've sent the shaking centaur aflight.

"W-wizard friend or f-foe?" he asked.

Drake raised an eyebrow.

The girl forced his bow down. "Forgive us, Lordling. We scented fired meat and thought you might be of the tribes."

"No need for forgiveness," Drake said.

Both jerked back as if slapped.

"I have no campfire, but," Drake said, "I'd enjoy company and local news."

Color fled from the male's face. "Great one, we would never deign to soil you with our companionship."

She slugged him in the side, scolding him in harsh whispers. "If he asks us to join him, we must."

Drake stretched. A great yawn evidenced his long labors. Both eyed him with the same frightened expressions worn by his dinner a moment before death. "Forgive me, I meant no threat. I'm just weary. Your company is welcome. What news in this area?"

The female mouthed soundlessly.

"Great things are at hoof, Lordling." He puffed his chest out. "The tribes rise up against the evil tyranny of our jailors."

Drake frowned.

"We refuse to accept imprisonment, fenced like normal horses," he stomped a hoof. "We've left our hidebound elders to join up and fight for freedom."

Drake chose his words. "There is great danger to the Fey should humanity learn of its existence. We might be eradicated or enslaved as curiosities."

"Perhaps they might try with us lesser Fey," she said. "But surely, normals wouldn't dare accost an Elder Fey like you."

"One did, nearly slaying me," Drake said. "Master Jedediah saved me."

The boy's bow snapped up. "You're wizard deceived, Lordling—by no less than the great deceiver and villainous despot Jedediah Two-Hawks who mocks us with his lies of friendship and protection."

"Take care, boy, and lower your arms." Drake growled, smoke escaping his nostrils. "Your words invite harm unintended. Provoke me again, and you'll end up half cooked like Sinesh Ena'Donishe— luckiest of my Wizard Bane foes."

He tensed to fire, but she slammed her arm down upon his. "You'd dare harm an Elder? Have you lost your mind?"

"He's wizard friend."

"He's Elder Fey." She bowed to Drake. "We hear your words in defense of Wizard Jedediah to whom you honor a debt. We thank you for your wisdom and will leave you to your rest."

She turned to go.

Her companion lingered.

"*Come on*, Glisyr Phri'Waph," she said.

Glisyr Phri'Waph's face set in a hard line. He inclined his head so stiffly cracks threatened to riddle his neck. "Lordling."

Drake's lingering appetite departed with them. If the evening's interaction were considered typical, Kane's description encompassed only a small fraction of the numbers flocking to Wizard's Bane's banner.

World's dropped into a hand basket right alongside hell. We need Jedediah back. If Mother can help me find O'Steele and get that information to Master, maybe he'll return.

❧

Billie Jo stormed out of the pastor's office. The insufferable man and his constant calm demeanor made her want to punch something. She'd wasted two more sessions. She'd laid out verse after verse, and still he refused to help them.

They'd argued grace versus law until blue in the face. He doggedly refused to accede that all magic rested in Satan's control, echoing Jedediah's question.

"Billie Jo, do you really think our Lord let Lucifer take something so wondrously created all to himself?" Pastor Fulton asked. "Don't you think it possible Mason's gift is Heaven sent?"

No. Absolutely not. Her gaze shifted to Mason. *You don't see the fighting, the sass coming out of my sweet boy. The evil is corrupting him more and more each day.*

Tears escaped her, running down her cheeks.

"Mom?"

"I'm all right, sweetie."

"No...well, good, but does something seem off to you about Pastor Fulton?"

She dragged him outside. "Of course there's something wrong with him. He's an idiot—or some witch sent to lead us astray."

"That's not it."

"Isn't it enough? You should be happy, he's defending you and that...that...." She couldn't finish the sentence. "At least until he suggested executing you."

"He didn't mean it," Mason said. "You kept quoting old testament to him. What choice did you leave him but to agree with you and suggest killing me?"

"There's middle ground, an exorcism—"

"Not according to those—"

"Don't interrupt me, young man," she snapped.

"He was doing the baby thing," Mason mumbled.

"That's enough. First, you embarrass me in front of my boss by fighting at school and now this back talk."

"That fight wasn't my fault."

"You must have done something to antagonize those boys."

"Sure, I got them detention by slamming my face into their fists," Mason said. "Thought I'd ruin their futures, bruise their knuckles with my jaw so they couldn't write, and they'd fail their college entrance tests."

"Before Jedediah and his evil, you'd never have acted like this." She slammed her car door, snarling at the steering wheel. "You're sick, Mason. It's not your fault, but we need to cure you."

She pulled out of the church lot with as much anger as the four cylinder minivan could manage. *One more session. Either he helps us, or we find a new church.*

Storms rode the horizon the next morning. Jagged shards of light tore across dark, twisting funnels of destruction. Drake circled around it, unconcerned that it put him off course. Once he flew sufficiently around, he could find his mother's draw once more. Drake generally stuffed down the thread of gravity which pulled child to Dame. It took a lot of effort, and the strength of the Dame bond they shared had interfered with his early lessons. He hated the connection. She'd abused it to control him more than once.

Soon my own strength will be enough to break it.

The wind coming off the storm slowed his progress, forcing

him to use more muscle to maintain flight at the lower altitudes. He climbed, not for the first time wishing he could just drive Jedediah's pickup or a motorcycle. Of course, their drivers followed roads.

Just need more practice. I've nearly got it perfect.

The wind dwindled, and he reached out for his mother's gravity, reorienting toward Silverthrone, a dormant volcano in the northern Rocky Mountains.

Only inactive until Mother's next tantrum.

Drake's neck scales prickled.

He turned a lazy circle, scanning above and below. Nothing threatened him. The storm remained where it'd been, neither approaching nor retreating.

He frowned. He circled back toward the storm, breathing deeply of ozone and fire. Something felt off about the storm ravaged area, but it stubbornly remained anonymous. Repeated lightning strikes left weak fires curling smoke up to his nostrils. A waft of it left the taste of burnt flesh across mouth's roof.

Drake flew closer.

Tingles flitted across his wings as if he'd flown through a curtain of static electricity. Wild aeromantic energies clustered around him, thick as fog even so far from the storm. He tapped into it, struggling to maintain flight, concentrate and keep his eyes open all at the same time.

Drake rose to keep above the lightning storm for a better look. The wild storm loomed over a farm in an almost symmetrical circle.

Too ordered, not at all like some impulsive elemental gone to town.

His gut told him to plunge into the strangely restrained storm. Taking that path to investigate meant exposing his wings to possible lightning.

And I still end up burned half the time when I skip lightning along their membranes.

Days separated him from his mother, business essential to the long-term health of his adoptive family. Drake circled back northwest.

It's not my problem.

A noise—weak mishmash of squeak and growl—reached him. Drake circled back, his gut knotted at the after the fact translation his ears insisted he'd heard. He heard it again, the almost inaudible draconic translating faster once expected. "Help."

He didn't think.

Drake folded wings and dropped into the storm. Jagged bolts of power exploded around him. Jedediah and Drake shared an affinity to air and its jagged biting power. His teacher loved throwing electricity at his students to keep them on their toes. It'd been too long since he'd played dodge bolt, but Drake's aerial skills had grown too.

Drake dove. His focus split between listening, feeling air pressures along his wings, and slipping past the lightning.

"Help...please?"

Drake landed hard. His talons dented muddy ground encircled by ruined buildings. Horse and magic choked the air. He rolled the pungent aromas over his tongue, adding subtler tastes of charred flesh and dragon to the warring list. He followed his nose to a little corpse so badly burnt he almost missed the scent of pending rain on the toddler's skin. His gut squeezed so tightly it all but imploded with agony. Another dead aquamancer only twice the toddler's age lay in three blackened pieces—a ribcage smashed so hard a centaur hoof imprint remained in the mashed flesh.

He sniffed back tears and recognized faun scent on the murdering magic. Heat built up inside Drake's gut. It belched in tiny angry roars from his flame lung, and sparks flickered in the rain like fireflies leapfrogging his scales.

The fauns had hunted Kane, but Kane, like himself, was almost an adult. The two little girls dead at his talons weren't old enough to have deserved their deaths. He found a boy child—dismembered and stomped despite his blood's compete lack of magic.

"Help me?"

Drake replied in a series of growls and snarls. "Hello?"

Excitement intensified a feminine dragon scent enough to draw Drake's nose. "Hello? Is someone there?"

Drake oriented on the scent. Pain and fear, excitement and

strangely attractive dragon blood rolled across the roof of his mouth. They drew him to a burned and blackened barn. Great, charred beams stuck up like stakes. Scent brought him to a root cellar door splintered open by one of the fallen beams.

Drake lowered his mouth to the doors, one claw peeling an opening big enough for his beak. For a moment, he nearly gave her his dragon name. His mother refused to honor anyone with her dragon name—afraid if any knew it they might over the course of their near immortality puzzle out her true Name as a means to control her.

"I am Drake, son of Stormfall," Drake said.

"Salyse, can you help? Please?"

Drake paced around the opening, examined the fallen timbers. "You're beneath the barn?"

"I'm pinned beneath its rubble." She sniffed. "One of my wings is broken, and I can't feel the other."

Drake grabbed a likely timber in his front talons and drew it back, wings beating for more pull.

Salyse shrieked.

He abandoned the first and attacked a second.

She screamed again.

He turned his back to the wreckage and slammed his tail and its growing spikes into the wood. His own pain felt more immediate than her cries, but he probably hurt her more than he did himself.

Drake lay on the ground, thinking with his beak in the cellar's entrance.

"Hello?" she asked.

"I'm still here."

"I th-thought you left," Salyse said.

"No, just trying to figure a way to get you out," Drake said.

"Please don't give up."

Drake grumbled to himself. "No one said anything about giving up."

The jumble of burnt timbers refused to offer him an easy solution. Drake disliked terramancy. Forcing his magic to bully the stubborn element left his shoulders stiff and skull splitting on the best of days—not that Jedediah cared about such. His master often declared Drake's discomfort with other elements a combination of mindset, laziness and a lack of practice. Under his tutelage, you learned and practiced everything—especially your weaker areas.

If I could complete a change into a human shape, this would be easier.

Drake stepped away from the fallen barn to give himself room, shook out his wings and compressed his form as small as he was able. He managed to stuff his bulk into a wolfish shape. The pressure of holding in all his mass left him on the constant verge of a sneeze. He shimmied into the cellar, scrapping off fur he didn't really need in the process.

Huge blue-silver eyes greeted him, followed by sharp, snapping white teeth.

Drake snarled in draconic, not an easy language for a wolf throat. "Do you want help or not?"

"Sorry, I'm s-so hungry," she said. "I saw you, and…well, your appearance and scent don't match."

"Shapechange." Drake examined the slightly roomier cellar, shifting again into an approximation of a chimpanzee.

"Wow," Salyse said. "You're really good at that."

Drake sneezed, cursing the pressure and the pungence of her blood. He tested both strength and stability of the beams. He cocked his head her direction, letting his eyes return to normal shape and function but not size. Wreckage and cramped quarters hampered his ability to judge the shape and scope of her body.

"I'm going to dig you out, but I'm going to have to concentrate, so keep quiet and no trying to eat me."

"All right," she said.

Drake settled down next to her frame. Warmth washed out from her slim lines and small tightly-layered silver scales. A headdress of frills and tapered ivory horns capped her silver head. Drake pushed her from his thoughts, sinking into a meditative focus.

I hate earth shaping. I should've brought Jordan…nah, Mother'd have eaten her.

<*What?*> She thought back at him.

He started, jerking away from her skin. "Nothing, sorry."

He sunk his senses into the earth around them. He tried searching for faults and seams, probing strengths and weaknesses, but it resisted him.

Curse it, I'm going to have to look for myself.

The thought of suffocating in earth knotted his gut, but he couldn't think of any other way to get the lay of the land. He slowed his breathing, picturing a calm lake. Mother birthed the dragons and their spring. She loved them best. She wouldn't hurt him. She wouldn't play favorites just because he flew with Father. *One with Mother, her body like water on my scales, air in me and around me.*

His tail slid in first, the ground's molecules sliding between the gaps of his own like sandpaper. His talons followed, dragging his head beneath the surface. A moment of panic seized his lungs. His body reacted, trying to expel the earth. He strangled the image of a calm lake. His lungs knotted. Lanea sprang from the lake's surface, glistening and gorgeous.

"Come on in, Drake. It's perfect."

He relaxed. Lanea'd taught him to swim. Sarah'd taught him this.

"Drake?" Salyse said.

He willed his head from the ground instinctively. "Yes?"

"Where'd you go?"

"Just earthswimming." *Yeah, like I do it every day.* "Give me a minute."

He slid back down and swam the area around her, learning what he needed to shift earth and set her free. He rose with a better picture and pitted his will against earth's stubbornness. Ground shifted agonizingly slow—not that earth did anything quickly.

A line of infinitesimal pebbles like sugar ants rolled up and out of the cellar. More lines formed. Pea gravel began its slow rollout. Loose debris dwindled. Bedrock, clay and stubborn dirt resisted him. Drake clenched his jaw and bore down on the terramancy in his center, squeezing it as if he could move soil and stone faster by wringing more earth magic out of his body.

His greater effort produced more significant effect, but it affected the wreckage above as well. He opened himself more fully to the Spring, struggling to rush earth by virtue of brute strength.

Earth respected nothing, particularly not strength. It deplored being hurried.

Mother punished his bullying with pain. His muscles burned as if he were shoving the earth with his back and legs.

He forced the ground away from beneath Salyse, easing her down and away from the timber piercing her wing. The beam followed before she slid entirely from its impalement. He shifted a few more times, using each shape to improve his ability to hollow out enough room for his natural form. With careful talons and jaws, he broke the timber spitting her wing and eased the remaining pieces from her silvery membranes.

A snatch of Salyse's thoughts washed over him when he brushed against her. *<He's incredible and so handsome.>*

Drake blushed, reminded of Mason's early hero worship. "I'm nothing special, just a good Samaritan."

"No, Drake, you're so much more."

Talons and magic shifted earth away until he released his terramancy with a body shuddering exhale. His every molecule demanded he drop and sleep. He ducked under Salyse's damaged wing and helped her from the ruin. He expected the building to crash loudly down the moment they narrowly escaped.

It didn't.

Drake collapsed. *Maybe Master's right. Maybe I watch too much television.*

Salyse giggled. *<Either way, thank you, Drake. I thought I was going to die in there, but you saved me. You're my hero.>*

Can you tell me what happened here? Drake asked.

Images washed from her mind over his. It replayed like a bad television show. Wizard's Bane arrived, accused Salyse's Mistress of crimes against the Fey—just as Kane had described. They'd attacked without parley.

A growl escaped him. *Where were you in all this?*

<Mistress Finerielle insisted I hide with her grandchildren when the border warnings went off. Why did she do that? Because I'm Elder Fey?>

Drake felt Salyse's terror as they both relived the sounds she'd heard of Finerielle's torture. He heard the familiar voice of Kiki demanding Salyse's whereabouts over and over. Finerielle's screams eventually drew out Sidney, Kimberly and their older brother Westin. Mimi used the children as leverage, but still, Finerielle insisted Salyse's Dame had summoned her back.

Anguish pierced Salyse's heart, memories of the two little aquamancers playing with her flashing through her thoughts. *<Why didn't she just give me up? They'd never have hurt me—not like they did... like they...>*

I didn't know her, but perhaps your Mistress cared about you like Jedediah does me. Master never would've sacrificed someone he loved, even under torture.

<She could've saved the little ones.>

She had perimeter alarms, which means she heeded Master's warnings about Wizard's Bane. She knew that they'd kill everyone anyway. She might also have been buying some of the others time to get away. There were not as many bodies as your memories tell me lived here.

<Payment.> Salyse shuddered. *<The head one ordered a storm spell cast and all survivors executed, but one of the females demanded they take a few alive as payment for someone named Master Remi.>*

Drake recognized both the voices in her head, the faun and the centaur—Sinesh Ena'Donishe. *You're going to wish you'd burned to your hooves on our first encounter, mule, once I'm done with you.*

Salyse snuggled against him and closed her silver-blue eyes. Comforting and yet uncomfortable—both reminding him of a nightmare-plagued Lanea curled tight against him for safety in an acorn-shaped bed.

Drake growled. *If I ever get my claws on that elf, I'll rip him to shreds.*

<Elf?> Salyse asked.

Treevoran—an elf that betrayed someone precious and later gave Dragonsteel to the very people that killed your family.

<They were human, not family.>

Did you love them? Did they love you? Did they treat you any differently than they did their little ones?

<They bowed and stuff, but otherwise no.> Warm images of Finerielle, her children and grandchildren washed through shared thoughts. Salyse's scent warmed, a hint of salt wafting into the air. *<Kimberly giggled every time she bowed.>*

Family.

Salyse drifted off into fitful sleep.

15

RUNNING OUT OF PATIENCE

The sun leaked through the boughs as it rose in the distance, striping the wild wood around Jordan like a zebra. She ran along a deer track. Cool soil met each bare footfall. Leaves whispering to her right marked Nip's stealthy pursuit. He'd pounced onto her twice, leaving her foster clothes coated in mud. The first one had been quite the shock. Anger caught her before she remembered Drake's tales of Wizard's Bane attacks. She'd needed the reminder, but the fun and challenge of evading him added to the run she'd also desperately needed.

She felt calmer, more centered. She'd started with knotted muscles and resentment circling her thoughts like endless, angry sharks. Mae offered her plenty of reasons for both, but running melted it all away. It also left her time to review and practice Mama Yamai's lessons.

Pending day and forest's edge blunted the joy pumping through her veins. Slavery, imprisonment and inappropriate touches awaited beyond the treeline.

I could turn around, run another couple miles...maybe just run and not come back. Crystal's pitiful expression peaked up from beneath thick lashes.

Arthur's continued "accidental" touches convinced her to ask

Crystal about Eve—the girl who'd apparently ran away before Jordan came. Crystal answered little. She suspected the younger girl had no real answers, the truth having been withheld lest Crystal say something at school to mar Mae's perfect public image.

Eve had been fourteen, petite and pretty—prey for someone like Arthur. Jordan had nothing but supposition, but her instincts told her Eve had suffered Arthur's attention more complacently than she'd ever tolerate. She also suspected that Eve's departure had turned Arthur's attentions to Crystal before Jordan offered fresh hunting.

He will probably leave her alone until he realizes I'm not prey. I'll have Nip guard her—except during my early morning runs. If I hadn't killed Nibble...

Jordan's breath caught. She slowed to a walk, wiping dust from her eyes. Nip eased into view and pressed against her side. "Good boy."

<Happy with sister two-legs. Happy with pack. Happy, happy, happy.>

A grin conquered Jordan's melancholy. "I love you too, Nip."

<More run? More Chase? More happy sister two-legs?>

"No, we're done running for today."

"I should say so," Mae snapped. "Faye Iris Jordan, come out of those woods this moment."

Jordan and Nip both let out low growls.

<Bite unwelcome predator. Drive her off. Defend pack. >

Jordan sighed. *No biting, Nip. This is her territory.*

"I'm waiting," Mae said.

Jordan tromped out of the woods to a crowd. Mae glared over folded arms, her displeasure set to heavy stun at the very least. Arthur towered over a miserable Crystal, his smug expression and possessive grip nearly making Jordan summon her staff before she mastered herself.

Mae tromped forward and snatched Jordan's hair, twisting to painfully assert dominance. "What do you think you're doing? You're covered in sweat and mud, dear lord you're barefoot like some savage!"

"I was running," Jordan said.

"You won't run away from me." Mae twisted. "Thank God Arthur saw you, or we'd never have known you were gone."

"Not running away, just running," Jordan said. "I'm on the cross-country team. I'm being scouted for the Olympics. I have to stay in shape."

"Not anymore," Mae said. "A lady should never sweat."

"How'd you end up with Arthur then?" Jordan snapped.

Jordan barely managed to harden her skin before the blow struck her. "I've tried to be kind to you..."

"Yeah, love by slave labor," Jordan said.

Mae struck her again, shaking her hand after each blow. "I've tried to be patient, but it's clear that idiot farmer either ruined you or didn't know how to fix what all's broken."

Jordan caught the next blow, her voice low. "Don't. Criticize. Jedediah."

"The cellar with you." Mae's voice shook with fury. "Crystal too."

Crystal shrieked. "No, please, no."

Jordan's gut tightened. "Why Crystal?"

"She didn't tell me you were running off into the woods."

"She didn't know," Jordan said. "I slipped out while she was asleep."

Mae licked her lips, eyes bright. "You and Crystal are sisters—a team. If one of you misbehaves and the other doesn't inform me, you're punished together."

"That's ridiculous," Jordan said. "Crystal had nothing to do with my choices. She was *asleep,* and why isn't Arthur being punished with us? We're supposed to be his sisters too."

"I told," Arthur said.

"Maybe this will get through to you," Mae said. "Arthur, take them to the cellar and lock them in."

Arthur grabbed Crystal. She struggled and flailed, giving him opportunities for accidental groping he didn't pass up.

"Let her go," Jordan said.

Mae twisted the hair in her grip. "You aren't in charge here."

"Can't you see how he's grabbing her?" Jordan asked.

"If she did as told he wouldn't have to fight her," Mae said.

"She's claustrophobic," Jordan said.

"She's faking to get out of punishment," Mae said. "I'm no fool."

The earth at Jordan's feet rumbled.

"Tell him to stop, and we'll obey. We'll go peacefully," Jordan said.

Crystal's look of betrayal squeezed Jordan's chest. Her fight weakened.

"You don't give orders here," Mae said.

Behind Mae, Arthur's grip around Crystal solidified. His attention focused on the young girl, a tip of tongue moistened his lips. The hand across one breast massaged it.

Jordan's voice rumbled, low and menacing. "Let her go, Arthur."

Arthur smirked. He groped Crystal more.

I'm going to wipe that smirk off your face, you little bastard. I'm going to break those fingers one at a time.

Mae yanked Jordan's face down to hers. "You don't—"

A deep growl rumbled the ground. Strength filled Jordan's limbs.

"Tell him to let her go, or someone is going to get hurt." Menace built in Jordan's tone. She took hold of the fingers in her hair. Her grip tightened. "He's got no business groping her like that."

Mae's face drained of color.

"I'm asking nicely." Jordan squeezed harder and dragged Mae's hand from her hair. "Don't make me demand."

Mae shifted her body, shying away from the pressure Jordan placed on her fingers. "I don't take orders from you."

"Tell him to let her go," Jordan said. "Or else."

Arthur screamed.

Mae whipped her head around.

Crystal lay a few feet from Arthur. His leg had sunk into the ground up to his knee. He fought to pull it out with both hands, face white with pain.

Too late. Jordan didn't fight the satisfaction his torment brought with it.

He lost his balance and fell. One arm yanked backward into the ground with a shriek-beckoning snap. His leg came free. Deep, bloody furrows peeked through the shredded pant leg.

Mae struggled to go to him.

Jordan let her. Someone had to wrap his wounds, and she had no interest in touching him. *Enough, Nip, let him go.*

Rather than descend on Arthur to help him, Mae seized Crystal's hair and started wailing on her.

"Leave her alone," Jordan shouted.

Mae ignored her. "How dare you attack my son, you ungrateful little—"

Jordan surged forward. "Let her go!"

Mae and Arthur, Crystal and various lawn furniture hurled across the yard. Mae slammed into the deck stairs. Arthur careened into the grill. Nip leapt from the ground like a dolphin, taking Crystal's impact against an overturned firepit.

Jordan's legs buckled, strong to noodle in an instant. She yanked magic from Mother in a panicked surge and reached Crystal. "Are you okay?"

"What happened?" Crystal asked.

"I'm not sure. Are you all right?" Jordan reached over her, ruffling Nip's ears. *Good boy, Nip. Hide now.*

Arthur's whimpers undercut Mae's groaning. Blood and unnaturally bent limbs filled Jordan's immediate concerns. She reached for the phone in her pocket. *Right, confiscated and smashed.*

Jordan hurried to Arthur first. From the purpling of one hand, the angle of his arm and bite marks on arm and leg, Nip had made her inner desires reality. "Crystal, go inside and call 911."

Crystal stared at her.

"Arthur needs a doctor," Jordan assessed Mae in a flash. She didn't see blood, and that made Arthur her priority. *Especially since his wounds are my fault.*

Mae tried to rise, but couldn't seem to find her balance. Her shrill tone cut through Crystal's shock. "Go get Louis, you useless waif, or you'll live in the cellar until you turn eighteen."

Crystal bolted for the house.

Jordan whipped her shirt off. She ignored her own relish as she ripped the pink tee and started wrapping Arthur's ravaged calf.

"Faye!" The railing helped Mae to her feet. "Put your clothes back on."

"I need to stop the bleeding." Jordan rolled her eyes. "And I'm wearing a sports bra."

She wrapped Arthur's leg as tightly as she could. She raised her focus from the work. His glazed eyes fixed on her bra-covered breasts. Jordan snapped her fingers in his face. "Yo, fat boy, are you in there? Stay with me. Are you dizzy? Do you feel cold?"

"Don't talk to my son like that, you filthy Jezebel." Mae fell as she reached them, using the momentum to shoulder Jordan to one side.

"We need to keep him talking," Jordan said.

Mae's demeanor offered no sign of distress. "Are you all right, sweetie?"

She's tougher than I expected.

Arthur reached toward Jordan's exposed chest.

Someone—Mae, Nip or perhaps Jordan herself—growled. Arthur snatched his hand back. Crystal emerged with Mister Bridgeport in tow. He took in the tableau and spoke more force-fully into his cell phone.

"Crystal, grab me a shirt."

Crystal raced off to the cottage.

"Don't bother hiding your sinful lusts now." Mae snarled. "All of you foster girls are depraved whores, taking advantage of my poor boy."

Jordan stood. "That what happened with Eve?"

Mae looked as if she'd been slapped. "Eve ran away."

"Where'd she run? Was it before or after she forced Arthur to assault her? How many other girls ran away?" Jordan glared down at them, all guilt for their injuries burned off. She strode away. "You know what, I think I know."

"Where do you think you're going?" Mae asked.

"The root cellar." Jordan kept walking, ignoring whatever Mae had to say. In any other foster home, she'd be worried about being thrown out. *My luck isn't that good. Besides, I'd need to be sure Crystal was thrown out with me.*

She met the other girl and took the replacement pink t-shirt. She threw it over her shoulder. "Come on, we're going to the root cellar."

Crystal blanched. "No. P-please, Faye."

"Jordan." Jordan gentled her voice. "Come on, Crystal, it'll be okay."

Crystal shook her head.

"Haven't I protected you?"

"Yes," Crystal said.

"Have I hurt you?"

"No."

"Then trust me," Jordan said.

"I'm…I'm…."

"I know." Jordan took her hand. "It won't be so bad this time."

"Because y-you're with me? There's barely r-room for one of us."

"It'll feel bigger this time," Jordan said.

"How?"

"Magic."

Zero levered his will, forcing the last and most stubborn of the four teeth into his desired shape. The earth-kindred tooth still connected to a living dragonling somewhere west fought the shaping magic. He refused to be balked.

After considerable effort, the tooth flattened into the blade of a slightly curved knife. It refused all but the roughest edge, but the talisman wasn't meant for hand to hand in any case. He bound the narrowed and stretched tooth roots between alder halves braced by silver crossguard and pommel. He wound satyr leather around the hilt. Crystal shards grown from his own power crystals studded the design, bespelled to resemble gems and enchanted to hide the magical link to their mother crystals.

He turned it over and over in his hands, meticulously verifying every inch. He made a small adjustment to the hilt wrap—aesthetic rather than to tighten it around the alder. He hung it from a wine glass rack beside its cousins.

"Bianca is quite insistent about speaking to you," Flash said.

"She must wait."

Zero turned his back to the knives and Flash, approaching another table filled with implements. He withdrew a bamboo skewer soaking in brine and dipped it in a small cauldron of bubbling, melted platinum. With practiced strokes, he drew precious metal onto a canvas of air. The floating portrait formed slowly—part rune and part symbol, ornate figure and calligraphy. He added layer upon layer onto the fragile artifice. A swipe of his hand shaved it long ways, leaving a flurry of eight identical figures spinning in the air. Another gesture heated the cooling metal, but not enough for its form to run.

He opened a small box of metal filings. He piled a pinch onto his palm. The tiny pieces alternately shone silver and darkened to old blood. He blew them gently into the construct, embedding the Dragonsteel slivers. He blew another pinch into the molten platinum.

I'd have painted with Dragonsteel itself if I could somehow melt it. This'll have to do.

The symbols floated over, pressing against the teeth. Dragonsteel and molten platinum embedded the symbols into grooves burned into the enamel.

That must hurt...though, perhaps not as much as this.

Zero misted the teeth with liquid nitrogen.

Hot to cold, poor dragonling is going to have a horrible toothache. Pity the sympathetic link to the Dragonsteel will keep it from healing while slowing the growth of a replacement tooth in that socket. He chuckled. *They're Elder Fey. They can take it.*

Velith'Seravin stepped from the cavernous fuel tank converted to his temporary headquarters. Other hooves echoed on the gradual ramps that spanned the huge iron cans. A whinny followed by laughter drew his attention to one side. A pair of yearlings chased wild horses that grazed the old oil fields offering his kind camouflage from eyes in the heaven.

Wizard lies, but the camouflage offered by the horrid creatures comfort those that fear Jedediah and his treacherous kind.

He left the children to harry the horses. Someone would stop them...eventually. Dry, scorching heat left the white, silver embroidered robes of leadership sticky and uncomfortable. Within the tanks, Lili and her sisters maintained magics to prevent them becoming ovens.

Valuable members, even if they aren't centaur.

A sleek black mare trotted toward him, vests like his covering her otherwise bare chest. Glent Se'Lailos tossed a raven mane over her shoulder and flashed him a white smile. An itch on his chest hidden by the robes reminded him that he couldn't get as close to her as he might like. Again, he didn't believe in the wizard's lies, but if he courted GlentLai and something happened to her, it might strike a crippling blow to morale.

"VelSera, the workers are done."

"Excellent, coordinate with SinDon. Move our prisoners to their new cells."

"I can handle it myself," she said.

"I don't doubt you, GlentLai, but dragons—even young ones—should never be underestimated. Let's go inspect the work."

"I already did," GlentLai said.

He smiled at her. *So eager to please. When this is done, perhaps I'll court her.*

A dun-colored sorrel galloped up to them in robes stretched across solid muscle and melted flesh. "I hear the cages are done."

"We're going to see them now. I don't wish to release Master Remi's dwarves until I've ensured their work flawless," VelSera said.

SinDon darkened, the expression adding menace to his melted

features. "I do not like trading captives with that satyr, I don't care what connections he has throughout the Fey communities."

"Mimi and her sisters more than earned our trust helping us capture the necromancer," GlentLai said. "A few prisoners are hardly too costly for the scouting and spell nullifications he's provided through the fauns."

SinDon shook his head. "I still don't like it."

"The satyr is useful to us. I respect your counsel and your warrior instincts, my brother, but his scouting reports have provided the means for the dragonlings in our...," VelSera grinned. "...protective care."

"Not to mentions teaching our faun sisters to amplify their magicks, increasing their value beyond when VelSera first recruited them," GlentLai said.

"I still don't like it."

"Our old friend Treevoran vouched for him as well. You know how valuable his help has been." VelSera slapped the other centaur's shoulder "I've made my own inroads with the dwarves. The fauns' strength grows heartily. We'll not need the satyr much longer. Would you like to slay him?"

GlentLai's voice rose in pitch. "Elder, you'd slay one who has helped us?"

"He knows we have the dragonlings, to merely cut off our association might leave us vulnerable to retaliation. I don't want the dragons catching wind of their children's predicament until it serves my plan."

"What if they out us?" SinDon said.

VelSera grinned. "They're dragons. We are beneath their notice. They'll never be able to tell their parents which tribe captured them. Their rescuers will thin the herd of old nags, allowing us to lead our kind into a glorious new regime with the normals serving us as their ancestors did before."

They reached the work area. Rows of tanks spread out in a cluster, surrounded by old rigs—only a few still pumping up oil to enrich Wizard's Bane and pay the dwarves for their work—and their weapons.

The dwarf foreman heaved open the heavy reinforced doors. Thick beams and sharp spikes lined its interior, cunningly positioned to slide between each other when the door was opened. A dark red glint shone on spike tip and reinforced beam alike—a thin coating of Dragonsteel.

An elevator lowered into position, and the dwarf pushed open its railing gate. They stepped out onto the platform to see depth once filled with oil, the barest layer lingering in its bottom.

"It's spell proof? Flame breath too?" SinDon asked.

"The Dragonsteel will foul their magicks, though extended exposure is not recommended. The iron would melt if your...," The dwarf chuckled. "...guests were able to summon enough fire, except the Dragonsteel will eat that heat to grow stronger."

GlentLai eyed SinDon. "Setting the ground beneath them aflame while wallowing in oil wouldn't be healthy either."

"I am pleased." VelSera let his smile grow teeth. "Very pleased. I'll inform your leaders such when I see them next."

A runner galloped up to them, passing a missive to SinDon. The sorrel read it, handing it to GlentLai. "We've caught the silver that escaped us in Kansas. May I suggest she be first in our new accommodations?"

The dwarf foreman stepped off the elevator platform and slapped a fist against a large red button. The oil tank's roof split open like spiked arms unfolding in welcome.

"Very pleased, Master Dwarf. You and your workman should join us to feast completion of your work, among other victories."

Mae's root cellar had once been part of the cottage's basement. The more time Jordan spent in the cottage, the more certain she became that it had once been the property's main home. It sat atop an incline, allowing the cellar subbasement to cut deep into the Georgia clay—probably meant for cool food storage in the hot summer months. She'd found the small room at the bottom of the basement stairs and its exit to the yard behind. It wasn't the Weems house, but it wasn't bad, and she told Crystal so.

She had shown Jordan the subbasement's back wall. Jordan had overlooked the newer brick. Crystal took her around to the iron hatch over the segmented section, though she refused to go within ten feet.

Jordan pulled open the hatch. Rope hooked onto the hatch's frame, stabilizing an otherwise rickety ladder. She descended, finding the small area suitable for three people without cramping them too much. A small iron door she'd taken to be an old furnace backed a rectangular hole not much bigger than a mailbox. PVC jutted through the newer wall, uneven on the inside where it was nicely finished on the public side of the subbasement. It reeked like a porta potty.

This woman is one seriously neurotic piece of work.

Broken clay pipes jutted into the other walls, chitters echoing in their depths. Old paper cups and bowls littered the floor. Small desiccated remains piled at the feet of a half full bucket long overdue for replacement. The thick contents oozed from rusted cracks.

She looked up. "Crystal?"

She heard a squeak that didn't come from the pipes.

Jordan climbed back up and extended a hand. "Come on, Crystal. I'll make everything right. I promise."

Crystal sniffed, wiping her nose on her arm. She made it three steps before her courage fled with what was left of her color. She wrapped arms around herself, shaking her head violently.

How do I help her?

Mae took things out of her hands. Louis scooped Crystal up into his arms. She shrieked and fought, but he dropped her at the ladder's top.

"Climb down." Mae cradled an arm, her fury and pain compressing her lips into a thin, bloodless line. "Or he'll push."

You and I are going to have a come to Jesus meeting when this's over. Jordan softened her expression, descended the ladder and extended a hand. "Come on down."

Crystal squeezed her eyes tight and very slowly descended until Jordan could help her the rest of the way down. Louis yanked the ladder up the moment she hit the ground.

Jordan embraced her. "See, this isn't so bad."

The hatch slammed with an ominous finality. Crystal jumped, tightening her arms to a choking grip that barely softened her shudders.

"You'll stay there until we come back," Mae yelled. The bolt slammed shut above. "You'll stay there all weekend. No food, no water, and no foster of mine is going to sweat in public view. You can forget the Olympics."

We'll see about that. Jordan raised her voice. "What about church?"

Chains rattled into place, and Crystal whimpered.

"Wasted on your likes, but we'll bring a preacher out to cure you," Mae said. "You'll be made right. You'll see."

Getting really tired of that woman.

"Love, the ambulance is here," Louis said.

Mae stomped away.

Crystal trembled around her. Jordan wriggled an arm free. She touched the walls and reached out to Mother. *Please let me get it right this time.*

She pushed the glamour into the walls for all she was worth, desperate to give Crystal an illusion of open expanses. She pictured the panorama from Jedediah's porch with a soft twinge in her chest. Magic pooled at her fingertips, but it refused to leave them.

Damn it. I just threw magic outside my body. Why can't I do it now?

She fought it until she shook as hard as Crystal—probably not helping keep her promise. She changed the push to a pull. *Come to me, Earth Fey. I bargain for a glamour...I can get candy.*

Nothing happened. No Fey arrived other than Nip who ducked in and back out of sight when she waved him off.

Maybe a little light will help while we wait. If I can't get the power out of me, maybe I can use it inside. She willed the magic inside her skin to glow like a flashlight beneath her palm. *That doesn't look demonic. Plan C.*

She summoned her staff, planted it in the broken earth and transferred her magic into its runes until a soft emerald light filled the small space.

Crystal's eyes opened. Her color became pallid in the dim light. "What?"

"Magic," Jordan smiled. "I tried to—you know what. It doesn't matter."

Crystal paled, shying away. "Is that what happened? You're a witch? You attacked them with magic?"

"I accidently hit all of you with magic when Mae started beating you. I don't know how, and apparently, I can't do it again," Jordan said. "I'm still learning."

"If you d-didn't attack Arthur, w-what happened?" Crystal asked.

"Do you like animals?" Jordan asked.

Crystal bit her lip and nodded.

"Nip?"

The mudpuppy slid into view.

Crystal shifted her grip, keeping the larger girl between her and Nip.

"It's okay, Crystal, this is Nip, my friend."

"H-how did it get in here? We're locked in, and the food slot's too small."

"Nip can swim through the ground," Jordan smiled. "And he can take us out of here if you trust us. How'd you like all the food you can eat and a nice soft bed tonight? Maybe a movie too, you choose it, we have plenty."

Nip wagged his tail.

"Where?"

"Home."

16

WAR RELIVED

Drake sunned in the rising dawn. Salyse's nightmares left him sleepless. He could imagine all too well the foster family he loved being slaughtered by Wizard's Bane. Lanea's lifeless body in the arms of a centaur left him cold even in direct sunlight.

Motion told him Salyse would wake soon. She'd be hungry, but his sleepless night had provided ample time to hunt her up a fresh buck. Her foster wizard's pond had been stocked with trout. He'd enjoyed them with a few rogue ducks for variety.

Salyse pressed up against him. Flashes of her recent pains proceeded warmer thoughts. *<Is that for me?>*

Drake shrugged.

Salyse shivered. *<Ugh, don't do whatever that was again. It's horrible.>*

He chuckled.

She fell upon the deer with abandon.

Maybe I should've saved her some trout too.

When she'd devoured the buck and licked the blood from her talons, he voiced the question he knew Jedediah would've insisted he ask. "Where do I need to take you? Where's your Dame's lair?"

Her frills bristled, sparkling silver in the morning light. She jabbed her nose against him. *<What are you talking about?>*

You're hurt and alone, someone needs to see you home.

She snorted. *<You're not much older than I am.>*

I've been fostered longer.

<If you can make your way places alone, there's no reason I can't.>

You're a gir-uh-gonna need to stay earthbound with that wing.

<I can't fly anyway. I'll make my way home in the rivers.>

What is it with me and water kindred? Drake asked.

<What?>

Nothing. He shook his head. *I don't know. I really should make sure you get there safe. Master would expect it of me.*

<I'll be fine, I promise. There's a dragon's lair between here and my Dame's.> Images washed through Drake's mind. *<He'll give me a place to rest if I flatter him right. He's sweet on me.>*

Drake's stomach tightened. *Are you sure that's safe?*

Warmth and amusement washed from her. *<Of course, boys are easy.>*

Zero settled into a café seat and glanced over the San Francisco Bay. Tourists bustled around the covered area, occasionally colliding with dock workers bringing fresh seafood to their employers and clients.

"Excuse me, I didn't see you there."

The tray in Bianca's grasp swept back down, having not spilled any of the chowder cradled in bowls of fresh sourdough. She snarled at the other woman. "Because you're an idiot paying more attention to your phone than people around you."

Zero smirked. It seemed her new dark red hair was more appropriate than he'd thought. She caught him smirking, eyes flashing behind fake glasses.

"You want to wear this food? I don't know why I had to fetch it, hell I don't understand why you've even got us down here. Surely your chef could have prepared better, and he delivers."

Zero moved the gift boxes onto a chair to give her more room to set the food down. "Perhaps. Thank you for fetching it. I find standing about in such crowds not to my liking."

She shot him a dirty look and dragged her food closer as she took a seat. She lifted a spoon to her nose, eyeing the wharf food dubiously. Zero watched her from across the table, amusement playing about his lips. She took a bite and froze. Her glare intensified, but her eyes softened as she worked the food around her mouth.

Zero saluted her with his spoon and sipped rich, buttery clam chowder. He closed his eyes, letting the blended flavors play across his tongue.

"Fine," Bianca said. "It's good."

Zero picked up the cutting of sourdough and dipped it into the soup. It didn't quite taste right, the restaurant having lost its original starter in a fire years before, but they'd restored an almost perfect level of tart to the bread.

"Try the bread."

She frowned but did so. Her eyes were closed when three women in business attire approached them.

Zero set his spoon aside. "Ladies. Have you caught the apprentice?"

"No," Kiki said.

"Almost," Lili added.

"Have you convinced Velith'Seravin to relinquish the necromancer?"

"Not yet," Mimi said.

"Do you have the talismans prepared?" Kiki asked.

"I keep my end of a bargain." He gestured to the stacked boxes.

Kiki snatched the top one. Lili and Mimi sucked in a breath, eyes on Zero. He took another bite of chowder.

"Apologies, Master Remi," Mimi said. "We're understandably eager."

"You should try the clam chowder. It's quite good. Isn't it Bianca?"

Bianca put down a chunk of empty bread bowl, swallowing hard. "Yes."

"We're not hungry," Lili said.

"That seems to be your biggest problem," Zero said. "Perhaps if you had a greater appetite you'd have accomplished more since our last meeting."

Kiki raised the boxes. "We can't fail now."

"Power is no substitute for desire, skill or planning," Zero said. "Set up a meeting with Velith'Seravin."

"He'd kill—" Kiki froze. "Forgive me, he'd attack you."

"It seems I must risk that to obtain what I desire. Fear not, I have skills enough that he'll not realize what I am."

Drake flew over the middle states, thoughts far behind on the silver-scaled dragon. He'd reluctantly left her to her own devices. He'd enjoyed having a dragon his age to talk to, even if they only discussed Wizard's Bane and their foster families. As much as he loved Mason or Lanea, they weren't dragons.

It shouldn't matter, and it doesn't really...except it makes a difference that I never realized existed. She was...she smelled like Lanea, but different. Her scales accentuated how sleek her limbs—

The roar of a twin-winged crop duster penetrated his forebrain. It sped toward him on a collision course. Drake dipped his right wing. He slipstreamed just under it.

"I've got you now! I told them you were real!"

Drake craned his neck backward, frowning at an old man in a leather pilot's hat. He stood in the biplane's cockpit, one fist raised at Drake. He dropped back into his seat. The biplane arched back toward Drake in a kamikaze attack.

"They said you were just another Jerry, but I knew the bloody Red Baron was no man!"

Drake cursed himself. He hadn't bother with glamour while above the clouds, but he'd been so preoccupied that he'd let his flight path slowly descend below cloud cover. The pilot seemed a harmless crackpot. Drake dodged another attack.

If I'd paid attention, the glamour would've hidden me from this normal—or in this case not-quite-normal.

Drake dove and slipped, barely staying away from the crazy pilot and his surprising dogfighting skills. Ten minutes stretched out, and Drake still couldn't slip the madman. Long distance flight wore on a dragon, but the constant shifts and changes required in dogfighting left Drake breathless.

The biplane sped up Drake's tailwind.

Drake dipped low and backpedaled with all his might.

The plane flew over as planned, but the crazy normal let loose with his crop-dusting chemicals right into Drake's face. He blinked tears from his burning eyes. Heat built in his gut. "Leave me be, old coot!"

The old pilot rose in his cockpit, pointing at Drake for no one's benefit. "See, I told them. They'll believe me when I wear your wings at my next lodge meeting by God."

Drake dove away, picking up speed.

The biplane's engine whined, pulling along behind with all its might.

Drake backpedaled once more, but only for a quick stop. He slipped around the biplane in an extended barrel roll and sunk his talons into its upper wings.

"Look, old man—"

"Betsy! Curse you, Baron, look at what you've done to beloved Betsy!"

"Shut up. I don't know what your problem is, but leave me alone."

"Kill me now like my wingmen, but we won't beg. No, we won't!"

"We who? What're you talking...you know what, I don't care." Drake crushed the plane's wings.

The old man raved, shouted and threw whatever was at hand. Drake tuned him out. His tail ruddered them downward. They hit the dirt road harder than expected. Betsy's landing gear crumpled. Drake flapped a hard reverse, tail twitching back and forth to control the sliding plane's grinding stop.

Drake leapt off.

The pilot glowered through his dirty goggles. "You killed Betsy!"

Drake closed his eyes.

Something hard struck his beak. A crescent wrench lay on the ground.

"Serve's you right, Jerry! If I had my machine gun, you'd have gone down in flames instead. Betsy, my sweet, sweet Betsy."

Drake opened his mouth to rebut, decided better and launched himself into the air. He climbed into a high cloud bank, cloaked himself in glamour and didn't look back.

Zero's plane landed in Kyoto, and a car met them on the tarmac. It took him to the rear of an old shrine. A blank wall opened a perfectly crafted door and offered passage below the temple to one of the few railroad stations which traveled to and from his destination. Had Bianca been able to accompany him, he'd have met his contact in Atlantis—just so he could show her the famed city.

I've another meeting there in a few weeks, perhaps then.

The station offered underground accommodations for business transactions and various Fey less capable with glamour or less comfortable above the surface during daylight crowds. He entered the hotel through a VIP door, swiping a gold inlaid card cut from ebony.

A dwarf woman rebraiding her dark hair leapt to her feet and rushed toward him, several of the newly introduced beads clattering to the floor in her haste. "Good afternoon, sir. Welcome to Laurelglade. We're glad to have you back."

"I have a meeting booked."

"Yes. Absolutely. Your party arrived early and is enjoying some refreshments. Would you care for anything?"

Zero stopped, looking down and giving her a gentle smile. "Are you on the menu, my beauty?"

She flushed, fussed with her skirt suit—showing a bit more cleavage than before, and pushed a half-finished braid out of sight. "Um, not officially? Sir?"

Zero exhaled loudly. "More's the pity."

Her cherubic cheeks reddened.

"I know the way. I believe you dropped a few beads."

The dwarf waiting for him wasn't young and curvy. He looked rough. Black peppered grey hair in need of a wash fell to his shoulders. A longer beard and half a handlebar mustache descended opposite a partially melted face. Dark eyes narrowed beneath dandelion fluff eyebrows. He set a half-gnawed something onto a small plate, revealing a crimson shirt and alligator-skin vest beneath bandoliers of shells and grenades.

"Mister Clutchanvil I presume," Zero said.

"You Remi no-last-name?" Clutchanvil folded arms bare from his rolled sleeves down. Scars and tattoos covered them so thickly they seemed impossible to separate.

"Yes."

"Call me Chicory." The dwarf tucked thumbs into an alligator skin belt dotted with machete-length knives and long fang-like teeth. "I hear you've got a dragon that needs slaying."

Zero's gaze went to the table behind Chicory. "Do you typically hunt dragons with an assault weapon and grenade launcher?"

The dwarf spit something dark onto the floor. "Depends on the dragon, his lair and whatnot. Whatcha got?"

"A juvenile behind a magical barrier. His teacher's missing at the moment, but considering, he might present a bigger challenge than most his age."

Chicory snorted. "You want the skin? Something for your mantle?"

Zero smiled. "Oh, no. I want nothing that can be tracked."

"Let 'em, rot. You got it."

Drake circled his mother's realm. He trumpeted, calling out for permission to enter and an audience. His requests remained unanswered. He spiraled slowly closer.

Either she's not in her lair, or she's in a mood.

Entering her territory without permission risked her displeasure even though her lair technically remained his home until declared adult. She'd made it clear the previous year he wasn't welcome. The slow spiral represented a gesture of obeisance, a groveling that turned his stomach but might sate her temper. Otherwise, he risked death.

I need her help with Jedediah. She won't kill me. It'd look bad.

Silverthrone rose in the distance, a forbidding mountain surrounded by only the barest traces of civilization. People in the surrounding area trudged hither and yon, doing their business weighted by an oppression they didn't recognize.

Mother's territory. Small surprise they feel oppressed.

He scanned the countryside, searching for a hidden entrance or a lava vent. He'd been flown out of it years ago barely awake and under cover of darkness. He'd been too young to think about paying attention, and even if he knew where the exit lay, she could've changed it.

Her age and subsequent size limited the kinds of entrances. Her age gave her plenty of tools to disguise her lair

Anything from magic to guile to camouflage. I know so little about her. I've no idea how she'd hide a lair.

Stormfall campaigned for a mass breeding to combat dwindling numbers. She'd pursued his Sire relentlessly until the elusive Lailos Prielaru capitulated. She'd taken Drake's egg to the Dragon Springs to strengthen him not once but twice. All that effort seemingly ended when Drake clawed his way out of his shell. Imperious and impersonal, she'd shown little patience even with her own son and his questions.

Drake didn't know her dragon name. He didn't know her affinity. He didn't know if she'd learned magic from a fostering wizard. No one he'd asked had even known if she'd employed 'talented kine' magic or eschewed wizards' ways. He wasn't even sure how she'd risen to prominence among their kind.

The mountain grew closer, and his search for an entrance continued without success. He found no waterways big enough to hide an underwater entrance. Endless circling showed him no caverns large enough for someone her size—not even in the old volcano's central crater.

Drake trumpeted once more, but silence doused his spirits.

All this way for nothing.

Stormfall's voice exploded in his thoughts. *<So this is the product of wizards. Rydari Phriel—a weak-willed failure given to retreat without even token effort.>*

Drake scoured the mountain beneath him. She'd never spoken to him mind to mind over a vast distance, only when in line of sight. *Mother, I am honored—*

<Save it. If you cannot find my lair, what good are you?>

I need help.

<Haven't I already lent you aid? Did I not bend minds you could not to save your precious teacher? What tribute have you brought to repay my largess?>

Someone altered the minds of judge and jury, but—

<Someone? You beg me for help and then refuse to honor me when I deliver it?>

I am sorry, mother. I received a message after, but it was too cryptic to be sure.

<Yet another reason to eat those lesser. I feared the messenger too stupid, but I left you another calling card.>

The farmhouse.

<Perhaps a lizard's brain worth of intellect in you after all.>

Drake bristled. The skin of his wings tingled.

<You dislike my words?>

Call me what you will, but please help me.

<Have you no pride? Have you no teeth in your mouth? Force your wizard to help. I have no time for worms.>

It is to help him that I came to you.

A hulking pressure speared into Drake's mind. His wings faltered, and he fell nearly to the treetops before catching himself.

<Ah, he is broken.> Her dark laughter reverberated through his thoughts. *<The mighty wizard is laid low by a normal's cruelty. How delicious.>*

Heat flashed through him, and ozone burned the air around him, but he forced his pain down. *Jedediah is needed. The centaur are slaughtering wizards.*

<Let them slaughter one another. A loss of a hundred kine more or less matters little.>

He's my teacher.

Anger slammed into his consciousness. Images of Jedediah on his knees ravaged through Drake's thoughts. The cherry scent of pleasure accompanied images of his master in torment. He reeled—unaware any dragon could project emotions into another with such strength. He slipped from the thermal lifting him back into the sky. *<Your continual sniveling for help, your inability to find me or my lair proves your tutelage worthless. Get a new teacher.>*

Those were images of you attacking and torturing Jedediah. Why?

<He's kine, I need no why. You're pathetic, unable to fight even so well as the wizard, and grown attached...> Anger lashed Drake once more, but he maintained altitude. *<You'd have bred with that half-blood abomination? You who are my son—twice taken to the Springs?>*

Jedediah is not kine. They're thinking beings with enormous potential who at least aren't callous, soulless creatures too lazy to care for their own child.

Stormfall's laughter thundered through his mind. *<Well, some bite after all. Fly away, beast lover. Grow stronger with haste before I tire of waiting, and hatch a better son to gnaw your bones and bring me glory.>*

Drake growled and wheeled southeast.

Drake rode a storm blown in from the west. Charcoal clouds painted his mood across the sky, thunder echoing his anger.

Let them slaughter one another, he mocked. *A loss of a hundred kine more or less matters little. She'd have cared if I told her about Wizard's Bane hunting Salyse.*

He'd flown all the way across the country. She refused to help, insulting him instead. She'd declared him useless. She threatened to replace him because he wasn't good enough. No human mother would've threatened to feed one child to another.

He'd tasted her pleasure as she'd shown him memories of torturing his teacher and called Lanea a beast.

I should've ripped her mountain apart chunk by chunk and showed her the worth of my teeth. How can any parent be so unreasonable?!

He'd pinned all hope of reclaiming his teacher on her. She'd, in turn, branded him as useless.

She's right. I haven't helped Master. I couldn't save Lanea. I couldn't even eat her killer.

He had to do something to prove himself, not just to his mother but to himself. It didn't matter how perilous the act. He needed to feel something other than helpless. Lightning danced across the undersides of the ominous storm, spreading like vast nets across the sky.

One of Lanea's novels spoke of Fire Runners—wild dragons that flew through storms acting as channel and conduit for heavens's fury. Wasn't his affinity air? Hadn't he done the same or similar with Jedediah's bolts? If those dragons could do it, then why couldn't he?

I'll show her. I can ride the lightning, can she?

Fury and elation, despair and exhilaration rushed across his scales talon to talon and wing to wing. Drake dove in and out of the darkest thunderheads. He knew it was reckless.

He didn't care.

The first strike lanced through the heavens. He slipped toward it, missing it by a wingspan. A tingle coursed through his flight hairs like he experienced working magic—though dozens of times stronger.

Drake chased another sheet of lightning, managing to catch the edge of the retreating wave. Burned hairs invaded the scent of ozone. Power washed over him, heady and heated.

He dove into the next thunderhead. A tickle coursed over one wing's hairs a moment before another arc lanced through the sky on that side. He wheeled toward it but proved too slow.

Drake closed his eyes, trying to focus on instinct and the pressures on those tiny hairs. The zing of power sung through him, making his focus as slippery as his wet scales. He missed two more lightning explosions. The brunt of cacophonous thunder left him feeling bruised, but with each near miss, he needed to catch the lightning even more.

A tingle of hair and a tickle of instinct, he slipped right.

Lightning burst around him in all directions, coursing along his wet scales. Euphoria and searing heat warred for foremost attention. Power pressed outward on his blistered skin, leaving him giggling, drunken and numb.

Somewhere in the back of his thoughts a voice much the mix of Lanea and Jedediah screamed warnings, tried to get him to acknowledge the pain beneath his pleasure.

He caught another half blast almost by accident. His scales tingled. His blood sang. A corona of sparks flicked along his length, no doubt making quite the spectacle for any storm watchers.

Drake rode the wind, gliding left and right through the storm in airborne drunken weaves.

Lightning exploded around him, cords of electricity tying him as if an actual net. Energy filled him and filled him as a thunderous concussion drove him downward. His vision blurred. The world went silent.

He felt so good.

He felt so powerful.

Invincible—with so much power I could cow Mother and force her help.

He truly was Elder Fey.

Lanea's musical voice broke the absolute silence. *<Remember what happened to that battery I tried to supercharge with magic?>*

Lanea? Drake strained to hear her through the quiet.

<Wake up, you great lizard.> Jedediah's voice snapped. *<Think! Why can't you hear the wind?>*

Master? Wind? Drake tried to focus through sluggish thoughts. *Why can't I hear the wind?*

Nausea shoved against his euphoria, parting the curtain between him and pain. He roared a moment before the sky did, a moment before lightning exploded through him.

17

SHOCK IN THE PARK

Jordan eyed Crystal. "I'm going to need you to trust me, can you do that?"

Crystal nodded.

"Please close your eyes and keep them closed," Jordan said. "Good. This will feel a little weird, but I promise you'll be fine. We'll be out of here and scarfing down goodies before you know it."

Crystal's voice didn't reach a whisper. "Thank you."

Jordan touched Nip. *Can you take us to Weems?*

<Weems? Little home. Yes, little home.> Nip wagged his tail.

She cradled Crystal, pressing the girl's face into her chest. She took hold of Nip and nodded. The mudpuppy slid them into the nearest wall. She shifted magic into her eyes, following how Nip swam through the ground with an educated eye. Earth passed through them, the sandpaper inside her skin sensation itching her nose. Earth muffled Crystal's voice. "Jordan?"

"You get u-us-use—" Jordan sneezed.

"Bles—" Crystal's screams split the air, deadened by the rock around them.

Nip hollow us out a cave like before.

Nip went to work, but unlike before he had to keep them with him as he hollowed out a space and burrowed small air tubes. The jerky ride stopped with them dropped into the egg-shaped hollow. The fall interrupted Crystal's screams, and Jordan took advantage.

She cradled the other girl, rocking her. "Crystal, calm down. You're fine."

Crystal shook her head violently, eyes squeezed shut and screamed.

"Walls...collapsing..." Crystal managed between sobs. "Suffocating..."

"Nip's made you a nice, solid cave," Jordan said. "He's bringing air in through little breathing tubes."

Crystal clawed at her throat, gasping even faster.

"You're going to hyper—"

Crystal's head lolled to one side.

"—ventilate." Jordan scowled. "This isn't going to work."

<Go? Home? Go?>

"No, Nip, I mean I'd like to, but I'm not sure how she'd take to another swim," Jordan said.

<Elves?>

"God, no, I can't even imagine how she'd take that—never mind Lirelaeli's reaction."

Nip whimpered.

Jordan agreed with his sentiment. "Can you move the egg slowly to the surface? Scout first."

Nip disappeared into the wall. The ground thrummed, but the low vibration didn't wake Crystal. An eternity later, humid evening air rushed into the disintegrating shell of earth. Tall pines clustered around them, an apartment complex visible between their trunks. Sweat teleported onto her skin. It glistened along her limbs, summoning a mosquito swarm. A trickle descended her spine.

Shadows shifted. Jordan struggled to her feet. She reached out and snatched her staff as it spit from the earth. The solid wood thrummed like a purring cat. Magic's rumble rose within her and pushed out at her skin. "Who's there?"

Brownish-yellow cat eyes reflected light from a moon nowhere to be seen. A feline body formed of smoke and menace sauntered out of the shadows.

A low growl like shifting rock escaped Nip's throat.

Another cat appeared followed by another.

"Unless y'all want cracked skulls, you'll hunt your fun somewhere else." She glared at them, resisting the urge to slap herself. *Mother's breath, I just said y'all, heralding the apocalypse.*

A fourth cat edged into view, moonlight striping its dark coat. It sauntered a circle of menace around them. As it circles, she realized the stripes were natural rather than lighting.

Nip's fur bristled, and his growl turned to a snarl of bared marble fangs.

Jordan lowered Crystal to the ground without taking her eyes off the cats.

Four more shadowcats edged out of the night.

Jordan grasped her staff in both hands. "You don't scare—"

Heavy thuds shook the earth—each harder, stronger and closer. Jordan tensed. Cats pressed ears to their head. Stripe hissed at the darkness.

A hulking behemoth stuttered to a halt. It pushed its way into the clearing, knocking trees to either side and making a gap for the sun. Shadowcats growled.

Jordan extended her staff.

Whatever this is, I hope I can protect Crystal. She's been through enough.

A shapely figure stepped into view, light sliding across smooth grey stone. Rose quartz laced it in a dainty fashion, reflecting shafts of light. The stone elemental gave each shadowcat a hard look. When her gaze settled onto Jordan, her lips parted into a smile. She inclined her head before moving on to the remaining cats.

"Hello?" Jordan said.

The elemental's voice slid from her lips smooth as river stone and soft as fresh-turned soil. "Is there trouble here, little mother?"

Jordan bit her lip. "I'm not sure. Are you here to cause me some?"

The elemental laughed, a tinkly sound. "I heard your summons, and come to serve—though I've no interest in candy."

"Oh," Jordan's eyes widened. "Oh! I'm sorry, I needed to glamour a cellar, but we left instead."

"No trouble. When you summoned your staff once more, I followed. It felt urgent. Shall I scatter these strays or would you prefer to crack their heads?"

"I'm Jordan." Jordan eyed the cats. "Who are you?"

"Kimberlite, once of your master's acquaintance." The rock woman leaned close, inhaling the air around Jordan. The elemental turned to Stripe, assumed a sumo stance and growled like an avalanche. "Something you want, fleabag?"

The cat flirted his tail and sauntered into the shadows without a backward glance. Shadowcats slipped between the trees, disgusted divas retiring from public view.

"You know Jedediah?"

Kimberlite traced the quartz lace across her bosom. "His generosity is as great as his power."

Jordan's stomach knotted. She looked down at her fidgeting hands.

Kimberlite curtseyed. "My pleasure to meet you, Mistress."

"Uh, I hate to bother you," Jordan said, "but is there any way you could maybe do me a favor?"

"What service may I provide?"

"I need help getting this girl home. I can't carry her the whole way, and we don't have a car or glamour for that matter."

Kimberlite scooped up Crystal. A soft thrum escaped her throat and calm washed from her over Jordan.

"Wish I could do that," Jordan said.

Kimberlite smiled. "Time moves mountains, little mother."

Mason glanced at the house before easing open the old shed door. The hinges squeaked. He froze. He didn't see any motion from his mom's upstairs bedroom. He waited a few more breaths then shifted it open enough he could squeeze inside. He turned into the shed's interior only to trip over something that clanged like a gong. He cursed, feeling around for the light switch.

His fingers found it, but the moment he slid it up the bulb above him popped. He swore again, this time at the bulb-eating outlet. He pushed the door open a bit more, cringing with each noise until light fell upon the old tool box. He crossed to it and started rummaging. They'd won the house through some weird sweepstakes his mom swore they'd never entered. It'd come partially furnished—all part of some dead guy's estate donated to a church then raffled off.

His search struck pay dirt. He crossed to the doors with the WD-40 can and sprayed the hinges before rocking the door back and forth to work it in a little further. When the squeaks died to his chemical assault, he tossed the can onto an old workbench and grabbed his bike.

He poked his head out the door and checked the house. His mom still wasn't up, weird, but a relief. She cried a lot lately, even more than when Jedediah had gone on trial. He wanted her to stop, probably even knew why but he didn't know how.

Not like I can be something other than I am.

He'd have asked Jedediah, but Jordan said the old farmer had disappeared. He'd gotten a few magic lessons from Jordan before something big had happened that no one explained. Since whatever, there'd been a girl stuck to Jordan at lunch like they were Siamese twins. The girl had been in his classes since the beginning of the year. He'd thought her stuck up, too good to talk to anyone. She still barely spoke, but opposite her and Jordan he noticed her eyes.

Deep blue like water, but kind of like from Jurassic Park. Rippled. Afraid.

Whatever was going on prevented further study in magic. They couldn't talk or practice in front of the girl, and both were whisked away the moment school ended. He'd gone by Weems to ask about it just after it all started, but the place seemed deserted.

Crystal came with an odd sort of consolation. Jordan bought

her more food than the quiet girl could eat during lunch. When the snobbish brother came over and threw some kind of fit about his mother disapproving of lunch, Jordan claimed the food was Mason's. He'd played along, and whether the older boy showed at lunch or not, Mason got the leftovers.

Mason missed Lanea. She'd been pretty cool—for a girl. Her dying made him a weird, hollow kind of sad that he didn't understand. He missed Jedediah, too. *Always gave me food when I asked even though Mom complains about how often I'm hungry.*

He really missed Drake. The dragon had to be the coolest kinda-brother ever, but the farm was too far to bike even if he hadn't been forbidden from going out there to visit.

Mason pushed the bike down the driveway at a run, getting it up to almost full speed before jumping into the seat and pedaling like mad. He relaxed once out of sight of the house and headed up the street to Heath Lake Park. The park was mostly wooded trail—cool for dirt bike riding and hidden behind enough trees he could do stunts without his mom catching him at a distance.

He stood up on his bike pedals, pushing them down with all the strength and speed he could muster. The wind tickled his skin, gooseflesh raising the hair along his arms. His bike hit a little dirt hill at speed. He hopped as the bike crested the top, giving him and his bike extra lift. His heart raced. There was nothing better than that moment of flight before his wheels hit the ground again. He rode at the hill faster, hanging in the air even longer. Exhilerated laughter escaped him. Mason ramped off the hill a few more times before deciding to ride deeper into the park so as to avoid easy discovery.

He rode slowly until he came to the stretch along the back of the lake. Wild ducks and geese waddled around the mostly clear area. Mason put on all the speed he could muster and plowed into their flock, sending them squawking and flying in every direction. He chased a few stragglers then raced toward where the group resettled down the lakeside.

He'd chased them into the water when he noticed a bulldozer

parked at the bottom of a steep embankment marking a barrier between park and houses. A pile of dirt had been pushed together a couple dozen feet from the embankment in almost perfect alignment with the Path leading down from the ridge's top.

Mason rode over to the dirt pile, leaping from his bike and letting it roll to a crash on its own. He rushed up the big dirt hill, stomping on it to find it solid after recent rain. He stomped some more to pack it down as best he could and grabbed his bike. He walked his bike down around the lake's end to the embankment's beginning and up atop it. He sucked in lost breath. The huge dirt pile didn't seem very big from his perch. It was a long way down.

Mason grinned.

He stood up on the pedals once more, getting as much speed as he could across the ridgeline. Cutting hard down the hillside path toward the new ramp slid his back tire out of control. He recovered and barreled down toward the ramp. A knot filled his gut. The ramp raced toward him. He tightened his grip on the handlebars and closed his eyes as his bike hit the hill.

Mason soared off its top, flying over the mud at its base and landing hard.

Exhilaration filled him as laughter escaped.

He loved the feeling of flight. Being airborne thrilled him. He loved the feeling of soaring off the high diving board at the public pool—even if he was afraid of heights.

This is better than even the high dive. I've got to do that again.

He rode it again. Braking before the hard cut saved him momentum. He hit the ramp with even more speed. He did it again, flying just a bit longer each time. Mason pushed his bike back up to the ridge and stopped to catch his breath for the next run.

Wait. What if I used magic?

A grin spread across his face. He'd practiced Jordan's lessons whenever he had the opportunity. He managed limited control of the air around him—better than Jordan could apparently do. She'd been able to teach him a sort of internalized magic which she did better. Mason closed his breath, heart beating in his chest. He extended his arms like wings, feeling the wind tickle the hairs on his arm. He sucked in slowly, not feeling the rumble Jordan described but rather a tingle. The more he breathed in, the more the hair along the back of his neck prickled.

He recited something Drake taught him. *The wind roars through canyons. The Zephyr races the eagle. I am the wind. I am the Zephyr.*

Mason pedaled faster than he ever had before. The bike practically flew across the ridge line. Wind braced him from every angle. He put a foot down and took the hard turn at almost a forty-five-degree angle, back tire sliding a little but not out of control. He rocketed down the hill toward the ramp.

A moment's fear gripped him, but there was no way to stop in time.

He soared.

The bike came down hard. Its back tire hit a protruding stone, shoving the rock to one side. The tire bounced the opposite direction. He lost a lot of momentum on the recovery and brought the bike to a stop.

He looked back at the ramp, heart thundering in his chest. He'd flown twice almost three times as far as any other time.

Drake, you're awesome!

He raced back to the ridgeline for another run, reciting the dragonling's little focusing chant once more. He raced along the ridge, down the path and up the ramp.

"Hey, Shiner!"

Mason's head whipped around as he launched. The bike struck ground. Its back wheel landed on the unearthed stone and bounced. Bike and boy jerked wildly, rolling sideways over one another. Shrieking pain lanced up his arm.

"Smooth move, Shiner." Roland sneered.

Tears rolled down Mason's cheek. He blinked them away to better see the approaching boys, but the pain kept them coming.

"Oh, did the wittle boy make himself cwy?" Edgar asked.

Mason cradled the burning arm. "Leave me alone."

Roland poked the injured arm. "Or what?"

Mason wasn't sure what. He couldn't think through the pain. Only the worst luck could've brought them and Mason together in an empty park after Mason had landed them all in detention.

Mason struggled to his feet.

Roland shoved him. "Or what, *Shiner*?"

"Why are you calling me that?" Mason asked.

Roland smiled. "Glad you asked."

He punched Mason in the face.

Mason tumbled backward, landing on his injured arm and squealed in pain. Edgar and Jimmy grabbed an arm each and yanked him off the ground. Mason's mind spun, and black spots edged his vision.

"I don't know, something about the name just fits your face." Roland's fist freed Mason from their grip.

Heat prickled his skin, herding the gooseflesh on it. He didn't want trouble. He'd never wanted trouble with them, but since Jordan and his mother stepped in they'd refused to leave him alone. In the park with no one around to stop them, they had every opportunity to punish him.

All I want in the world is for the pain to stop.

Edgar yanked him up by the injured arm. Blackness swallowed him. When it retreated, Jimmy helped Edgar hold him upright. Roland hit him again.

"Stop, please," Mason said.

They laughed. Jimmy kicked him where he lay.

"You asked for this," Roland said. "We're only giving you what you deserve."

They weren't going to stop. They had no reason to leave him alone. They'd keep tormenting him, keep him from going home. They were going to kill him.

He wrapped himself into a ball, cradling the injured arm at his center. They kicked. Heat flickered in the ball's center. They laughed. His fists itched. They pried at him, trying to lift him back up for Roland to hit once more.

He blacked out.

He woke in agony, eyes opening to find Roland's fist speeding toward him. He slammed into the ground, landing on his uninjured arm.

They laughed.

Something snapped.

Mason exploded up off the ground, throwing all his momentum at Roland with a single punch from his good arm. Rage colored his vision red as he slammed the punch into Roland's face. His wrist exploded in agony like a supernova. His tucked thumb burning like he'd stuck it in lava.

Roland went backward, head over heels.

Mason seized his wrist with his injured arm, redoubling his pain. Darkness swam a tight orbit around Mason's already whirling vision. Edgar and Jimmy grabbed him, keeping him upright when everything in his head demanded falling over. Blackness blinked.

Roland righted himself, face twisted in fury. He spat blood. A flash of white shooting onto the ground between them. His face reddened almost enough to match blood dripping down his chin. He lurched up onto his feet. "You're dead, Shiner. I'm going to hurt you over and over until—"

A calm baritone interrupted Roland. "Good day, gentlemen."

Edgar and Jimmy let Mason collapse.

Roland wiped his mouth and glared.

Stay awake. Help's here. If I pass out again, Roland will make some excuse, and I'll wake up to more torture.

A tall, dark-haired man scrutinized him from outside Roland's line of sight, a strange smile curling the corner of his mouth. He stood, somehow looming over the three teens without actually being near them. "You boys might want to take your friend home to his mother. A trip to his dentist is no doubt in order."

"I'm not going anywhere," Roland said.

The man tilted his head side to side, the sound of his neck cracking giving Mason a chill. "I see I underestimated your bravery. Few your age are so willing to answer to the police regarding their actions."

Edgar and Jimmy edged away from the man toward Roland.

Their ringleader didn't budge until the other two dragged him away.

Roland spat more blood. "I'll see you later, *Shiner*."

The man bent over Mason and extended his hands. "May I see?"

"Ar-are you a doctor?" Mason asked.

"No." He smiled, but it didn't quite reach his blue eyes. He adjusted his wire-rim spectacles. "But, I've had plenty of experience with injuries."

"It hurts," Mason said.

"I'll bet it does." Gentle but cold hands probed his injuries. "Keep still, I don't want to hurt you more than you make me. I'm Sensei Truth. What's your name?"

Sensei Truth's fingers moved to the next injury. Pain flared, sending black spots scurrying into Mason's vision. He wrestled his name from beyond the pain haze and offered it.

"Well, Mason, this probably won't surprise you, but you need a doctor. I'm pretty sure your arm and thumb are broken, but the wrist might only be a bad sprain," Truth said.

Mason managed a nod

Truth slid behind Mason and grabbed him beneath his arms. Every hair on Mason's body stood up straight.

A girlish, immature voice yelled at them. "You leave him alone."

Mason tilted his pain-clouded head. It lolled to a stop with his gaze pointed in the general direction. Spiders raced up and down his spine. Shimmering blue light shrouded a naked toddler and her pony where they stood atop the water's surface. She seemed familiar. She looked really, really angry.

Wish I could think.

Truth snorted. He lifted Mason to his feet. "Come on, Mason."

"Do you see that, Mister Truth?"

"I see nothing of consequence."

"I see a blue girl riding a pony across the lake. Don't think she likes you."

"You're delirious with shock," Truth said. "Let's get you to a doctor."

The pony stomped, rippling the water. "Let him go."

"Can you walk, Mason?" Truth asked.

"My bike?" Mason said.

"I'll come back for it."

Mason nodded.

"Someone your size should avoid fighting, but that was one hell of a hit you gave that older boy. Also, never tuck your thumb."

Mason nodded again.

18

UNREASONABLE ATTITUDE

Billie Jo pulled into the high school parking lot. She'd gotten up early for the team's cross-country meet. She didn't attend as a teacher supporting her school's team or because she was a rabid fan of running. She'd come to see Faye. The girl had been distant after she and a truant officer had tracked her down for not attending class. Distant had transformed into graveyard iciness since Sheriff Dunford drove her from Jedediah's farm to a halfway house. She'd refused every attempt Billie Jo made to talk at school. She'd tried visiting at one of the cross-country meets, but when rebuffed had backed off to let Jordan calm down.

Billie Jo hadn't been deterred. She'd visited Faye's new foster home several times. Mae Bridgeport insisted each time that Faye wasn't home.

It's possible she told Mae to keep me away.

Girls got like that in their teens, stubborn and standoffish—things Faye had been before either of them had met Jedediah. Faye acted as if Billie Jo had betrayed her, but no girl of seventeen should be living on her own. She'd had to report Faye to the state. Billie Jo probably should've left well enough alone now Faye had a family, but she needed to convince Faye it'd been in the girl's best interests. She also needed to be sure Faye wasn't infected like Mason.

That and I can't shake the feeling that something is wrong.

Miss Setter stood next to the bus behind the gym, arms folded across her body. She surveyed the stretching team with a regal expression. An African woman stood opposite Miss Setter, shifting back and forth from small talk to worried glances at the nearby parking lot.

Setter inclined her head. "Miss Bartlett, come to see us off?"

"I wanted a word with Faye."

Heads around the team rose.

"Jordan hasn't shown," the African woman scowled. "No note, no call, no answer at her house."

"She said she'd be here," Miss Setter said.

"I'm Billie Jo Bartlett, Faye's…chemistry teacher."

Setter gestured. "This is Marnie Hepp, an agent friend of mine intent to take Jordan to the Olympics. Marnie this is Jordan's former foster-father's former fiancé."

"Girlfriend," Billie Jo said. "The Olympics? You think she has a shot?"

"I think she can win," Marnie said.

Billie Jo closed so she could lower her voice. "She's in a new situation, maybe…"

"Well, she needs to sort things out. She knew how important today was." Setter turned to the team. "Stop gawking at conversations that ain't your business. Warm up!"

Billie Jo grimaced. "I know she's a valued member of the team, but—"

"Team needs her, sure, but Marnie needs to see if she can repeat what she did during the last two meets," Setter said.

"I'm pretty well convinced," Marnie said. "So I arranged for a contact of mine to come see her. I told her well in advance and even reminded her this week."

"She's that good?" Billie Jo asked.

"Jordan's not good, she's incredible. Had her run four speed-races in addition to her cross-country last week," Setter said.

"She won them?"

Setter snorted. "She beat all five records. Smashed two of them. That girl's plain magic."

A knot tightened in Billie Jo's gut. "Any way she…uh, cheated?"

Marnie's expression tightened. "Please tell me you don't think she's on drugs."

"No, not drugs per se—"

Setter's glare scattered the attention of the rest of the team. "I'll have her tested this week."

"If you can get her new family to approve it," Billie Jo said. "They haven't seemed very open to visitors."

"The consent we have on file covers the test. If Jordan wants this shot, she'll cooperate," Setter said.

"All right, I'll go give Jay the bad news." Marnie headed for the stands.

Setter swore. "You sure this new family wouldn't accept a visit? This is the Olympics, surely they'd support that."

"I'll talk to Angesa, see what she can arrange."

"Let me know when you're headed over," Setter said. "I'll chew their ears myself. Girl with talent like this needs parental motivation."

Billie Jo opened her mouth, but her phone rang. "Hello?"

"Ms. Bartlett?" a woman asked.

"Yes?"

"This is St. Francis ER. Your son's here and—"

"Mason? Is he alright?"

"I can't talk about it over the phone."

Cold welled up in her.

"He needs you to come down here right away."

Billie Jo bolted across the parking lot without saying goodbye. "On my way."

Bianca answered her cell phone on the third right. "Yes?"

"There is a property across from the airport next to the north-bound interstate on-ramp," Zero said.

"Yeah?"

"Buy it."

Bianca frowned. "Why?"

"Opportunity," Zero said. "I've sent you a text file. Fill the request and courier it to the address listed."

She checked her phone. "I've got it. When do you need this?"

"Immediately."

Her phone went dead.

ॐ

Under normal circumstances, Billie Jo wouldn't have let anyone drive her van. That Saint Francis Hospital offered valet parking at the emergency entrance had always seemed odd to her—until she needed it. Billie Jo pulled up in front of the valet podiums and was out of the car before an attendant reached her. Without word or question, the lady in dark blue Saint Francis polo swapped a ticket for her keys.

She rushed past a gift shop, snatching directions from signs and resisting breaking out into a full run with all her might. As is, when she arrived, she didn't have enough breath to address the nurse. The ER was primarily a long hall with a sitting area on its right side. It didn't look like an emergency room. There wasn't the slightest feel of urgency. A male nurse in lavender scrubs watched her with a benign smile.

A smooth, gentlemanly voice addressed the nurse. "This is Ms. Bartlett."

She turned toward him. Déjà vu left her breathless.

He gestured. "Please provide this young man your information so they can see Mason."

When she didn't move, the man's light touch on her shoulder turned her back to the admissions desk and a waiting clipboard.

"They took him back initially thinking I was his father," he said.

Heat rose, launching her back into motion. "Marcus caused this?"

"No, ma'am, just mistaken identity," he said.

"Where is he? Is he all right?"

"He broke his arm and probably a thumb," he said.

"Who are you?" Billie Jo scribbled on the clipboard without regard to her penmanship.

"Just a concerned citizen," he said. "I'm a teacher too."

"Do I know you?"

"No, but Mason talked about you. I found him in the park—"

"What happened? Some fool stunt on that bike of his? I swear I'm selling that thing—"

"There was a fight," he said.

"Another one? I wish I'd never met that-that farmer."

Truth's brows pushed together. "I'm not sure what you mean. Mason was fighting three older boys. He's brave, got in a good hit—three on one are ugly odds. With a little instruction, he'd have won."

Billie Jo shoved the completed clipboard at the nurse and narrowed her eyes. "Fighting's wrong, and Mason knows it. Who are you?"

"Sensei Truth, I teach—"

"Nothing Mason needs to learn," Billie Jo snapped. "Thank you for bringing him to the hospital, but I doubt we'll need any more of your time."

Truth smiled, something warm yet patronizing, safe yet hungry. He maintained eye contact with her in such an intense way she felt nearly violated.

"Obvious where Mason gets his temper. He defended himself against three much larger bullies and kept his head despite a broken arm. You should be proud. He's a very strong boy in here," Truth tapped his chest. "A bit of formal self-defense training and he might not be here."

"I don't believe in fighting, Mister Truth."

A corner of Truth's mouth twitched upward. "Martial Arts are about discipline, inner strength, confidence and the ability to defend one's self if the situation is forced."

"Well, be that as it may, Mister Truth." Billie Jo glared at the man. Her tone would have made a king cobra pause. "Was there anything else?"

"I have his bike in my car."

"Keep it, good day." Billie Jo turned to the nurse. "Take me to my son. Please."

❧

Jordan dropped to a walk outside the Weems house. She needed to get to the track meet, but first she had to take care of Crystal. Kimberlite tromping up behind her with Crystal still asleep in her stony arms. The halo of walnut-sized pixies slowed to a hover around them all.

Jordan dug a newly purchased box of candy from her pocket and handed it to the nearest pixie. "Thanks, we should be okay from here. Keep it."

They streaked away, fighting over the Raisinet's box and taking their glamour with them.

Nip's hair bristled.

Eerie music escaped the supposedly empty house.

"Wait here." Jordan approached her front door. Her gut clenched. *Who could be using the house? Is Drake back? Has Jedediah finally returned?*

She raised a hand to knock, deciding instead to center her focus and summoned her staff. Drake and Jedediah always complained about feromancy, but it was one of the few magics she could manage outside her own body. She extended her right hand and twisted it at the wrist. The lock clicked open. She repeated the spell with the deadbolt, but it wasn't locked.

Opening the door changed the quiet music into a blast of noise.

She crept forward, staff in both hands.

The kitchen to her left was trashed. Garbage piled on the pool table and trailed into the living room. Cups and plates lay dirty on every surface. Take-out wrappers and pizza delivery boxes formed pyramids of garbage in every available theater chair. A Resident Evil loading screen blared from the entertainment center.

"Mason?"

No answer.

Jordan crept down the hall, checking the bedrooms one by one. Every bed was slept in, but none were occupied. The closet door hung open, allowing quick exit to the farm.

"Why do I feel like I'm in a horror film rendition of Goldilocks?" Jordan mumbled.

A whimper brought her up short. She followed it down the hall. Inside the very back of the closet, a tiny mudpuppy with a swollen stomach lay tail tucked and ears pressed. She pawed the wall, howled a short cry and turned sad eyes up to Jordan.

"Aw, poor baby. How did you get here? I closed up that door." Jordan touched it. "Do you want to go back to the farm?"

<Sick. Mama. Sick. Mama.>

Jordan stood, exhaling a rise of warmth. She touched the fridge screw that opened the gateway. The puppy appeared in the bone-yard. She gave Jordan one tail wag and hustled out of sight.

She'd hoped Jedediah had returned—though she knew it a small hope considering the mess and his preference for cleanliness. The puppy nailed that coffin tight. Jedediah would never have left the animal ill and in distress.

Jordan marched back to the master bedroom. The master bed's sheets were wrinkled and piled to one side. Jedediah's bathroom door stood closed. She approached it, unsure if she should knock or throw the door open to surprise whoever lay beyond. The choice fled her control as the door flew open.

A lanky boy stepped out and screamed like a girl.

She yelped.

An almost physical wave of stench followed an instant later.

Jordan gagged. "What the frak died? Forget it, who the frak are you and what are you doing in my house?"

Kane held a hand to his chest. "This is Drake's house, and what the hell are you doing? Trying to scare me to death?"

The wall exploded in a rain of wood and brick as Kimberlite charged into the room. "Little mother, are you under attack?"

"Now look what you did," Kane said. "There's no way the AC

will be able to keep up now, and the neighbors are going to complain about the noise again."

Jordan tightened her hands around her staff. "If you're Kane, I'm going to beat you black and blue."

"If I'm not?" he asked.

"I'll murder you. What did you do to that poor puppy?"

"I didn't do anything to it."

"She was sick."

"She didn't have to eat all those leftovers. That was her choice."

Jordan blinked. "I'm sorry, did you just blame an infant for eating what you gave her?"

Kane shrugged. "It's not like I threw whole boxes of food on the ground. I gave her something when she asked for it."

"She touched you? Thought to you that she was hungry?" Jordan asked.

"Hell, no. I didn't want that thing touching me at all," Kane said. "It whined, and I gave it food."

Mason scowled at his casts.

"You know how I feel about fighting, Mason."

"I didn't mean to fight," Mason mumbled.

"So your arm just swung at that boy all by itself? You could have hurt him."

Mason shot her a look. "He was hurting me."

"And that makes it okay to fight? To break your hand?" Billie Jo snapped.

Her phone chirped. She snatched it off the top of her purse. The minivan edged toward the cars parked along their street.

"Mom!"

She dropped the phone and jerked the van back into its lane.

"Texting and driving is illegal," Mason said.

"I wasn't texting," she said. "I just read the message."

"And I wasn't fighting, I was defending myself."

She scowled at him. "That's still fighting."

"What was I supposed to gorram do?"

"Mason! You know how I feel about cursing."

He opened his mouth, but she cut him off.

"It is too cursing. They may not be considered curse words by most of society but they still are, and I don't care if Jedediah let Faye get away with it."

"Jordan," Mason mumbled.

"That's the last time you're going to correct me. Do you understand, young man?"

He folded his arms across his chest, trying but failing to find a way to do it with the various casts. He gave her one nod, satisfied by the way she pressed her lips together but couldn't yell at him.

"You're not getting your bike back either," Billie Jo said. "I told that man to keep it."

"My bike?! Why'd you give him my bike?"

"You broke your arm."

"You didn't see him after you came in to see me. How'd you know I broke it on my bike instead of during the fight?"

"It doesn't matter. You shouldn't have been fighting, and you know it."

"So what?" Mason snapped. "I'm supposed to lie there and let them beat the hell out of me."

She whipped the minivan into their driveway, slammed on the brakes and slapped him across the face. "That's it! Go inside and straight up to bed. In my house, you will not fight, and you will not have a foul mouth, and you will not talk back. You're not allowed any of your books or electronics and no dinner. Only sweet little boys get to eat the food I paid for, do you understand me?"

Mason glared at her. He fumbled with the door, got out and slammed it.

Billie Jo started the minivan.

"Where are you going?" Mason asked.

"None of your business. Do as you're told." She pulled out of the driveway and sped down the street.

Mason trudged toward the door. His stomach gurgled. He called his mother a dozen names she probably didn't realize he knew.

She'd been nicer when she was dating Jedediah. Hell, everything'd been better. He stomped up to the front door and cursed.

She had his keys. They were in the envelope of personal belongings the ER had given her—including his phone.

He sat on the stoop, glaring at the driveway.

His stomach grumbled again.

Mason lurched back to his feet. "Screw this."

He headed down the street. The Weems house was only a few miles away. He had a room there so he could do exactly what she said. It also held food and electronics she hadn't forbidden him.

❧

A huge hole gaped in the Weems house's front wall. Resident Evil music boomed from inside. Mason's imagination conjured images of a zombie Kool-Aid guy crashing his way out of the house. "Oh, brains!"

He chuckled, deciding to go inside through the hole since he wasn't sure how well he could manage the door. He stepped inside and stopped short.

A rock woman rose from beside Jedediah's bed. She glanced him over, seemed to sniff him—a ridiculous conclusion since rocks couldn't smell. She sat back down.

"Uh, hello?" Mason shouted.

"Hello, Mason," the rock elemental shouted back.

The music stopped.

"You were expecting me?" he asked.

"No," she said.

The game music started again.

Mason waited for more. He noticed a shape beneath Jedediah's covers. "Is that Jedediah?"

"No."

The music went off then started back up. Mason glanced toward the hall. He walked to the bed and threw the covers off Crystal. The elemental rose to her feet and growled like an avalanche.

193

"You protecting her?" Mason asked.

The music stopped.

"Yes."

"For who?"

"Whom," Kimberlite corrected.

"Whom?"

"Yes."

Mason's stomach growled. "Look, what's going on here? Why are you here? Why is she in Jedediah's bed? Who are you? Why is there a hole in the wall?"

"Her name is Crystal, great name if you ask me. I made the hole to save the little mother you know as Jordan when she warred with the death mage in this room..."

"Wait, Jordan's here?" Mason asked. "Maybe she can heal me."

He didn't wait for an answer but sped down the hall into the teeth of the noise. Jordan stood near the drink machine. He rushed forward so relieved to see her he didn't realize she was yelling at someone.

Jordan glared down at a boy his age, remote in her hand. She clicked it, and the sound turned off. The boy waved a hand, and the sound came back on.

She turned it off again. "Stop that, I want some answers."

He waved his hand. The music started again. He glared at her and snatched up a controller.

The music went silent.

"They still war," Kimberlite said, driving Mason into a panicked sort of jump spin.

"Don't do that!" Mason said. "You're too quiet for a rock."

Nip sidled up to Mason, wagging his tail and pressing his head into Mason's hand.

"Mason?" Jordan seized him in a hug before he could turn around. Pain lanced up his arms.

"Ow, ow," Mason said. "Not so tight."

The music came back on.

Jordan snarled, snatched her staff of petrified wood from God only knew where and hurled it at the wall of televisions. The dense wood slammed into the center screen, shattering it and driving its halves into the wall. The other units sparked and popped, falling one by one to the floor.

Mason and the other boy groaned simultaneously.

Jordan gave the other boy a smug look before addressing Mason. "What happened to you?"

Mason opened his mouth to answer when a half-naked girl poked her head and breasts through the front door. "Don't mind us, wizards. We're just here for the necromancer."

Billie Jo pulled up and parked behind a pink metrocar that didn't seem to fit Miss Setter at all. The coach stepped out of her car, heavy metal music booming out only to go silent when she closed the door. Billie Jo rolled down her window.

"No answer at the house," Miss Setter said. "I waited until you got here, but I'm not sure how long we should wait."

"How important is it Faye be on the team?" Billie Jo asked.

Miss Setter leaned against the van. "I've got time."

Billie Jo stared up at the house. The front yard was bigger than her whole property. She could park the van in the fountain and have room for a splash. She'd done right by Faye. The girl would prosper here, even if she hated Billie Jo for it. Hatred wasn't so bad, better to be a good parent and be hated than be their friend and let them become worthless, entitled burdens on society.

Or let them dabble in evil.

Billie Jo wasn't Faye's parent. She was just her teacher—a teacher that could have been her mother if things had gone differently with Jedediah.

"So how's your sex life?" Miss Setter asked.

The question broke Billie Jo's reverie and left her spluttering in shock.

Miss Setter laughed. "Sorry, but I had to. You looked buried in unpleasant thoughts."

Billie Jo forced a laugh.

"Worried about Jordan?"

Billie Jo gestured at the house. "I shouldn't be."

"Money doesn't make family."

A Mercedes pulled past them and into the drive. The garage door opened in response to some signal but the car stopped outside. Billie Jo got out of the van and with Miss Setter headed up the driveway.

Mae got out of the driver's side. For a moment Billie Jo thought she caught a glare across the top of the car before Mister Bridgeport's head blocked it. A smile rested on Mae's face when he shifted out of the way to open the back door. Louis extended his hand, receiving a crutch first and then helping Arthur rise from the back seat.

Billie Jo stopped, eyes on the boy's casts and the mud stained tatters of his lower pant legs. She glanced around at the bushes, checking for danger in the manner of Faye's mud wolves.

"What happened?" Miss Setter asked.

Arthur refused to meet her question, muttering something.

"What?" Billie Jo asked.

"He fell in a hole," Mae said. "Can I do something for you Miss Bartlett? Perhaps you'd introduce your friend."

"I'm Miss Setter, physical education teacher and Jordan's coach."

Mae's brows rose. "Faye doesn't have a coach."

Setter cocked her head to one side. "Yeah she does, me, for track and cross-country."

"A lady should never perspire, especially on purpose," Mae said.

Setter opened her mouth, but nothing came out.

"Faye's an important part of the team," Billie Jo said. "In fact, she's the subject of quite a bit of interest."

Mae frowned. "Very well, we'll move her to a different school and see to it her trampish ways are quashed before she earns more interest. Good day."

"What?" Billie Jo said. "No, Olympic interest."

"As in a scout for the Olympics," Miss Setter added.

Louis and Arthur focused on Setter, identical surprised expressions on their faces.

"Sports are not appropriate for a young lady. My son's been injured, and I suffered a broken arm rescuing him. If you'll excuse us, we'd like to get inside," Mae said.

"Love," Louis said. "The Olympics."

"I've made my feelings on this matter clear," Mae said.

"Are you out of your mind?" Setter asked. "You're fostering an Olympic hopeful, and you'd stand in the way of her chances?"

Mae glowered at Setter.

"Imagine the prestige," Louis said. "the glory—Faye Bridgeport, Olympic Gold Medal Winner."

Billie Jo opened her mouth to correct him, but Mae cut her off with a single sharp word. "Louis."

Louis opened his mouth, closed it and inclined his head. "Yes, love." He turned to them. "My wife knows best how a lady should be raised. I'll thank you to respect her wishes. Good evening."

"Now wait a damned moment," Setter charged forward.

Billie Jo grabbed her arm, surprised by the amount of momentum the coach managed in only a few steps.

Mae fixed Setter with a furious glare. "You will keep a civil tongue on *my* property, or I'll see to it your position as a suitable educator is thoroughly investigated."

Billie Jo positioned herself in front of Setter and eased her toward the road.

"You can't threaten me, you uppity bitch. I've got tenure." Setter said. "This isn't the eighteenth century. Women have equality now. What's wrong with you? How can you stand in the way of Jordan reaching the Olympics?"

"Miss Bartlett, if you and your coworker aren't off my property in thirty seconds I'll have you both arrested for trespassing," Mae said. "Furthermore, Faye is no longer your concern. You're not welcome in my home or near my daughter."

Billie Jo fought back tears she hadn't realized were so close to the surface as she steered Setter toward the road. "Come on."

"This is stupid," Setter whispered. "Hell, stupid on steroids."

"I know."

"Jordan could represent her country, win gold, set herself on a path to an incredible and prosperous future."

"I know," Billie Jo said.

"We can't let this happened," Setter said.

"We won't." Billie Jo glanced up the driveway at Mae's glower. "I know who to call."

❧

Mae watched the two women drive away, manicure of her uninjured hand digging into her palm. That they'd dare interfere with her parenting was unconscionable. Busybody though Bartlett might be, Mae'd intimidated her sufficiently to send her running in tears. She wouldn't be back.

The other teacher still needed to be taught a lesson. She'd challenged Mae in her own home. A woman like that, well she was probably a lesbian and a Satanist—totally unfit to teach children. Hell, totally unfit to live with good Christians. She'd see that woman ostracized and exiled from her town if it was the last thing she did.

Mae strolled into the house, mindful to keep her every step measured and graceful. No matter who drove by or looked out their window, Mae Bridgeport was and would always be the picture of ladylike beauty to be envied by women and desired but never conquered by men. Her home was perfect. Her husband was perfect. Her children were perfect. They would always be perfect— or else.

She entered her foyer. "Louis."

She didn't need to yell. The foyer would amplify her voice perfectly, and her husband was listening for her or else.

Louis appeared. "Yes, love."

She narrowed her eyes. "You contradicted me in front of the help."

"I'm sorry, love, but imagine what people would think of you if Faye was in the Olympics."

"No."

He adopted a falsetto. "Mae saved that girl, and through her tutelage molded her into an Olympic champion."

A shiver went through her at the thought. She'd not just be a gorgeous Mother of the Year to the affluent. She'd be a savior, singlehandedly responsible for winning the nation a gold medal.

"No," she said softer.

His brows rose.

"No." she repeated.

"Would you like a massage, my love?"

She smiled. Louis remained well trained. He knew he'd been wrong to speak out and proper spoiling would follow as amends. She toyed with denying him, making him stew until the efforts he planned to repair his mistake grew monumentally.

"Very well," she said.

He smiled. "Just let me release the girls to start dinner and I'll—"

"No," Mae snapped. "Order something catered. They're not getting out of that cellar until Monday."

"Yes, love, whatever you want."

19

REUNION

Jordan marched to the faun as she slid fully into the open door. An ornamental dagger and sheath strapped around its bicep glowed softly even in daylight. Her staff ripped free of the wall. She caught it as she armored her skin. "Who are you, and what do you want?"

"Mimi. We've come to slay that little necromancer." Mimi pointed.

"I sympathize, I really do," Jordan said.

"Hey," Kane said.

"Unfortunately, Drake asked me to protect him," Jordan shrugged. "Kind of means neither of us are allowed."

The sliding door opened behind her and another faun positioned herself to block access to the deck. "Then the dragon is away?"

A third faun stepped in through the hall. "Yes, Kiki, it seems he's all ours."

Mason shifted his gaze from chest to chest.

Nip slid between Kiki and Kane, marble teeth barred.

"You're outnumbered, Earthsister," Mimi said. "Surrender him, and we go in peace."

Jordan allowed a grin to fill her face. "You think so? Kimberlite?"

"If you're summoning the stone elemental, she's bound and unable to move," the hallway's faun said.

"You?" Jordan asked.

"Lili isn't responsible," Mimi said. "I am."

Iced adrenaline shot through Jordan. She glanced at Nip and Kiki, Mason and Kane, Lili and the hall. She closed her eyes and inhaled. *Ozone, rain and growing things. The terramancer is strong enough to immobilize Kimberlite. How the hell do I keep the little brat from them?*

She swept her gaze around the room once more.

"We'll take our sister's murderer now," Kiki said. "If you like it or not."

"Do you plan to slaughter him here or take him elsewhere?" Jordan asked.

"You're not just giving me up. Drake said you'd protect me," Kane said.

"Why do you ask?" Lili said.

"There are young here that I'd rather didn't witness whatever you have planned for him," Jordan said.

"This is a valid concern, but we do not intend to give him another chance to escape us," Mimi said.

"Could I send the children away first?" Jordan asked.

Kane lowered his hands to the ground, his jaw clenched in concentration.

Fauns raised hands filled with glowing energy.

Nip snarled.

Jordan dropped her staff and held up both hands. "Stop, please. Let me send them down the *hall* first."

Kane blinked at her.

"Mason, take Nip and help Crystal down the hall. Good boy, Nip." Jordan ruffled the mudpuppy's ears, pushing an image of the linen closet trigger into his mind. Another flash showed Mason leaving a bit of Nip's mud on the screw. *Show Mason, take them through.*

Nip whined.

"Follow Nip, Mason," Jordan fixed Nip with her gaze. "Go."

Lili stepped to one side as the two headed toward the hall. Nip knocked into Mason, and he gasped. Lili frowned at them.

Jordan backed up to the yellow metal spiral stair rising next to the hearth. She reached into it, trying to use the conductive metal to pass her will into the concrete it was bolted to and back to the master bedroom. She didn't know what she was doing, but she hoped she could persuade the elemental to lend a hand. *Kimberlite. Get up. I summon you, release you to serve me as you offered.*

Kane resumed his casting, sweat beading on his upper lip.

"No time, boy," Kiki stalked forward. "But you'll be with the dead soon enough."

The ground rumbled.

It wasn't Jordan, but she took advantage. She summoned her staff and hurled it with all her strength at Kiki's ankles. She snatched up the fireplace poker and swung it at Lili's legs.

Kiki crumpled with a scream of pain. Both of her doe ankles broken at odd angles from the impact. A blast of ice magic slammed Jordan backward against the stair with a reverberating clang. Mimi charged Kane.

Jordan tossed him the poker and summoned her staff. "Kane, hallway."

At such close range, it rocketed to her hand. She caught one end and swung it at Lili once more. Lili dodged backward and threw another ice bolt at Jordan.

"Kane, behind you," Jordan shouted.

Kiki shot a bolt of electricity from the floor. He parried it with the metal poker. He screamed like a girl, and the poker flew from his hand. Mimi's hands filled with a mahogany light. Jordan threw her staff at the terramancer. It bounced off her hardened arms but succeeded in knocking what looked like a thin stalagmite off course enough to prevent it impaling Kane. Lili hit her with another bolt, this one a sharpened icicle similar to Mimi's spell.

"I've had enough of you," Jordan snapped, willing her staff back so she could hit the Aquamancer. The stair against which she'd been thrown groaned. It ripped itself from the upper floor and whipped out at Lili. The faun leapt back, but the stairs unwound as it struck and slammed her into the pool table.

"Kane, down the hall or I'm leaving you behind."

Kane sprinted past her. Mimi caught him in the back of his head with Jordan's staff. He flew into the hall door jam.

Mimi raced after him. Jordan yanked her back by her hair. "That's mine."

The faun terramancer swung it into Jordan's teeth. She hit the floor, willing the staff to hit Mimi. The stairway slammed Mimi back into the wall of broken televisions. Jordan scrambled up and bolted for the hall, scooping up her staff as she ran.

Lili hurled a swarm of ice spikes. They didn't penetrate Jordan's skin but threw her off balance. Jordan snarled and flung her staff at Lili. Lili put together a shield of ice before the staff hit her. Jordan summoned the staff from behind the faun, willing enough force to spear her with the blunted wood.

Her staff disappeared, reappearing from the kitchen as Jordan commanded. It flew at Lili accompanied by Jedediah's Henkel knives.

Lili turned, wrapping the shield the rest of the way around herself.

Jordan didn't wait to see if she succeeded. She sprinted down the hall and hoped Lili's scream meant the Fey was distracted enough for her to escape. Kane beat at the towel shelves in the closet.

"Go," Jordan shouted.

"How?"

"What do you mean how? Haven't you been going back to the farm where it's safe?"

"Not since I got here."

"Didn't you think knowing how to get back might be important?"

"Figured I had time to work it out later."

"No," Mimi leveled her arms. "Hourglass is empty for both of you."

Jordan hardened her skin, but she was pretty sure whatever the faun threw would skewer them both.

Kimberlite slammed both fists down against Mimi. The impact drove her through the sheetrock and framing into the smallest bedroom.

Jordan slammed Kane backward, the skin on her forearm crawling with the contact. She reached up above the door, activated the gateway and threw him through by his shirt.

Jordan whirled and pointed at the closet lintel. "Kimberlite, in two seconds destroy this then find me."

She didn't wait for a response. She raced through to the farm, slammed the door shut and barred it with her staff. "Sarah, Nip, help."

The mudpuppy matron raced to Jordan, followed by a pack of mudpuppies from the newest to those older than Nip.

"If anything flesh and blood comes through this, rip it apart." Jordan collapsed next to the nearest pile of toilets. A lid opened and something very fast yanked a few hairs from her head.

"Hey," Jordan said.

Nip growled.

The sick pup from Weems planted herself awkwardly in front of Jordan and growled at the fridge door.

Jordan looked up at the others. Crystal cowered into Mason's shoulder. From his expression, he was uncomfortable and unsure what to do about it.

Kane straightened his hat and glared at her. "You were gonna sacrifice me."

"Are you really that stupid?" Jordan asked. "Oh, right, you stayed at Weems where the barrier didn't protect you without even learning how to get back to safety. Why was that?"

Kane gestured. "What am I supposed to do around here? Plant things? In case you couldn't guess, I don't exactly have a green thumb."

"Oh, I don't know, you could've *stayed alive*," Jordan snarled. "Drake told me you were only using Weems for food."

"You had the new Resident Evil," Kane said. "Mistress doesn't even have a DVD player."

Jordan started laughing. She couldn't help it.

"Stop laughing at me!"

Jordan wiped her eyes. "Mason? What happened to you?"

"Bullies," Mason said. "And a bike accident."

Jordan's laughter died. "Roland?"

Mason looked at his feet. "No. Different bullies."

"Drake never told you magic can let you know when people are lying?" she asked. *Never told me either, but he doesn't know that.*

"Fine, it was Roland, but please don't do anything I'm going to regret."

"Why'd you come over?" she asked.

"Mom locked me out on accident." Mason glared at Kane. "I was hungry."

Kane held up his hands. "Hey, don't blame me for the titty sisters, I didn't kill their sister. There wasn't any food left in that place anyway."

"None?" Jordan asked. "There was plenty when I left."

Kane shrugged. "Do they deliver pizza out this far?"

"No," Jordan said.

"Can you maybe heal me?" Mason said. "I'm never going to keep up with homework like this."

Kane snorted. "Use it, bro. Milk it, and you won't have to do homework."

"My mother's a teacher."

"Oh," Kane said. "You're screwed."

"Says the guy with half-naked girls trying to kill him," Mason retorted.

Jordan heaved herself to her feet. "And I'd like to know why? Why are those...girls trying to kill you?"

Kane described the Wizard's Bane assault on his mistress.

"Damn," Mason said. "You can actually, like summon dead? Why didn't you do that back at the house?"

"I tried," Kane said. "I'm not good under pressure, and I couldn't find any bodies beneath us."

"None?" Jordan asked. "Surely something's died there."

Kane shrugged.

"You couldn't even find a hamster?" Jordan asked.

Kane reddened. His expression hardened "I didn't see you doing any big fancy magic. All you did is throw a stick around."

The puppy growled at him. Jordan bent and stroked her head.

<Happy. Happy. Happy, Sistwo, happy.>

Glad someone's happy with me.

"I'm hungry," Kane whined.

"Me too," Mason said.

"And bored," Kane said.

"Really?" Jordan leapt back to her feet. "Fighting for your life makes you bored? That was my home they damaged, you inconsiderate little brat. Mason could've been hurt, hell, I could have been killed fighting those fauns to save your gorram neck."

"No, the fight made me hungry, being here makes me bored," Kane said

Jordan threw up her hands and paced with her back to him. *Damn it, Jedediah, I'm not...enough. I don't know how to keep everyone safe. I can't throw magic around like those fauns.*

"This is a farm, right?" Kane asked. "Aren't there any chickens? Maybe fish in the pond."

Jordan whirled. "Will you stop whining about your stomach? Look at Mason, he's torn up, but he's not constantly going on about himself."

"Why should I care if he'd fed," Kane asked. "He's going to be dead...."

Mason paled.

Jordan grabbed Kane. "Why would you say something like that?"

Kane's color washed away like showering off body paint. His eyes rolled back into his head. He convulsed. "Let me go! No more, please, let me go!"

Jordan let him jerk out of her grasp. He stumbled to the ground, looking up at her with abject horror. "I didn't do anything to you."

Kane crab-walked to the toilet pile at high speed. He snatched a length of leather from one pocket, bit down on it and curled up into a ball with his hat pulled down to hide his face. He didn't even flinch when a tiny Fey plucked hair from behind his head.

"Um," Crystal said. "I'm kind of hungry too. Sorry."

Jordan gave her a soft smile. "I'm the one who's sorry. Crystal. None of this has gone as I meant it to, but I promised, and I'll deliver, just give me a minute...please."

Crystal nodded.

Jordan looked at the three twelve-year-olds. Sanctuary, beds, food, they were all easy. More than a dozen homes hid only a refrigerator away. She had to keep Kane from them if she wanted the properties to remain undamaged. Being tracked by competent sorceresses meant he was only safe on the farm.

Unless they find one of the gaps.

Kane had proven less than wise where it came to creature comforts. Until he figured out the other portals led to other furnished houses, he'd stay safe.

Maybe the fact that none of them has any better electronics than the farm did when I first came will keep him from lingering. She eyed him. *Maybe not. I never thought of Mauve as someone who'd be soft on her apprentices. Mama Yamai sure wasn't.*

Traveling to another of Jedediah's properties satisfied her promise to Crystal. Some of them had vehicles, but only Weems was close enough to take Mason home. There was the parking lot of Jedediah's formerly shrunken vehicles, but she didn't have their keys and had no idea if any of them worked. Mason had come after food too, but mostly healing.

Kane had to be kept on the farm, but Crystal needed some safety that included a real bed and food to fill her. Jordan's gaze shifted from one to the other trying to choose which action would offer the most good.

"Kane." He jerked at the sound of his name. She softened her voice. "Drake said you stayed at Baba Yaga's hut."

Kane stared wide-eyed, mouthing. When he finally found his voice it stuttered. "T-that w-was...she *eats* children."

Jordan rolled her eyes. "How many huts do you know that walk around on chicken legs? Jedediah bought it from her. It's safe. Do you have any idea where it is or was at least?"

She took his glare as a yes.

"Take Mason to where the hut last rested," Jordan said. "There should be healing potions in there somewhere, just don't wander off the property. You can feel a magical barrier, can't you?"

"Yes," he responded in a petulant tone. "Why do I have to take him? There isn't any food there."

"Crystal and I will see to food while you help Mason," Jordan said.

Kane folded his arms. "I'll wait for the food."

Jordan growled. A chorus of throats added their growls to hers. Nip and the little pup bared teeth.

"Nip, go with them to keep them safe." Jordan hardened her expression. "Take him to the hut, Kane, or you're on your own."

"You and that damned lizard are peas in a pod, aren't you? Bossing people around? Acting all greater-than-thou?"

"Mauve sent you with a message, right?" Jordan asked. "You've given it to both Drake and I, right?"

"Yes," Kane said.

"Good job. Message received. Your task here is done. Have a nice life."

"You're kind of a bitch, you know that *right?*" Kane asked.

"No more than you and half as whiny."

Kane stomped off in a well-practiced sulk. "Come on, whoever you are."

"Mason," Mason said. "I'm an aeromancer."

"Yippee for you," Kane said.

The two boys trudged out of the boneyard with Nip on their heels. Despite his surly oh-so-teen-boy attitude and a massive case of the stupids, Jordan kind of liked Kane—or would once he'd grown up.

Problem is he's not grown up. None of us are, and yet I'm stuck with taking care of them. It's not like we're stuck in the wild in some post-apocalypse zombie show, but we are under real attack and I haven't the faintest idea how to keep everyone from getting killed.

She sighed and scanned the boneyard trying to remember which portal led where she wanted to take Crystal.

❧

Kane trudged away from the annoying girl. *Think's she so smart.*

His stomach grumbled. The other boy's answered with equal hunger. He glanced at the other boy out of the corner of his eye. He looked friendly enough, not too tall, too strong, too anything really. Light brown hair hung above simple features, cut recently.

"I'm Kane."

"Mason. My mother thinks I'm demon possessed."

Kane inhaled through his nose. "I don't smell a demon."

Mason laughed. "Magic is evil, and since I'm Saved, it has to be a demon."

"Oh, she's got *religion.*"

"I didn't use to think so, but lately it seems more that than faith," Mason sighed. "She's had a hard life—especially this last year."

Kane reached a familiar field and turned them. "What happened?"

"She fell in love."

"Damn," Kane snorted. "That sucks."

Mason chuckled, but it died suddenly. "My Dad's, well, he's...not around much. He took me out to a Renaissance festival to piss her off. Not sure where he got the idea. I never asked him. He always made snide comments about Mom's love of old world things like that. That's where I met Drake and Jedediah the first time."

Jedediah again. For a guy no one seems to be able to locate, he sure seems at the center of things. "How does falling in love figure in?"

"Mom fell for Jedediah, like instantly. I didn't realize it at first, but when I thought about it. It seemed almost like they'd both been really old friends, you know? Like they'd known each other in school or something."

"Sure."

"So Mom doesn't have any excuses about me not being old enough to go to Renfests, and she has to equal out if not one up

Dad, so we go up to the new Medieval Times while they're doing some kind of winter solstice thing."

"Reenactment, right?"

"Yeah, kind of dorky, but you can watch knights joust and fight, and you can buy swords—well, if you have a Mom that doesn't freak about fighting," Mason said.

Kane smirked. His mother had almost grown a second head when Mauve showed up at their door dressed in—well, a lot less than most gardeners usually wore—and announced he was a necromancer. *As if the butler's zombified cat following me around hadn't been a clue. Should've thought to check for animals too when the fauns attacked. That was stupid.*

"So, you guys went up there and what?" Kane asked.

Mason sighed. "She asked him out, like right there after his magic show with me standing there. It was so embarrassing, worse she almost got a ticket taking me to the salad place—"

"Salad?" Kane asked.

"Yeah," Mason said. "Wall to wall salad."

"Torture."

"Tell me about it, but she almost got a ticket so she could find a CVS and buy makeup. She never wore makeup, not before anyway, not really."

"Grownups," Kane said.

"Yeah."

Mason stared off into space. Kane took the time to check their progress. The mud dog followed along at an easy lope. Kane drew on the frigid knot that nestled between his stomach and lungs, reaching out for something he could summon to protect himself.

"So, Jedediah was the best. Mom was happy. I got to play with Drake—"

"Play? With a dragon?"

Mason laughed. "Mom didn't believe he was a dragon at first, but Drake told me later she can't see all the things I do because she's got no magic. Probably a good thing, too."

"Why?"

"She's convinced its evil."

"Right, *religion*. Let me guess, everything went south when she found out this Jedediah was a wizard."

"Actually, it started going bad when he was accused of being a serial killer."

Kane gestured, and they turned at a boulder beneath a small group of trees. "Is he?"

"He was acquitted." Mason shrugged. "I'm pretty sure he's killed people before, and would again if he had to."

A skeletal animal about the size of Nip trotted up their back trail. Nip growled.

Kane gestured it closer. It stopped near him, shook dirt from its bones and sat with a wagging tail.

"You did that?" Mason asked.

"Yeah."

"Cool," Mason said. "Can you make it look alive, like with glamour or maybe fake skin?"

"Maybe," Kane said. *I've never tried that, might be cool.*

"What are you going to name it?" Mason asked.

Kane shrugged. "It's a servant, it doesn't really need a name any more than our maid does."

"He's your dog, like Nip is Jordan's. He's got to have a name." Mason's mouth twisted to one side. He smiled. "How about McCoy?"

Kane groaned. "He's a Guardian, right?"

"A doctor, on Star Trek."

"No, Jedediah."

"Not that he ever told me. Jordan might know."

Kane's voice gained heat. "I don't like her."

"She's okay. Not as cool as Lanea...."

"Who's—"

"Hey," Mason blurted. "You're a necromancer. You could bring back Lanea. She could help us get to Jedediah, and everything would be great."

"I...uh, could try, but she wouldn't be able to do any magic." Kane adjusted his hat.

"That's okay, Lanea knew stuff. She was old."

They cleared another group of trees to find the hut nestled atop a hill where he'd last seen it. Mason smiled and increased his pace.

"Hold up, there's a barrier here somewhere."

"I don't see anything."

"Are you seeing with magic?" Kane asked.

"I haven't learned that yet."

"What? That's magic 101."

"I got like half an hour's lessons from Drake and few basics from Jordan."

"She didn't teach you Sight?" Kane asked.

"She said her magic and mine are different."

"Can you reach your magic?" Kane asked. "Find it in your core and use it."

Mason beamed and held up one cast. "That's how I got this."

The other boy bombarded Kane with the story of flying off the jump. Despite the broken arm, it sounded pretty good. Kane cupped his hands. "Hey, shack, could you like come over here a minute?"

The hut didn't move, but Kane got a distinct impression that had it owned feathers, it would've ruffled them at him. He invoked the Sight, but couldn't see the barrier that had been there when Drake found him. He eased forward, hands out to find it. He felt it prickle his skin. He gave Mason a little tutorial on magical sight and gestured. "Right here. Do you see it?"

Mason shook his head. "I don't see anything. What does it look like?"

"I don't know." Kane groused. "I can't see it either. I guess we run for it."

Kane judged the distance, glanced side to side and sprinted. He pumped his arms and legs for all he had. Breath and pulse thundered in his ears as he raced across the intervening distance and slammed into the barrier.

Mason caught up to him, equally out of breath. "What was that?"

"The barrier," Kane clutched his face. "Damn useless dragon."

"You can't get in?" Mason asked.

"Apparently not," Kane said.

"So sad," Kiki said.

Mason's head shot up. His color fled. "Kane, when you said something about me being dead, did you mean like right now?"

"No." Kane stood up, summoning the skeletal animal and reaching into the ground for more. "Leave me alone."

"No can do," Kiki said.

"Where are the others?" Mason asked.

"Around. Mimi's a good tracker. She smelled you here with the dragonling, but since invisibility is one of my strengths I got to be the one waiting for you," She beamed. "Lucky, lucky me."

Kane reached into the bones near the surface of the ground, forcing the old fragments to come together just under the turf.

"What, you're not happy to see me? Both of you were gawking pretty hard before." Kiki hurled a ball of writhing sparks.

Kane yanked, pulling the shield of earth and bone into place.

Mason tackled Kane, yelping with pain as they both hit the ground.

"What did you do that for?" Kane asked. "You ruined my spell."

"You were just standing there."

Kane growled. "Fine, throw a lightning blast at her already."

"I can't do that."

"They didn't teach you?" Kane asked.

"That and Mom says it's never right to hit a girl."

"She's trying to kill us, besides she's a faun."

Kiki threw another spell. Mason and Kane leapt separate direction, Kane's leap ricocheting off the barrier spell. McCoy slammed into Kiki, biting and tearing at her like a pit bull.

Mason pointed at Kiki's breasts. "Pretty sure those make her a girl."

"Are you inside the barrier?" Kane asked.

"How the hell should I know?"

Kane hurried over to him. He found the barrier with his hands, grimaced and extended one. "Pull me in."

"What?"

"Just pull me in. Hurry."

Mason grabbed him and pulled. Cold welled up out of his core, setting his skin aflame with vampiric gooseflesh. Images washed over Kane's eyes, growing stronger and stronger as they had when Jordan had seized him and not let him go. His eyes fogged over as Mason's deaths flashed through his mind, dire omens tumbled unheard from his lips.

Mason let him go. He stared in horror not at the bloody faun pounding the barrier in shrieking rage with a dog skull shaking itself on one thigh but at Kane.

"You said it again. You said I was going to die." Mason reached out for him. "How do you—"

"Don't touch me." Kane shrieked.

Mason stopped short.

Kane looked through the barrier as Kiki shattered the skull to release its locked jaws. She glowered at him and hurled a huge blast of lightning stronger than anything she'd sent at him before—even more powerful than when she and her sisters had attacked Mauve.

"Come on," Kane said. "Let get into the damned shack."

He had to fight the door but won out against its stubbornness with more of his own. He climbed into the cavern filled with alchemical ingredients and paraphernalia. He shivered, wrapping his arms around himself and checked once more to see the exit still there.

"You said I'm going to die," Mason said.

"We're all going to die." Kane opened up a small refrigerator and cursed. None of the little sports bottles on the shelf labeled potions had anything to describe their variously colored contents.

"No, you said it like you knew when it was going to happen."

Kane didn't answer. *If I stay silent long enough maybe I won't have to.*

Mason grabbed his shoulder and whirled him around. The cold reached up in a flash, suffusing him faster along the recently energized pathways. He shoved Mason away. "Don't touch me. I hate being touched."

Mason careened into an alchemy table, knocking half the tubes and beakers to the floor. "Why?"

He wants to know? Fine. "Because I see deaths, okay? Every time something touches me I see their death. It's horrible. Death, death, death, I can't hug or be comforted or anything without seeing the person die, all right? The longer it is, the clearer it grows until I feel them dying, as if I'm dying too."

"I'm sorry."

Kane waved him away.

Mason approached, but Kane backed off. The other boy reached into the fridge and pulled out a red bottle. He pulled off the foil seal and drank it with a grimace. "Raspberry with an aftertaste of burnt gym sock."

Reddish magic spread out across Mason's body. He drank a second, intensifying the glow. They stared at one another in silence for several minutes. "When?"

"I don't know," Kane said. "It's not always the same. Sometimes I see dozens of deaths, all dependent on what you do. It's not like the future is a stationary target. How come you can get in the barrier when I can't?"

Mason pulled a thin rod from his arm cast and went to work scratching his broken limbs like mad. "Mom and I used to visit all the time. Jedediah must've done something so Mom didn't kill me driving through it. Lanea said it didn't hold back mortals when I first asked her about the barrier, but no one told me I had magic until later."

"You want me to help you take the casts off?" Kane asked.

"Nah, I'll milk it like you said. Once it stops itching it'll be much better, besides if I show up healed Mom may stone me."

ROUGHING IT

Jordan set a platter of cinnamon rolls down on the table, drawing Crystal away from a bowl of oatmeal with double helpings of raisins and brown sugar. She'd called a number on the corkboard pointed out to her when she'd first bumped into the caretakers of the Cheraw farmhouse in South Carolina. They'd gone to town for fresh groceries. She'd made do with the pantry and the deep freeze of staple meats, a thing of frozen cinnamon rolls and a tube of cookie dough.

"I'll be back in a couple minutes. You remember how to come back?"

Crystal smiled around cheeks stuffed with hot cinnamon goodness.

She stepped back onto the farm while Crystal ate, checking for the boys. She'd considered bringing the oatmeal, but she didn't want any of the mudpuppies or varied Fey getting into it.

She set up the piled camping gear inside the u-shaped alcove made by the greenhouses. There was only one tent, but she could buy more if need be. She looked at the spot she intended for the firepit and reached for her magic. The rumble rose with little effort, but the ground didn't turn itself over.

Come on, this is the first magic I ever did, not feet from where I am right now.

The mudpuppy pup cocked her head, ear shifting forward. She waddled over to the spot and started to dig.

"No, little one—you need a name. I'll have to think about that, but for now, please don't help. I need to do this myself."

Jordan focused on the spot. She'd gotten better under Mama Yamai's tutelage—particularly after she believed in her own magic —but something blocked magic use outside herself.

I can do this. I know I can do this.

Nothing happened. Heat bubbled in her gut. Her magic rumbled harder. The earth sat under her glare, unmoving and unturned.

Barefoot, check. Connected, check. Visualizing, check. Calm, check, well mostly.

She pushed at the ground with all her will. *This is ridiculous! I'm alone and being attacked and I can't even move a little dirt? Frak, frell, gorramit Jedediah. I need a teacher. I can't get to you or Mama Yamai. I've been trying. Where the hell are you?*

Jordan grabbed a shovel from the collapsed tool shed and dug a fire pit in the ground. It resisted the spade, but she summoned strength enough to cut through the turf. *At least that's one thing I can manage.*

She returned to find Crystal knotting and unknotting her hair on the bed next to the Cheraw portal. She reversed her direction into the bathroom doorway she'd just stepped from but not exited and ran the water. She wiped sweat and dirt from her skin with a damp washcloth. She paused to give Crystal a smile. "Is there something you want to talk about? Magic maybe?"

Crystal shook her head. "There's someone at the door."

Jordan straightened. "The other side of the portal?"

"Front door. He has groceries. I made him wait on the porch."

"If he brought the groceries why'd you make him hold on?"

"I don't know him."

Fair enough. Jordan hung the washcloth and trotted down the stairs. *Why didn't Dave let himself in? He has keys.*

She reached for the door but looked out the window instead.

The barefoot man outside wasn't Dave. Jordan looked him up and down, enjoying muscles exposed by his denim cutoffs and absent shirt. He smiled, juggled the grocery bags and pushed a brown lock away from his forehead.

Jordan stepped over to the door, summoning her staff but setting it in the umbrella pot at the door's right. She opened it. "Can we help you?"

"Groceries, M-mistress? Dave said I could deliver them."

"Mistress?"

He dropped his eyes. "I'm frightfully sorry, Dave said I should call you Mistress. I didn't mean to anger old man Shine or his witch."

Jordan planted hands on her hips. "His what?"

"I'm doing this all wrong. My name's Jed, what should I call you?"

"Jordan. Are you related to Jedediah?"

His face paled further. "No, Mistress er Jordan, nothing like that. I got the name from my father. Old man Shine ain't my daddy. I'm sure. I've met both."

Jordan almost laughed. She searched his face, finding no resemblance at all. *Probably just a weird coincidence.*

"You can ask him if you don't believe me."

Her stomach tightened. "He's not here."

"Miss Jordan, can I put these in the kitchen. Some of it's melting." He turned the paper bags to show soaked areas threatening to release their tide of groceries to the floor.

She led him into the kitchen.

He set the bags down, but before he could unload, Crystal started transferring food into the fridge, beaming at many of the items.

"Okay, food's taken care of. Why did you call me a witch?"

His hands twisted through a peasant ward pointed at both Crystal and herself as he backed away. "I meant no wrong. I figured, you know magic, and you being the old man's wife, and your daughter there."

"Crystal's not my daughter. That's not even possible."

Crystal laughed.

Jed frowned. "How old are you?"

"Aren't you southerners supposed to know better? You're not supposed to ask girls that kind of question."

He stammered another apology. "S-sorry, you're right. Ma says women get prickly about that when they get old, not to say you're old Mistress. I just wondered, and it wandered out my mouth before I could stop it. I mean old man Shine is like two hundred. I didn't think he, well, you know."

"I'm younger than you are," Jordan said.

"Oh." He brightened a moment before it died. "You can do the magic, though, right?"

"Yes, why?"

"I talked Dave into letting me bring the groceries on account of hearing y'all were in residence and all. Hoped the old man might do me a service like he did my Dad, but you said he wasn't here." Jed fidgeted. "If you do magic too, then maybe I could ask you. I'm pretty desperate you see, assuming you're not in a mood to turn a man into something not natural."

Jesus, where exactly is this town, the middle ages?

Jordan glared at him.

The big country boy fumbled through another apology, looking so like a beaten dog she felt sorry for him. She thought for a moment, fiddling with her fingers before taking a deep breath. "I'm just an apprentice, but you can ask."

"Great, um, you might not have a...," He gave her a bashful smile, complete with a blush. "You wouldn't have one of old man Shine's love stones you could give me? Please?"

"Love stone?" she asked.

"See, there's this girl I like." Jed smiled. "My Dad came up for a stone when he wanted to court my Ma. She's smart, and Dad and I were out at the football game the day they handed out brains, so he got a stone to bewitch her heart."

Flush rushed over her face, heat collecting at her fingertips and ears. She curled her hands into fists.

Jed stepped back.

"I'll kill him," Jordan said.

⁂

Jordan sat opposite Crystal, stirring the pot of oatmeal on the low campfire to keep it from burning on the bottom. She'd told Jed she didn't have any stones, then hired him to pick up an order at the closest Walmart.

"You're sure you'd rather camp out than have a real bed?"

"I want to stay near you," Crystal said. "I've never been camping."

Jordan focused on the popping fire, occasionally glancing at the setting sun. She heard Kane and Mason before Nip trotted around the corner. The boys followed, Mason floating a few rocks through glowing orbits.

"Yeah, that's it. Now you're getting it," Kane said.

"Hey, Jordan. Look what Kane taught me." Mason beamed. "It's a lot easier to move stuff when I can see the magic."

"Why didn't you teach him that?" Kane snatched the lid off the pot, dropping it to the dirt and shaking his hand. "Oatmeal? We trudged all the way out to that hut, and you made oatmeal?"

"Shut up, Kane," Crystal said. "This is a good meal compared to most I get. Count your stupid blessings."

Kane stared at her. "Um, okay."

Mason chuckled.

Jordan blinked. "Okay...what took you so long?"

Mason shrugged. "We got attacked."

Tension knotted her shoulders. "What happened? Are you both all right? Were they on the property?"

"They can't get through the barrier," Kane said. "Hell, *I* can't get through the damned barrier."

Mason and Kane took turns gorging themselves on oatmeal and telling the story. Crystal leaned forward as they described their heroics. Jordan's mind spun. The fauns weren't going away. They'd tracked Kane back to the farm and could probably follow him to any of Jedediah's properties.

And only this one is protected. I can't let him in any of the others.

She rose and excused herself into the boneyard. She crossed over to the Cheraw house, called up a local pizza place that delivered and looked out the window. Jed had left the purchased camping gear on the porch as instructed, so she relocated all of the equipment load by load back to the farmhouse's back porch while she thought. Drake had gone off in hopes of finding a way to Jedediah. She had no idea when he'd be back. She was on her own.

A sardonic chuckle bubbled from her lips. "Got to watch those wishes."

She thought over the fight at Weems once more. Most of what had happened was luck, surprise and throwing around her petrified staff. She didn't really know how to fight with it...beyond what she knew about quarterstaff combat from Robin Hood movies and a few Daffy Duck cartoons. She'd done a few things she hadn't understood, but it wasn't the first time she'd done something weird in a panic.

"Not that I wouldn't like to know *how* I managed them."

She continued moving the new gear until the delivery guy rang the bell. She thanked him for being so quick and tipped him the order's amount—it was Jedediah's money after all.

A thought stopped her at the boneyard's edge. *What if I couldn't turn the firepit because I kind of burned out my connection?*

She summoned strength, making the pizzas easier to carry. She needn't have bothered. Mason and Kane, led by their respective noses, appeared out of nowhere to take the boxes from her hands.

Kane paused a moment, wrinkling his nose in disgust. "No Cokes?"

Jordan folded her arms. "With the gear on the back porch, feel free to fetch it all."

"Nah, I'm good. All I need are the Cokes."

"You drink anything out of that pile before the gear's moved, you better be able to cure ingested poisons," Jordan said.

"You're bluffing."

She smiled.

Mason finished the last marshmallow in the bag. He'd won it from Kane with a swirl of wind, but Kane's retaliation left the gooey sweetness more blackened than Mason liked them.

He smacked his grinning lips. "So good."

Jordan smirked at him.

He glanced at the stars. The sky on Jedediah's farm was always so cool, like floating in outer space. He grimaced. *Mom's gonna kill me.*

"You all right, Mason?" Jordan asked.

"Feeling sick from too many marshmallows?" Kane asked.

Mason chuckled and rubbed his stomach. "Mmmm. Actually, I need a ride home."

"You're not staying?" Crystal asked.

"Can't. I was sent to my room."

"You disobeyed?" Crystal asked.

"Not exactly, she locked me out, so I went to my room at Weems, but she has no idea where I am."

Jordan sighed. "Yeah, you're screwed. I don't even know if any of those cars still work."

"I need to use the restroom." Mason walked out of the firelight. Once out of their sight he headed to the cars Jordan had pulled out of the farmhouse. Trucks, muscle cars and a few weirder items like a cart-drawn chair sat side by side like a strange parking lot. He checked an old truck like the one Jedediah wrecked. It wasn't locked, but the keys weren't in the ignition. He checked the next car and the next. None were locked. None had keys hanging ready. Mason turned his hands over.

Did Jedediah use keys? Older cars were simpler, could he have just used magic to hotwire them?

He wished for his phone. Surely Google could find directions for hotwiring an old truck. The little pup Jordan'd named Beryl nudged his calf, startling Mason into a leap. She whined at him, wagging her tail.

"Sorry, girl." He bent to pet her.

Her tail wagged so hard it took her butt with it side to side. She ducked her head from his petting and chewed on his fingers.

<Play? Play? Play?>

"Sorry, I need to go home."

<Home?> Beryl darted toward the greenhouse, stopping with her wagging tail high in the air daring him to chase her.

"My home, where my mom is." Mason went back to the first truck, sitting in the driver's seat with the door open. Beryl stood up on her hind legs in the doorway and whined. He picked her up, deposited her on the seat next to him and examined the controls. She hopped to the floorboards sniffing around.

Jedediah had given Mason some basic driving lessons—until his mom objected. He pushed in the clutch and put the car into gear. He shifted his foot from the brake to the gas and focused on what he knew about magic.

Magic did stuff. It sounded like it helped to know how something functioned when you used magic to do it, like how a deadbolt worked for unlocking it. He didn't have any idea how a car ignition worked beyond push in the clutch, turn the key and give it gas. Some stuff, like throwing lightning or moving objects seemed more about telling the magic to make it happen and letting the power figure out the best way.

Mason rubbed his hands together like paddles for shocking people to life, reaching for the magic. He felt it under his skin, tingling his fingertips. He grabbed both sides of the steering column. *Start.*

It tried but didn't turn over.

He rubbed his hands again and tried to push more power into the truck.

The truck roared to life. He got so excited he forgot to keep his foot on the clutch. The vehicle jerked forward and stalled.

Mason cursed.

Jordan appeared at the open door. "It works? You found a key?"

Mason grinned, eased his foot off the gas a bit and shoved the clutch all the way down. "Nope. I hotwired it."

"How?"

He threw another charge into the column. The truck started, rumbling unevenly as his foot shifted a bit.

"Put it in neutral and move over, squirt,'" Jordan said.

"I can drive," Mason objected.

Jordan laughed and shoved him over. Mason hurriedly shifted to neutral and bent his legs around the long shifter in the center of the floorboards. Beryl leapt onto his lap and put paws on the dashboard. Jordan took his seat in a hurry, getting the brake down to stop a slow roll.

"I'm taking Mason home then stopping by the store. Anything you want?" Jordan asked the other two drawn by the noise.

"A game system, big TV, drink fountain—"

Crystal shoved Kane. "Shut up. It's your fault those are all gone."

"How about a real bed?" Kane asked.

"Crystal?" Jordan asked.

She shrugged, shaking her head.

"Okay, be back soon."

Mason pet Beryl while they drove. When she crawled onto Jordan's lap to get at the window, he rolled his own down a little so she could stick her nose into the wind but couldn't jump out.

He thought while they drove in silence. "If that fridge leads to Weems, don't the others do too?"

Jordan didn't answer at first. "Yes."

"So why not have everyone sleep there?"

"Kane."

"Because the fauns want to kill him?"

"And outside the barrier, they can track him," Jordan said.

Mason considered it. "Why can't the rest of you sleep there then?"

"They don't lead to Weems, but if we went to one of the houses I have no doubt Kane would sneak in behind us—leading the fauns straight to us."

"You think they could find you that fast?"

"I'd rather not risk it." Jordan turned off onto Moon Road.

They turned right onto Weems toward Heath Lake Park and

home. Mason's stomach tightened. His mom was going to be so mad he might need to hide out with Kane and the others.

"Hey, what if you put beds in the shack thing? In that cavern? Maybe even a TV or something."

Jordan chuckled "The beds are a good idea, but there's no electricity."

"How does the fridge get it then?" Mason asked.

"No idea, one more thing to ask Jedediah when we get him back." She turned off the lights and pulled into the driveway. All the lights burned inside the house.

Mason scowled at his home.

"Do you want me to stick around?" Jordan asked.

"Nah, it'd probably only mean more trouble." He got out of the truck.

She gave him a bright smile. "All right, tough guy. See you at school."

Mason squared his shoulders and trudged up the drive.

Jordan swung by the Weems house on her way to Walmart. There'd been a few things she wanted out of her room, only her room wasn't there anymore. She pulled to a stop. She stared at the ruin as completely destroyed as the farmhouse.

She got out of the truck, forcing down her own temper. Beryl followed to the edge of the seat and whined to be lifted down.

"No, stay here, girl."

The fauns had destroyed her home. The boneyard offered her other houses, but Weems had been her second home. She'd spent hours on its couches with Lanea, sharing movies and throwing popcorn at one another. It was gone.

What am I going to do now?

Her gaze shifted to the short driveway. The Charger she'd been driving wasn't there anymore. She'd been so intent on the music coming from the house that she hadn't glanced at the driveway earlier. She didn't know if the Sheriff had taken it or the fauns or neighborhood thugs out for a joy ride.

She had only the Bridgeport clothes on her back, a debit card which might stop working at any point and three, no two twelve-year-olds to watch. The time to run away was long up her back path. Even as desperate as things were, she belonged on the farm even if it was crushed, even if it was empty.

A tear escaped Jordan.

She didn't want to be alone. She didn't want to be responsible. There were good things on her horizon, like the Olympics. *Why do I have to be stuck in the middle of some war? It isn't even mine? Is it?*

Beryl nudged her boot. She picked up the puppy, stroking its muddy fur.

The centaurs had almost killed her. They'd killed Nibble who'd protected her and ran with her and loved her. He'd helped her try to free Jedediah. He'd helped her survive Sinesh Ena'Doniche's first attack on her and maybe the second, she couldn't remember.

No, I'm confusing that one with the one...with where Velith'Seravin... where I got Nibble killed.

The *Namhaid* killed Lanea. They'd killed Joe Franklin and his girlfriend. They'd almost killed Drake before she'd gotten to know him like Lanea had. Their sniper shot her in the head. In a way, they'd even taken Jedediah.

None of it had been her fault—except Nibble's death. It hadn't been her war. They'd declared war on the only people in existence that gave a damn about her.

Jordan looked at her ruined home. *It's my war now. I've just got to figure out how to fight it.*

She marched forward intent to dig into the ruin for the screw that made portaling to the farm possible, but she stopped. It'd be easier to find in daylight. Right now, they needed beds and Mason's suggestion had been a good one. Jordan turned back to the truck. It gave a hiccupping rumble and died.

"Frell me." She bit her lip to keep it from quivering and wiped her face. *Not a problem. I know it runs. There's a slope. I can jump start it.*

Jordan set Beryl into the passenger seat, released the brake and pushed with one hand on the door frame and the other on the wheel. As soon as she got it up to speed, she hopped in, shifted to second and popped the clutch. It jerked back and forward, shaking her like a bulldog's toy. Beryl careened into the dash and huddled in the floorboards with a disgruntled bark. Its engine rumbled, but it didn't start. She tried again with similar results. The third try brought the engine to life. She slammed the door shut and shifted down to first.

It died.

Oh, God, gas. She checked, finding the tank more than half full.

She got out of the truck and pushed it through a stop sign and around the corner to avoid a dead end. The hill in front of her was steep, but if she didn't get the truck started, there was little chance she'd be able to push it back up the opposite hill. She tried anyway.

Jedediah's heavy old truck rolled over the hill's crest. She quickened her steps to keep up. Gravity took hold. She tried to keep up. Her foot caught. She hung suspended from the door frame a moment before finding her feet. A little magic sped her steps and launched her into the cab. She shifted to second and popped the clutch. It roared to life.

Yes!

It coughed and spluttered.

No! She floored the gas pedal, pumping it madly. *No, no, please don't stop, please.*

The truck died. The scent of gasoline filled the cab.

"Gorram fraking hell!" She slammed a fist into the roof, denting the old metal. A set of keys dropped from the visor, bouncing off her lap into the floorboards. She grimaced and slammed her fist into the roof cursing her way through several more dents.

Beryl cowered next to the keys.

DEBTS PAID

A gloved hand wrestled the pixie doll from Jedediah's hands. It tossed it across the room into the far corner and shifted to cradle the ragged wizard's shoulder.

"Your children are under attack."

A rasped whisper escaped his dry throat. "Protected."

"No, Two-Hawks. Weems is destroyed. The barrier fails."

"They'll manage." Jedediah licked painfully cracked lips. "Go away."

"No. If you do not rise, Stormfall will kill them all."

Jedediah looked up into an empty room. He harrumphed and crawled toward the fairy doll.

NECESSITY & LEATHER

rake awoke to pain, leaves and nostrils filled with the scent of burnt skin. Flashes of the storm, lightning shrieking through him and desperate last minute efforts to soften his landing crossed his memory. He turned his gaze on a stiff neck, the pull firing up its ache to something loud enough to barely hear over his body's other complaints. Shattered wings bent shredded membranes over the surrounding branches. One foreleg felt nothing at all, but the bend it made to fold into the large tree joint foretold a broken limb.

I'm not dead. That's a start.

He shifted his weight, intent to gather his whole limbs beneath him. His deciduous savior teetered. Drake's maw shot downward. Half his perch's roots stuck out of ripped ground in gnarled, broken knots. The other half struggled to keep it rooted to soil.

My impact must have partially—

The tree lost its fight and fell. It slammed the rest of the way to the ground with a bone-jarring crash.

Ow.

Drake dragged himself from the branches, talons tearing up loosened ground. Wings refusing his every command scraped along bark and splintered wood, shrieks of pain amplified a hundred fold. His forelimb woke, aflame with agony. He flopped down only half way extricated but unable to bear any more pain. He tried to push it aside, tried to block it out.

Something dug into his chest. He tilted enough to drag it out, finding an ivory curve of bone. His tongue probed the recesses of his mouth, assuring him that he'd not lost any teeth. It wasn't dark enough to be a talon.

I lost one of my horns. Teeth would've been better. They regrow faster —though it hurts.

Drake reached for dew and lingering rain in the damp ground. He begged and cajoled it up over his scales and membranes. He sunk into his air magic, using it to press the water tight against him.

Heal.

Pains eased, but by the barest margin. Bones shifted, invoking more pain. He struggled to move one wing. The agony all but knocked him cold.

No way I'm flying home. I should've practiced aquamancy more.

He slid the water off of his body, gathering only a fraction of the initial. He spread it—suspended in air—into a rippling upright mirror.

Drake sank into his power, spreading tingling magic to every corner of his body. It coursed up and down his limbs, from talon to talon, beak to tail, wingtip to wingtip. Heavily damaged areas stung like a sleeping limb struck against something. He held the magic there, drawing more from the source. Despite all the practice intended to help him hunt down Lanea's killer, he'd never tried the whole shift at once.

Drake focused on the picture he'd built in its mind, rotating it like Mason did a new character generated on one of his computer games. *Get this right, and I can play too.*

He focused on the image, making little corrections that he'd learned from copious mistakes to make the new shape better. He screwed his face up against imminent pain, squeezed the core of power into a tight ball and let go. The compressed energy exploded outward over the energized cells of his body.

His reflection rippled as if in a heat haze, only his illuminated brown-flecked golden eyes in focus. His frills shortened, multiplied and darkened. His eyes shrunk and shifted together on opposite sides of a beak that seemed to flow backward into his rounding head. His neck thinned. His scales softened, lightened and grew a thin coat of fine hairs.

Talons shifted shape into large, long-fingered hands and five-toed feet. His tail shrunk into his body mass as the rest of his frame stretched and reshaped until he stood erect—a well-muscled adolescent with broken dragon wings and short-spiked, dark hair.

Much the way he always felt that his feet or hands were shoved into shoes or gloves several sizes too small, his face now felt similar as if he were stuffed up or congested. He could still smell almost as well as normal, but it was really uncomfortable.

He smiled, managing more of a grimace and exposing short, sharp teeth

Drake cursed.

He focused on his teeth and corrected their shape, being sure that they were white, straight and close together like he'd seen. They joined the too-tight feeling plaguing his body. He turned his focus to his eyes. He closed them for a moment and then opened them to reveal dark brown flecked with gold rather than the other way around. He nodded to himself.

A husky voice escaped his new throat. "It'll do."

He focused on his wings. After an eternity of daggers, they solidified into a long trench coat to otherwise hide his body until he obtained clothing. He stood still, easing the magic back into his core. The slippery feeling that'd washed over him with the first motes of change magic faded, leaving him feeling settled and centered.

Drake sighted the sun and resumed his southeast trek, this time on scale-tough bare feet. His stomach growled, and pain lingered beneath his new skin. Occasional stabs jolted up and down his left arm, but the limb no longer felt broken.

I changed its shape, did doing so form it whole rather than busted?

He walked for hours, coming at long last to state highway. He followed it more or less the same direction. A roadside bar presented itself just as Drake's hunger reached the point where tree bark edged onto the menu. He quickened his pace, slipping inside past a line of motorcycles.

Smoke and darkness fouled his eyes for three blinks. He scanned a rough looking clientele, found a bar and headed over.

"Please tell me you serve food," Drake said.

"You best walk right back out that door, boy, and find yourself a McDonalds."

Drake turned from the bar to a large enough man to look down on Jedediah. The thought brought a snarl to Drake's lips. "I wasn't talking to you."

The biker shoved a finger into Drake's chest. "Well, I was talking to *you*. This here's our place, and Road Dragons don't share with sniveling millennials too entitled for their own good."

Drake smirked. "Road Dragons?"

Both of the man's huge hands slammed Drake back into the bar. Pain lanced up his altered wings and dug into his spine where it'd struck. Drake met the man's gaze and shoved his mind into the normal's skull.

Kneel.

The biker shook his head like a dog trying to clear his ears.

Kneel. Now!

The biker knelt. His fellows rose to their feet with a scraping of chairs and the sounds of various weapons coming free.

Tell the man behind me to make me food.

"Yo, Lees, make the kid some food."

"Damien?"

"Do it," Damien said.

"What the hell's going on?" another biker asked.

Tell them to look and see, I am not touching you. Tell them everything is fine.

"Look, everything's cool. He's not touching me, see?" Damian said.

"What're you doing on your knees?"

"Just felt like it, Nat, everyone back off."

The bikers looked at one another, a few stepping back toward their chairs while others froze where they stood. Drake considered. He'd caused himself quite a problem with his choice of commands.

Get up. Pretend the kneeling was a joke with an old friend's son.

Damien rose. He slapped Drake painfully on the shoulder and laughed. "Good to see you...kid. How's your dad? Last time I saw you, we'd have been eye to eye with me on my knees."

I need clothes. Make it happen.

"Hey, anyone got something more appropriate for the son of a Road Dragon? Let's get..."

Drake.

"Let's get Drake here dressed right," Damian said.

The bikers relaxed. Several fetched clothes from outside. Drake dressed in the bathroom—using alteration magic to get a t-shirt on over his wings. He used the faucet to bath in healing water once more, donned the clothes and changed his wings into a leather coat. After the second excruciating shift, his wings hurt a bit less. He checked the biker logo on the back, remembering to reverse the design, then went over the rest of his shape. He could've used the spare jacket they'd given him, drawing in his wings as he had his tail, but he preferred the armored version his enhanced wings afforded him.

Plus once my wings are whole I can fly in an emergency.

Few of his kind practiced the shaping magic, using it more and more only as camouflage as they grew larger and larger.

He changed his face, hair color, and complexion a few times, trying out different looks. The first one was definitely his favorite, but Jedediah always said options and imagination are the hallmarks of good wizardry. He reset his face to the original teenage bad boy look he'd chosen.

The newer shape felt strange, confining, but never again would he be forced to sit on the sideline like a good dog while the people he cared about were in danger. He could walk in the world of normals, go where they went, do what they did. Whether by talon and teeth or magic and fingers, he could defend his family on any battlefield.

Kill Lanea's murderers and disappear in a crowd. The hunt is on.

Drake ran a hand through his spiked locks and showed off a devilish grin. He walked out of the bathroom to a line of armed, angry bikers.

"I told them you controlled me," Damien said. "I'm ready for you this time, we all are. You won't get away with it again."

Drake lowered his hands to his sides, drawing in power. "I don't want to hurt y'all. I just want some food."

"He doesn't want to hurt us," Nat said.

Drake inhaled. The scent of roast beef and brown gravy wafted from the bar. "Sit back down. Enjoy your drinks. Live another day."

<*Or he'll devour you like the worthless kine you are.*>

Drake stiffened.

Damien gestured with a tire iron. "You made me kneel."

Heat and ice fought a tug of war in Drake's gut. "I apologize. Hunger makes me grumpy, and you were being an ass. It's been a long day."

"Get him," Damien charged forward.

I won't be like her. I won't kill them. Drake stretched out his mind and threw the entire weight of his personality into the room. *Sleep.*

They all kept coming.

Drake slapped his arms together. A massive wind threw the bikers, the chairs and tables against the far wall. He slid the wind into his limbs and moved with zephyr's speed. He leapt into their midst, sliding around blows and striking his own. Pain dulled by healing and time raised its voice. A blow caught him. He yelped. Someone laughed. Fire gurgled in the neck of his flame lung.

He dodged again and again, the free-for-all ranging all over the cleared floor. A tire iron rebroke his arm. The answering blow raked sharp talons across the man's leathers. The shock of the shredded skin beneath and the sudden tang of hunger summoned by beading blood cost Drake a bat to his wing.

He ducked from the fight, wrapping himself in glamour.

"Where the hell'd he go?" Damian snarled.

Drake threw glamour over Nat like a web.

Damian saw Drake and struck. Nat went down. The other

bikers pursued. He fought back. Drake hit them with another toppling gust and moved the illusion of himself to another biker.

Roast beef drew him to the bar. He shifted the illusion every few moments, keeping the brawl chaotic. He extended his invisibility around the food ever so glad of the times Jedediah forced him to use layered or multiple glamours. He sat cross-legged on the pool table, eating the incredibly delicious feast while the Road Dragons beat each other into submission.

He finished half the plate before they stopped fighting altogether.

Drake set the plate aside with a soft belch. A chair slammed into a biker's back. A stool hit the next. Wind swirled. Furniture flew. His illusion lay over bloodied faces, but no one struck it.

So be it.

He lurched off the pool table, letting the wind die. He waded into their dwindled number. He glamoured them all to look like him, punched Damien's face and dropped his invisibility. He reduced their number to half before they bothered throwing another punch.

Speed. Deception. Confusion. Drake rifled pockets, collecting money from the fallen bikers. He slapped it on the bar. "More of the same, and Cherry Coke if you've got it."

"P-Pepsi all right?" Lees asked.

Drake sighed. "Fine."

He took a bottle, picked up a table, added a chair and fetched his remaining food. He sat positioned to watch both bikers and entrances while he ate.

Drake chose the motorcycle to his liking and crashed it almost at once scratching the fire breathing dragon painted across its body. The old 2007 model Suzuki Boulevard M109R started again. He drove it more slowly onto the highway. He hit the brake too hard. The bike toppled.

Drake growled. *This shouldn't be that hard.*

He crashed three more times in various ways before storming back into the bar and up to Lees trying to revive Damian. "Tell me how to ride a motorcycle."

"What?" Lees said.

"Tell me how to ride a motorcycle without crashing and falling over."

"Um."

"Motorcycle for dummies?" Drake asked. "Just the basics."

Lees fidgeted. "I-I guess."

Lees's instructions were haphazard and a bit confusing. Drake took the directions on the road, crashed again and summoned bracing winds to keep him upright. *Screw it. I'll figure it out on the way.*

❧

Zero stepped from a portal in the brickworks basement into a ruined castle—at least ruined from the outside. He descended from the parapet tower down winding stone steps and restored tapestries depicting clan tartans. He continued past several floors deep into the underground. An old oak door bound in pitted iron blocked his way. He waved a hand, a thick bar sliding out of the way on the opposite side. The reek of unwashed guests hit him. He shifted a bit of air magic to protect his nose, folded hands behind his back and strolled down the path between the cells. At the very end, another door swung from his way. A rank old satyr hung in chains against the round wall.

Grey horns curled twice upon themselves in slate curls. A bare sunken chest showed off the creature's ribs, its arms and furred legs thin enough to see their individual bones.

"Good afternoon, Meikra."

"I'll." A coughing fit consumed the satyr. "I'll have to take your word for it, wizard."

"It seems you have some strength left in you, so much the better. I shall need you a while longer."

"Maybe you should feed me then."

"Perhaps, just a little. For now, though, I need only your company."

Zero set a hand on the brittle, grey chest hair caked in vomit. He sent magic down his arm into the creature, drawing not life energy but the essence of the satyr. Limbs stiffened. Muscles knotted. The skin on Zero's face sloughed as if rotted from his skull, as a thousand spiders swarmed his flesh, pushing and pulling the muddy flesh into the satyr's shape.

❧

Velith'Seravin watched the bent old satyr make his way across the surrounding scrub. He leaned against a staff nearly as gnarled as the old horns curling atop his head. He glanced at SinDon then the fauns on his opposite side.

Everyone's tense. SinDon doesn't like the thought of double-crossing the old satyr, but what's making my sorceresses uncomfortable?

Zero stopped a respectful distance away, bowing with both hands on the staff to keep him upright. "Prelate Velith'Seravin, leader of the Wizard's Bane."

"Master Remi," VelSera inclined his head. "Your help has been invaluable to our cause."

Zero smiled, a wicked, angry expression that caught VelSera's breath. "The wizards have done irreparable harm to us. I am glad to help see them dead and the wasteful, polluting normals they protect put in their proper place."

"The dwarves you sent our way provided valuable service in securing our guests," Velith'Seravin stepped toward the old satyr, closing to within reach of the blades hidden beneath his Robes of State.

The fauns stiffened.

Zero narrowed his eyes, wrinkles redoubling. "I'm here for the necromancer, as agreed."

"We've given you many wizards in tribute."

"Do the Wizard's Bane hide behind false faces like the Wizards I've helped you hunt? My contribution to you and yours." Zero gestured at the fauns. The dragon tooth talismans strapped to their arms glowed. "So we agreed in exchange for the necromancer Mauve."

237

"She's too valuable to me, right now," Velith'Seravin said. "Once Jedediah is dead you can have her."

"No good," Zero said. "I take her now, or I take what I've given."

"Master, no," Kiki cradled the talisman.

"You're threatening me?" VelSera asked.

The worrisome smile returned. "I keep my bargains, centaur. I've given you help to penetrate wards. I've given you maps that led you to fostered dragonlings. I've not told the mothers what you do with their hatchlings. If you are to break your word, why should I keep mine?"

VelSera darkened. "Turning against us would risk grievous consequences."

Zero's imitation of Meikra's voice dropped. "Think you betraying me comes with none? How many curses can your flesh bear? Give me the necromancer, and you ensure my assistance in your long campaign, *Leader.*"

Heat fueled Velith'Seravin's voice. "You cannot have her."

"Lord VelSera, please reconsider," Mimi said.

"You've betrayed me, Velith'Seravin," Zero said.

"You won't live to tell another," VelSera said.

Zero smiled. "So be it."

The talismans jerked free of the fauns. They flew across the intervening distance, taking up orbit around the satyr. Velith'Seravin signaled his archers. The air talisman spun up wind, catching the arrows and throwing them skyward toward the centaur who'd fired them. A ridge of earth rose around Zero, obsidian spears stretching from the mound long and wicked. Zero stretched out his arms, his staff standing unsupported as lightning swam around him in the swirling wind.

Zero built up magic within the fortress of energies. Velith'Seravin sent a charge of lancers at it. They tried to leap the barricade, but the obsidian shards launched themselves with enough force to impale their bellies and send them flying backward.

VelSera pointed. "Fauns, kill him."

The sisters hesitated. Before they could react, the satyr shot into the ground in a spear of writhing black tendrils. Talismans vanished. The barrier crumbled.

"You've made a mistake, brother," Sinesh Ena'Donishe said.

"Silence," Velith'Seravin whirled on the fauns. "Why didn't you attack?"

Kiki glared up at him, hands on her hips. "He had all three talismans. We couldn't have touched him, and it'd have been stupid to try."

Fury heated VelSera's cheeks.

"Kiki speaks wisdom," Mimi said. "If you wish us able to help you defeat wizards, we cannot just throw ourselves at so powerful an enemy."

"I see cowards hiding behind excuses while my people bloody themselves striking at an enemy," VelSera said.

"An enemy you created," Lili said.

"Get out of my sight," Velith'Seravin said. "Do not come back without proof of your worth."

23

NEW ARRIVALS

Kane awoke to the caustic scent of half-brewed potions. The frame of the futon Jordan had brought back dug into his ribs. He'd have suggested she set it up wrong on purpose, but he'd been forced to build it himself.

It's just cheap.

Jordan and Crystal shared one, the bed built to house Crystal all but unslept in—if you ignored the big and tiny paw prints. He climbed the curling cavern steps to the shack's door. No one seemed sufficiently concerned about the hut sacrificing them to its former mistress as breakfast munchies.

He stepped outside to find the greenhouses just beyond the pond. He'd laughed when Jordan asked it to move nearer the farmhouse.

I probably owe her an apology. Wait, if we're near the farmhouse, we're near the boneyard.

He held the need that brought him outside and hurried over to the first available refrigerator. A large mudpuppy, easily twice Nip's size, rose from the dirt with its teeth bared. Kane picked up a stick, waving it. "Doggie want to play? Fetch the stick, come on, fetch the stick. Go get it."

Sarah didn't bother following the thrown wood, instead curling her lip.

"Come on, I just want to use a real bathroom. I'll come right back."

"She doesn't care. Jordan told her to protect you." A brownie with grey shot through his fur glared through spectacles. He chuckled. "From your own idiocy."

Kane clenched his jaw and reached for his magic. He'd been attacked. He'd been carried across the continent on a rotting zombie. He'd been ridiculed and lectured and forced to sleep in a carnivorous, child-eating shack. He was not going to be kept from a bathroom with real toilet paper.

"I'm not letting a ball of dirt with rocks in its head tell me what to do." Other mudpuppies rose from the ground around the boneyard. Their hackles bristled, and snarls showed off marble teeth in many colors.

"How about packed dirt?" The brownie asked.

Kane growled but turned from the boneyard. One foot didn't lift right. He fell flat. His nose splashed into a puddle that had been dry ground only moments before.

"Well, dang, did I retie your shoes incorrectly?" The brownie's mole nose wagged back and forth. "You know us earth Fey, dumb as rocks."

Kane yanked his laces apart and marched off across the fields toward trees with sufficient leaves for his needs. He found a likely spot, dropped his trousers and set about his business. He hadn't finished when another copse of brush parted, revealing a young centaur filly with a brown coat that blended perfectly into the trees around her.

Kane lurched to his feet, drawing on his power. "Oh, no, not again you don't."

He threw both hands at her, nearly losing his balance. A thick ray of dark energy hit her. It shifted oddly like a swarming conga line of fruit flies. Her knees folded and color fled from both her coat and the skin visible beneath a pale leather shift.

Kane grabbed his hat, covering himself as he let a fierce grin show on his face. "That's right, mule. Kane Batson is no pushov—"

His trousers fouled his legs, tumbling him to the ground. The spell slipped from his fingers, and both scrambled to get their hands up. Kane managed his knees and threw the magic at her once more. A pulsing white mist swirled up to interpose itself.

"I'm not your enemy," the filly said.

"Sure you're not, *Wizard's Bane*."

"My name is Chieru E'Riel of Fleet Hoof, formerly Wood Courser. Waphri Ah'Raemyn sent me to seek after Rydari Phriel."

Keeping the spell up grew harder. "Who sent you to who?"

"My teacher sent me to check on a dragonling."

"Drake?" Kane asked through gritted teeth.

Her strained expression shifted to include surprise. "He lets you speak his common name?"

"Sure, we're old buddies." Kane dropped the spell and smirked. He grabbed his trousers. "Drake and I are thick as thieves. I even do him favors…."

She raised a finger. "Um, you might not want—"

"…I pick him up some Cherry Coke and he—" He pulled up his pants.

Chieru E'Riel cringed.

A squishy warmth arrived with his trousers. His expression soured. *Oh, crap.*

Jordan woke with a knot in her gut. She rubbed sleep from her eyes, focus shooting to Kane's empty futon. *Gorram it.*

She lurched out of bed, rushed up the stairs and sprinted for the boneyard. A figure hunched over last night's campfire caught the edge of her vision. Relief washed over her. "Kane, I…who are you?"

The bulky man dressed in alligator and blood tipped up a black wide-brimmed hat she'd mistaken for Kane's. Half his face had been melted just like Sinesh Ena'Donishe.

"Name's Chicory. Hear you've got a dragon hereabouts."

Jordan summoned her staff. He laid a massive steel revolver onto his lap and sipped a pewter mug. "Be careful making sudden moves around some, girlie."

"I don't know who you are, Mister, but Stormfall hasn't been back since she crushed the house."

The melted lines of his face tightened, making the scarred ridges even sharper. "Stormfall. You friends with that bitch?"

Jordan gestured at the house. "What do you think?"

Hooves drew her attention away from the stranger. A young centaur trotted to a stop with an odd bowing gesture, Kane walking oddly in her wake. Kimberlite unfolded from a tumble of stones Jordan'd passed without even noticing. The stone elemental barred the centaur's path.

Frak, Grand Central around here.

She turned back to Chicory to find him removing, inspecting and reloading shotgun shells into his revolver with casual ease. His face rose back into view, chewing the corner of his long mustache. "Centaur."

"Dwarf," the filly said.

"Human," Jordan said. "Who are you people, and what do you want?"

"Told you, girlie, I'm here about a dragon. Juvenile, not old Skyraker."

"I'm protecting you," Kimberlite said.

"Really?" Jordan gestured. "What about him?"

"He's dwarf, salt of the earth, why would you need to be protected from him?" Kimberlite asked.

"Ain't interested in human hides," Chicory said. "She'd only need it if she insisted on protecting the dragonling. Where is it?"

"That's what I came to find out," the centaur said. "Waphri Ah'Raemyn sent me to see if he'd returned."

"How long's it been gone? Which direction did it wander off?"

Kane stepped up into the tableau. "I need new clothes. These are dirty."

"Bit busy here, Kane," Jordan said.

"Having a tea party?" Kane asked.

Jordan fought down her frustration. Beryl appeared at her feet, growling it at him. "Not now, Kane. Mister Chicory, I'd like to know how you got onto this property through the barrier."

He patted a huge knife. "Cut through. Where did it go?"

He cut another hole in the barrier. Great. Jordan tightened her hands on her staff. "I don't know where Drake's gone, but—"

"He flew home to see Stormfall," the centaur said.

Jordan and Chicory narrowed their eyes in unison. Chicory had more practice.

"Home, horsie? To Stormfall?" A wicked grin cut a jagged line. "As in the bitch's get?"

"Who are you?" Jordan asked.

"Chicory Clutchanvil."

The centaur pushed hair off her face. "Chieru E'Riel, Fleet Hoof Acolyte of *Lah'Phriel.*"

"Wait, wait," Kane grinned. "Your name's Chickery? Like Chick for short?"

Chicory's bushy brows narrowed until his eyes were mere slits. "To my friends, whelp, what of it?"

"You like movies, Chick? Got any favorites?" Kane asked.

Jordan lowered her voice in warning. "Kane."

"You and the other dwarves all hang out at your place Friday nights? Pass around the jug of moonshine and watch Chick's flicks?" Kane asked.

Chicory pulled a second massive steel revolver from behind his back. "You ain't my friend. Now, where's the lizard?"

"What do you want with Rydari Phriel?" Chieru E'Riel asked.

Frelling hells, she just gave this...whatever...Drake's real name?

"New boots." Chicory's thumb stroked melted jaw. "And it's mama's head."

"Get off our property, Mister Clutchanvil," Jordan said.

"You going to make me, mageling?"

"No, if you're not honorable enough to respect my request or our property then I won't make you leave. I'll inform Jedediah and let him deal with you."

"Are you saying I've got no honor, girlie?"

Huh, you can actually learn things from the Lord of the Rings. Jordan shrugged. "You're trespassing, and you've been asked to leave. Whether or not you have honor is yet to be seen."

❧

Sensei Truth pulled up behind his tan dojo. A small plane roared from the nearby airport, fighting physics to rise from the runway to the sky. Truth unlocked the back door and saw the crowd waiting on the front mats. Parents clung to the room's edges, though not so many as students for the new class.

He folded hands behind his back and entered. "Good morning, class, parents. I'm Sensei Truth. The attractive woman you've already met is Sensei Yves. We shall be your instructors."

A hand shot up. "Where are your trophies?"

Truth offered the anxious girl a smile. "Do you need to see others' achievements to encourage your own?"

An Alpha Barbie at the back resembling the adolescent asking the question spoke out of turn. "Your ad said your classes would compete."

"Are you suggesting that I display no trophies because our students don't win?" Sensei Truth asked. "Elaine, slide open the wall behind you, please."

The auburn haired woman eyed him. He inclined his head toward the wall. She placed her hands flat on it and slid away panels to reveal a glass fronted display filled with trophies. Gasps ran through the room.

"It's unwise to keep what's precious in harm's way," Truth said.

❧

Jordan held herself still, watching the dwarf stride over the horizon. Fear and anger fought to control her thoughts. She exhaled them, drawing strength not just from magic or those around her but from herself. She marched over to the only partially excavated farmhouse ruin and assembled molding for a single door frame. She grabbed a tool belt, ensuring a hammer and nails in its recesses. She marched it all up to Nip, laid it on the ground and touched him.

Can you take this to where you helped us? Mae's cellar?

<Yes, sister two-legs.>

They must be whole. This is important.

Nip's ears perked. He held his head up. *<Understand.>*

Jordan ruffled his fur. "Thank you. Kimberlite, before the fauns destroyed the house, there was a lintel I pointed out to you."

"Begging Mistress's pardon, but the fauns did not destroy your home. I did. As you directed."

Cold flashed through her. "I only wanted you to destroy the lintel, the top of the door frame."

"Oh," Kimberlite said.

Jordan closed her eyes. *Weems is my fault. I wasn't clear with her... though to be fair I was in a bit of a hurry.* She took several deep breaths. *Live and learn not to order obedient Fey to destroy your house.*

"I need you to find a screw that was in the drywall inside the closet just above the door frame. Can you do that, Kimberlite?"

"What the hell are you on about?" Kane asked. "Who cares about doors and screws? I need clean clothes."

Jordan pointed. "There's a pond, help yourself."

"I don't know how to do laundry. That's maid's work," Kane said.

"You can raise the dead, figure it out." Jordan turned to Kimberlite. "Please bring me that screw. It should feel like Jedediah's magic."

Chieru E'Riel edged closer. "Have I done something to displease you?"

"You told that dragonslayer Drake's real name. You told him about Drake's mother and that he wasn't here. I might not know much about dragon slaying—well, okay anything at all—but I've seen enough CSI to know you just gave the dwarf help in killing my friend."

Chieru E'Riel took a step back. "I'm sorry, Mistress, but—"

"Call me Jordan, all right?"

"I offer my most sincere apologies, Jordan. I meant no ill. Acolytes of the Path are taught integrity and impartiality are crucial."

"What's your name again?" Jordan asked.

"Chieru E'Riel. You may call me ChiRie."

Jordan smiled. "You're ChiRie?"

"Yes."

"ChiRie." Jordan shook her head. "ChiRie, I need your help."

"I must remain impartial and do only as my teacher instructs," ChiRie said.

Jordan snorted. "Sorry. We're not quite so obedient around here. Drake needs Kane looked after. He's not here, and I have to be elsewhere. If I asked you—in the name of Rydari Phriel—to guard the boy, would that be possible?"

"I have to check with Waphri Ah'Raemyn, but she's not refused the Elder Lordling before."

"Go find out," Jordan said. "Please, hurry."

Jordan marched toward the boneyard. Kane knelt on the opposite side of the pond, his lower half naked and his pants floating untouched in the water. He shifted his hat over his privates when he realized Crystal and Jordan were watching him.

Jordan shook her head and led the younger girl to the refrigerator leading to China. "Remember this fridge, okay Crystal?"

Crystal nodded.

They stepped through. Orange juice and toothpaste hit her at once. Jordan dug out a pack of gum ordered in Cheraw and offered Crystal two pieces. She chewed three pieces of grape lemonade gum herself in flavor defense. The light in the small garden seemed late afternoon. The old man she'd met before knelt in the garden tending who knew what.

He looked up and inclined his head.

"Hey, can you staff fight?" Jordan asked.

He blinked at her.

Jordan picked up a garden tool with a long blade, kind of like a hoe with a fang. She swung it a few times and pointed at it. "Can you do this?"

He took it from her and showed her how to dig in the garden.

Jordan bit back an angry comment, smiled and patted him gently. "Thanks."

"Where are we?" Crystal asked.

"Somewhere in China."

"But I don't have a passport."

Jordan laughed. "Me either. Let's see if Jiang Wen is here. She speaks English…mostly. "

"Great," Kane covered himself with soaking pants. "They can do my laundry."

Jordan whirled. "Get back on the farm where it's safe. These people don't need you bringing an attack to their doorstep."

"I need clean clothes," Kane said.

"Then clean them *yourself*. Didn't you do Mauve's laundry as part of your apprenticeship?" Jordan asked.

Kane blushed. "Um, s-she, well, I t-tried…her unmentionables, b-but—"

Jordan threw up her hands. "You're pathetic. Get back to the farm."

"They're Chinese, though, right?"

"They do live in China," Jordan said.

"So they can do laundry," Kane said.

Crystal stomped up to him and slapped him across the face.

He stood there with his mouth agape. "What?"

"What the hell is wrong with you? Do you have one brain cell or considerate bone in your body?" Crystal asked.

"My father said the Chinese did the best laundry just like Mexicans do the best gardening."

Crystal narrowed her eyes.

"It's a compliment," Kane said.

"You need help." Crystal glared. "Can I slap him again?"

"We can do laundry, Mistress Jordan," Jiang Wen said.

Kane beamed.

"Thank you, Jiang Wen," Jordan's smiled shifted to scowl at Kane. "Apprentices do their own laundry. Master Jedediah's orders."

"Would you eat with us, you and your guests?" Jiang Wen asked.

Kane and Crystal brightened together.

"Kane will tend his laundry on the farm. Once that is done, he may return for some food—if that isn't an insult," Jordan said. "Crystal and I can stay, but I actually came to ask if your grandfather might be able to teach me staff fighting."

"We are farmers, Mistress Jordan. Why would we know how to fight?"

"You're Chinese," Kane said.

Jordan's stomach fell to her feet, tempting her to stomp it. She'd made a stereotypical assumption just as Kane did. She considered bowing with an apology, but that too was something she knew from television and probably just as stereotypical. She fidgeted with her fingers. "I apologize, Jiang Wen. My ignorance led me to assume you might. Forgive me for being insensitive."

"You thought us monks?" Jiang Wen smiled, shifted through a few martial art gestures. "Like Chan Kong-Sang?"

"Who?" Jordan asked.

"You know him as Chan Jackie?" Jiang Wen asked.

"Jackie Chan?" Crystal asked. "How do you know about him?"

Jiang Wen blushed. "Master Jedediah knows I think he's handsome. He brings me movies we don't have in China."

Love stones and Jackie Chan movies...you're a strange old man.

Jordan followed Jiang Wen into the house, stopping when the bridge creaked behind her. She spun, pointing. "Farm, Kane. *Inside* the barrier."

"I'm hungry," Kane said

"Go."

Kane skulked back, stymied by the portal trigger. Jordan growled and hit it, sending him back to Georgia. *Maybe I should buy him a book on sensitivity. Can he even read to himself?*

Jordan allowed Kane fifteen minutes to eat. An hour later, she allowed him fifteen minutes to bathe, hoping the gaps would foul any tracking at least temporarily.

ChiRie awaited them when they returned, chatting with Kimberlite.

"My mistress says we will shelter him. It may even be possible to offer similar protections on his person to enable time outside the barrier." ChiRie lowered her voice. "And outside our village. He's quite pungent."

Jordan smirked. "Sounds good. Is there any way to send a message to Drake, warning him about this hunter?"

"Fleet Hoof is still under censure. We may not travel outside certain distances, but I will ask Waphri Ah'Raemyn."

"Great." Jordan slapped her hands together. "Kane, you're going to go live with Fleet Hoof. If they figure out a way to shield you, you can go to school with Mason and Crystal."

"School?" Kane asked. "With ordinary people?"

"Going to school means processed food. If you'd rather eat fresh game, that's your call." Jordan forced a smile. "Crystal, we'll sleep in Cheraw and go back to Mae's in the morning."

"I don't want to go back."

"I'm sorry, Crystal." Jordan folded her arms. "We have to go back."

"Why?"

"Mostly because we've nowhere else to go that they won't search."

Crystal wrapped her arms tighter. She turned her eyes onto Kane then to the mobile hut. "Why can't we stay with him? Maybe go to another property? Maybe your hut could hide out in the woods."

"Mae will open up the cellar and find us gone. She'll call the cops and—"

"Maybe she won't want to admit we left."

"It won't matter. Billie Jo will call the cops if Mae doesn't."

She turned away, her voice dropping to a whisper. "I don't want to go back, don't want to be hungry."

"You won't be hungry." Jordan offered an expression she hoped would encourage the younger girl. "I have a plan."

Crystal brightened.

Mischief played on Jordan's face. She shifted her gaze to include Nip and Kimberlite. "We're going to be bad…a lot."

❧

Bianca stood in the circle hidden beneath the Brickyard complex. Energies played across her skin—energies she'd never knew existed before, but that filled her with a euphoric sense of power beyond even murder.

Unlike when she drew from the magical batteries, the energy seemed caught in an identity crisis. It shifted from hot to cool, electric and weighty. She envisioned its play across her fingers and focused like Zero instructed.

Blue flame erupted around her hand. Instinct caused her to shake it off, and rather than flick away a jet lanced down to the floor. A grin filled her face. She shifted into a fighting stance, practicing moves while willing the flame to extend her reach.

A slow clap drew her attention to the doorway. Flash eyed her, Zero at his side offering the applause.

"I see you've learned how to manifest ambient power and apply it to martial combat. If you can do so in areas without power crystals, you will prove a useful ally."

"I thought I'd already proved how useful I can be, lover."

"Looked more like flailing around," Flash said.

Bianca glowered at him. "I'd like to see you do better."

Flash stepped forward, but Zero restrained him. "Your bedroom weapons are well practiced, are they not?"

She stiffened a moment as compulsion stole her breath. She unfurled a seductive smile. "You know they are."

"And you employ them to my pleasure for the purpose of manipulating me, isn't that correct?"

Flash smirked.

"Yes," she admitted.

"The curse upon you is a useful one. I'll have to research it if it can keep a scorpion like you honest." Zero smiled. "I mean that in the best way."

The compulsion drove her. "I want to laugh it off, but I know you're lying."

"Exceptional bit of magic."

Anger flooded Bianca's features, but it cleared as quickly as it had come. "I have no need to lie to you."

"No need, at the moment," Flash said.

"Guards should be silent," Bianca said.

Flash's brows rose.

"It's time to see how you fare with this weapon," Zero said. "Proceed."

"Without the toys?" Bianca asked.

"As you are."

Bianca extended her senses. She willed the power in the room to collect within her, similar to how she'd channeled it when in physical contact with the crystals or their surrogate batteries. Runes along the walls illuminated, dimming a moment later to coals on the edge of dying out.

"What was that?" Bianca asked.

"Nothing you need concern yourself with at this time."

She wanted to object but focused on restoring the fire to her hands. She fought with it a moment until Zero's impatient expression encouraged her to shift fire to a glove of crackling electricity. It behaved in a more erratic manner. She got a feel for it and traded portable lightning for a sheen of ice. She launched long stilettos at the targets, pleased to successfully curve the shards despite her inclination to will them straight.

"Good, now earth," Zero said.

"How would rock spears be any different that ice?"

"You think rock is earth's only natural weapon?"

Bianca searched her brain, trying to determine what other resources seemed part of terramancy. Zero yawned. His hands flexed. A small demonic-looking fairy erupted from nowhere in a gout of flame.

Its eyes flashed around the room. They settled on her with abject hatred. It shrieked and drove at her, small yet powerful fire bolts lashed out from its tiny flaming fists.

Bianca raised a defensive shield almost in time. Flesh along one bicep crisped and bubbled. A moment later the pain drove a blade into her nerves. She lost her sense of magic. Her shield fell.

She threw herself sidelong, barely avoiding another firestorm. The little beast rocketed toward her, jaws drooling green slobber with anticipation. She rolled the other way, spinning a kick into its side. It careened away, and Bianca used the time to draw up her focus once more.

Blue flame launched from her hands. It struck the creature square and anticipation of victory exhilarated her. It took her a moment to recognize the creature's screams as laughter and a second to see her flame feeding the Fey's growth.

She switched to ice, showering it with shards. Even as a bigger target, the thing's speed made it almost impossible to hit. She threw a spiked wall into its path. Cold magic warmed around her. She glanced to see the water crystal dim to dangerous levels.

I'm using too much power. She growled at herself. *Just like he's been telling me.*

She shifted to air, arcing electricity at the darting beast. Fire slammed her shields. Razor talons cut lines across its surface, cracks spreading out from the deepest gouges.

It retreated, settling behind the fire crystal breathing hard. Bianca smiled and stalked forward. She drew earth magic in preparations to skewer the little beast. It sprang from its hiding space, both claws wreathed in white-hot flame. It slammed through her shield. Claws slashed her, cutting and cauterizing most of the wounds delivered. She kicked it away and ripped off her melting practice shoe.

"That wound's lethal," Flash said.

"Eventually," Zero said.

He's going to let it kill me. She cradled her side. *Jesus, it burns like...*

The beast charged her once more. She launched walls of stone out of the floor, not shielding herself but cornering the thing against her to cut off its escape. Acid sprayed from her fingers in a swirl of putrid greens. The beast screamed. Flesh melted from its bones. She closed the cage to keep it from lashing out and collapsed to the ground.

Flash inclined his head with grudging respect.

Zero smiled. "Resourceful, though you're still draining too much power. Skill not muscle is the path to victory."

"You would have let it kill me."

"What would you have done in my place?" Zero asked.

"Right."

"Let's work on healing magic," Zero said.

"Now?"

"Seems like a good time. Otherwise, you'll be dead in the next ten minutes."

LAST STRAWS

"Do you understand me, Mason?" Billie Jo asked.

Mason hunched his shoulders. "Yes, Mother."

"Explain it back to me."

"I'm late for class."

"I'll write you a note."

Mason glared at her, gesturing to the other cars lined up for drop-offs. "You're holding up the line."

"They'll wait."

"Fine," Mason grumbled. "Don't leave school. Don't talk to Jordan. Don't get beat up."

"No, don't start fights."

He glared through his lashes. *I hate you.*

Mason marched off into the press of bodies. She called after him, but he'd had enough. She didn't spank, and she'd already cut up all of his cords. There wasn't really anything else she could do to him.

The stubborn combination on his locker worsened his day, joined by classroom doors and ultimately any attempt to take notes. He tried writing with his off hand, tried writing with a pen between two fingers of the hand in a wrist-thumb cast. He even tried cupping his arms around his work and moving the pen via magic. He couldn't read any of it.

Kane's an idiot. I should just take the casts off.

A shadow drew his attention. Crystal pushed hair from her face. "I forgot the other night, can I be the first to sign it?"

"Sign what?" Mason asked.

"Your cast, silly."

"Oh, right, sure."

Crystal bent over his left arm, hair hung down so close he could smell her shampoo. She stood a moment later, exposing her signature surrounded by little firework shapes. "Thanks."

Mason spent most of their class together paying attention to the little starbursts. It wasn't hearts—not that he wanted to wear hearts on his cast—so he wasn't entirely sure what they meant.

He smiled. *I'll ask her at lunch.*

The intercom crackled. "Mister Spade, can you please send Mason Bartlett to the guidance counsellor's office?"

The class erupted in jeering noises. Mister Spade silenced them with a look. "He's on his way."

The counsellor burned up the rest of the morning, trying to get to the root of Mason's anger. Despite the calm badgering, Mason didn't give the school shrink the real answer. Telling the school his mother thought him perverted by dark sorcery and in need of an exorcism didn't bode well for her job. She didn't deserve to lose her career even if she had sicced the counselor on him

Mason marched across the dining courtyard to see his spot taken by the plump, obnoxious Arthur. "That's my seat."

"You're not allowed to sit with them anymore," Arthur said. "Mother's orders."

Mason snorted. "Your mother doesn't control me."

"She controls them." Arthur smiled. "Mother knows best."

Mason lunged forward, nose to nose over a corner of the table. "Your mother doesn't control shit, *fatso.*"

Crystal gasped.

Arthur rose, reminding Mason that he wasn't the biggest at the table even if he hadn't been handicapped by sparsely signed casts. "Mother's word is law."

Jordan cut off Mason's response. She shot Arthur a dirty look. "Sit down, Mason. We've saved *most* of your lunch."

Mason narrowed his eyes. "You ate my food?"

"Finder's keepers," Arthur said.

The hair on Mason's skin rose, tingles prickling his fingers like pins and needles.

"Mason." Jordan shook her head. "Jedediah taught us to give to those less fortunate. You can always buy more."

Mason followed her eyes to the debit card tucked on the far side of her tray. He rounded the table, kissing Jordan as he reclaimed the card. "You're the best sister."

"Mine," Arthur growled.

Brows shot upward around the table.

"Excuse me?" Jordan said.

Arthur hesitated before drawing all the food on the table to himself, leaving none for Jordan, Crystal or Mason. He popped a Coke and smiled. "Mine."

You want my food, fat boy? Have it all. Mason grabbed the magic brought to easy reach and shoved it at the food. Wind gusted into the courtyard. Chilidogs and ketchup-coated fries slid across the surface into Arthur's face. Other foods hit him, most still in their wrappers. The open soda flipped onto its side sending drink into Arthur's lap.

"Did you?" Crystal asked.

"Freak gust of wind," Mason said.

"You're the freak," Arthur retorted.

"I'm going for more food. Anyone want any? Spaghetti maybe? Soup?"

Crystal laughed.

Billie Jo pulled into their driveway. Heavy silence and simmering anger filled the van. Mason hadn't argued. He hadn't said anything

—despite her railing at him for more than half the trip. Mason unhooked his seatbelt, jumped out, and slammed the door before she'd fully stopped. He sulked toward the front door.

Billie Jo rolled down the window. "Go to your room. I'll be back in an hour or so."

She waited a moment for his response, but he didn't even look back. *Whatever happened to my sweet boy?*

She pulled back out onto the street, mulling over the things her coworker had related after the counselling session. Between Betsy's attempt and Pastor Fulton's failures, she was losing more ground than gaining. She'd considered changing churches—she couldn't really change schools—to get Mason help, but every time she seems on the edge of leaving she suffered guilt so intense it almost caused a panic attack. She'd been with her church family since not long after Mason was born. She couldn't just abandon them.

Miss Setter's little pink car waited a street away from the Bridgeport home. She leaned against it, talking with Angesa, Marnie and Agent Ridley. Billie Jo pulled up behind the government vehicle. All heads turned her way.

"Good afternoon, Billie Jo," Ridley said.

"Thank you for coming, Agent," Billie Jo gestured to the others. "I know this is none of our business, but we don't think it's right to keep Faye—"

"Jordan," Ridley, Setter and Marnie corrected.

"It isn't right to keep her from an opportunity like Marnie is offering her," Billie Jo said. "Something just doesn't seem right in that house."

"Have you been able to come up with any specifics since our phone conversation?" Ridley asked.

"No. I'm sorry."

"Very well. Ladies, I'd appreciate it if you waited here while Angesa and I have a chat with the Bridgeports." Ridley held up a hand to forestall their objections. "We can legally enter their home. You might muddy things if she decides to call you trespassers."

Mae Bridgeport opened at Ridley's knock. Her eyes narrowed, but her face shifted into a smile. "Miss Cooper, Agent Ridley, to what do we owe this surprise?"

Ridley glanced at Angesa.

"Home inspection," Angesa said.

"I wish you'd warned us," Mae said. "The place is a disaster."

"Surprise inspections suffer when you advertise them," Angesa said. "I'd like to see Faye Jordan and Crystal Potter."

"Arthur, fetch your sisters," Mae called into the house. "What brings the FBI to my door then? Surely you have better things to do than inspecting my home."

"Angesa agreed to my presence. Jordan is—"

"Faye," Mae corrected.

Ridley removed his glasses, cleaning them in slow, methodical motions. "Jordan is still connected to a person of interest."

"In my house, you will address my foster daughter as Faye," Mae said.

"Technically, I'm on your doorstep, Miss Bridgeport, not in your house."

"You're on my property."

"Within the bounds of these United States," Ridley said. "I'd also like to inquire about Eve Russo."

Mae stiffened infinitesimally.

"Missing person cases are my specialty," Ridley said.

"Eve was a troubled girl, agent, wayward. I've no idea what happened to her after she left. I'm sorry she ran, but I'm not entirely sad to see her out of my house."

You are hedging the truth. What are you hiding?

"Why is that?" Angesa asked.

"She...well, what she did isn't suitable for polite conversation," Mae said.

Arthur appeared in the back foyer, shifting his weight from foot to foot. "Um, I...I can't find them."

Mae whirled. "That's not possible. You know where they're supposed to be, Arthur. Fetch them."

"They're not in there."

Mae flashed Angesa a nervous smile. "Girls have taken to locking themselves in their room. They're probably just refusing to answer because of an argument with Arthur at school today. I'll fetch them. Arthur, see our guests to the sitting room."

"That's all right," Angesa said. "We'll accompany you. I need to inspect the premises anyway."

Something hot flashed through Mae's expression, but it softened as she led them through the house. "This way."

Mae led them through an immaculate house marred only by dirt tracked across its floors by Arthur-sized shoes.

Ridley catalogued the furniture, its placement, the knick knacks and the way she treated those around her. The new information evolved his working profile, adding to research into past fosters and interviews with those of adult age he'd tracked down. They hesitated at the foot of a staircase.

She's thinking hard. Why?

"Their room isn't upstairs?" Ridley asked.

Mae's shoulders tightened. Extra cheer layered her voice. "After Eve, we decided it best to let foster daughters live in the back cottage. We're still moving them."

"But you said after Eve. Crystal's been in your care for months since then," Angesa said.

"I...well...it wasn't as much of a problem before Faye joined us," Mae said.

Ridley glanced from Mae to Arthur and back. "What problem?"

Mae smiled. "Sometimes misunderstandings happen. Accidentally walking in on one another, unintended flirting. It seemed best to avoid the situation."

"Are you suggesting Eve sexually assaulted your son?" Ridley asked.

Angesa opened her mouth but closed it at Ridley's gesture.

"I certainly wouldn't know, would I, Agent? If I were in the room when these misunderstandings occurred, they'd have been nipped in the bud before anything could've happened. Eve's tendencies brought unsavory ideals into my home. I never found any evidence of drugs or alcohol, but I fear whomever she hung around in school gave her inappropriate ideas she brought back."

Ridley removed a picture of the girl from a file, displaying a timid fourteen-year-old. "This girl?"

"Pictures can be deceiving, Agent," Mae said.

"You're right. Things are not always what they seem. Let us continue to the girls' room."

Mae led them out the back and across the yard. Once off the stairs, Ridley shifted position closer to her side. He studied her profile, trying to get a sense of the woman. Her eyes moved several times toward one side of the sizable cottage. Nothing seemed out of place to him, but she kept looking anyway.

They climbed the cottage stair to a series of bedrooms. Two cots made up as if by experienced soldiers and a small bureau were the solitary contents of the spotless room.

"Cots?" Angesa asked.

"As I said, we're in the process of moving them," Mae said.

An inspection of the door offered an older style lock easily opened from either side. He checked but didn't find a bolt to over-rule the handle lock. "May I use the restroom?"

Mae blinked. "Arthur, take Agent Ridley back into the house."

Ridley smiled. "I noticed one at the end of the hall. That's more than sufficient."

Before Mae could object, he entered the bathroom, shut and locked the door. He lifted the seat to provide auditory confirmation of his activities and scrutinized the empty room. He opened the old medicine cabinet and frowned. *Cheap toilet paper. No makeup. No extra toiletries. No feminine products.*

He checked behind the opened shower curtain. *Hotel soap and shampoo. No razors. What am I seeing? Their financials provide no reason they're fostering for the money. Using hotel toiletries isn't criminal, maybe just frugal.*

He flushed the toilet, put down the seat and washed his hands. He smiled at Mae's scrutiny when he exited. "They don't appear to be in there."

"Mae suggested Jordan might be running in the woods behind the house," Angesa said.

"She likes to run," Mae said. "Crystal might have gone to emulate her big sister."

"So I understand she's been approached about competing in the Olympics," Ridley said. "You must be very proud."

"An Olympic Athlete is definitely something to be proud about, but Faye isn't my own—no matter how much I care about her—so there's only so much credit I could claim in that situation."

"This is a very special case," Angesa said. "I think we should discuss her competition options more thoroughly. Why don't we chat while Agent Ridley and Arthur see if they can't find the girls?"

Mae looked as if she'd object.

"Don't worry, I won't let him get lost in the woods," Ridley said. "How about you give me a tour of the cottage, Arthur. Show me where they might hide."

"You are not granted permission to interrogate my son, Agent," Mae gave the boy a significant look.

"I give my word I won't ask him a single question, but if you'd prefer, your husband can give me the tour."

"He's working," Mae said. "No. I'm afraid I can't permit you to explore my home unescorted."

"I'm investigating a missing person, Missus Bridgeport. Surely you want me to find and help a wayward fifteen-year-old girl," Ridley said.

"Do you have a warrant?" Mae asked.

Ridley smiled. "No, I have an invitation to accompany a state inspection of your home. Angesa, let's inspect first while we wait for the girls to turn up. You can *instruct* Missus Bridgeport in the state's expectations regarding this Olympic opportunity later."

Mae bristled.

"After you, Agent," Angesa said.

Ridley led them on a room by room inspection. Angesa made copious notes she didn't hide from Mae Bridgeport while he collected information inside his head. Once they'd gone through the cottage, he turned them to the wood's edge. He knelt several times and inspected the ground, but he found no recent evidence that anyone had entered the woods. His roundabout course back to the main house circled the cottage. Chains and a heavy iron door brought him to a hole in the ground. A ladder leaned against the nearby wall. He double-checked its position against their original route to the cottage.

Maybe.

He produced a flashlight, shining it into the hole. It appeared empty. A reek of human waste lingered. Small wrapper scraps and some bones dotted the floor's edges. He leaned in, finding a door frame leaned up against one wall just out of easy sight of the entrance. He shifted his light to the opposite wall. *That brick seems newer. PVC instead of old clay. What's going on here?*

"What do you use this for?" Ridley asked.

"It's an old artifact from the previous owners. We've been cleaning it out to store garden tools."

They finished the exterior tour, took a lap through the house and ended up in a formal sitting room. Mae refused to let Arthur answer any of Ridley's questions about Eve. She listened to Angesa's instructions to let Jordan train and compete, countering them with concerns regarding poor school performance and disciplinary issues.

"Fine. I'll check those as part of my review," Angesa said. "But unless I find evidence that indicates more than the standard disruption caused by a new fostering, I expect her to be allowed to compete in school track and field, train, and audition for a position on the US Olympic team."

Mae fairly crackled with anger. "Thank you for clarifying the state's expectations, Miss Cooper."

"We'll still need to interview Crystal and Jordan," Ridley said.

"Angesa may do so when she likes," Mae said. "You're not welcome on my property without a warrant, Agent."

"Unless I invite him," Angesa countered.

"I'll clarify that too, with my lawyer," Mae said.

"Why?" Ridley cocked his head. "Are you hiding something?"

Mason trudged up the road, sipping on a Mountain Dew bought at the Texaco beside the park. His feet seemed incapable of rising off the ground more than absolutely necessary to move them, toe scuffing the ground with each step. He couldn't remember ever feeling so tired.

His stomach rumbled.

Maybe I should've bought food with the coins I scrounged up.

He'd have grabbed food on his way out the door, but his mother had already caught him sneaking food—though he wasn't sure how unless she was photographing the fridge, pantry and the insides of boxes. Jedediah used to feed him whenever he wanted.

"Boys your age need to be sure they keep their tanks full," Jedediah said. "Good for keeping them growing strong."

Jordan had complained about Jedediah's absence while they roasted marshmallows. She needed him back for more important reasons than her stomach. *Where are you, sir?*

Hollowness filled his gut, bigger than his stomach. He'd used a lot of magic against Arthur. Even Jordan's debit card hadn't been able to refill him. The walk to the park only made it worse, but he couldn't stand to be in his Mother's house any longer.

Guess if I'm going to run off I might as well take food too. I'm just so tired of this whole thing, the arguing, the punishments, the dirty looks when she thinks I don't notice. I've had enough of being 'evil' just for how I was born...and that part is her fault.

Some nights had been like the day's lunch. The table couldn't hold enough food to fill the emptiness. He felt empty all the time. The afternoon wore down, but the heat didn't, adding its sticky oppression to fatigue and hunger. He'd only recently started sweating, but he knew he'd be soaked and miserable long before he got home.

Wish I still had my bike. Why'd she have to give it away? On the bike, the wind would cool me. A thought struck him. He sipped his drink, closed his eyes and reached for his magic. He felt it, but it kept just out of reach too far for the strength he had to draw it near for a cooling wind.

His stomach complained about his failure.

His feet drew him to lake's edge—the same spot he'd broken his arm. He pulled off shoes and dropped his feet into the water. He stared at it, remembering the strange hallucination. He leaned back on his cast-covered arms, kicked his feet and thought about Crystal and Kane.

Kane understood about having magic and keeping secrets. Crystal knew about having a pain in the ass Mother. He liked them, felt comfortable talking with them. They didn't seem the type of friends to drop him when his Mother publicly humiliated him.

He sat on the bank, idly ripped free clumps of grass and threw pebbles or twigs into the water. Maybe it was having his feet in the lake, but the bank felt cooler.

Maybe I should jump in. He glanced around and started shimmying out of his cast. The wrist brace went next followed by his shirt. He checked his surroundings once more.

"Good afternoon, Mason. Aren't you suppose to wear those until your arms are healed?"

Mason started. He whirled around to find the martial arts teacher holding his bike. "How'd you sneak up on me? I didn't even hear the bike's clicking."

Truth chuckled. "Maybe you were lost in thought. Why are your casts off?"

"I heal fast?" Mason said.

"You might not stay healed if I give this back to you, but it isn't mine."

Mason took the bike from him, laying it on the ground. "Thanks, Mister Truth."

"Sensei."

"Sensei," Mason said.

"You also might not stay healed sitting out here alone where those bullies can find you again. Don't you have any friends to hang out with?"

Mason shrugged.

Truth glanced at the lake. A loud, powerful sneeze exploded from him, almost sounding as if he'd sneezed while trying to say something.

"I'm sorry, what was that?"

Truth shook the mucus from his hands.

Mason's neck tingled. For a moment he thought he smelled impending rain. He glanced at the sky to find it empty of grey clouds.

"Something wrong?" Truth asked.

"Bless you," Mason said. "Nah, just wishful thinking."

Truth took a seat on a low, flat stump opposite the lakeside path. "We started up a new class at my dojo. Got a spot for you, if you're interested."

Mason shuffled his feet. "Mom's not going to pay for that."

"Must be a mother thing, pity though. With a little practice, you'd be able to defend yourself from those bullies."

"Mom hates fighting."

"Defending yourself isn't fighting."

"I know, right, but she doesn't see it that way."

A corner of Truth's mouth turned upward. "I don't think she's thought it all the way through."

"What do you mean?"

"Well, she doesn't want you hurt—that makes sense, right? That's why she didn't want me returning your bike."

"Sure."

"She doesn't want you to learn martial arts because she's afraid you'll use it to start fights."

"Because I'm evil," Mason mumbled.

"Pardon?"

"Nothing."

"My point was that if those bullies catch you again, what does she expect you to do? Let them hit you?"

"Yes."

"How does that keep you from being hurt?" Truth asked. "There's only two ways to keep bullies from being bullies. Avoid them or teach them that messing with you will cost them more than it's worth—in defense, of course."

"Of course," Mason chuckled.

Truth's jaw clenched as he looked out over the lake. Mason turned to look, but Truth's powerful sneeze snapped his attention back to the teacher. The faraway expression changed. He opened his mouth to speak, shook his head and closed it again.

"What?" Mason asked.

"Nothing," Truth said. "Bad idea."

"What was it?" Mason asked.

"You could always just watch the classes. Maybe ask questions about how the moves are performed. You wouldn't exactly be in the class."

"Mom might figure out if I got the clothes all dirty, and besides I don't have any money...she stopped my allowance."

"We've got spare gis and such. They get left behind when a kid gets tired of studying sometimes. It'd be better if you could participate...."

Mason sighed. "Yeah."

"But you can't...not without a parent giving permission." Truth stood. "Well, I should get going. You'll be all right here? Don't need a ride home or anything?"

He really wanted to learn any martial arts. Ninjas were the coolest thing on the planet after all, even cooler than wizards.

But I could be like a wizard ninja if I could just get Mom's...wait. Mason brightened. "Mister, I mean Sensei Truth, could I borrow your phone?"

"What for?"

"Call my Dad."

It took very little convincing to get his Dad to give Sensei Truth permission to teach Mason. He explained about the bullies, but in the end, it was telling his Dad that Mom didn't want him to learn how to defend himself for his father to acquiesce. He gave Sensei Truth verbal permission and promised to sign the forms and mail them. Mason thanked his Dad, lock the phone and beamed.

Sensei Truth took it. "See you in class."

Jordan stepped through the fridge into Mae's cellar. The hatch gaped open, and her stomach plummeted. She glanced back through to Crystal, hesitating before motioning her through. Nip and Beryl followed her, the former licking his chops and the latter rolling on the ground pawing at her muzzle.

"Nip, go see what you can and come tell me."

Nip slipped into the cellar's brick wall. Beryl lunged after him. She bounced off the brick, shook her head and dove into the loose ground beneath the bricks.

"What's going on?" Crystal stared at the opening.

"We'll find out in a minute."

"They came looking for us, didn't they?" Crystal asked. "We're going to be in trouble."

Jordan sidled closer to the younger girl and took her hand. "They don't believe in magic, Crystal—not real magic. Mae's worst punishment is the cellar. She'll probably just double up the locks, maybe check on us more often for a while."

Crystal seemed to shrink. "Does that mean we have to stay in here next time?"

"No. I'll sit on this side to listen for them. You can remain on the farm near the entrance."

"How will you eat?" Crystal asked.

"We'll work something out."

Nip slid back into the cellar. He nuzzled Jordan, licking Crystal's hand.

<Billie Jo. FBI. Others. No one watches.>

Ridley came to check on me? With Billie Jo? Why?

Beryl slid up out of the floor, pressing into Jordan as she dropped something from her mouth. *<Ball. Ball. Ball.>*

Crystal giggled. *<She's so cute.>*

Beryl pounced onto Crystal's foot. *<Love. Love sis-two-sis. Love.>*

Calm down pup, we love you too. Jordan laughed. *Guess there's no point hiding down here if we have guests.*

Jordan realized the ladder hadn't been lowered. She considered having Nip fix it but instead filled her legs with strength and jumped to the ledge. She overdid the jump, landing with her stomach rather than her arms on the metal frame. Despite driving the breath from herself, she caught hold, wedged a leg and dragged herself the rest of the way up. She lowered the ladder.

Jordan led their way into the house.

"Good day, Miss Cooper. Agent."

The front door shut as Jordan entered the foyer. Mae whirled, eyes holding enough fury to suggest flames. "You wretched, ungrateful child. I will not be ordered around."

"I didn't say a word."

Mae charged her, slamming her uninjured hand against Jordan's hardened face. "Who did you talk to? That nosey redneck teacher? The dyke coach?"

"I'm getting tired of you hitting me, Mae. I *highly* suggest you stop."

Mae struck her.

Jordan lowered her voice. "That was the last one."

"I am in charge. I will not be questioned. I do not take orders from public servants, slovenly cops or impertinent little girls."

"And you don't learn from your mistakes." Jordan shoved Mae across the foyer and into one of the side tables, toppling a flower arrangement. Mae slipped on the spilled water and fell flat on her back.

Hands seized Jordan from behind, pinning her arms and latching onto her breasts. "I've got her, Mom."

Louis appeared at the top of the stairs. "Mae!"

Crystal shrieked, and more weight pulled Jordan backward. She pushed power into her limbs and stabilized her footing. Arthur let go. Crystal yelped.

Jordan turned back toward them. Blood beaded in scratch marks along Arthur's cheeks. He whirled and slammed a fist into Crystal's face. The foyer's sunny tones went scarlet. Hardwood creaked under Jordan's fingers. Arthur leapt toward her, eyes widening. Jordan's staff swung an upward arc. It cracked against Arthur's face. Bones broke.

Hands seized Jordan again. She threw the attacker off and raised her staff to strike.

"Jordan! Stop," Billie Jo yelled.

Shapes charged Jordan, but they didn't grab. Miss Setter, Marnie and Billie Jo formed a semi-circle, empty hands stretched out each saying words that didn't seem to register. She choked up on her staff like a bat and turned to the most recent attacker. Agent Ridley struggled up from beneath dented wallpaper.

She checked Crystal. Half the girl's face seemed swollen, the rest tear streaked. She curled up in a doorframe, Nip and Beryl snarling between her and the puddle of blood haloing Arthur's head.

Oh, God. Oh, God.

White overwhelmed scarlet in a blizzard of roaring wind. A dented lower jaw spilled blood and teeth, rattled by labored breath.

Voices whispered in the distance.

Mae's hushed screams echoed Arthur's name over and over

Billie Jo and Marnie blocked the Bridgeports, both urging Louis to hold Mae, to keep her back. Miss Setter barked urgently into her phone.

"Jordan," Ridley said. "Please, put the weapon down."

Jordan's eyes flicked to him. He tensed, every inch of him ready to attack. She turned back toward Arthur. *What did I do? He needs help. Why aren't they helping him?*

"Jordan."

She met Ridley's eyes. Something in their depths drew her. Understanding and sympathy lurked behind a wall of fear. Her attention shifted to her hands, travelling up the staff to dark, wet blood.

She dropped it and jerked backward away from it.

Oh, God. Oh, God, what have I done?

25

FROM DEATH'S GRASP

Drake pulled up the farm drive, gravel crunching beneath his confiscated motorcycle. A weak tingle of the barrier's energies washed over his tanned skin. He parked at the porch's foot. More excavation had finished clearing the area in front of the den's hearth.

"Hello?" Drake called.

No one answered.

He dismounted, stretching to loosen limbs stiff after hours riding in human form. He strode toward the greenhouses.

"Hello?"

The hives buzzed angry warning, but no bees flew out to meet him. He peeked inside. The spot reserved for Sarah and her litter was empty. Drake narrowed his eyes. *Something's wrong.*

He changed direction into the boneyard. The yard, beyond holding Jedediah's portals and other spells, offered refuge to countless Fey. None poked their heads up when he called. A whimper drew him to the Weems fridge.

A small girl curled in its entrance. Her face had been severely bruised, and the warm sun above seemed to intensify. "Hello?"

She looked up. Her eyes widened. She crab walked away as fast as she could scramble. "Don't hurt me. Please. Just leave me alone."

Why would she be sitting in the Weems fridge? Drake approached the refrigerator, leaning forward to look through the portal. Instead of a closet, a dark hole gaped in its depths. He turned his attention to the girl once more, evoking her squeak.

Drake crouched, not a very comfortable position in the long run, but less threatening. "My name's Drake. Who're you?"

"Drake? Jordan's brother?"

Drake smiled, glad to have changed his teeth to something more human. "That's right. Where is she?"

"She's in jail," Crystal said.

"Jail?" Drake surged to his feet. "Where? For what?"

"The FBI guy didn't want to do it, but Mistress demanded she be charged with assault and battery."

Drake licked his lips. "Who'd she hit?"

"Arthur. He was grabbing her and me, and I think Eve and he hit me—"

A growl rumbled out of Drake's chest, cutting off the girl's patter.

Sudden fear drained off the girl's expression. She cocked her head. "That's glamour, isn't it? I forgot, you're supposed to be a dragon, right?"

"I'm a dragon, yes," Drake said. "Do you have magic?"

"No, I don't have magic, silly." She laughed. "Jordan said you were funny."

"Glad I amuse someone. Why are you here and where's Kane?"

"Kane's with ChiRie and the centaurs. Mae threw me in the cellar again." Crystal studied her feet. "I'm afraid of it, so Jordan made it so I could come here, you know, and get food from Cheraw when Mistress starves us...well me."

"How'd Jordan set up a portal? Why aren't you getting food from Weems?"

"Weems got destroyed when Kane played too many video games, besides he ate everything in the house."

"I don't understand."

"Jordan said he was supposed to come back to the farm after short visits—that's why she has the mudpuppies guarding all the portals—she didn't want the sisters tracking him and destroying any more houses. She used the portal there to set up one in Mae's cellar."

"Weems is gone?"

"Yeah, the day before the dragon hunter—oh, God, Drake you're in danger. There's a dragonslayer guy who's hunting you."

Dragonslayer? Drake blinked at her. *Who'd hunt Elder Fey? She's got that wrong.*

"Wait, is that why you're hiding with glamour? Will that keep that dwarf Chicory from finding you? Jordan was worried because ChiRie gave him your real name. He didn't seem to like your mom very much."

"Nobody does," Drake grumbled. "Come on, we need some help."

"But you're a dragon."

Drake considered her a moment. He'd had a lot of time to think on the road. "Sometimes problems are just bigger than me."

"I have to stay near the cellar. Mae will beat me if I'm gone when she comes back from the hospital."

He bristled. He started to tell her not to worry about it, but he had a pile of his own problems apparently topped by a dwarven dragon hunter. *Yippee.*

Drake returned to the farm house. He lifted magic to his eyes and examined the hearth. Part of him wanted to run off and rescue Jordan from police custody, but the other part knew finding a trigger to grant him access to Sanctuary Hole could bring a bigger, better solution to all that plagued them.

When the search offered him nothing, he shed his clothes and shifted back into his own shape. The change hurt less than the last time, and he found his wings all but mended. He trotted down to his motorcycle for a Cherry Coke before invoking Sight to search for Jedediah's trigger with sharper dragon eyes.

Kane lounged on a pile of cushions. Two fillies flanked him with platters of food and wine. He nibbled a grape off the fingers of a centaur who never wore anything over her perky breasts. The other offered him a morsel of goat cheese. She was prettier, not that he had any intention of asking a horse out on a date, but she kept herself covered to his disappointment.

"Should I peel this one too?" the topless centaur asked.

Kane swallowed the sharp, salty cheese. "I didn't really taste a difference."

"They why did you ask it, Rydari Phriel's friend?"

Kane shrugged. "I heard kings and sultans liked them that way. Figured that made it good enough for me."

Sheriff Dunford stared across the table at Jordan. He said nothing. He couldn't, not until Angesa arrived. They'd been through the process several times. A deputy picked her up from juvenile detention, brought her before the sheriff, and he asked her questions—mostly about Jedediah.

Dunford's interrogation technique seemed learned from bad spy films. He kept asking her to confess her attack on Arthur in a way he could use to pursue Jedediah, unwilling to accept she'd only been defending Crystal.

If it wasn't for Crystal, I'd just leave. Hell, if Arthur wasn't in the hospital, I'd leave just to make sure she was safe—not that Nip and Kimberlite can't protect her if something terrible happens.

The sheriff drummed his fingers on the table.

Where is Angesa?

As if a granted wish, the door opened. Her blonde caseworker entered, pressing her lips into a tight smile. She stepped out of the doorway to let a woman dressed in expensive clothes enter the room.

Dunford shot to his feet. "This meeting is not open to the press."

The woman smiled and extended a hand. "It might be soon. Meadow March, Miss Jordan's attorney."

Jordan blinked up at the woman. It took a moment to place her. She'd ran a booth at the Renaissance fair, dressed like one of the gypsies and cackling like a mad hen.

The sheriff didn't take her hand. Meadow sighed. "I see. Well, if we're not going to be friendly, Sheriff, get out."

"Excuse me?" His barrel chest swelled, rough air rippling his mustache.

"Get out. I'm not saying it in Japanese. You are not permitted to stay. Client-attorney privilege? Surely you've heard of it."

"This is my—"

Meadow raised a brow.

Dunford slammed open the door and stormed out.

Meadow took his seat. "Nice to see you again, Jordan. You might not remember me, but I'm a friend of your father's."

"She doesn't have a father," Angesa said.

"Yes and no," Meadow said.

Jordan turned to Angesa. "Did you call her? Agent Ridley?"

"I thought you contacted her," Angesa said. "Though I've no idea how you expect to pay for such a high-end lawyer."

Meadow patted Jordan's hand. "Don't worry about that, dear. It's all in the family. Just tell me what happened."

Jordan told her everything she remembered and everything she suspected. "Please, Angesa, you have to get Crystal out of there."

"You need to be more worried about yourself," Angesa said. "We'll review Crystal's situation, don't you worry."

Jordan examined her fidgeting hands. "Angesa, could I please speak to Meadow alone?"

Angesa hesitated but rose from her seat. "I'll be right outside the door."

Meadow raised both perfect brows. "What can't you say in front of your case worker?"

Jordan took a deep breath and a bigger chance. "Do you know about magic?"

The other woman frowned. "The stage stuff Jedediah does?"

Jordan's hopes fell. Tears edged out of her eyes. "You said it was in the family, I thought maybe you were a wizard too."

"I'm not sure I understand."

"Magic's real. Jedediah's a wizard. So am I."

"Jordan, honey, you don't need an insanity defense. This was clear cut self-defense," Meadow said.

Jordan looked down at the cuffs restraining her hands. She drew the rumble of the Dragon Springs into her being and focused on the cuffs harder than any other spell she'd ever tried before. They clicked simultaneously, unwrapping from her wrists and floating off the table.

Meadow gasped.

Jordan focused for all she was worth, speaking through gritted teeth. "Magic is real. You have to believe me."

"I'm listening."

The cuffs clattered to the table.

"Crystal is claustrophobic. She's in danger. Mae is holding her in a small underground cellar. I can prove it if you'll just take me out to the farm."

"We can get a deputy to go out to the Bridgeport house," Meadow said.

Jordan shook her head. "They'll cover it up like when Agent Ridley came out the day I...t-the day I h-hurt Arthur. There's another way. A magic back door. Please, you have to believe me."

Drake rounded the farmhouse to a pistol barrel.

"Don't move," Ridley said.

He looked up at the FBI agent, a snarl rumbling from his beak. "Go away."

Ridley stiffened. "You're under arrest for the murder of federal agents. Furthermore you're charged with assaulting and interfering with said agents in the execution of their duty."

Drake snorted. Smoke curled from his nostrils.

"I'm serious." Ridley glowered.

He considered the man. Fear wafted off of him, sharp and spicy, underlaid by a note of sword steel. The scent of air magic wafted out of every exhaled breath. He'd testified in Jedediah's defense. He'd helped Jordan. *He's a good man. He doesn't deserve to die.*

"Agent," Drake said. "I'm not subject to your laws."

"No one is above the law. Come quietly, you'll...," Ridley trailed off.

"Get a fair trial?" Drake asked. "How would that work?"

Conflicting emotions orbited the Agent on winds of his inner turmoil. Fire suffused them as the Agent's voice hardened. "You *murdered* my people."

"Not me alone, but that doesn't matter. I'm sorry you lost people you cared about, but I'm not sorry for killing them to defend Jordan."

"You admit it," Ridley said.

"Why wouldn't I? I'm outside your laws, well, that's not even true. I'm above your laws because you fall under mine and my kind. We are the supreme law in this world," Drake said.

"God is the highest law."

Drake considered Ridley's scent. The absolute conviction. Jedediah had spoken little of divine magic, but he had included it in the complicated model describing the many magics in the world. Drake didn't know everything, hard as it was to admit the difficult lesson learned in Jedediah's absence.

"I cannot restore your people to life. You cannot drag me into one of your courts. I—"

"Watch me," Ridley tightened up on his pistol grip. "Lay on the ground with your limbs where I can see them."

Drake rolled his eyes. "This is stupid. You can't handcuff me. They won't even fit."

"Do it."

"I've got more important things to do." Drake turned his back.

Ridley leapt atop of him. Drake snarled and whirled. The FBI agent clung on, arms locked beneath Drake's chin. He whipped his tail into Ridley's side. The agent grunted, and the smell of blood joined the breeze. Explosions of sound deafened Drake, pain lancing along his scales with a tailwind of gunfire.

Drake bucked and spun, whipping his tail.

Ridley locked legs around him. "I'm sorry to do this, but justice is justice."

He brought an arm back and fired bullets point blank into the scales between Drake's shoulders. Pain shot through him as bullets perforated one lung and his flame lung. Heat seared Drake, flaring from each wheezed exhale.

Drake threw himself over, landing atop the agent with all his weight. More gunfire punctuated the air, bullets ripping wing and a lucky—or unlucky—bullet spearing through one talon. He roared with pain and rolled.

Ridley lost his grip somewhere in the roll. The combatants managed their feet, a magazine falling to the ground and replaced with inhuman speed.

They circled.

Drake blew flame, but his damaged lungs failed to push it fast enough. Ridley rolled out of the path and fired three shots.

A car crunched up the drive. Jordan threw herself clear before it stopped. "Stop! Don't hurt him."

Drake didn't ask which him she meant. *This isn't any of her business.*

He filled his limbs with magic, sinking into wind's speed as he had with the Road Dragons. He lunged, slashing a talon. Ridley leapt clear with only shredded suit shirt and shallow tears from the razor-sharp, serrated claws. He shot Drake twice more, two hits to the high left chest.

"Stop! Stop!" Jordan screamed. A wall of stone shot out of the ground between them.

Drake put all his power into a leap, flapping torn wings for enough lift to clear the barrier and drove Ridley into the ground. The semiautomatic flew from Ridley's grasp. Another gun barked fire into Drake's stomach.

Drake tilted his head and opened his jaws.

"Please," Jordan sobbed. "Don't do this to me. Please, Drake, not again."

"Drake?" Crystal appeared from around the greenhouse.

All fire vanished within Drake, quenched by the pain in her

voice and the curdled milk scent pouring off her like a flash flood. He held his strike.

"Dear God," Meadow said. "Jedediah's dog is a dragon? You weren't making any of it up, were you?"

Drake turned toward them in time to see Jordan's ivory face shift left to right and back. He looked down at the man beneath his talons. One squeeze would disembowel him. One bite would take his head.

He hurt, but no anger heated his core. "You're a fool, Agent. You should be a dead fool, but I won't make Jordan or Crystal watch me kill you."

Anguish filled Ridley's words and Drake's nostrils. "You have to pay for what you did. They deserve their killer brought to justice."

The almost silent hum of the barrier's power hiccupped.

Jedediah's willful hut sprang up onto chicken legs with a squawk. It tore across the fields as fast as its feet could take it, terrified clucking noises fading with astonishing rapidity.

"Did that hut just run away?" Meadow asked.

Distance wings beat massive amounts of air. Drake's head shot up to see his mother's silhouette flying their way from the horizon.

"Get behind me," Drake leapt off of Ridley. "Stay with Jordan. Don't speak."

He drew on the Dragon Springs and ideas only newly considered. He pushed shape change magic into his injuries, reshaping damaged flesh into whole with skull-splitting pain.

Stormfall landed with a resounding boom, a hurricane of wind ripping up the ground as she back-winged to a stop.

Drake lowered his head. *Mother.*

<Child, I see you've prepared morsels to replenish my strength.> Stormfall stepped toward the group of humans.

Drake stepped into her path. *These are not for you.*

<You ask for my help and then refuse to share your meal?>

They are not my lunch.

<Is not your blood on that one marked by your talons?>

Training.

"Drake, what's going on?" Crystal asked.

Stormfall whirled to the solitary girl. Her voice thundered through the area. *<Not DRAKE, petulant kine.>*

Everyone but Drake crumpled to their knees under the assault of her mind. He darted in between Stormfall and Crystal, barely covering the girl with his wings before Stormfall's teeth snapped her up.

No!

<No? You dare tell me no?>

These are not kine. They are not meat for your belly.

Stormfall's massive teeth snapped at him. Her house-sized jaw could've snapped both Crystal and him up in a single mouthful. *<I decide what fills my belly and no one else.>*

These are not for you, Mother. I will hunt you meat enough to fill your stomach, but not these.

<I hunger for human.> She showed her teeth in a menacing grin. *<Mageling.>*

"Go to Jordan," Drake whispered. His frills bristled, and he puffed himself up.

Before he or Crystal could do anything, Stormfall slammed a talon into Drake. He flew into the farmhouse ruin. Crystal squeaked.

Stormfall licked her lips. *<Delicious little mouse.>*

Drake shook off his disorientation, gathering feet beneath to leap to Crystal's defense.

A pillar of stone shot out of the ground into Stormfall's beak, slamming it shut. "Leave her alone."

Stormfall's eyes narrowed, hatred focused on Jordan. Dragon-fear swamped them all. She stalked toward the group

Jordan whitened, fists tight enough to cut into her apparently armored palms. "Leave her be."

"Jordan," Drake shook his head, but too late.

Flame the width of a highway streamed out of Stormfall's maw. Drake's heart leapt into his throat. He pushed it with all the wind he could summon, knowing that it would be too little too late. The wind curled her flame, revealing a wall of melting, molten mud and the stone elemental holding it upright.

Stormfall charged forward. One talon swept the elemental and her shield into the farmhouse ruin. The next sent Jordan flying into the parked cars.

Mother, stop, please.

<They dared strike an Elder Fey. All will die who witnessed this crime.>

Drake leapt onto her back and sank talons into her scales. The thick hide resisted his claws. She whirled, her tail sweeping his position. Drake leapt it and dug claws in once more, teeth latching onto a wing joint.

Stormfall roared. *<Worthless, petulant failure, you'll learn a lesson once and for all.>*

Sarah, her siblings and her older children rose out of the ground. They bit and harried her, disappearing into the ground to leave her uselessly gouging earth to hit them.

Stop this, please, Mother. I don't want to hurt you.

Stormfall roared and leapt to wing. From the height, Drake saw Jordan crumpled at a wrong angle in the back of one old truck. The sight wrung all the blood from his heart. She blew fire across the circular drive, catching several mudpuppies in the flames.

She shook Drake from her back before he could determine if the fires had slain any of Sarah's family. A massive talon chased him through the air. Drake slipped sideways, rolling around it only for a second to slam him downward. He caught the wind and furiously beat upward. Stormfall dove toward him.

Drake dodged, but Stormfall's tail slammed into him as if she'd know exactly where he'd wanted to be. He recovered, pushing shape change magic into the rent scales and diving across her back to rake her wings.

She flipped midair. Her talons snapped in on him from either side. He slipped her grip by diminutive size and pure luck. Climb and slash, dive and rake, Stormfall caught him over and over, tearing flesh from him faster than he could shift it back. Her talon shattered one wing.

Drake tumbled a crazy spiral, drawing magic like a desert absorbed rain. He repaired it and caught wind in time to see his mother dive, wings folded tight They flipped out for a moment, whipping her around herself. Her tail slammed into him, spikes bigger than his limbs slicing scales from his either side.

The force of the blow drove him to the ground. Bones and pain exploded much as they had during Muler's attack.

Stormfall slammed into the ground, her rear talons and tail smashing a greenhouse. She lowered her beak and opened her mouth. *<I only wish I could've fed you to your replacement.>*

Her head snapped upward, roaring in pain.

"Get off my student," Jedediah said.

Hope surged through Drake at Jedediah's voice. He drew power in to repair himself, but it resisted, coming in only a barely sustaining trickle—as if he'd become saturated. The old man stood on the edge of the porch, little more than a grizzled skeleton in swallowing robes.

<No one tells me what to do, wizard, least of all you.>

Jedediah uncupped his hands. Something tiny flashed past Drake. Stormfall screamed. Her blood sprayed tiny geysers around him.

<How dare you assault me?>

"This is my land. Drake is my pupil," Jedediah rasped. "I protect what's mine. Back off, Stormfall. I do not want to war with you just because you're set on being stupid."

<He's mine.> Her jaws snapped downward. The tiny object rocketed across the space, lancing between her nostrils and exploding blood out the bottom of her jaw.

"Get off my land," Jedediah said. "If you don't want the lazy lizard anymore, I claim him."

Stormfall's neck arched back. Her chest swelled. Drake tried to call out a warning, but before his Mother unleashed her fire, a Dodge Ram slammed into the side of her face.

"I said get," Jedediah snarled. "Don't make me kill you, Elder."

Stormfall threw herself into the air. *<This isn't over, kine.>*

"Y'all come back if'n you want another tail whooping."

<Keep the wretched child. I have another.> She flew toward the horizon.

Drake's eyes closed, opening a moment later to find his mother out of sight.

Meadow rushed to the porch. "Oh, my God, Jedediah. She was...and you...but how...Jedediah?"

His master collapsed like a stringless marionette. A moment later darkness took Drake too.

26

TRUTHS REVEALED

Jedediah woke to whispers and pain.

"Are you sure this is Jedediah?" Ridley asked.

"He might look like an extra from The Evil Dead, but that was Jedediah's voice coming from his lips," Meadow said.

"I can't argue. He needs a hospital, if not a morgue."

"You're not looking too healthy yourself, Agent."

"Potions," Jedediah rasped, unable to open his eyelids. "Where's Jordan?"

"Injured by that big dragon," Meadow said. "She won't come around."

"Drake?" Jedediah said.

"Same," Meadow said.

"Lanea?"

Jedediah's memory filled him with pain a moment before Ridley's whisper. "I saw her die, Mister Shine—unless you know something I don't."

He shook his head, exhausted by the effort. His voice barely managed a whisper. "Honey."

Meadow leaned closer. "Jedediah?"

He licked his lips. His connection to the Dragon Springs felt wide open but scorched and cracked liked a dried riverbed. He drew a sip off whoever's hands touched him, adding it to his voice. "Honey."

He heard the buzzing before the two huddled over him reacted. Bees arrived first in ones and twos that became a swarm. Meadow slapped back and forth in a defensive retreat, helping the injured agent away.

Jedediah felt them on his cracked lips, tiny motes of sweet stroked across his dry tongue. He swallowed tiny deposits of raw honey.

"They're swarming him," Meadow said. "What do we do?"

"I think…nothing," Ridley said. "I believe that they're feeding him."

Jedediah's stomach recoiled, cramping at the foreign invasion. He rolled, retching and curling into a ball. The stream of bees returned the moment he stopped. For an eternity, he ate honey and vomited most of it back up, but strength crept into him—disgorged one bee at a time.

"Mason?" Jedediah forced his eyes open.

"Billie Jo's son? Why do you need him?" Meadow asked.

"My shack. He can find it," Jedediah said.

"It ran away when the dragon showed up."

"The shack ran away?" Ridley asked.

Jedediah grunted. Weakness crippled him, leaving him barely able to stay conscious, but Stormfall wouldn't stay away forever. Drake and Jordan needed him, as did the injured FBI agent.

"Those are talon blows," Jedediah said.

"Drake's." Ridley's jaw tightened. He looked toward the injured, unconscious dragon. "He killed my people. I came out here to bring him to justice."

"Bad idea," Jedediah said. "Worse timing. Help me sit."

Meadow helped him up. "Dear God, Jedediah, you nothing but bones. What happened to you?"

I tried to die.

Jedediah searched Ridley's eyes. "I can help you, help all of us, but only if you can keep it off the record—and stay away from Drake."

The man's expression hardened, but as with so many encounters, a storm raged behind his eyes. "I'm on extended leave."

"Your word. Man to man."

Ridley looked at Drake.

"I'll help," Meadow said.

Jedediah shook his head once. "He'll see too much. Can't endanger others."

"I won't harm the innocent," Ridley said at last.

Jedediah thought through sluggish pathways. He knew the agent to be honorable, but he also knew by his words that he'd not quit his claim on Drake. Jedediah struggled to rise. Meadow helped him to his feet.

"I need to get to the boneyard."

"Weems is gone," a small voice said.

He turned toward it to find a mousey girl on the precipice of womanhood. "Who are you?"

"C-Crystal, Jordan's foster sister. You have to help her."

Jedediah reached out to cup her bruised face. She flinched back from skeletal fingers. "I'm trying, little one. Help me to the boneyard. I have no strength."

"Do you need food?" Crystal asked.

"He can't keep anything down," Meadow said.

"Milk maybe?" Jedediah asked.

The girl vanished ahead of them. They followed, the trip exhausting his reserves. Despite the shallow cuts on his chest, the FBI agent flagged worse than Jedediah did. He collapsed just as Jedediah pointed to a pile of toilets.

Meadow helped him down and returned for Ridley. "He needs a hospital. You both do."

"Beauregard," Jedediah rasped.

"Pardon?"

Crystal appeared with a half-gallon of milk and a glass. She poured some and offered it. Jedediah took it, but it fell from his fingers.

She picked it back up, added more milk and lifted it to his lips. "Here."

Sweet and cold, it soothed his throat, simultaneously like liquid lead in his gut. "Beauregard. Rent's due."

Meadow and Crystal made a sound when the old brownie poked his head into view. "This better be important."

Jedediah didn't have the strength to grumble or roll his eyes and Ridley didn't look like he had the time. "Quick as wind, fetch Waphri Ah'Raemyn."

"Wind's not my thing," Beauregard said.

Jedediah growled.

The brownie slipped into the ground.

"Did it, I mean he just?" Meadow said. "Is he going to help?"

"Yup." Jedediah closed his eyes. A glass pressed to his lips. He sipped twice. Consciousness faded from him. He awoke to find Waphri Ah'Raemyn and a young brown filly tending him.

"Help the others, WaphRae."

A white-bodied mare smiled at him. Silver-white braid framed her face—feathers and polished stones swaying side to side. "We already have. What have you done to yourself, *Feihtor Ah Mythe-la'Raemyn?*"

"Nothing."

She pursed her lips, nodding. "You must be tended. It will take long weeks to recover your strength."

"Ain't got time for that, been out of things too long as is. Where are my clocks?" He asked.

No one answered.

"Well, who the heck cleared out the den?" Jedediah asked.

"Rydari Phriel was moved to our camp," the younger centaur said. "And the injured normal took Jordan back to incarceration."

"What's she doing incarcerated?" Jedediah asked.

The young woman who'd brought him milk raised a hand. She spoke when his attention shifted to her. "She defended me from Arthur. Mistress pressed assault charges."

"Who're you, girl? Who's your Mistress? And what's she doing letting normals police us?"

"Um, Crystal?"

"Right, sorry for not remembering."

Crystal smiled. "Mistress is Mae Bridgeport. That's what she makes us call her, but she's our foster mom."

Jedediah chuckled. "Bet Jordan liked that. She's not a wizard I take it?"

"No, thank God. No offense, sir."

"You just call me Jedediah, little one."

"We will bring you to our camp," WaphRae said. "Drake and your other apprentice are already there."

"What other apprentice?"

"Kane," the young centaur said. "Best friend to Rydari Phriel."

Jedediah opened his mouth, but WaphRae spoke first. "This is my acolyte, Chieru E'Riel."

"ChiRie," ChiRie said. "If *Feihtor Ah Mythela'Raemyn* would honor me."

"I don't recall having an apprentice named Kane—unless Drake or Jordan decided to take students while I was gone." Jedediah frowned. "Mauve had a boy, name might've been Kane."

"Come with us, and you may see for yourself," WaphRae said.

"I can't come," Crystal said. "Mistress will beat me if she finds out I'm not locked in the cellar. I've been away for too long as it is."

Jedediah struggled to his feet. "You've disobeyed your mother, girl?"

Crystal nodded. "Jordan said it was okay if I sat this side of the portal."

"Why'd she tell you a damn fool thing like that?"

"Easy, Jedediah," Meadow said.

"I-I...I'm c-claustrophobic."

He darkened. "Tell me true, girl. Don't lie to me."

"I'm n-not lying," Crystal sobbed. "I s-swear."

"She's not," ChiRie said. "They discussed Crystal's illness in my presence."

"I hear truth's chime," WaphRae said.

His fingers prickled, tiny tingles wreathing his hands. "I got no problem with taking a child over my knee when the occasion calls, but if she's locking a claustrophobic in a cellar and beats you if you flee your terror, your mistress and I are going to have words in short order."

"She doesn't like being told what to do," Crystal said.

"I don't like child abuse." Jedediah turned to ChiRie. "You go with this girl and layer a glamour only she can see."

WaphRae tone hardened. "Jedediah."

Jedediah rolled his eyes. He performed a painful, elaborate bow. "Waphri Ah'Raemyn, for the love of this sweet child, send your apprentice to do as I asked…please?"

WaphRae inclined her head, and the two youngsters headed for the boneyard. "That wasn't so hard, now was it?"

"Gorram nag," Jedediah grumbled.

§

Mason checked the small locker room to ensure he was the last. He changed out of the sweaty, second-hand gi and wrapped a fresh towel around his slick skin. He entered the shower cubicle and hung the towel over the frosted door to further obscure his nakedness.

Hot water sluiced over warm muscles only just starting to ache. Martial arts didn't look that hard, but repetition after repetition of unfamiliar moves left his arms almost too heavy to lift. He cleaned up slowly, washing his hair with the bar soap in the stall.

He'd have to sneak the gi into the laundry, but his body would be cleanish after the sweltering walk home. He dressed in his street clothes, restored his casts, balled the gi and exited right into Sensei Yves.

"Oh, sorry."

She glowered down at him.

"Sensei."

"I don't like you," she said. "You're lazy and well behind the class."

"I-I just started." He studied her super serious expression. *She's screwing with me. It's like an initiation or something, to prove I'm tough.*

"I'll get better," Mason said. "Good enough to kick your butt, Sensei."

"I'd kill you."

"Elaine? Mason?" Sensei Truth said. "Problem?"

"No, Sensei," Mason said. "I bumped into Sensei Yves coming out of the locker room. It was all my fault."

"Fault's not important, Mason. How about you come up front with me, and we'll drill you a bit more," Truth said. "Catch you up."

"I'd like to, really, I appreciate it, but I just cleaned up, and besides I have to get home," Mason said.

"Need a ride, son?"

"No, thanks though." Mason exited through the front door, bell ringing as it shut. He glanced back to see Sensei Truth pressing Sensei Yves against the wall. *Guess she's irritated because I was keeping them from making out.*

❧

Jordan sulked in a corner of the common area. Other girls chatted, glared or otherwise banded together for mutual protection and entertainment. A small group clustered around an ancient television behind steel grating.

Her shoulders started to relax, but she focused on her anger to strengthen the sulk. Letting herself relax meant thinking about Arthur's unknown fate and her attempt to kill him.

A thick-limbed girl with a buzz cut approached her. "What're you in for?"

"Assault." Jordan shrugged. "Maybe attempted murder."

The girl smiled. "You don't look that tough."

Jordan started to roll her eyes but took a moment to examine the other girl instead. *She's me. An ogre smacking people around because she can't get anything else in her life to work.*

"What're you looking at?"

Jordan turned her hand over, concentrating on the rock in her palm. It didn't move, despite her assault on Stormfall with a column of the stuff hours before.

The other girl slapped the rock from her palm. "I'm talking to you."

"I was just thinking. Don't worry, you're tougher than me—queen of the hill. You've got nothing to fear from me."

"If I'm tougher, you have to do what I say."

Jordan met her gaze. "If that's how it works, then we'll have to see who's really tougher."

She slapped a fist into her palm. "Bring it on."

Jordan stood, drawing on her magic to armor her. The girl slugged her. Jordan waited. The next hit slammed into her jaw.

"Man, Terra's the coolest," one of the television watchers said. "She's got the coolest powers."

The body blow drove the air from Jordan's lungs. She doubled over in pain The ogre girl hopped around, gesturing at Jordan. "Third time's the charm. Knew I was tougher than you."

Jordan ignored her, pushing the girl to one side as she moved closer to the television. A cartoon about superhero kids played behind the metal.

A hand whirled Jordan around. "You have to do what I—"

Jordan's palm knocked the other girl head over heels and into the far wall. "Later, I want to see this."

She slid into a seat near the television. "Is she moving earth around?"

"Yeah," the Terra fan said.

"With magic?"

"It's her superpower."

"Is she floating on a rock?" Jordan asked.

"Cool, right?"

"Her power's Earth. She's floating, that's air. How is that even possible?"

The other girl shrugged. "Gravity? That's Earth, right?"

Another of the girls shifted her smile from the television to Jordan. "This is cool, but if you like element stuff you've got to watch Avatar."

"That cartoon is for little kids," the first complained.

The second shrugged. "Still cool."

Jedediah took another sip of WaphRae's sludge, the peppery flavor intensified by its sharp aroma. Magic trickled back into him almost as if uncertain of its welcome. He scrutinized Fleet Hoof's two unexpected guests. They'd been prohibited from leaving, Fleet Hoof's elders weathering Ridley's objections about false imprisonment with good graces.

On the one hand, the FBI agent had a touch of magic. That inheritance came with a right to see the world where it originated. On the other, he worked for the same government Jedediah feared might show up with mobile dissection teams and harm his Fey charges. Meadow was as normal as they came despite her mad witch persona at Renaissance fairs. She had no right to see beyond being Jedediah's family. Just the same, she'd never tell others.

He lurched to his feet, his staff appearing in a flash to help him rise. "Y'all are here, and you might be tempted to tell others what you've seen. That's a problem."

"Planning to imprison us indefinitely?" Ridley asked

"No. I'm planning on giving you the whole E-ticket." Jedediah's gaze bit into Ridley's. "I'm going to show you what's really going on, why what I do is so important and why people murdered to steal away my property."

Jedediah took hold of the reading glasses hanging on a chain around Meadow's neck, infusing them with magic. The spell fought him, but in the end, he handed back lenses which let her see true. Ridley offered his glasses. Jedediah shook his head.

"You've got the gift, Agent, so with your permission, I'll turn up the volume so to speak to help you."

"Agent Ridley's a wizard?" Meadows asked.

"He's got a whisper of the gift. Even untrained, it helps him see and notice things better than other agents. See what others miss." Jedediah smiled at Meadow. "I've met few normals with as much romance and magic in their hearts as you, Meadow, but your blood's got about as much magic as beer in a college dorm keg Monday morning."

"And if I refuse?"

Can I trust him if he doesn't see it all? I could work a seeing on his glasses, but I want him to understand that he's connected to this world.

"Then you refuse," Jedediah said. "I ain't going to shove magic down your throat. You're not a strong enough talent that I'm responsible to teach you."

"Teach, like wizard schools?" Ridley asked

Jedediah barked laughter. "What is it with law enforcement and that damned book? No, Agent, like Merlin and his apprentices."

"Merlin was real?"

"How should I know?" Jedediah asked. "I look that old to you?"

Both replied in unison. "Yes."

Meadow continued. "How old are you really?"

"Four hundred and twelve."

Her expression shifted, disbelief hard in her eyes.

"You remember when we first met?"

"When I first opened up my stand at the Georgia Renfest," Meadow said.

Jedediah shook his head. "You were seven. You told me it was your first time at a Renaissance fair. I gave you a little necklace."

Meadows eyes shifted out of focus. "A North star, but that can't have been you. That man looked...."

"Ancient?" Jedediah asked.

"You're immortal?" Ridley asked.

"No. I live longer, but not forever. My clocks let me change which age I am. It's a rather complicated mix of life magic and chronomancy."

They stared at him.

"Is it so hard to believe after what you've already seen?"

"This could be an elaborate scheme," Ridley said.

"To what end? No, I give you my warrant that you'll get nothing but truth from me—possibly more than you can accept. Follow me."

Jedediah led them into the woods.

"Jedediah, this isn't one of those tell us and have to kill us things, is it? You're not leading us to some blood sacrifice to Satan or anything like that?"

"Meadow, how long have you known me?" Jedediah asked.

"That's a bit close to asking a lady her age," Meadow said. "Besides, the polite agent wasn't going to ask."

"Infernals are generally a bunch of selfish, arrogant bastards, and I've got no truck with bending knee—especially to their lot."

"The Devil is real?" Meadow asked.

"He is indeed," Ridley said.

"No, I mean, Jedediah, have you…met him?" Meadow asked.

"Not the kind of company I generally keep."

Shadowcats slunk into view on either side, pacing them from shadow to shadow. Bright lights flickered behind leaf, branch and stick bugs the deeper they got into the wood—only the bravest pixies staying visible for more than a heartbeat.

Meadow tried to approach one of the cats, jerking back a hand when it barred sharp teeth. A low growl followed into shadow, fading slower than the cat itself.

"They're not kittens, Meadow."

"You're a dog person, so obviously you wouldn't understand."

Skeptical and awed silences filled Jedediah's wood. Meadow's gaze flitted from point to point almost as much as the darting sprites. Ridley watched, his expression reserved. He started with basic questions typical of skeptics when faced with what they couldn't explain. Jedediah answered, reigning in his patience and explaining until Ridley seemed momentarily satisfied. He'd seen Stormfall, but a stubbornness Jedediah commonly attributed to terramancers stiffened his spine when it came to the magical world —right up until a flurry of sprites kissed him in a giggling chain of land and fly pecks.

Ridley's shoulders eased. His expression brightened.

Jedediah stopped them. He narrowed his Sight at the FBI agent, checking to see if the pixies had dusted him with enthralling or mischievous magics.

"Something wrong?" Ridley asked.

"Nope."

27

TYING LOOSE ENDS

Ridley followed Jedediah as he continued down a rabbit path. Cats in shadow and delicate pixies the size of pecans —some in a kind of bark armor—circled them. Larger fairies about the size of Skipper dolls peeked behind leaves or swung on silvery Spanish moss. None of which made sense against everything he'd ever learned, but just the same he couldn't dismiss the truth of his unaugmented eyes.

They strolled deeper into the woods, coming to twin oaks leaning together. Jedediah gestured to the few lurking Fey. "I am Guardian, and beyond dwell my charges. Woe to any who threaten or bring them harm."

Jedediah stepped through the arch made by the two trees vanishing from sight. Meadow rushed to follow. Ridley stepped up to the tree, setting a hand on its bark. He stroked it, feeling a tiny tingle like an electromagnetic field.

A stick bug poked its head out of a knot. Ridley noted its human-like limbs and realized it wasn't an insect at all. It peered down at him, cocking its head before shaking a fist and clicking angrily at him.

A face slid from the bark above his hand, beauty carved in pale wood by a master's master. Moss clung to her head in a pixie cut, framing a bright smile and chocolaty eyes. Her body slid fluidly out of the tree, one breast obscured by his hand.

He snapped it back. "Sorry."

A playful pout shaped her lips into a mahogany heart. "You'd prefer my bark? You won't enjoy it nearly so much as—"

"As your bite?" Ridley asked.

She curled her strategically moss covered body against his. "As the smooth touch bestowed upon those that love the wood."

Ridley smiled. *Talk about tree hugging.*

<You've no idea, lover.>

Ridley jerked away from her, but rather than be offended she let out a musical laugh that tingled his entire body.

Jedediah appeared once more. "Should I leave you with Dixee, Agent?"

"No, charming though she is."

Ridley followed Jedediah through the tree arch guarded by Dixee's sultry defenses. A world of light and color exploded as if he'd stepped into Oz or Willy Wonka's factory. Scallop mushrooms climbed trees at either side in pastel stair steps. Entire pixie communities swarmed through the fungal high-rises, laughing children playing a high-speed tag trailing neon rainbows.

The children's game turned abruptly toward Jedediah. They tittered greetings and questions.

A larger pink one landed on Ridley's nose. Her glow faded to reveal a tiny winged fairy the size of his thumbnail. "Did you bring candy too?"

"Um, no?" Ridley said.

She scrutinized him a moment with hands perched on her dainty hips, inhaling deeply. She gave him a bright smile, kissed his nose and flew off giggling.

"My God, it's all so beautiful," Meadow said.

A cheer squad's worth of adolescent pixies darted in out of nowhere with the little pink pixie. They landed on Ridley's shoulders and looked dreamily up at him. Another landed on his head, her upside down face smiling into one eye.

Jedediah cleared his throat, one hand open. "I do."

Pixies and sprites reoriented on the pile of Lemonheads, M&Ms and cinnamon imperials. Countless trails of blazing color dive-bombed Jedediah. In moments, his hand had emptied of all but a pitiful looking green pixie with tears in her eyes.

"Aw, poor thing," Meadow said.

Jedediah smiled at the little Fey. "Darling, I'm pretty sure if you asked that lady over there, she's got a bit of candy tucked behind one ear."

The pixie whirled toward Meadow.

Meadow reached up to her ear.

"I don't have...," She drew out a Lemonhead.

The pixie eyed her warily for perhaps two seconds and dove for the candy. The tiny thing hugged it kissing Meadow's thumb and the huge yellow candy in turns.

Jedediah passed her a Ziploc bag of candy. "Just put a few on your palm, not too many though or you'll be swarmed."

Meadow dropped a few candies on her palm and extended it. Pixies came from every direction, taking candy and kissing her in thanks.

Meadow giggled. "It's kind of like those butterfly exhibits where you bring them nectar."

"Yup."

Three gnomes clustered together on a pile of rocks vaguely body-shaped. Smoke curled from their pipes. One by one they took pipes from their teeth to salute the group. The last clenched the stem in his teeth and addressed Jedediah. "Come for a game of Grotch?"

"Not this trip, Cognas," Jedediah said.

"Can't beat me if you don't practice."

"Doubt I'll ever be able to beat you."

The gnome nodded. "True. True."

Jedediah touched fingers to his head and led them on into various avenues within the wood. They strolled through colonies of Fey, gnome and fairy, brownie and oakmite. They encountered more centaur and dryad. Everywhere they went, the Fey treated the old farmer with courtesy and respect—many going so far as to bow.

Two lean, beautiful figures stepped in front of Meadow, cutting her off from the glowing flower garden tended by a pair of doll-sized fairies.

Meadow gasped.

Grace swept up their features like a perfumed wind, bending flesh to perfection and stretching their ears to points. Bright eyes flashed and noses wrinkled.

"What are you doing here, *normal?*" the taller elf asked.

"They're with me, Thestle," Jedediah said.

The elf stiffened. After an instant's hesitation, both swept around in a flourished bow, silver-green silken garb fluttering and long, flaxen hair falling to hide inclined faces.

They spoke in unison. "Guardian."

"What're you boys doing on my land?"

"They're boys?" Meadow asked.

Jedediah smirked.

"Thestle and I have leave to traverse these woods."

"Not from me you don't, Chalet."

Ridley swept his gaze back and forth. Both elves rose, their jaws tight and words held back. They covered with smiles they didn't mean. *They're afraid of him, and they don't like it.*

"Rydari Phriel," Chalet said.

"An Elder Lord of Fey," Thestle added.

"And my apprentice. These lands ain't his to grant passage."

"They're Mother's," Thestle said. "He is Mother's chosen."

Jedediah moistened his lips. "They are Mother's, yet it's my strength that guards these borders and my job to decide who travels them."

"A job you left forsaken," Chalet said.

"I grieved your cousin, but I left protections in place," Jedediah said.

"The half-breed was a distant cousin at best," Thestle said.

"And holes riddle your protections," Chalet said. "Perhaps age catches you, Wizard."

Jedediah's face darkened and with it, the day's light waned. The air thickened. Hair along Ridley's skin rose, and little sparks seemed to cling to Jedediah. Fey scattered in all directions. Thunder rumbled, and dark clouds rushed in to fill the clear sky.

Ridley stepped forward, drawing Meadow back from coming conflict. His motion drew the elves' attention.

Thestle shook his head. "Why bring normals and near normals into this sanctuary? Don't you recall how they treated your kin?"

"White man's sins rest on the perpetrators, not their children. I've trusted these because they've earned it."

"And if they betray you like they did your tribes?" Thestle asked.

Tribes? White man? He's... Ridley tried to fit Jedediah's reported age into historic terms. Unease crept into him as the number settled. *He lived through the slaughters. The forced relocations.*

"You know full well, youngster, if you heeded your elders. Which begs the question, what're you doing on my land without permission?"

"We depart, offering no offense. May your grief wane and your days brighten. Good day."

They continued on through the colors and light of the Fey world. Homes and artistic works, inhabitants and plants, a creator's joyful brush painted everything. More candy brought he and Meadow close examination of diverse clothing and wing designs. They met creatures never described in fairy tale.

No wordsmith could've done them justice.

Earth Fey in dozens of shapes kept a respectful distance, some barely more than pebbles and others cousins to the Jolly Green Giant. Tiny campfire mote sprites Jedediah called rexies flew swarming sorties, only one landing on them and burning Meadow's nose. Ponds and streams offered figures of sculpted water and half-height, liquid versions of Dixee—dewdrops and naiads respectively. Air Fey in many flavors rushed to greet Jedediah and Ridley, most interested in candy but some lingering as if being near them granted some intangible gift.

Jedediah led them from a grove. Sunlight cast beams of light in the rustling leaves, but the light seemed washed out. Ridley glanced behind them. Forest replaced fairyland they'd only just departed.

"We're outside it now?" Ridley asked.

Jedediah nodded, scratching his beard. "A single small refuge, and one for gentler Fey. There are many more, some protecting far more powerful creatures from humanity."

"Why hide them?" Meadow asked. "They're so beautiful."

"Remember the Indians," Ridley said. "Think about zoos and circuses, butterfly museums. As a species, we have no respect for life, even our own."

"So Guardians protect and hide the Fey."

Meadow frowned but didn't argue.

Ridley glanced back once more, a sense of loss he'd experienced before. His voice wavered more than he wanted. "Saw photos of a beautiful reef full of color and life once. It was so fantastic I took a special trip there."

"How was it?" Meadow asked.

"Nothing like I'd hoped. It'd seemed subdued as if the photographer had brightened his pictures."

"No," Jedediah said. "Vision is akin to air magic. The pictures would've seemed crisp and vibrant. Seeing the reef through water would've hampered your sight a fraction."

Ridley gestured back the way they'd come. "What you protect...I could never have imagined it existed anywhere in our world. It has to be protected."

"It's not all Tinkerbelle and cotton candy, Agent. Those bodies you dug up all over, they weren't my doing—outside the burying. They were normals run afoul of the Fey."

Ridley considered it. Sharks killed, alligators and bears too. There was no way to tell if the bodies dug up had belonged to innocent or deserving. There was nothing to do about it now—well, almost nothing.

"Do you protect us too?" Ridley asked. "Try to keep these Fey from hurting regular people?"

Jedediah's tone hardened. "Of course, I do. What do you think I am? Some unfeeling monster? It tore my heart when that son-of-a-bitch and his idiots killed Ronnie Gerald. The man had a family to feed, little ones that'll have no memory of their Da."

"Ronnie Gerald was one of the deaths we couldn't connect to the *Namhaid*." Ridley narrowed his eyes. "You know who killed him."

"I do. They've been dealt with for now—at least to the extent I could."

"Give them to me. I'll see them imprisoned at the very least."

"Aren't you paying attention to what he's been trying to show you?" Meadow asked. "This is a world of magic, fantastic things that can do what we'd never dream. Jedediah said he dealt with them best he could, which means they weren't human like us."

"She's right. You haven't the knowledge or prisons to hold these bastards. Some people died because of a Fey temper tantrum."

"The others died because the *Namhaid* wanted to steal all this," Ridley said.

"In a way," Jedediah said. "It was about a specific piece of land, but all this would have come to harm."

"You led us to those you could, in person unless I misjudged Agent Pine."

Jedediah smiled.

"You assembled all this land using your magic? Fairy gold for hospital bills, cars and houses?" Ridley asked.

"Nah, gold's real."

"Where'd it come from?"

"I can make it, Agent," Jedediah said. "From dirt."

"Then why do you live in that old farmhouse and not some mansion?" Meadow asked.

Jedediah bristled. "I like my farmhouse."

"Be that way," Meadow said.

"Yup."

"Children?" Ridley said.

"Now you know who we are," Jedediah said. "I'd like your help. Jordan needs taken out of your foster system and given over to my care. No normal parents are going to be able to teach her what she needs to know so that she's not a danger to others."

"Is she that much of a danger?" Meadow asked. "She seems sweet enough—for a teenager."

"She's got a solid talent despite her learning troubles. She needs teaching."

"I'll consider it," Ridley said.

Ridley stared at Jordan's records. A few keystrokes would remove her from both trouble and the foster system. Jedediah's request stuck with him. He'd considered it. He sat before his computer considering it once more. The whys of the request made sense, but something about deleting a federal record just didn't sit well with him.

Our laws aren't equipped to handle this world—for now, but even so, Jordan or others like her just can't be exempt from those laws serving everyone's benefit. We'll all just adapt.

A window popped onto his computer screen. "Agent Benjamin Ridley: Report immediately to Director Laru, FBI Headquarters, Washington D. C."

Angesa arranged for the jelly-stained social services slob from the halfway house to drop Jordan off outside the school. He waited while she went inside and would be waiting—if he wasn't late again—to take her back to juvenile detention. It took a moment for the first student to recognize her, but the moment they did, an expanding wave of frozen motion rippled out from her.

She rolled her eyes and headed toward her locker.

I was only gone a week.

Motion resumed, but with it came a thousand whispers she could almost feel crawling across the back of her neck. She fetched her gear from the locker and turned straight into a dozen suddenly fleeing eyes.

Don't let it get to you, it's all just stupid adolescent gossip.

Jordan entered her class, passing by two girls huddled head down with their backs to her.

"I heard she gave him her V and then killed him for cheating on her."

Jordan froze.

Both girls looked up. Jenny turned away a pixie nose to match her blond hair. Teesh offered a guilty smile. "Hi, Jordan."

Jordan growled. "I would *never* sleep with Arthur."

Jenny turned back to them. "Okay, makes sense, but then why'd you kill him?"

Frustration spiced her tone. "I didn't kill him."

I hope he's still alive.

"Take your seats," Mister Dirk said.

Jordan hurried to her seat, trying to figure out her next maneuver while fending off sly glances and outright curiosity. She survived to lunch. Crystal jumped her from behind, saving herself from attack by speaking once she'd wrapped arms around. "Jordan, you're here. I thought they sent you to prison."

"Only kind of," Jordan said. "Juvie."

"I heard it was a real prison on account of you killing Arthur."

"I didn't kill Arthur, you were there," Jordan said.

"I saw what you...," Crystal faltered, her face reddening. "Hi, Mason."

Mason grinned at Jordan. "Welcome back. Heard you killed Arthur."

Jordan's tone lowered. "I didn't kill Arthur."

"Pity," Mason said. "He kind of deserves it. Holy shit...."

Jordan and Crystal followed Mason's attention. An ancient looking Jedediah hobbled across the lunch area in new overalls. Warmth spread through Jordan. Weeks ago, Nip had snuck into juvie and told her about Jedediah's return and all about how he'd saved her and Drake. She hadn't entirely believed until that moment. Her happiness faltered.

Where's he been all this time? She smiled. *It doesn't matter. He's here. I don't have to take care of everyone anymore. We all survived. It's all going to be okay now.*

Another flurry of movement stole her joy. Billie Jo stormed across the courtyard on an intercept course. They met mere feet away.

Jedediah's eyes softened. "It's good to see you, Billie Jo."

"You're not welcome on school property," Billie Jo said.

His jaw drew a hard line. He tapped his staff, a soft wind caressing Jordan's awareness. Jedediah turned around, letting Billie Jo escort him away while Billie Jo stared from Jedediah to the copy her own copy escorted away.

He turned to Jordan.

She leapt from her seat, tears tumbling as she embraced him.

He grunted. "Little looser, girl."

Jordan felt her face heat as she loosened her hold. Arms around him registered thin limbs and emaciated frame. Billie Jo grabbed her arms and pried her from him.

"You leave her alone, *Satanist*."

"She's hugging me." Jedediah ruffled Mason's hair. "How're you, boy?"

Billie Jo struck him. Her voice pitched to pixie range. "Don't touch him."

Mason glanced at his lunch. "Shit, it's going to be evil tuna all over again."

"Mason, language!"

Mason gestured. "He raised a glamour. No one's going to hear."

"I heard you, and how do you know...never mind." Billie Jo pointed. "Go to my classroom this moment."

"But, Mom, I'm hungry."

"You're not eating anything that came within five feet of this monster."

Mason looked up at Jedediah. The old man gave him a sympathetic smile and inclined his head slightly the direction his mother pointed.

Mason cradled his stomach and grumbled away. "Yup, evil tuna."

Jedediah took Mason's seat, an uncharacteristic relief on his face as he sat. "Jordan, girl, do you know where my clocks are?"

"I told you to go away," Billie Jo said. "Crystal, I want you to go—"

Crystal blinked up at Billie Jo. Jordan narrowed her eyes, a skin of magic glowing almost imperceptibly around her.

"You freeze her or something?" Jordan asked.

Jedediah looked at Billie Jo, expression somehow hard and soft at the same time. "I love the irritating bitch, but I don't have time. Where are my clocks?"

Stupidity welled up around her. "Oh, I'm so sorry, no wonder you look so old. They're in the Cheraw house's den. I moved them there to keep them safe."

Jedediah cupped her cheek. His wrinkled fingers felt cold, but warmth filled her. He'd tried to touch her the same way on their first meeting. She'd slapped his hand away and accused him of being some kind of freak. Jordan placed her own hand upon his.

"I'm so glad you're back."

"Yup," Jedediah whispered. "I meant to come back earlier, I swear I didn't abandon you, girl."

"I-I...," the lump in Jordan's throat slowed her reply. "I know... mostly. What's important is that you're here now. There's so much going on. We need you...I need you here so badly."

"Meadow made mention of something about Olympics?"

Jordan nodded.

Jedediah hugged her. "I'm so proud of you. We'll celebrate later. I've got to go grow down a bit."

Jordan's laugh stifled her tears.

"I'll be back before you know it."

She forced a mock glare. "You better."

He laughed, a warm, wonderful sound that proclaimed all right in the world.

Jedediah pulled up in an old dented pickup, surveying the address Meadow had given him. The large house and its yard looked immaculate, but something made his beard itch. He shifted his eyes but found no signs of magic that didn't feel like Jordan or her mudpuppies. He got out, glancing at the expensive cars in the open garage.

What's the point in a garage door if you're letting everyone see they can get at your car?

A woman stepped onto the front porch, pulling his attention away. She wore a simple dress reminiscent of those half a century before—though certainly not old enough to have been bought in the era. She scowled at him, an arm folded over its bandaged twin. "We already have lawn care. Leave this neighborhood. Nobody would offer work to someone like you."

Jedediah marched up the walk, a thick oppression he couldn't pinpoint in the air. "Guess it's a good thing I'm independently wealthy."

She snorted. "I asked you to leave."

"Actually, you didn't, and it doesn't matter much if you do. I've come to palaver regarding Jordan."

"Faye," Mae corrected.

Jedediah's brows rose. He stopped in front of her, forcing her to look up at him even though he stood a step below. "Jordan's—"

Mae's voice hardened. "Faye. You're the farmer, the murderer."

Jedediah pushed down rising temper rose. "Jordan's special to me. I'd take it as a kindness if you'd drop the charges against her so I can bring her home."

"She tried to murder my son."

"Jordan hasn't a killing bone in her body. If he got hurt, he had it coming."

"How dare you?"

"How dare *you*," he growled. He stopped, drawing in his anger once more. "That boy grabbed her in an inappropriate way."

"Lies and over exaggerations. He's not to blame," Mae pulled out her phone. "I'm calling the police."

Mae's phone sparked, flying from her hands when she flinched.

"I agree. It's not his fault. It's yours—and his Da's. In fact, boys with grabby hands lost one to a hatchet back when."

Mae stepped into Jedediah, jabbing a finger just above the bib of his overalls. "You are an uncouth, ignorant nothing. You've obviously no idea how to raise children. Faye assaulted Arthur, and she'll pay for it—one way or another. You can forget getting her back, hillbilly. Now get off my property."

Jedediah met her unflinching gaze. Hitting women wasn't appropriate, though her Da should've done the job in spades when she was young enough to bend over a knee. He stepped back from her. "I've asked you for a kindness. If you're thinking to do otherwise, that's your call and your consequence."

"Go away."

Jedediah turned back up the walk. He felt her gaze on his shoulders. He paused. "A piece of neighborly advice, don't push Jordan unless you want the bed next to your boy."

"She won't get the drop on me."

"She's not your only worry," Jedediah turned back, tipping his hat before returning to his truck.

❧

Jedediah dragged a battered and faded board game from the farmhouse ruin. He dusted it off, frowning at the scars left on the venerable box from exploding model case shrapnel. He tucked it under an arm, strode into the boneyard, and walked into the Cheraw farmhouse.

As promised, his clocks lined the bookshelves of the well-appointed den, tucked between leather-bound first editions from previous centuries. He scanned the clockworks. Each bore a design which symbolized the stage of life stored within its innards. A slightly bent key lay next to a leather chair and a copy of Harry Potter rested half read on its pages.

He picked up a clock decorated with gay colors, a baseball glove and bat. The décor fit seamlessly to the casual eye, but he knew the cracks and seams where he'd added handcrafted carvings atop his first rough clockwork. He set it down and replaced it with one covered in sailing ships—their rigging intricate. A scent of salt air wafted out of his memory. He heard gulls cry, waves splashed against hull and the pang of leaving his homeland behind for the Old World.

Its casing had been crafted of driftwood collected from British shores as he walked the western beaches longing for his tribe and forest during the few idle moments stolen from his apprenticeship. He turned it over, marking the tiny imperfections of his third clock and remembering the Dutchman's guiding hands and encouragements.

He brought clock and board game to the hand-crafted dining table. A smile touched his lips. He ran a hand over the old wood, crafted for Elsabeth in this their first real house. Their children had run across floors he'd laid with bare hands rather than magic, carpentry skills garnered during his apprenticeship with the Dutch clockmaker.

Thoughts of children long gone turned his mind to playful little Lanea and his smile vanished. He laid out the Risk game and brought magic to bare. He dropped a black square of wood into its Atlantic Ocean.

"*Artog il Terra, nal rieken tal moor.*"

The wooden square melted, forming first a skeleton and then a small blond man. It glanced left to right before setting off at a jog across the painted countries. Jedediah watched it go, the intensity of his gaze nearly carving a burning path across the map like a giant magnifying glass with sunlight fury behind it.

The tiny figure stopped in eastern China, folded its arms and glared.

Jedediah glared back. "Your days are numbered, boy."

THE CATCH OF THE DAY

Drake licked his beak clean of fresh blood and sucked the marrow from a buck's hip bone. His stomach bulged from the three deer Fleet Hoof hunters brought at his request. The full stomach felt good, but a part of him felt sorry for sending them out so often.

Master is back. I have to heal before he leaves on his own hunt.

Drake shifted, stretching as much as was possible with broken limbs and without damaging the hide pavilion set up around him. He drew upon his magic, reached out for the Dragon Springs and filled his skin until it too felt uncomfortably stuffed. He pushed the magic into every inch and focused on himself. Scales prickled like a thousand porcupine quills shoved beneath them. The pain intensified. Muscles burned. Bone ached. He pushed magic harder, not shaping into another form but into an image of himself hale and whole.

Wings shrieked. Smoke and snarl roiled from his beak. Worse than any shedding, it felt as if his furiously itching scales struggled to shred themselves away in every direction at once.

He let go of the magic. Strength and pain fled together. He slumped, stomach notably emptier. A shift of wing shot pain through him, but less than before. He snapped up the last of his meal, drawing on magic again.

He shifted his shape again and again and again.

Ravening hunger dragged talons through his gut. He crawled onto his feet. His head swam. His legs wobbled and gave out. Drake flopped to the ground with a drunken grin.

Nothing hurt.

He resisted calling for more food. He wouldn't burden them anymore. He'd hunt for himself. Then he'd hunt for Lanea's murderer. He hobbled from his pavilion. Centaur at the village's edge rushed to his side offering help. He sucked in what strength he could, making the best show of it possible.

I'm thirsty. He projected at those in view. *I'll make my own way to the creek.*

They fell away as he stalked into the woods. Drake lay next to the creek, beak in the water guzzling madly. He drank and drank, noticing only the cool refreshment and not minnows, tadpoles and other foreign debris racing down his throat. He raised his beak, snorted water from his nostrils and drew in a deep breath. Deer some distance upwind brought a grumble to his stomach.

He leapt into the nearest tree. Bound by bound, he rose in the old arbor's branches, finally jumping from its leaves and snapping open whole wings. He circled higher, eyes on the forest upwind. Breeze and current tickled the tiny hairs on his scales. He listened to them, listened to his nose and pointedly ignored his grumbling stomach.

Drake flew over the forest canopy. He shifted his eyes to a variant of Sight that offered him a view of heat and cold. A small deer herd entered his vision. A large buck's head shot up. Others repeated the movement. They sprang away.

He checked the ground but saw no other predator to drive them so.

I must've given myself away.

He beat wings faster. The deer broke from the treeline, bounding across empty farmland. A huge shadowcat with a striped coat sprinted out of the trees. It hissed, growling frustrated fury as it darted back into the cover of shadows.

Drake dove. Eyes flicked from deer to deer. None seemed injured, so he hit the large buck, driving it to the ground and snapping its neck in his jaws. Luscious hot blood washed through Drake's maw. He sucked its neck as if it was a Cherry Coke can, trying to savor every drop. The blood stopped spurting, and Drake relaxed on the ground to eat. He finished the last haunch, hunger still rubbing his belly like a genie's lamp to wish for more.

My stomach will wait. It's time to find Master and hunt Lanea's killer.

A large cool shape appeared on the northwest horizon.

Drake rose to his feet, kneading ground with his talons. It was downwind, but it kept charging him. Drake shook away the thermal sight and narrowed his gaze. A horse galloped toward him. The brown of muddy water, its graceful muscles pumped with all the speed it could muster. A long, flowing mane flew behind it, the frothy white of river rapids.

Drake crouched, readying to pounce.

It shimmered. Its shape blurred. It became a naked mocha-skinned woman, lissome and lithe. The frothy mane folded over her skin into tumbling curls and a gossamer shift. She raced to him, dropping into a skidding bow at the last moment.

"Rydari Phriel." Her alto carried no breathlessness. Her skin offered no sheen of sweat. "I bring tidings. A group of centaur attacked our home. They slaughtered many, taking an Elder Lordling prisoner. Prisoner, my Lord!"

A deep dark growl rumbled from his stomach.

"We were too few to stop them, but I remembered the memories of you she'd shared when we shared our meal. I've run sunrise and moonwake to find you. You must come. You must help Lady Salyse."

Drake's breath caught. His stomach hollowed, the buck's carcass teleported elsewhere by unknown magicks.

Wizard's Bane has Salyse. She needs my help. He rose to help but stopped. *Lanea's killer. I've waited so long to taste his blood.*

His chest ached.

Jedediah wouldn't wait now that he was healed. He'd hunt O'Steele with or without Drake. Salyse had felt a friend almost at once. It'd been his duty to see her to safety, but instead, he'd let her go off on her own. Her capture was his fault. He had to help her.

There's really only one choice to make...isn't there?

❧

Yves checked the coast clear, touched the trigger point with a toe and stepped into the wall between locker rooms. She descended with rapid steps, stripping the jacket off to let the growing field of magic roll over her skin.

She stopped short.

Flash knelt in the center of the magical circle beneath the dojo class floor.

She narrowed her eyes. "What are you doing?"

"Enjoying the quiet, Bianca," Flash said. "It feels almost like listening in a forest with those crystals here."

She stepped into the room and glanced at the smaller power crystals syphoning off energy from the class above. Power filled her like air her lungs. She gestured. "My spot."

Flash moved off the center without complaint. Bumps and thumps sounded above her.

"Quiet?"

He shrugged.

"He's up there you know?"

"Who?"

"Shine's boy. It's so hard not to just kill the arrogant little snot, preening about how fast he's learning. One blow, that's all it would take."

"He's an adolescent, arrogant and preening come with the package," Flash said. "I feel no desire to prey upon twelve-year-old boys."

"He's one of the enemy, a way to hurt Shine," Bianca said.

"He's a child quickly displaying advancing skills."

Bianca checked her back path, finding Mo Sha shadowing her in silence.

"Flash honors his enemy," Mo Sha's voice seemed too small for her frame. "He is right to do so. The boy moves faster and better than any of the others, more instinctually. If not culled, he will become a skilled combatant and worthy opponent—a good mate to females of his kind."

Bianca scowled. "He's not going to live that long."

"We'll see," Flash said. "As long as he serves his purpose, Zero will not let you slay him. If that is too long, your attentive young pupil may learn how to perpetuate his own survival."

Bianca closed, looking up into the Samoan's calm expression. "What's going on with you?"

"I serve."

"No, something's different. You never offered opinions before, weren't so disagreeable," Bianca said. "You don't like working for me? For a woman?"

His lip curled. "I work for Zero, not you. Now that you're One you're almost equal to me, so I suggest you don't throw weight you don't have."

Heat flashed through Bianca and out her fingertips. She thrust a burning hand into Flash's chest. "I've got weight and fire and her. You're outclassed, Flash, lower in pack."

"I'm not a wolf, Bianca, even if you are a bitch."

"Get out," Bianca snapped. "Get him out of here. I want to meditate alone."

Mo Sha showed her teeth.

Flash exited, showing his own.

Bianca knelt in the center of the circle. She reached out to close the engraved pentacle and concentrate the power. The circle lit, followed by parallel lines which reached out to encircle each power crystal. She frowned.

Was Flash trying to work the magic? Can he do that? She examined the illuminated construct. *The circle wasn't energized. He couldn't have been.*

Bianca closed her eyes and reached out to the concentrated

power. It had a different feel to it when a class fed it, more alive somehow. Meditations at such times proved better, allowing her better control and helping her store magic inside herself longer.

Maybe I should retire the old man once Gordon proves ready.

Flash climbed into his jeep, closed his eyes and took a deep breath. It'd taken all of his control not to rip her throat out. Only the reality of Zero's wrath kept him from proving how little weight her magic and bodyguard offered.

Curse Zero and the day he captured mama and us.

In the wild, he'd not have surrendered territory to a weaker bear. He hated letting Bianca order him around, trading on Zero's strength as if it were her own. *I'm tired of Zero's tramp barking orders like some yappy poodle.*

Flash started the jeep and threw it into gear. If he didn't get some distance, he'd go down into that basement and show her real strength. He backed up, but before he could pull out of his space, some soccer-mom road-warrior cut him off—with a minivan of all things. He whipped out a pistol. Slow, deliberate breathing calmed killing fury and slid the weapon back into the concealed holster. It took so long that the clear parking lot teamed with exiting students. Adolescent boys talked and laughed, unconcerned about blocking a man very much in the mood to shoot them.

He moved the jeep slow enough for them to get out of his way, forcing the issue with a particularly arrogant girl and her alpha Barbie mom. Mason came abreast of him, and Flash rolled down the window.

"Hey, kid."

"What?" Mason asked.

Mason's tone told Flash a lot about him. If the kid were a wolf, an alpha who didn't kill him young might lose his place. "Saw you going at it in there. Looking good. Keep it up."

Mason's ears reddened, but he smiled. "Thanks."

Flash drove away. *Watch out, bitch, that pup might be too much for you soon.*

Jedediah stepped out of the bright hallway into Arthur's darkened hospital room. Electronics he didn't understand surrounded the boy. Frameworks cradled his head, and bandages covered half his face.

Dark eyes opened, swimming a moment before locking onto Jedediah. He met the boy's gaze. Arthur made a noise. Jedediah shook his head.

He swept a hand, tinting the inside of the darkened windows to prevent casual observation by passing nurses. "We ain't going to have a conversation, so don't bring harm to yourself. You've caused enough as is."

Arthur's brows wrinkled.

Jedediah set a disposable phone into Arthur's fingers. "Agent Ridley's number is already programmed. I'm thinking you two need to have one of those text-it conversation...a little heart to heart chat, maybe tell him how you really ended up with those injuries."

Temper rose up, summoning magic beneath his skin. He considered the electronic equipment a moment and then forced the sparks manifesting his anger into a corona of flames.

Arthur paled.

Jedediah smiled. "Confession's good for the soul, boy."

Marc O'Steele exited his hotel. His grip tightened around a briefcase handle. He squinted, scanning the street through the glare of the setting sun. He hailed a cab. The driver dropped him off at the entrance to a suburban community. The main cities in China offered modern thoroughfares and amenities, but outlying regions offered narrower streets and cluttered alleys.

He checked his suit free of the flaking cab's interior and tipped the driver. A tension pinched his shoulders. He scanned the street, noting the decorations hung in the waiting community—preparations for who knew what celebration.

I need this deal. One more and I can contact Zero.

Just inside the arched community entry, rickshaw's lined either side of the narrow street. Cracked roadway mostly bereft of litter stretched into a veritable labyrinth. He scanned the bicycle drawn cabs, noting an old style muscle-drawn rickshaw edged in gold and silver designs. A venerable man who appeared short on the requisite muscle waited in its plush, cushioned seat.

Something about it appealed to him—a figurative return to a time that was.

Marc negotiated a trip with the old man and took his seat. The old man started slow but soon managed a smooth stride. People clustered in the streets, an excited air on adult and child faces alike. He chattered about the festival, but Marc paid no attention. For the former head of the *Namhaid's* American cell, whatever they celebrated offered only camouflage for his deal. He focused on that— one more success to restore him to the Board's good graces. They'd wanted the proposed relationship for some time, but the Chinese cell leader hadn't managed to deliver.

I might not be One, but I'll have a cell again. From there, I'll take back what's mine one step at a time.

The rickshaw turned hard, throwing him out of his reverie as it pulled down a cluttered alley. It wove between old crates and garbage cans. Building walls rose to either hand, forming a narrow, laundry-roofed canyon.

A figure blocked the alley ahead. Black robes cloaked it. Hands tucked into their opposite sleeve. Its woven bamboo hat bowed forward.

Marc leaned out of the rickshaw, looking back up the alley. The mouth seemed as close as the far exit and turning the old cart around might prove challenging. "Talk to him. Ask him to let us pass."

Marc's driver laid the cart's handles down, inclined his head and trotted up to the stranger. He bowed low to the man and slipped down the alley beyond him.

"What the hell?"

The hat rose. The robe sleeves parted. Jedediah glowered at Marc, fingertips sparking. Cold shot through Marc. He whipped a pistol from inside his jacket and fired.

Jedediah raised a hand, stalking through the bullets as if they didn't exist. His voice cracked with rage. "Marc O'Steele."

His name fell like death nails. He leapt from the cab. His gun barked twice more as he raced back up the alley. Jedediah's stalk picked up speed.

Marc knocked crates over as he passed. He charged into the busy streets, using the crowd to slow his pursuer. He dodged down another alley, forced to leap an inconvenient stack of boxes. He leapt a short wall, raced passed an open cooking pit and its tenders, jumped another wall and ran down an alley. He turned right into a dead end. He hurried to a ladder, taking it twenty feet before jumping to a ledge on the opposite building. He climbed onto the low roof and searched the horizon.

Jedediah turned his direction, racing atop rooftops with feet that seemed to only touch down every dozen feet like some bad martial art's film.

Marc raced the other way. Low walls, laundry, old chimneys— he sprinted across the rooftops, dropped into an alley, bounded over more crates, another wall and into the street.

Crowds pressed tighter, slowing him as he forced his way through. Breath raged in his chest. He searched for a place to hide, considering crowded shop fronts and more alleys. He glanced over his shoulder. Jedediah stood atop a peaked roof, scanning the crowd.

Marc hunched low and wiggled upstream. *If I get under him without him noticing, he'll probably head the wrong way to find me.*

Marc reached an intersection, the crowds bending right rather than continuing away from Jedediah. He glanced up but didn't see the farmer. A solution danced into view. A Chinese dragon, red and gold and welcome mobile hiding place turned the corner. He rushed for the float, ducking under curtains of fabric to join those carrying it.

It stopped its dance.

The crowd screamed.

Marc looked backward, finding no men in dragon-leg pants holding up its end but a scaled, anatomically correct and obviously male creature. He looked up. Reddish brown scales formed a roof above him. Every inch of his body went numb. Something drew his gaze forward. A dragon's massive beak hung upside down between front legs. Fire lit its eyes. Smoke curled from its nostrils.

Marc threw himself from beneath the beast that'd once chased him down Georgia back ways. He snapped off a few bullets, sprinting for everything his legs were worth. Jedediah settled onto the recently emptied street ahead of him. Lightning flickered around him.

"You messed with the wrong farmer, boy."

Jedediah threw his hands forward and with it a barrage of electrical energy. It slammed into Marc, burning and tingling and filling his every inch with unimagined agony. An echo of his own torment exploded from the wizard's mouth. Smokey tendrils sprang from the ground. They lashed at Jedediah, wrapped his limbs and drawing him down in a cocoon of shadowy power. Marc wrenched himself away from the pain and hurdled up the side street.

A massive weight slammed him to the ground. He gasped, sucking in pungent smoke. The dragon pressed its scales against him, talons piercing into him in an uncomfortable but not cutting way.

"Oh, no, little soul," Drake said. "You're not going until Master's done with you."

Marc glanced back at Jedediah to see his own body between him and the wizard's crumpled frame now freed of the tendrils. He raised a translucent hand before his face.

"That's right. Master promised. Death only begins your punishment."

Jedediah awoke to darkness. Pain lingered, a constant thrum throughout his body. He blinked, but the darkness didn't clear. Hands found cushions beneath him, and a rocking motion accompanied by creaking wood suggested he rode in his old rickshaw.

"Drake?"

Something light and thin settled onto Jedediah's arm. *<Here, master. There's something wrong with your eyes.>*

"I noticed. Where's O'Steele."

<His body's been disposed.> Drake belched. *<I stopped his soul's flight.>*

"I see you've been practicing in my absence."

<You don't know the half of it.>

"Drake?"

<Nothing. What's wrong with you?>

Jedediah slipped into his power, stretching it through and around his body. He probed with magical senses, but whatever had attacked him as his lightning slew O'Steele, it seemed gone even if its effects lingered.

"I'm not sure."

Sha Hung Wu spoke in Chinese. "We are almost home, Master."

Jedediah replied in the same tongue. "Thank you for your service."

Fabric rustled and the breeze of motion slowed. "I am honored to have served well in righting the treacherous wrong committed against your honored household. Birdsong was dear to all of us."

Birdsong, their nickname for Lanea. Pain stabbed Jedediah's chest. Other pain mimicked his own. Flashes of Lanea playing her flute, feet dangling in a river splashed through his mind's eye. Birds answered her notes, and she raised her voice to sing with them.

<Birdsong.> Drake's thoughts caressed and mourned the nickname.

The rickshaw pulled to a stop. Hands drew Jedediah from the

seat, guiding him up a walk. Shifting panels slid against lubricated grooves, a soft shushing sound Jedediah recognized without knowing he'd known it so well.

"Master Shine?" Jiang Wen cursed in whispers. "What happened?"

Jedediah focused on her voice and how it lilted as she translated her thoughts from her native tongue. "Victory with a catch. Can you lead me through the portal?"

Her voice guided his feet. An assault of orange juice and mint and a sudden oppressing humidity signaled his return to the farm.

"Drake?"

<Here, Master.>

I don't feel your touch.

<I'm not touching you. What may I do for you?>

"Lead Jiang Wen to the Cheraw portal. I need my clocks to escape this spell."

He tasted the portal once more. Something knocked hard against a piece of furniture, rattling china plates. "Be careful, you big lizard. There's a key on the table. Put it into any clock but the sailing ships and turn it clockwise."

"It won't turn," Jiang Wen said.

"Let me." Jedediah felt his way to her voice. He found her arms with fingers and traced them to the key. It didn't turn. He pushed strength into his limbs. It still refused to start the clock. He moved it to another clock, fumbling to get the key in. It also declined to turn.

Jedediah cursed. *Someone knows me too well....*

Watching his master struggle pained Drake. Whatever had attacked Jedediah and robbed him of his sight twisted Drake's guts too. He'd put off rescuing Salyse to see Marc dead—the hardest and probably most selfish decision he'd ever made.

Master?

"What?!"

Forgive me, but I have a friend in trouble. I'd like to go to her aid now that our business with O'Steele is in hand.

Jedediah's expression changed, but he shielded his inner thoughts from Drake's awareness. He felt Jedediah's barrier but decided not to push at it.

"I'm sorry I snapped at you, Drake. If you feel you must assist this friend, then you have my blessing. Be safe. Wizard's Bane is still out there, and I trust not VelSera to abide by any moral convention."

Tell me about it.

Drake departed through the portal, rubbing his tongue on the roof of his mouth to be rid of its flavor. He shifted into his human self, dug clothes from the saddlebags of his motorcycle and drove away from his afflicted master—torn in two directions by his sense of duty.

Jordan sat alone at a picnic table in the rear courtyard, absorbing her government-permitted minutes of sunlight. Her feet itched for a run, but she kept the bare appendages pressed against the rough earth. Her rumble played about her skin. She concentrated on the ground, trying to raise a stone from it like the cartoon character seemed able. She chose a small stone, suitable for launching at certain thick-headed adults of her acquaintance.

Angesa Cooper seated herself next to Jordan. "How're you doing?"

Jordan glowered. "I'm locked up in here for defending myself. I'm the target of rumor and ridicule, and I'm not getting any practice time."

"I think we can change that."

Jordan sat up.

"If you'd like, I'm here to take you to Marnie for some track time."

A grin turned up Jordan's lips. "I can run?"

"Yes, and you won't be here much longer."

"Why? What happened? Where am I going?"

"Arthur confessed to attacking you before you hit him. You can go home soon," Angesa said.

Home. A weight lifted from her that she hadn't realized she'd carried. Jedediah's return had lessened it, but it'd lurked upon her shoulders. His return meant him taking care of her. Jedediah could take care of Mae and Crystal. He could help find Eve to set Crystal's worries to rest. He could help Mason and keep Drake safe, and he can deal with that idiot Kane.

I can be a kid again...well, an almost adult.

"We should be able to take you back to Mae—"

Jordan snapped to her feet. "Mae? You said I was going home."

"Yes." Angesa nodded. "Home to the Bridgeports."

She flopped back into the seat. "I'd rather you sent me to the Chair."

Jordan jogged to a stop, placing her hands on her head. "How was that?"

Angesa smiled up from her phone.

Marnie gazed lovingly at her stopwatch as if a Cheshire cat about to swallow a particularly obese mouse. "Fantastic, especially since you haven't been able to train."

"She'll get more training once she's back at Mae's," Angesa said.

Marnie darkened. "I don't like that woman."

"Why can't I go back to Jedediah's?"

"He abandoned you," Angesa said.

"He was grieving, besides I'm old enough to babysit by state law."

Angesa set her phone aside. "You're not supposed to babysit yourself."

"But I can. He didn't leave me homeless or hungry or naked."

"You were left unsupervised."

Not exactly true. Jordan squared her shoulders. "I'm seventeen."

"Exactly," Angesa said. "You're still a child. Children shouldn't be abandoned to their own devices. I'm sorry. I know you prefer Jedediah. If I was honest, I think we all do—except maybe Billie Jo, but bad breakups happen. It doesn't matter. You can't go back with him. No one would approve that request."

Jordan turned her back, stomping in a fit of temper. The asphalt cracked beneath her sneaker. She cursed, checking the other women's reactions. Both frowned at the damaged ground.

"I better run the outer lane on this next run," Jordan said.

QUESTIONABLE CHOICES

Kane trudged across another field. ChiRie chattered about something girlie—or horsie. He wasn't listening. The shaman WaphRae insisted she escort him. He didn't see the point, but adults seldom made sense

Exhaustion warred with fury. His Mistress was in danger.

She's been in jeopardy for...months? Well, I've waited long enough.

It'd taken the old wizard long enough to return. The centaur had prevented him from seeing the inconsiderate old man as if Kane weren't the personal confidant of Rydari Phriel. They'd claimed the *Feather of Mythdom* or however they said it required time to heal. He'd been injured, starved and then fought a dragon.

Any wizard that can do that can damned well save my mistress.

He'd disappeared without warning, leaving with Kane's message unheard. Kane had been patient, but enough was enough. He marched around the pond and greenhouses to see the farm ruin. Palettes of construction materials sat in the grassy space circled by gravel drive.

Good, I'm tired of tents.

"Is that him over there?" ChiRie asked.

Kane looked. The man being led from one of the refrigerators was old, but not the ancient old man Mauve sent him to find. A young woman helped him walk—Jiang Wen from China.

He doesn't look that frail. Kane shrugged. *Maybe he's got answers.*

He turned toward the boneyard and hurried his steps. Jiang Wen looked up at them, her face filling with delight. She whispered to the man in her care.

Jiang Wen bowed to her knees, a grin stretching her lips wide. "I am so honored to meet a follower of Lah Phriel."

ChiRie laughed. "I'm just an acolyte."

"Still," Jiang Wen said. "I've read—"

"Cut the how's your mom and them crap," Kane said. "Does your husband know where Jedediah is? I'm tired of waiting on the old man."

The man turned toward him. The air filled with power, pressing against Kane's skin as if someone pushed him downward with a gigantic thumb. Milky eyes looked through Kane, and for the first time, the death he foresaw might've been his own.

"You'll watch your tongue and mind your manners, boy. Apologize."

Kane balled his fists. "I'm not apologizing when I've done nothing wrong. My mistress is in danger, and I'm tired of waiting for your master to stop playing patty cake. I demand to speak to him."

The old man's head cocked. "You are."

"No," Kane said. "You're not fooling me. I won't be put off anymore. I want to talk to Jedediah Shine."

ChiRie touched Kane's arm. "That is *Feihtor Ah Mythela'Raemyn*."

"Feather of Mythdom is an ancient, lazy old vagabond—"

Lightning shattered the clear sky. Thunderheads formed like some sped-up movie. Power doubled the pressure on Kane's skin. "Be silent, boy. You don't know enough magic to dry behind your ears, and I have half a mind to yank your britches down and switch you until you learn to respect women."

Britches? Switch me? What's he talking about?

The old man bowed before Jiang Wen. "I thank you for your

help. Your family serves honorably as they always have. If I can grant you any boon, you need only ask it."

"Master Jedediah is as generous as he is gracious, but I cannot abandon you while you cannot see," Jiang Wen said.

It really is him? How did he get so young?

Jedediah gestured. "The boy will serve me."

"The boy has a name," Kane said.

The glower turned his direction made him step back. "The *boy* will be silent. I will tell him when his name matters."

"His name's Kane," ChiRie said.

Jedediah inclined his head to her. "All will be well soon, Jiang Wen. Where I go, you are not suited to travel."

She bowed. "As you wish, Master. I shall return to my family."

Kane rolled his eyes. *Come on, move this shit along already.*

Jedediah turned toward Kane. His eyes flashed gold a moment. He extended a hand. "Lead me before the farmhouse."

"Before?"

"In front of. Creator's breath, child, Mauve said you had brains."

Kane set his shoulders and marched toward the farmhouse. *I've got brains, you worthless old fart.*

"Boy?"

Kane looked back. "What?"

"*Lead* me."

"What, let you touch me?"

"Yes."

"Do I look like a seeing eye dog to you?" Kane asked.

"Do you want to?" Jedediah asked.

Kane glanced around. He found a long, slender piece of wood. He shoved one end into Jedediah's hand. "Hold onto this, and I'll *lead* you."

They made it half-way to the pile of construction materials before the old man spoke. "You have Gravesight."

Kane's tight shoulders knotted. "What of it?"

"Mauve hasn't taught you how to shield against it?"

"She was busy being captured by centaurs, not that you care.

You're off doing who knows what while they're torturing her. She might even be dead by now."

The stick connecting them stopped moving, almost yanking it from Kane's grip. Jedediah's blank eyes stared off toward the Southwest. "She's not dead."

Kane's pulse quickened. "How do you know?"

"I've known Mauve a long time. I can feel her magic still part of the world."

"Is she hurt? Can you save her?"

Silence filled the space between them.

"There's something strange about her—something mussing her magic, but she's not hurt badly."

"Come on. We've got save her."

"Other priorities must be addressed first."

"What? The house?" Kane asked. "Just magic it back together and let's go save Mistress."

"I cannot assault those that took her until my sight has been restored."

"All right, let's go. Where do we go—"

Lightning crashed around him. Every inch felt bitten by a thousand mosquitos. Blinding light faded to reveal a grassy glade at the bottom of a massive well, a waterfall and a mage tower.

"Holy shit! Does Mistress have one of these?" Kane asked

"Mauve prefers the beach."

Kane helped Jedediah into the fortress. The wizard disarmed magical wards and opened locks while he served as the old man's guide. *Bark.*

Ornate stonework and old tapestries, silver and polished wood decorated the tower's interior. They climbed stairways passed rooms—some centuries out of date and others with modern conveniences only a few decades old. The stairs ended in an empty round room.

Kane put hands on his knees, trying to catch his breath.

"You need to go outside and play more if such a small climb has you out of breath," Jedediah said.

"Why would I play outside, the good stuff is inside," Kane said. "Besides, that was like three hundred thousand steps."

"One hundred sixty-four."

"See."

Another flash of light made Kane flinch. He looked around expecting to see someplace new. Instead, the only thing that had changed seemed to be the staff in the old man's hands. He tapped it twice, spun it around and tapped it twice once more. An ornate, silver-bound door appeared in the room's center.

"Take me to the door."

"A please wouldn't go amiss," Kane said.

"Once you've earned one, you won't miss it."

"Earned it? I'm doing all the heavy lifting here, dragging you around, doing what you tell me—"

"Not to mention complaining about every small thing," Jedediah said.

"There's a lot to complain about."

"You're an apprentice. Suck it up, buttercup."

Buttercup? Who does this bastard think he is?

The door opened as they approached, revealing a massive room twice the size of the one they left. A silver pedestal stood sentinel in the chamber's center surrounded by countless chunks of dark, broken crystal.

"Damn. You need to get some Mexicans up here to clean u—"

Jedediah's blow sent Kane to the ground, face on fire.

"What the hell was that about?" Kane said.

"I tire of your disrespectful attitude."

Kane climbed to his feet. "Disrespect? Father says Mexicans make—"

Another blow heated the opposite side of Kane's face. He stepped out of reach. "Stop that. It's a compliment."

Jedediah loomed over them. "It's an insult, careless and thoughtless and you'll learn better starting now."

"I'm not your apprentice."

Jedediah gestured around them. "Just who do you figure is going to hear your case? I will not tolerate prejudice, boy, thoughtless or otherwise."

"What do you care? It's not like you're Mexican or Chinese—" Kane broke off and ducked under the next blow. *He's targeting me by sound. I'll just—*

The old man's staff hit the ground. Thunder threw Kane and crystal shards outward in a huge circle. He shook off the after-effects, looking up into angry, glowing eyes.

"I was born Shawnee, boy. I've lived through centuries of small minded *compliments*, watched my people suffer because they were *lesser* than so-called privileged white man."

"I didn't know."

"It shouldn't matter."

"I didn't mean anything by it," Kane said.

"That's what makes your hatred so horrifying."

"I don't hate minorities."

Jedediah bent close to him. The air crackled with energy. "You want to talk about minorities, boy? Let's talk about why most of Fleet Hoof gave you a wide berth."

"They were respectful because of my friendship with Rydari Phriel."

"Bullshit. You stink, boy. You reek of death. You terrified and repulsed them. There are few true necromancers—the ultimate minority. If you don't want to be treated like a pariah the rest of your life, then you'd better learn how to respect the differences of others—really respect them."

I repulsed them?

Jedediah picked up a crystal shard. He ran hands over it, sculpting hard edges into smooth curves. It formed into an orb then took on the aspects of an eyeball the size of a coconut. Jedediah lofted it into the air. It looked side to side, fixated on Kane and blinked.

"Better." Jedediah waved a hand, and the eye faded from view.

"Problem solved, now we go save Mistress?" Kane asked.

Jedediah approached the pedestal, a somber expression that knotted Kane's stomach. He picked up a fairy doll as if it were finest China. He set it with a tumbled collection of oddments, placing each at the apexes of a five-pointed star inscribed in the tabletop. He added a dark chunk of crystal in their center.

Cold plunged the room into an icy fog. Power around Jedediah changed, transforming fog into shadows. He cupped hands around the crystal. Old mausoleum scent filled Kane's nostrils. A sharp aroma of embalming fluids cut across it. The crystal didn't smooth. It glowed once, then again. A slow throb filled the room—a dark heartbeat of lesser darkness.

A phantasm's scream echoed off the walls.

"Seal it, boy."

"Seal what?" Kane asked.

"Seal the soul into this stone," Jedediah said.

"Why don't you do it?"

"You're the apprentice. You'll do as you're told."

Kane sighed but stepped closer to the table. He drew up the cold power deep in his center. It came quicker than it ever had. A ghostly veil descended over his eyes, letting him see the construct Jedediah had built and the soul writhing beneath. The necromantic energy of the old aeromancer seemed incredibly powerful, but something equally compelling fought against it.

He scrutinized the soul encased in the working. Dark tendrils lashed out from it, but the specter didn't seem to have any magic of its own.

"Today?" Jedediah asked.

Kane set his hands on the crystal. He jerked them away from the burning cold rock. He cupped the stone once more and wrapped his power around it.

"More."

Kane added another layer. Jedediah demanded more. Layer after layer he mummified the soul in necromancy, leaving no chance for escape. Jedediah collapsed.

"Jedediah?"

"Is it sealed?"

"Best I can?"

Fury exploded in the old man's face. "If that soul escapes I'm taking it out of your hide, boy, so you damned well better *know* the soulstone is sealed tight."

"It's tight, it's tight. Are you okay?"

Jedediah struggled back to his feet. "Marc O'Steele, come forth."

The phantasm of a handsome man younger than Jedediah but still old appeared above the altar. Barbed chains forged of ghostly links held it to the stone. Expanded from its minute prison inside the soulstone, Kane recognized intermixed chains of almost every kind of magic possible.

Jesus. He seriously doesn't want whoever this is to leave.

"What did you do to me?" Jedediah demanded.

"I didn't—"

Jedediah shushed him. "Marc O'Steele, I compel you to answer."

"Fuck off—" Marc screamed, doubled over and writhing in pain as the chain's barbs gleamed bright.

"What did you do to me? What spell did your wizard hide in your skin?"

"I don't know." Marc doubled over again.

"Tell me," Jedediah said.

"I don't know," Marc said. "I don't have a wizard."

Jedediah gestured. Different chains lit. Ghostly flesh ripped from phantom muscle. Ichor leaked down the spectral flesh.

He's torturing a soul.

"Um, Jedediah?" Kane asked. "I'm not sure we're supposed to treat the dead like this. It isn't right to—"

Jedediah pointed. "There's the door, boy. Kitchen's on two. Get out."

Kane fled the room, chased by agonized screams unlike anything he'd ever imagined. Mauve had taught him to imprison spirits, even to punish if they forced him to make them behave. He'd never experienced anything like the torment the non-necromancer inflicted.

He sat just outside the room, arms wrapped against a cold that refused to go away. He wiped itchy eyes. He couldn't hear the screams anymore, but somehow deep down he still felt the man being tortured.

This isn't right.

⚜

Mason bounced on the balls of his feet, facing down a much bigger boy on the dojo mats. The older boy had two belts more than he did, but the others at his level couldn't keep up with Mason's speed. Another flurry of blows followed him across the mat. In the background students cheered and Sensei Truth spoke instructions to both of them in turns.

He sank into his power, drawing it over his skin. It always came quicker when he sparred, as if his wind magic liked fighting. Mason slid around Terry, under a blow that stood still a moment. He swept Terry's legs, but the older student hopped it.

"Not this time, Mason," Terry spun a kick Mason barely dodged. It dropped hard on the follow through, barely missing the spot Mason ducked down into a moment before he rolled away and back to his feet.

Mason charged with a flurry of punches. They didn't have the strength Terry did, and even fighting he'd been unable to make himself stronger like Jordan said she could.

Strike and dodge, kick and block, Mason and Terry ranged over the mat. Sweat poured off of Mason, the salty liquid fouling his eyes. Terry's breathing didn't sound nearly as ragged, and his face was definitely drier.

Mason threw himself forward, catching a windstream between Terry's legs. He swung blows to either side as he passed through, striking the backs of Terry's knees, slapping hands on the mat and flipping over in a series of wind enhanced moves that drew appreciative noises from the rest of the class—not to mention a few utterances of, "How the hell did he do that?"

Terry pitched forward, but caught his balance and kicked backward. His injured leg didn't hold him up. Mason spun and leapt into a move he'd watched a thousand times on DVD. He reared back his right fist, bringing all his weight and momentum down behind the blow.

The other boy rolled sideways with more speed than Mason thought him capable. Mason pulled back on the blow at the last minute, but not enough. His fist hit the mat, and the previously sprained wrist exploded with pain.

Mason clutched it, rolling around the floor in agony.

Terry knelt next to him. "Mason, are you okay?"

"Serves him right," Sensei Yves said. "This is real training, not some subtitled movie."

Sensei Truth cleared his throat, checking Mason's arm with gentle fingers. "I think you broke it this time, Mason. I guess that means you won't be able to practice anymore for a while."

No practice? But practice makes me feel like myself, like a ninja-wizard that can help Jordan and not worry about Roland. Mason gritted his teeth, tears squeezing by his eyes despite his best efforts. "No! No, Sensei, it hurts, but I'm sure it'll be fine."

"I don't know, son."

"Good fight, Mason," Terry said. "Where'd you learn that between the legs thing?"

Mason looked at Sensei Yves through hooded eyes. "A movie."

"All right, go clean yourself up, and I'll take you home," Sensei Truth said. "Your mother can make the final decision."

Mason cleaned and dressed the best he could, struggling with his clothes but eventually managing. He had to keep learning, but if his mom found out he'd been fighting—let alone broken his wrist fighting—there'd be no way she'd let him out of the house before he was thirty.

What am I going to do? If I let Sensei drive me home...wait. What if Mom's not home? A smile grew across his face. *What if she's visiting her good friend Mae Bridgeport?*

Sensei Truth dropped Mason off in front of the address he'd gotten from Jordan. He pulled Mason's bike out of the SUV trunk and handed it over.

"You sure you'll be okay? I don't see your mom's van."

"Yeah, Missus Bridgeport picked up Mom early this morning for some shopping."

Sensei Truth scrutinized him, a smirk on his lips. "If you say so."

As soon as Sensei's car was out of sight, Mason walked his bike down the street and around the corner out of sight of the Bridgeport house. He snuck into the woods behind the house, circling to the back of the cottage Crystal had told him about. He got to the door, checking for movement from the big house.

Do I knock? Just go inside?

He knocked with his uninjured hand. No one answered. He knocked again, glancing at the big house. She'd told him about all the chores Mae forced her to do. If she was busy doing chores visiting might get Crystal in trouble. He'd enjoy her company—not to mention her help, but what he really needed was the root cellar.

Mason circled the house trying to find the metal hatch they'd described. It didn't take long. Chains crisscrossed the lid. Mason frowned. It took a long time to unhook and untangle the chains. The heavy lid didn't want to lift with only one hand and trying with two shot horrifying pain up his arm.

I wish I could do that strength thing.

He managed to get it open and peeked inside. "Crystal?"

No one answered. A ladder leaned against one wall. He looked down.

Doesn't seem that far.

Mason sat on the hole's metal rim, feet dangling. He rolled over onto his stomach, sliding his legs in a little bit at a time. His stomach caught the edge. He wiggled. In a flash, he slid wholesale into the hole. His arms scrabbled for purchase to stop the tumble but pain stole his breath and grip. He hit the ground with an oof.

He cradled his wrist a moment before struggling to his feet. He glanced around at the dirty, stinky hole. *And I thought my mom was bad.*

"Mason?"

He turned toward the sound of Crystal's voice, seeing her through the leaned door frame. He waved his right arm, wincing and cradling it once more. "Hiya."

"Are you hurt?"

"Yeah, but that's okay."

"It is not. Why'd you jump down?" Crystal asked.

"I need to find the chicken hut, and using this way made more sense than bicycling out to Jedediah's farm."

"Chicken hut? Oh."

"Yeah. Jedediah keeps healing potions out there."

"How did you know you were going to hurt yourself visiting me?"

"I didn't," Mason said. "I broke my wrist sparring."

"You should go to a hospital then."

"If I did that my Mom would find out, then I wouldn't be able to fight at the dojo anymore."

Mason stepped through the portal. He rubbed his tongue against his teeth to get rid of the taste. Crystal giggled at him.

"Hey, it tastes horrible."

"I know," she said. "But you made such a funny face."

"Come on," Mason led her over to the greenhouses. "Hello? Nip?"

A little mudpuppy poked her head out of the door. Mason went up to her, stroking her puppy-soft fur. "Hey, Beryl, is Nip around?"

Beryl rolled onto her back, legs spread so he could rub her belly. *<No Nip. No Nip.>*

"Do you know where the hut is? I need to find it."

Beryl flipped over onto her feet, tail wagging her whole back end. She nipped and growled. *<Hunt. Hunt. Hunt.>*

Before Mason could answer, she bounded off across a field. He glanced at Crystal, shrugging. "Follow that dog?"

They followed Beryl's winding course across the fields, laughing and talking about everything and nothing. They stopped when the mudpuppy put her nose to the ground, butt high in the air wagging her tail like a flag. Mason almost forgot about the throbbing pain. Hours later Beryl sprinted back over a rise to them, bouncing a circle around them yipping.

Mason grabbed her. "What's going on? Did you find it?"

<Yes. Yes. Hut. Yes. Centaurs. Chase. Centaurs. Chase.>

"Centaur? Here?" Mason walked up the rise to find a group of centaur slamming sword-tipped spears at nothing. Nothing flashed an energy shield each time they struck.

"Um, what's going on?" Crystal asked.

"They must be Wizard's Bane."

"Who?"

"Bad centaurs."

"Should we run?"

Mason smiled. "Nah. They're outside the shield."

"We're not going to run?"

"I need what's in that hut," Mason said. "Besides, Jedediah's back so the protective barrier should be just fine."

Worry clung to her tone. "Are you sure?"

"Trust me." Mason took her hand and led her forward. One of the centaur pointed their direction. The assault stopped. Mason strolled past them headed for the hut which seemed their intention. He waved. "Hi. Nice day?"

"Not when we're done with you, wizardling," a palomino stallion said.

"Barrier giving you trouble?" Mason asked.

"What're you doing?" Crystal whispered. "I thought you said they were the bad guys."

Mason puffed out his chest. "They're outside the barrier."

"What if they get inside?"

"Won't happen," Mason said.

"Preen all you want, arrogant child. Wizard's Bane will rule all of these lands. VelSera has proclaimed it, and when we do you will die, and normals like the whore will bow down to us."

Mason stopped, his skin suddenly alive as if his knotting stomach somehow wrung electricity out through his pores. He turned their course toward the centaur. "Leave her out of this, jackass."

The centaur group stomped and glowered. Beryl rushed through the barrier, growling and nipping at the centaur. He tried to stomp her, missing by the barest margin. She darted away, ears back and still yipping.

"Beryl, come," Crystal said. "Mason, let's just go."

The mudpuppy raced to Crystal, but once there turned to growl and yip.

Mason focused on the power clinging to him with all his might and pushed it at the stallion. Sparks erupted from his fingers with a small pop. The centaur laughed. Heat filled his face, burning a path to his fingers.

"Mason, come on."

"Run away, *Mason*, like the cowardly two-leggers your kind are," the stallion snarled.

Mason's fingertips itched. The blood warming his cheeks seemed to wash over his eyes, tinting everything crimson.

"Shut up, horse," Crystal put a hand on his arm, jerking back when she got a shock. "Ow. Come on, Mason."

The centaur's jeering face blurred, resolving into Roland. A roar of wind in his ears drowned it out, a subtle melody he didn't recognize coming to his attention nearly too soft to hear. Fury exploded from Mason's fingertips, searing his skin. An arc of electricity lanced through the barrier into Roland's face. It burned a jagged line across the flesh as the centaur reared back and away. Mason stared at his hands.

Crystal screamed.

The injured centaur snatched an arrow from the quiver around his waist. He shoved its tip through the barrier, jerked it back so that the tip touched the magic and dragged it across the power's surface. A small rend formed where the arrowhead cut.

The stallion's arm reached through, but Crystal snatched Mason backward. "Come on, Mason. Please!"

The centaur tried to force his way through, blood trailing from the burned cut across his face. The barrier's energy collected, a thrum filling the air. It threw the centaur backward.

Crystal dragged the stunned Mason toward the hut.

"This isn't over, boy. Rhinlar E'Hynar does not forget an enemy."

"Screw off," Crystal said.

Her scream snapped Mason out of his shock. She crumpled to the ground.

"VelSera ordered us not to waste the arrows, RhiHyn," a brown mare said.

An arrow jutted out of Crystal's back, its bloody tip exiting her sternum. Rage and panic overwhelmed him. He scooped her off the ground without respect to the pain it shot through his arm. Wind wrapped him in speed and propelled his sprint to the hut. He'd charged into the hut and down into the cavern before he realized he'd kicked the door hard enough to make the hut squawk. Mason set Crystal down and yanked a bug juice bottle of red liquid from the fridge.

He turned to give it to her, cursing over and over. *What do I do? What will the potion do with an arrow in her?* She lay quiet, too quiet. *Crap, did she stop breathing?*

Mason dribbled potion into her mouth. Red light spread across her skins at a snail's pace. He bit his lip hard enough to draw blood. He shoved his injured hand into his pocket, pain screaming from his wrist as he dialed Jordan.

"Mason, what's wrong?"

"Crystal's got an arrow in her chest."

"What?"

"I think she's stopped breathing. What do I do?"

"Where are you?"

"The hut."

"Are there potions?"

"Yes, I gave her a little, but—"

"You have to break the arrow and pull it out," Jordan said.

"Pull it out? You're sure?"

"Shut up and do what I tell you."

Mason dropped his phone and grabbed the arrow. Tears ran down his cheeks. "I'm sorry. I'm so sorry."

Jordan's voice came from the floor. "Do it."

Mason broke the arrow.

Crystal screamed.

She's alive.

Beryl whimpered, ears pressed to her head.

"Did you pull it out?" Jordan asked.

Mason rolled her over enough to get at it. His blood-slicked left hand grabbed the arrow. Crystal yelped.

"It's hurting her."

"Do it fast, Mason."

Mason yanked the arrow out of Crystal's back. Crystal's body jerked away from him, bowed away from the pain. He kept pulling. It seemed a thousand miles long. The end finally slipped from her shirt. She collapsed, whimpering with blood pooling around the wound.

Mason snatched up the potion, clumsy fingers sending it rolling across the stone floor. He ran fingers through the spilled mess, touched the potion to the wound on her back and raced to get a new one. He wrenched the lid off, spilling a third before he poured it onto the wound.

Mason didn't wait for the glow to start. He flipped her over, shocked by the amount of blood staining her chest. He cradled her to him, dribbling potion onto her lips. "Drink, please, drink."

She convulsed, choking on the potion. He fed her more. Crimson magic darker than her blood spread across her body.

Crystal's frame fell limp.

He shook her. "Crystal? Crystal?!"

"Mason? Mason, what's going on?"

He bent his ear next to her mouth. A heavenly whisper of breath blew across him. He closed his eyes, squeezing more tears out.

"Mason? Talk to me," Jordan said.

Mason picked up the bloody phone and pressed it to one ear. "I think she's going to be okay."

"Good." Jordan exhaled on the other end. "Now what the hell were you doing that Crystal got shot with an arrow?"

RISKY DECISIONS

Drake tracked down the river courser who'd brought him word of Salyse's abduction. The battleground stank of Sinesh Ena'Donishe, faun and magic. Under it all, he scented Salyse's anger, her fear and her blood.

He'd considered his options on the long drive, choosing his motorcycle over flight to help him track back to the battle site. Salyse hadn't given him her dame's name, but she'd told him about another dragon to the North that she'd befriended.

He faltered. He wanted nothing more than to track the centaur who'd taken Salyse and rend them limb from limb, but helping Jedediah had meant letting them return to their stronghold. He couldn't survive in a headlong assault on a stronghold filled with Dragonsteel-armed defenders. He needed help.

I could ask Jedediah. Drake pulled on his power, forming a mist in preparation for a mist mirror. He shook his head and let go of the magic. *No. This is dragon business. I should've killed VelSera when he ordered his warriors to attack me. He must be taught the meaning of crossing our kind.*

He headed north to find a dragon known as Gilrender, chaffing at taking the long way to vengeance but all too aware that his prudence was the best course. It was also lined with convenience stores and truck stops filled with treasures worthy of a dragon's trove.

Drake leaned against his motorcycle atop a hill overlooking a Michigan coast. He crushed another empty Cherry Coke can. Several cases worth lay discarded around his bike. He stopped eating the cans, preferring to save room for more of the sweet intoxicating elixir.

Thick purple-black clouds overcast the sky. Lightning flashed within them, preferring to dance along the clouds rather than descend to the ground. Rain damped his hair and dripped beneath his jacket. He raised his face, relishing the feel of wind and rain on skin. Human form offered advantage and disadvantage.

Buying my own Cherry Coke is definitely in the advantage column.

He'd experienced plenty of disadvantages. Clothes stuck uncomfortably against him, tight with water making them cling like a second less comfortable skin that needed shredding away. Speed traps had proved troublesome too. Not stopping for the first had sounded a fox hunt, bugling out to an army of cops with nothing better to do than chase him.

Thankfully none saw through my camouflage.

Stopping hadn't improved the roadside traps. The sentinel enforcing too slow speeds had demanded identification he hadn't possessed. He'd tried to incarcerate Drake. The arrogant normal seized him, and it'd taken all his willpower to not bite the cop's head off—literally.

If I can save Salyse and punish Wizard's Bane, it'll all be worth it.

Drake scanned the lake—he didn't remember its name and didn't care. His eyes settled on an empty, half-rotten fishing dock. It matched the one in Salyse's memory.

There were other memories too. She hadn't been fostered long, and her Mistress had treated Salyse as if she were fragile—something Jedediah definitely didn't bother doing. He'd augmented Salyse's information by talking to people, asking questions like a television detective. The fishing dock and those nearest had been abandoned. Gossip blamed commercial fishing companies for depleting the local fish and putting local competitors out of work.

Except it's nothing more sinister than an empty belly. Why did this dragon settle so near people?

Drake drained his last Cherry Coke, distractedly bit a hunk from the can and discarded it with the others. He stomped down-hill in the heavy, sloshing boots. A broken chain pretended to hold the gate closed.

A minivan slowed on the road. Its old driver squinted at him through busy wipers. Drake smiled at her, adding a little wave. She sped off to bingo games beyond the horizon.

He left the chain dangling and clomped down the longest of the nestled docks. Old death, sex and blood clung to the wood of a half gutted office.

Someone chose the wrong place to mate.

Old shredded clothes and long-deceased campfires showed it a haven for homeless that'd ended up on the menu. He continued onto the long pathway stretched out into the water. The dock shifted beneath his feet, knocking against rotted pillars to either side that no longer held it in place.

He'd learned to balance on two legs, but the wind and wave rocked dock challenged his skill. Drake drew upon his magic, raising pale icy fingers that never seemed to get enough blood to warm properly. They flashed through a series of spells he'd studied before he had fingers and practiced after he'd managed to make some.

Living in the normals' world had served as a crash course in practical necessity. The wards and detection magic from old lessons flowed off his fingertips with ease. Thoughts about how Jedediah might've reacted brought a snort that leaked smoke.

Still probably complain that I needed more practice. Warmth filled Drake. *Or he'd tell me he knew I had the ability the whole time as if he'd figured out that I was holding myself back to keep him from sending me away...like Mother did.*

The magic he'd invoked had gone missing by the time he jerked himself back into the world. He performed them again. Water bubbled despite not having anything to do with his magic. Some-thing oppressive pressed against his mind, growing with each popped bubble. He wanted to leave, to put as much distance as he could between himself and the dock

Drake snorted. *You're going to have to do way better than that.*

He glared down into the muddy depths. A glance overhead at the storm left him sure it'd had a hand in the brackish water, but he felt just as certain the water remained muddied in service to the dragon far below.

Fear? Fog? Simple tricks for someone who so obviously doesn't like to be seen. How old were you when your master sent you into the world?

Drake folded his arms and waited. The other dragon had to know he was there, so he waited for invitation or challenge. They didn't come.

He sighed. "All right, Gilrender. If you've no nerve to face more than drunks, drug addicts and teenagers in heat, I guess I'll have no choice."

Drake wrapped a glamour around the dock's end and stripped.

"Last chance. Face me up here, or I'm coming to you."

Uncertainty whispered. *What if he wants me to come to him, to some kind of trap? This isn't a centaur or a normal. It's another dragon in both lair and preferred element.*

Drake counted to ten, each number a rung upon a ladder of gathered energy and squared metaphysical shoulders. The last number fell from his lips. He took a long breath, leapt into the water and shapeshifted midair.

Mason led Crystal back to the farmhouse, feeling like the biggest jerk in existence. She carried her bloodstained shirt in one hand, his shirt covering her.

"There isn't even a scar, Mason."

He shriveled inside. She'd made an effort to cheer him the whole way back toward the farm. She didn't yell at him for ruining her clothes. She didn't scold though he knew them being away all night meant trouble from both their mothers. She didn't even complain about their stomachs grumbling in chorus.

Beryl leapt from the soil like a dolphin, pouncing on a loose shoelace with all the ferocity she could muster.

"You didn't mean for them to shoot me. You were defending me."

"Yeah," he said. *And almost got you killed playing the bigshot...same kind of thing that broke my wrist. It's all my fault.*

The greenhouses came into sight. Beryl raced toward them and Sarah's silhouette—another worried mother. She barked. Beryl stopped. The puppy whirled, nose in the air and yipped.

Mason followed their attention. High in the sky, a red, winged shape circled.

"Is that Drake?"

Dread crept into Mason's gut. "I...don't think so. Crystal, run."

Mason sprang to a full sprint toward the boneyard, jerking Crystal forward with him. The circling creature drew nearer. Wind whipped the dusty fallow fields, sending up a cloud of debris. He let go of Crystal's hand. She yelped, but he didn't look back.

Mason slowed enough to scoop up Beryl, turned back and grabbed Crystal once more as she caught up.

<Cower and worship, worthless kine.>

Mason started to say something snarky, but the blood-soaked clothes left in their wake kept his lips closed. He ducked through the farm equipment, the sound of Jedediah's hives buzzing behind the greenhouse wall.

"Little distraction would be great," Mason said.

"What?" Crystal asked.

<You cannot escape me.>

Fear pummeled him. Crystal's hand tightened around his and Beryl whimpered. Every cell in his body wanted to cower, to give up, but something hard in him kept his leg moving. *I'm not letting Crystal get hurt again.*

"The fridge, go," Mason pushed Beryl into her arms and sprinted back the way they'd come. He waved his arms in the air. "Hey, fatso! Should you knock off the junk food? Maybe get a little exercise?"

Stormfall roared.

"Mason, no!" Crystal shouted.

He glanced her way to be sure she was still running toward escape. He sucked in all the magic he could manage and wrapped the Zephyr around himself. *All I have to do is distract her long enough for Crystal to escape.*

Stormfall's consciousness slammed into him, driving him to his knees. She dove toward him, careening into the ground and flattening another section of greenhouse.

The bees roared out of their damaged home. Stingers were no match for scales, but the bees targeted eyes and exposed skin. Mason struggled to his feet, racing toward the fridge. He glanced backward.

Stormfall reared back, her chest swelling.

Mason dove behind a combine.

Heat washed over him in a massive roar. The combine melted to slag, hot metal flying overhead. Mason ran for the fridge, dodging puddled metal. He stepped onto a small hunk. Heat stabbed his foot, rubber soles igniting.

Mason yelped, kicking off the shoe. *Good thing I never tie them tight no matter how many times Mom complains about me slipping them on and off.*

Crystal extended her hand at the fridge's entrance. "Come on."

"Just go."

Tears ran down her face. "No."

Stormfall slammed into the ground between them. She blinked her large eyes, red spots visible on her eyeballs. Mason threw himself between her talons. They rose and slammed down as he tripped, scrambled to his feet and dove behind one back leg. She slammed her bulk down a moment too late. The impact threw him from his feet.

Crystal darted away from the portal, yanking him onto his feet.

Stormfall whirled. *<No!>*

They dove through the doorway, slamming into brick and falling to the ground in a heap. Breath tore at his chest. His heart slammed at his ribs demanding escape. Mason gasped, curses rolling off his tongue in an endless litany of survivor's shock.

Crystal laughed at a particularly awkward profanity.

Her laughter ignited his own. *We survived. Holy Jesus, we escaped a dragon.*

Kane shoved in another mouthful of food he didn't want, not actually tasting it. He'd been over the whole place a thousand times, but he couldn't find anything to do but sleep and eat. The one old iPod he'd found rummaging through drawers had been out of power. He'd searched high and low for a charger. When he'd finally found one, he'd been unable to plug it in because the tower had no outlets.

Kane ate more pie. *Not even in the kitchen where the fridge is running. I don't know how they've even got power.*

There were a ton of books, but reading was hardly better than staring at the stone walls around him.

Too much effort for something without explosions or cool special effects. Why can't something interesting happen? I thought we'd at least be off to save Mistress.

A cacophonous boom shook the tower, knocking the spoonful of pie down his shirt. He raced to a window. A second boom knocked him from his feet before he got there. A swarm of centaur sieged the tower far below.

Another boom rocked the tower. Kane raced up the ten thousand stairs. "Jedediah! Jedediah, we're under attack!"

He found the old man leaning out a window in the big library.

"Quick, Jedediah, Wizard's Bane is attacking."

Jedediah raised his eyebrows. "We should go talk with them then."

"Talk? How about raining down fire and brimstone and hurricanes and lightning and hell, I don't know, exploding frogs."

"Ain't no reason to abuse frogs."

The infuriating old man headed down the stairs as if browsing a grocery store. They made it without another boom, Kane's shoulders tight in anticipation. The doors swung open. Behind them a mob of centaurs milled in a half circle, their skins so dark brown as to nearly mimic black. A massive woman with breasts bigger than Kane's head perched hands of cascading layers of flab in the general vicinity of her hips.

"*Jedaiha*, what the meaning of what you been doing up there?"

Kane reached into himself and down into the earth, power seeking something dead he could animate. Jedediah put a hand on his head, and the gathered magic just vanished.

"What the hell?" Kane asked.

"What do you mean, Mama?"

"Someone been shaking the spirit pillars." She cocked her head. "Voices be crying foul in Mama's dreams, and it looks like whatever you be about, it's sunk fangs into you."

"What's with all the nice? They've got Mistress. Kill them or something."

"It's a curse of some kind," Jedediah said.

"The boy?" Mama Yamai asked.

"No, just a spoiled nuisance," Jedediah said.

"Hey!"

"You want I should take him with Mama like your girls, *Jedaiha*?"

"Thanks, but Mauve sent him to me. I can't rightly pawn him off."

"He's standing right here," Kane said.

"Mama Yamai has eyes, boy, ears too. You be straining them with your yearling whines."

Kane folded arms across his chest. *I'm not whining.*

She scowled at Jedediah. "A lost Jewel come crying to Mama Yamai, begging me to knock on your door and stop the harm you be doing."

Jedediah's voice cracked "Jewel? No, that's impossible. She's been dead...."

"Maybe not possible for young *Jedaiha*, but Mama Yamai knows the Mother and the children she's taken back. Many spirits know the path to my lodge. Many come to Mama Yamai in a terrible fury, crying out for vengeance against wrongs you be guilty doing."

"I don't harm those that don't deserve it," Jedediah said.

Her face smoothed, her eyes glazing almost to match Jedediah's. She frowned. "You might believe it so, but maybe you be lost in the savannah too heartsick to see the lion in the grass."

"What do you want, Mama?" Jedediah asked.

"You be coming with me, *Jedaiha*. You must dance with the spirits."

Jedediah shook his head. "The dance nearly killed me last time."

"You be dancing without old Mama, clumsy boots stomping ripples in the resting places like a legion of Rome, forcing me to reach across Mother to save you from fool grief and worse stupidity."

He looked away from her. "I remember."

"You be remembering also the debt you be owing Mama?"

He replied with a whisper. "Yup."

"Then you be remembering to obey when Mama call, and I say you dance."

"Get your things, boy. We won't be back for a while."

"Where are we going?" Kane asked.

Mama Yamai smiled at him. "We be walking the African steppe, little death, putting sun on your skin that none be mistaking you for staking."

"Walking? Outside? In Africa?" Kane asked. "Can't I just wait here?"

Both answered. "No."

Mason stepped out of the dojo locker room, pleasantly sore and feeling more confident than ever. Roland, Edgar and Jimmy wouldn't walk all over him if they showed up now. He glanced at his phone and cursed. He had to hurry if he was going to get home before his curfew.

"Mason."

Sensei Truth's smile met his own.

"How'd I do today?"

"Remarkable," Truth said. "Flexible, quick—you're a born fighter."

"I mostly just don't want to get my butt kicked anymore."

Truth laughed. "I doubt that will pose a problem, even three on one."

Mason checked his phone once more. "Was there something else? I need to get home."

"Week after next is your Spring Break, isn't it?"

"Yeah."

"There's a tournament going on in Atlanta. If you're interested, I'd like you to come."

"Watching a tournament would be epic," Mason said.

"Probably, but I'd like you to compete." Truth smiled. "With your father's permission."

Mason fidgeted. "Yeah. I don't know. I have to ask."

"I understand. Let me know by next week, all right?"

Mason nodded. He bounced out of the dojo, letting the door close on its own to tinkle the bell. He skipped toward the street's edge, remembering proper decorum for a man of his age in time to stop before being seen.

He thinks I'm good enough to compete! Mason groaned. *How am I going to go? Mom's not going to let me out of her sight for that long.*

He crossed a parking lot into a Walmart, beelining for the bakery discount rack. He bought a dozen after holiday cupcakes, a Mountain Dew and continued up the long road toward home.

He called his dad.

"Hey, Mason. Bit busy here, bud. What can I do for you?"

"Are you taking me during Spring Break like the court order says?"

"I'm not sure your mom's going to want to let you go," Marcus said.

"It's law, right? Judge signed and all that?"

"It is…."

"I'll arrange things with Mom, you won't have to do anything," Mason said.

"If she says no, I think it might be best to let her have her way. She's been under a lot of stress lately."

Mason licked his lips, considering his plan.

"Mason, bud? You still there?"

"Yeah, let me ask. okay, Dad?"

"Call me back," Marcus said.

Mason crossed the busy road to the airport side, avoiding a section of street with yards ending in curbs and no safe place to walk. He dialed his mom's number.

"Mason? What's wrong? Are you in the hospital?"

Mason rolled his eyes. "No, Mom. I was just talking to Dad on the phone about Spring Break."

"Spring Break?"

"Yeah, he wants to pick me up so we can do something together."

"I don't think so," Billie Jo said. "Not after you staying over at your friends without telling me."

"The court order says I get to spend time with him during the break, doesn't it?" Mason asked.

"Yes, but—"

"Great. I'll tell him you said it's okay." Mason added the finishing blow. "Thank you, Mom. I love you so much."

"I love you too, honey."

Mason called his father. "You were right, Dad. She's not happy with the idea."

"So she vetoed it?" Marcus asked.

Mason fought rising excitement to put disappointment into his voice. "Yeah, you could fight her over it, but—"

"No, sport. It's probably best just to let her have her way."

Mason grinned.

"Maybe we'll do something big this summer if things work out."

"Great. Talk to you later." Mason hung up.

I'll hide out at Jedediah's, hanging out with Kane—and Crystal if she's been sent to the cellar for misbehavior, then I'll go to the competition. Mom'll never know I was gone.

BEATDOWN

J ordan folded her arms, glaring at the empty driveway. Her meager belongings leaned against one leg on the drab tiles of juvenile detention's floor.

Come on, Angesa, I could be studying more Avatar.

She closed her eyes and summoned her magic. She sent it seeking into the ground, trying to feel the earth so she could somehow bring it up to her. She didn't actually try to bring it up inside the building—not that it mattered. She'd never succeeded.

Yeah, the crap floor is safe from me.

Angesa's car pulled up. Jordan grabbed her stuff and headed for the door. One of the cops stopped her.

"What? That's my ride," Jordan said.

"It is if she comes in and signs for you."

Jordan rolled her eyes.

Angesa took her to lunch before dropping her off once more at the Bridgeport house. The sight of it knotted Jordan's gut. She wanted to return to the farm, to Jedediah, but the State of Georgia assumed they knew better.

Mae appeared on the porch. A malicious anticipation all but radiated off of the woman.

"Now remember, Mae's been gracious enough to invite you

back, so no hitting people," Angesa said. "If something happens that violates the things we talked about, you are to be allowed phone access, or you can reach me from school."

"Great."

"Marnie is allowed to pick you up three times a week plus Saturdays for practice. If Mae offers any problems with your training, please let me know."

"Okay," Jordan said. *At least they're twisting Mae's arm on that one. Wonder what it's going to cost me.*

Jordan grabbed her stuff from the back seat and trudged up the walk. She passed Mae without a word and headed through the house to the back door.

"Where are you going?" Mae asked.

"To my room?" Jordan said.

"You've been moved upstairs," Mae's tone sounded brittle. "The State objected to you being so far from supervision."

"Crystal, too?" Jordan asked.

"Yes."

"How's Arthur?"

Mae bristled. "Put your things away and come down to start dinner."

Crystal was already hard at work chopping vegetables when Jordan entered the kitchen. The younger girl squealed, embracing Jordan with the chef knife still in her hand."

"Careful," Jordan said.

"I missed you so much."

"Have you been getting sent into the cellar a lot?"

Crystal smiled, but it slid from her face.

"What?"

"I was, only, well last time I got shot in the chest by a centaur, and then Drake's mom tried to eat us—though Mason distracted her by calling her names and setting bees on her."

The room spun. She'd known about the arrow and had every intention of slapping his thick head next time she saw him. She hadn't known about Stormfall. "He taunted a dragon?"

"He was so brave."

Taunting Stormfall can't bode well. Jordan balled her fists. "Damn it, Mason."

❧

Stormfall tired of waiting for a morsel to scurry out of one of the metal mouse holes. She glanced up at the setting sun. A storm lurked in the breeze. She loved storms.

She lowered a nose to inhale the scent of the boy and girl that's taunted her and leapt into oncoming twilight. She'd come to destroy the petulant wizard, his ilk and her disrespectful offspring. Their actions couldn't be tolerated.

Glamour tinted her glorious scales a flat grey to match the dark, pendulous sky. She flew low, wind from her wings throwing debris in all directions. There were few scents in the sparsely populated areas around the wizard's farm, but more and more caressed her nose as she neared their warren.

Flying low to scent her prey offered challenges in the stormy sky. She rose and fell, her wings stronger than any push of intemperate wind. She flew back and forth over the city. The coming storm arrived, filling her flight with rain and more powerful winds. A scent caught in her nostrils, the petulant boy that'd escaped her.

She circled, found its path and winged along in its wake while steel birds took off and landed to her right. Lightning cracked the sky. She flew over houses with tiny yapping morsels, parkland and eventually found more dwellings. His scent clung to a cluster of them.

Stormfall dropped, her bulk smashing through a tree onto the centermost house. Talons crushed the paltry dwelling. The screams she wanted didn't rise from the building. Heat rose in her chest. She sucked in air and blew out the contents of her fire lung in a wide circle.

Houses caught fire despite the rain. Screams joined the thunder, and the scent of fear bathed her tongue. A young morsel ran from a house. She pounced, snatched it up in one talon and shoved it into her mouth. Blood laved her tongue, but its taste mismatched the scent she desired.

More kine fled their dwellings. She leapt on them, shoved some into her mouth. Others she batted, letting them find their feet before she snapped them up in her teeth. Joy filled her. She slammed talons into burning houses. She ignited more of them—including the first—driving more snacks into the street.

None of the kine tasted as they should. None were the boy she wanted most to roll across her tongue and crush between her teeth.

Sirens wailed in the distance, drawing nearer. She considered eating their bearers, but noise, fire and death would keep her prey from returning.

Besides, there are other kine to hunt.

Billie Jo stepped out of Pastor Burton's office, Mason sulking behind her. *That's it. That's the last chance I give him.*

Her phone rang. Marcus's number knotted her gut. She let him feel her frustration. "What do you want?"

"Are you and Mason safe?" Marcus asked.

The question threw her off. She gathered her anger back up. "What do you care, and why do you even want to know?"

"Your neighborhood's on fire."

Cold washed over her. "We're fine. I'll call you back."

Billie Jo hung up, pulling up the local news website on her phone. The camera panned through her neighborhood. The anchor said something about missing presumed dead, but she barely heard it. Her crushed house burned in the center of a fire the reporter blamed on lightning storm and tornado.

Mason looked over her shoulder. "Shit. She found the house."

"Watch your mouth, young man. She who? Who found the house?"

"Drake's mom," Mason looked away. "I may have pissed her off."

Hot and cold, anger and disbelief whirled around her like a miniature hurricane. "You brought a dragon to my home?"

Mason frowned. "Not exactly?"

Billie Jo grabbed his arm, threw open the pastor's door and dragged him inside. She shoved the phone screen forward. "You idiot! This is your fault. If you'd just performed the exorcism, my son wouldn't be consorting with the Devil, and I'd still have a home."

Pastor Fulton darkened. "Mason, please wait outside."

"He's not going anywhere," Billie Jo said. "I want you to get off your lazy, ignorant ass and perform an exorcism on him right this moment."

Mason turned around and marched woodenly out the door.

"Come back here," Billie Jo said.

The door slammed itself behind him.

"Sit. Down."

Billie Jo whirled, a rejoinder on her lips. Pastor Fulton's eyes glowed like coals. They locked gazes. Her limbs moved without her, and she found herself sitting in the chair gripping its arms in a death grip.

"I have had enough of you." Pastor Fulton growled. His appearance melted away, revealing a tall, fit and very imposing figure. Fury bent an otherwise handsome face, the light in his eyes almost making his wavy, crimson shoulder-length hair glow. "I didn't draw your soul back from death, lug the soulstone around all those centuries, engineer your birth and manipulate your introduction to Jedediah for you to screw up everything with ignorant zealotry."

"Who are you?" Billie Jo asked.

"The question is who are you?"

Her chair slid away from the wall. The desk flew out of the way, making way for her chair to stop centered in the room. The man circled her.

"Elsabeth, I command you to come forth."

"I don't—" Billie Jo's world tilted. Her vision blurred. She rose, the action feeling as she were somehow tearing herself in half. She looked down to see her body still in the chair, slack-jawed and drooling. She lifted a transparent hand. "What've you done to me?"

"Separated your soul from your newer body so we can have a

chat which you'll share with no one. You're instrumental to my plan, and I've had enough of you fucking it up." Zero threw his hands forward. Tendrils of magic stabbed her insubstantial body. Pain shot through her. "You love Jedediah."

Billie Jo opened her mouth to object, but she did love him—deep down.

"You will accept his magic as you did before. You will encourage Mason's lessons in both fighting and magic. You will *beg* Jedediah to take you back if that's what it takes."

She wanted to object. Her parents had taught her the horrors of witchcraft and tried to drive the evil from her as a child. No, her parents had taught her to make a good house, preparing her to marry well for the clan. Conflicting memories dizzied her. She remembered meeting Jedediah for the first time—twice. She seemed two women, born centuries apart.

"You will be a warm, supportive, loving and compliant mate from now on. If something upsets your world view, you'll deal with it without complaint. You'll...," Zero smiled a malicious grin. Something yanked her back toward her body. "You'll bake like a good little woman should, *Mother*."

Jedediah stared into the small valley from beside a baobab tree. Kane fidgeted behind him, surrounded by a silent, deadly escort of African centaur. Silver tattoos marked the dark skin of their human counterparts. Their intermixed scrutiny itched his trimmed beard.

Predators one and all should I threaten their little Mother.

Jedediah felt kindred to them. He'd grown up with a few of the older centaur, hunted with them, learned their lore. Mama Yamai shouldered a decade of his training for the Dutchman—much as he'd sent Lanea to learn from Mauve.

Kane approached him, clothes dirty and sweat soaked. "Are we done wandering around the continent with a bunch of savages? I want air conditioning."

A shift in Jedediah's hand sent the young apprentice flinching away.

"Sorry, sorry," Kane said. "Month-long walks makes me grumpy."

Jedediah shook his head. "Ought to turn Mauve over my knee."

"Excepting she be wanting that for ages, *Jedaiha*."

Jedediah's own childhood among his mother's tribesmen had instilled great respect in the wisdom of so-called savages. Both groups survived without bullets or lightning for attacking anything that moved. They'd lived and flourished—the only predator in their homelands without natural claws, testifying to their ferocity and brilliant simplicity.

Dark expressions followed Kane. Nights in camp, many freely spoke derision at the two newcomers and their ways. Older, wiser centaur warned them against angering an enemy who could break their strength like thinnest twigs.

The warning had almost made Jedediah laugh, but a seditious response of hotheaded youth told him how far Velith'Seravin's poison had traveled. The elders quashed the rebellious claims, spinning tales of generosity granted their tribe by magic users.

The young complained further until Jedediah uttered a question in their tongue. "You would murder your little Mother in the cause of an honorless warrior who'd kill a dragonling lord?"

One young warrior refused to relent. A warleader challenged him to something akin to the Rite of the Long Knives. Blood flowed, but only in contest. No one died.

Jedediah considered the tiny mud hut at the depression's base. It'd faired poorly, evidence of patches and reconstruction scarring its walls. He touched the baobab tree, feeling the life force of the veritable ecosystem alive in its nooks, cracks and crevices. It had born witness to all—shorter on his last visit but no less impressive.

"Have you caught your breath, *Jedaiha*? Are you able to keep pace with Mama Yamai now?"

Jedediah smirked. "Ask the kid. He's the reason we're resting."

'What have I got to do with this?" Kane asked.

"We're doing a spirit dance," Jedediah said. "Sounds like an educational opportunity for a young necromancer to me."

"Both boys be learning much if Mama reads the next world true."

Jedediah shook his head. "You are one insufferably arrogant woman."

"Mama Yamai is not arrogant." She preened. "She's far too good to be so. Let us seek the spirits and dance to their song."

A shiver ran along Jedediah's spine. *Jewel is here. I never spoke to her after she died. I couldn't bring myself to call her until long after her spirit would've passed beyond the veil.*

Jedediah gestured Kane after him downhill to the hut's opening. The tribesmen fanned out along the ridge. They wouldn't descend to court the dead and angry, but they would be on guard against assault—from living or dead.

Temperature dropped with every step, kindred to descent into his ice house.

Kane moaned. "That's better."

Gooseflesh ran rampant across Jedediah's skin. It bothered neither Kane nor Mama Yamai, though their breath blew thick and white in the graveyard cold. Jedediah steadied himself.

Death is. It bears no evil intent. Fear turns its indifference into a malicious predator stalking man and child. Jedediah rubbed his arms, dreading the embarrassing discomfort to come. *I've met true evil. It smiled a lot and spoke beautiful words—implacable but not patient.*

Jedediah squared his shoulders and stared the hated hut in the face. Near to its entrance, the squat structure seemed grown rather than built of mausoleum marble. Polished wood beads curtained the doorway. It bore no skulls, no evil marks, no runes, no finger bones, no Halloween horrors, no malicious ornamentation. It was merely a hut that terrified him.

Mama Yamai disappeared inside. Kane moved to follow, but Jedediah restrained him. She reappeared with a tray of implements. She flipped woven grass mats out, laying them in the hut's shade, set small pots beside each and stripped off her already sparse clothing.

"Wait, what are you doing?" Kane stared at dark-skinned evidence of the temperature. "What is she doing?"

"Take your clothes off, boy." Jedediah kept his gratefulness from his voice. The boy's acute embarrassment having distracted him from his own.

"What? Why?"

"Nothing of this world goes beyond," Mama Yamai said. "Besides, little death, why so shy? Many brave warrior has begged Mama to dance with them in nothing but moonlight."

"I'm good," Kane said. "Not really the dancing kind."

She laughed in her childish way.

"Just strip, boy." Jedediah glowered. "Tormenting the boy with such images isn't funny, Mama."

"It isn't the boy in my sights, *Jedaiha*. Make haste that I may mark us as friends to death while sun yet shines."

"What if they can't read?" Kane asked. "What if they don't want friends?"

Jordan escaped through the portal early the first Saturday of Spring Break and drove a Charger out to the state park she loved best. It'd been forever since she'd last run in the woods near the elven city, Lynelaen. She fidgeted, staring at her hands. *Avoiding Lirelaeli Ermyn'Phir and how she'll remind me of her daughter Lanea.*

Before Billie Jo's intervention, she'd run along the railroad track converted to running path that headed downtown to the Riverwalk. She faced out into the beautiful woods, grief drawing wet lines down her face. She'd bottled it up, much as she'd bottled up the fear Jedediah wouldn't return and her own unease at being responsible for Mason, Crystal, Kane and the rest of the world.

Maybe it was a mistake to come here.

She wiped her eyes and opened the back door. "Come on then."

Nip hopped out, and Beryl tumbled after him. He nosed the puppy over onto her feet and shared an exasperated look with Jordan. He leaned his head into the car and licked the mud she'd left on the seats—as if he hadn't been guilty of the same at her age.

Jordan sat on the clean back seat, tossing her shoes to the floor. She crossed hot asphalt to dew-damp grass and stretched out. She drew on the Mother until it felt as if she'd gorged at a Sunday bake sale.

Monday lunches often included Mason complaining about their weekly get-mason-an-exorcism meeting, but Billie Jo had apparently experienced a bizarre reversal. She'd given him permission to learn magic and martial arts and topped it all off with dozens of cookies. She'd come up to Jordan at lunch. The woman had begged Jordan to help her make up with Jedediah and then practically shoved a cake and a plate of brownies down Jordan's throat. Mae, the news of Stormfall destroying Mason's house and Drake's disappearance—she really needed a good, solid run.

Glad Marnie agreed to meet me a bit later. I need to burn off all this crap in my life where no one can see.

She looked at Nip and Beryl. The latter raised her wagging butt to the sky and yipped while the former thumped his tail against and occasionally through the ground.

"Think she can keep up?"

Nip answered with a doggy grin, leapt up without warning and bolted into the woods. Beryl froze, ears forward. Her head shifted back and forth between Jordan's position and where Nip had run.

Jordan laughed. "I was going to do that to both of you."

She dashed after Nip, leaving the excited, yipping puppy scrambling to catch up. Magical power pulsed through her, pushed hard to enable her to catch her surprisingly fast companion.

Guess I'm not the only one who's improved their skills. She laughed again. "No fair holding out on me."

Sounds of excited, frustrated puppy followed her, but she had no intention of letting Nip show her up. Trees and bushes whipped past. A few grabbed at her, trying to catch her or at least leave their mark. Earth-hardened skin deflected their petty grasps.

Jordan pulled on the Dragon Spring and her own reserves,

bolstering the rumble with power from Mother whenever a foot touched ground. Exhilaration better than any runner's high coursed through her. The wild wood, augmented by the presence of elves and Fey, filled her with joyful contentment. Wind caressed her face, flying her hair like a banner. Magic pulsed through her bones. Everything felt right, perfectly simple and straightforward—a life she could handle with no more burden than placing the next foot on the path.

She'd spent a lifetime in foster homes keeping herself distant and disconnected. She'd refused friendships and even parental concern, divorcing herself from connections that allowed others to inflict pain. She'd dropped those walls for Jedediah, for Drake and Lanea.

Ache stabbed her chest, causing her to falter for a step. It pierced her to the depth her love of Lanea had rooted inside her. Sorrowful tears joined the joyful. War, fear, the Bridgeports, Lanea's death—so much pain burned into her like blazing metal. Mason, Drake, Jedediah, even Crystal and Kane balmed the pain. Love brought hurt, but it so overshadowed the bad she wasn't sure why she'd pushed it all away for so long.

They're worth protecting even if I'm not sure how.

Jedediah's declaration of pride filled her as if she'd swallowed a warm spring sun. He'd declared his pride in her accomplishments. She wouldn't let him down. She'd run hard. Train hard. Do well in school. She'd be the daughter he wanted her to be—not Lanea but equally loved.

Jordan passed Nip. Her long strides finally if slowly outpacing him. He pushed faster, keeping them even and then slowly regaining lost ground. She smiled at him and pushed herself even faster. They were in a section of wood she'd never entered before, and certainly never at this kind of speed. Her pulse raced in her ears, and she felt wonderful.

Nip barked.

His bark directed her attention to a large ravine slashing across their path. He slowed. She stuck her tongue out and put on more speed with the tip of her tongue peeking. She reached out, trying to bring the wind coursing by under her control, trying to add it to her reflexes

She leapt, not over the ravine but a zig-zag course from tree to tree like a pinball. She hit ground on the other side and kept running. Nip barked again, but he could catch her if he earthswam.

But Beryl can't.

Jordan slowed. A deep, warm ache clung to her limbs. It felt good. The success of her complicated leap added to her elation. Part of her wanted to keep running, but she felt guilty leaving the pup behind.

They might've found something interesting to sniff, but just the same I should go back. The shadowcats haven't exactly been warm and fuzzy lately.

She dropped to a walk, shaking her arms out and circled back the way she'd come. She halted, the three fauns that'd been hunting Kane stood in shafts of early morning sunlight.

"He's not with me." Jordan shifted the rumble of her magic, stealing some from her strengthened limbs to toughen her skin. "Kane's not the running type."

"We're here for you," Kiki said.

The three closed the distance and started a slow circle around her.

Three on one. Talk your way out of it. Jordan's stomach tightened. "You need help or something? Jedediah's not around either."

"You stood in our way last time," Lili said. "Hurt us."

"What choice did you give me? We had to defend ourselves."

"Our master wants wizards," Mimi said. "We were directed to you."

Her staff leapt to hand, runes igniting along its length. "I don't care what Velith'Seravin wants. Just go on your way, and I won't have to hurt you again."

Unfriendly eyes assessed her, sizing Jordan up for a fight she'd hoped to avoid. Their circling picked up speed. It turned into a dance that bounced their shoulder-length curls.

Jordan shifted her sight, seeing the trail of magic left by their hooves. It thickened into a ghostly wall as they walked. She drew on the Dragon Springs, but her generally reliable connection wavered as if she wasn't able to tune it in. *They're trying to cut me off. What do I do? Run? Attack?*

They raised pipes to their lips. Melody circled her like they were Disney sharks preparing for their big musical number. Her skin crawled, nausea washing up to push bile into her mouth. She drew more power from Mother, pushing it against her skin until her whole body tingled.

Kiki lowered the pipe from her lips, a birdsong voice singing while the other two continued to play. "Fear ran away, and sorrow fled."

Magic swirled from her lips like milk drops in water, clouding the interior of the circle. Jordan studied their movements, watching the way they set their feet.

Lili's contralto took over. "All your worries take to wing."

Jordan's tension eased as more power trailed off them like ribbons fluttering in a breeze. The song called out to Jordan. The magic caressed her, feeling every bit as if Mother's gentle touch while making her teeth vibrate.

Mimi raised her voice in dulcet soprano. "Lil birdie you twirl and dance,"

"All your foes are safely dead," Kiki sang.

They're trying to charm me or something. Jordan relaxed her body, lowering the staff and shifting her gaze to a wider, softer focus while still tracking them.

Lili took the next verse. "Of victory joyous sing."

Wait for it.

"Forest child we do entrance," Mimi sang the last line. The three stopped, hands extended. Subtle ribbons of energy fluttered out, wrapping gently around Jordan's skin. Their touch fogged her thoughts, trying to lull her as elemental energy built up in their opposite hand.

Three energy bolts shot toward her.

Jordan flattened herself to the ground, thrusting fingers into it.

She sent energy into kudzu on her side of the circle. "Really? It's obvious you *farbot* bitches ain't never tangled with a Jersey girl."

The invasive vines exploded with growth. Leaves and vines grew out of everywhere, quickly wrapping furry legs as it did everything else in the south. They stepped from the plants as easily as a dryad.

Jordan cursed.

The three sisters attacked.

Jordan had a sudden urge to kiss Mae and Arthur—no, definitely not Arthur—and the geeky girls in juvenile detention. She sidestepped, swung her staff into a whirl, and knocked away Kiki's electrical blast with the petrified wood. She gouged a chunk of earth from the ground. A shot of ice flew over her head. She lobbed the ball of earth like a coach at softball practice and drove a line drive into Lili's gut. Spikes of rock shot out of the ground. Jordan jerked from their sharp tips and swung her staff once more, sending broken stone knives at Kiki.

More spikes shot out of the ground at her. They stabbed her gut, but her armored skin reduced the attack to pinpricks leaking tiny red, beads.

Jordan's mind raced. *Earth, air and water. Earth grounds electricity and earth to stone is pretty much a stalemate.*

A globe of water flew across the intervening space. She batted at it, exploding the ball into a burst water balloon that only soaked her t-shirt. Jordan congratulated herself for quick reflexes and kicked at a rock spike. It broke but wobbled a sideways flight that didn't match the cartoon attacks she'd watched.

I seriously need to go to classes with Mason.

A serrated stone shard cut across her midriff, leaving a trail of blood. A spark of lightning arched at the wound a moment later. Jordan sucked in her stomach and cursed.

Blood, on the other hand, won't cancel a shock. Stone had no problem exiting, I wonder.

She hurled her staff into Kiki's face and drove a fist into the ground with as much power behind it as she could muster. A wave of earth and rock rippled outward in all directions, a call for help embedded in the shockwave.

Mimi leapt it with ease. Lili stepped over it, and Kiki seemed to float a moment over the wave, a condescending titter bubbling from her lips. Jordan's staff shot out of the ground behind Kiki, coldcocking the stupid grin from her face.

Jordan snatched it from the air, orange runes glowing brightly at her touch. She charged the circle, readying to beat Lili down Jersey style. She rebounded off the wall. Another shock of electricity slammed into her. She convulsed, the taste of blood on her bitten tongue.

She rolled to one side barely ahead of a flurry of long, frozen stilettos. She reversed the roll, drawing up a handful of grassy turf like a blanket's edge. She sent power into it. It hardened into a waist height dome of ground. Mimi's magic battled her own in the shield, Lili wetting it to further weaken the barrier.

Kiki said something. Another blast slammed into Jordan's midsection, driving the air from her lungs. The water in her t-shirt slithered up her neck in a rush.

Jordan slapped at it, but the coating reformed and rallied in its attempt to envelop her face. Panic washed through her as it cut off her air. She slapped dirt into her face, caking it in mud. Fingers and power pushed the dirt from her mouth and eyes.

Nip drove himself into Lili, marble teeth splashing blood everywhere.

"Nip." Jordan gasped. "Get the elves."

Nip snapped at Lili's face and slid into the ground a pixie's breadth ahead of an icy blade of power.

Jordan struggled to her feet, driven sideways by another shot of electricity. Mother's strength poured into her, hot as her fury. She snatched up a spike of rock, dragged its fat end in the muddy ground and shoved it against her staff. She drove the makeshift spear at Kiki.

The aeromancer slid around it with speed Jordan couldn't hope to match. Mimi grabbed the staff, yanking it from Jordan's grip and casting it aside. It shot back into Jordan's hand in time to shatter an icy wave.

Jordan spun, gasping and shaking with rage. They couldn't cut her off from Mother, but she couldn't escape the circle. Three on one they'd consistently kept ahead of her and her attacks had only managed marginal effect.

Nip's gone for the elves. I only have to survive. She planted her staff. *I can't throw magic around like they can, but I can draw the Mother into me...literally.*

Jordan pulled earth into herself. Rock and Georgia clay flowed up through the soles of her bare feet. It filled her body until it extruded from her pores like a thousand Play-Doh strings worming out of a press.

Ice, stone and electricity slammed into her. Mimi's magic seized her growing shield, but Jordan held her ground in the sorcerous tug-of-war.

Jordan drew more and more earth into her body. It hardened layer after layer into a shield they seemed unable to penetrate. In many ways, she wrapped herself in a reverse earthswim, thankful for the time she'd spent studying the way Nip had made air channels for Crystal and her to breathe. She built an inner cave around herself, lit by the deep orange glow of the staff's runes.

The Earth endures.

"What's going on here?"

Treevoran? Jordan's heart skipped a beat. Desire filled her body. She shook it off. *I call for help and get that ass?*

Jordan shifted earth from her face, turning to see a group of six elves—Treevoran at their head with Chalet and Thestle to either hand. "Treevoran, I call for sanctuary, invoking the protection of the House of Lirelaeli Ermyn'Phir."

The elves looked to Treevoran.

He smirked. "Well, look who it is. Little Jordan, the wizard's castoff."

"Treevoran?" Jordan said.

Velith'Seravin's words echoed in Jordan's mind. *<Dragonsteel. A rare gift from our new benefactor. Perhaps you know him, Treevoran?>*

"Hello, girls," Treevoran said. "Enjoying playtime?"

Kiki blushed. "Oh, yes."

"Mind if we watch?" Treevoran asked.

Jordan didn't wait for a faun to reply. She yanked earth over her once more, piling it on as curses spilled from her thoughts. More power attacked her shield, the elves either cooperating with Mimi or adding to her strength. Jordan fought them, knowing that she was dead if she didn't come up with something.

Pain shot into her gut. Something lodged in her stomach. Something she hadn't felt since the day Velith'Seravin had nearly killed her. She looked down to find an arrow lodged in her midsection.

Her shield started to crumble.

She fought the pain and redoubled her efforts to build and harden the shield.

Another arrow sliced into an arm. Another lodged in her.

Tears muddied the earth shielding her eyes. *I'm dead. I can't leave the circle. I can't fight so many, and they're just going to keep shooting me until they kill me.*

Slow, pervasive heat seeped into her with the drawn earth. Orange runes grew brighter. *No. I am not just going to give up. If I'm going down, by God, I'm going to make it cost them.*

Jordan drew magic into her. The rumble built beneath her skin until her body seemed to vibrate with the pressure.

An arrow sliced into her chest.

Jordan screamed.

Rock and stone exploded outward in all directions.

She sprang to action, arrows lancing pain through her while shifting limbs broke others. She charged...no one. Faun's and elves lay in disarray around her. Rock shards bloodied them.

Jordan turned her charge into a full on sprint. The elves come to her rescue might not be willing to help, but she'd been claimed. If she could reach Lynelaen's treetop civilization, she could claim her place—no matter how tenuous it might be in light of Lanea's death.

She collapsed at the base of a winding stair at the settlement's roots. She'd pushed everything she had in her, adding all she could beg, borrow and steal from Mother. Dark swirls clouded the world and its merry-go-round forest.

Feet rushed down the stairs from above. Beauty incarnate bent over her, a melodious voice perhaps more beautiful for the concern in it. "You are injured, wizard."

"Cousin," Jordan gasped. "Lirelaeli's da—"

DEATH STRIKES

The colorful lines drawn across his skin made Jedediah feel like a mostly plucked parrot. Considering how they looked on the red-faced boy, he had no idea how they proclaimed the two anything other than idiots. Mama Yamia's lecherous grin and warm fingers hadn't improved the finger-painting session, particularly when she offered the paints to each of them to paint her.

He entered the hut. Candles in strategically placed windows replaced the setting sun, casting light inward like sword blades trust into a stage magician's basket. He'd snuck into the hut once before, confirming the mathematical precision employed in setting each window—all but the one he just knew Mama Yamai added to irritate perfectionists.

Soiled rugs dotted the floor, an occasional snatch of color somehow unfaded despite countless butts over the years. Baskets holding dung, grass and wood interspaced the rugs around a ring of large quartz stones. Varied herbs filled smaller baskets hung above the quartz—some for the dance, others merely offering Mama's favored scents.

Mama positioned herself on the far rug, gesturing for them to stand upon two others. Her fingers twirled, magic warming Jedediah's bare backside. A glance showed the beaded curtain growing into a leafy, intertwined thicket.

"Why's she doing that? What if we need to," Kane blushed. "You know."

"Should've gone before," Jedediah said. "There's no leaving until the dead've had their say."

If they let us go at all.

"They're say? Mistress told me we say and they obey."

"In our world, it may be so, little death, but not in theirs."

"I don't want to go to their world then. I don't even have a hat to cover...."

Jedediah pinched the bridge of his nose.

The fire burst to life, filling the hut with heat and herb-heavy air. Mama began the dance. They moved slowly at first, stepping right and repeating the first line of her mantra. They stepped again, intoned again and spun upon the balls of their feet.

Jedediah watched Kane for mistakes, but the boy's feet somehow knew the dance, and his lips knew every intonation.

Smoke and scent filled the small hut. They sang as one, chanting as they stepped and turned. Hands rose heavenward then touched fingers over the fire before withdrawing and alternating. They stepped forward. They jumped back.

The dance accommodated dozens or could be performed alone. Each dancer added their own essence to the ritual, preparing the way into death with a custom audience drawn for their individual soul. Larger groups often put enough energy into the spell that the spirits drawn to the threshold brought words for the dancers.

This time I was summoned—didn't know that was even possible.

Thick aromatic smoke and exertion dizzied his mind. A pounding drum marked the song in a double beat he eventually recognized as his heart. Painted lines on his flesh tingled. They itched. Mama Yamai's lines ignited like flaring neon. Kane's gleamed a rainbow halo around his features.

Caesar's Palace presents Tribal Dances of Disco.

Jedediah's eyes pressed closed. He fought the impulse like an exhausted infant resisting sleep it didn't understand. It took a moment to realize closing his eyes didn't matter and another to recognize the wizard eye had either closed or gone. Bodies pressed against his, none of them Kane or Mama Yamai. It didn't matter that the hut had been sealed. An invisible host pressed against him, turning ritual into a dance party.

The touches he felt varied. Some shoved and jostled. Others pressed tenderly close. Yet more seized him with hungry, furious insistence.

"Stop." Mama Yamai's voice echoed in the sudden stillness. "We are here, see what is to be seen."

Her insistence compelled him, but he resisted. *Don't like bullies, besides won't change anything if I do.*

"Jedaiha!"

Jedediah opened his eyes, and they widened at once. He could see. Spirits in numbers never before encountered surrounded them. They filled the vast savannah depression—no sign of the hut or the guarding tribesmen.

They stared at him, barely an eye shifting to Mama or Kane.

Why are they here for me, I don't recognize any but Marc.

O'Steele's broken, warped soul glared at him. The condition of Lanea's killer's spirit brought a satisfied, malicious smile to Jedediah's lips.

"You have something to say, Murderer?"

"You did this to him?" Mama asked.

Jedediah's smile grew. "That I did."

"Why?"

"He deserves it."

Mama Yamai shook her head. "This is not good, *Jedaiha*. It stains you, cuts at your soul. Release him."

"Not so long as I draw breath."

"What you've done to him isn't right," Kane said. "And you made me help you."

"The child sees right. Why cannot the wise man I taught?"

"He murdered my Fey Lily to service his greed. He cursed me, stealing my sight and my years." Jedediah willed electricity to lash Marc, but nothing emerged from him. "I'll torment this soul until my last day in the sun and pass his spirit on to my replacement to continue his punishment."

"This is not like you, *Jedaiha*." Mama Yamai's lips pressed together into a thin line. "You are not thinking."

"I've thought of little else."

Kane turned away. "What happened to them?"

Jedediah turned his attention to the assembled spirits. First glance painted them as children, but focus brought a dual nature to the fore. Small and wrinkled, their after-shadows resembled undead pygmies. Girls pressed dolls against hollowed cheeks. Ravenous, rabid eyes ignored wooden toys and plastic as if they could consume him with their anger.

What has happened to them, and why are they angry with me?

At the far edges of the spirits, old enemies jeered and snarled. They urged the pigmies closer. Childish smiles overlaid fangs and pointed teeth. He'd nearly died in his attempt to find Elsabeth beyond the threshold, but even then he'd never faced something as sinister.

A tall, thin beauty stepped through the crowd. Long scarlet hair lay across a shoulder opposite the sleeping face of an infant cradled against her.

Jedediah's breath seized in his chest. *Jewel?*

"Hello, Da. Meet your granddaughter Pearl."

Jedediah gasped. "My Jewel, you were pregnant?"

She smiled. "You'd have made a good grandfather."

Anger twisted Jedediah's features. "But I never got the chance because you refused to hear me."

"I heard you, Da, and did as you taught. I loved with my whole heart and did as I knew was right."

"Right?" Jedediah stormed toward her. "He stole centuries from you."

Anger murmured among the pigmies. The fury in their face tugged at his memory. It didn't surface but sent unease through his soul.

"He didn't mean to hurt me, and he gave me Pearl." A man appeared at her side. She wrapped her arm through his and leaned closer to him. "What harm would you have done to Elsabeth or Mother? Ever? Under any circumstance?"

Anger exploded through him. He cast it at the man, but no magic lanced from his fingertips. Pearl cried. Jewel shielded her. "You've already killed him, Da. You can do him no more harm."

Jedediah jerked a thumb over his shoulder at Marc O'Steele. "Think so?"

"I won't allow it." Jewel stepped between them, eyes a hot echo of his own—the same anger in the pygmy faces. Dread nestled into Jedediah's gut for an extended stay.

"I be thinking this is not the message you wanted to deliver."

Jewel set a hand on Jedediah's arm. Cold, ghostly fingers sent warmth into him. "Mama is right, Da. I love you. Will you forgive me for my choice?"

"I forgave you already," Jedediah said.

Mama Yamai's tone hardened. *"Jedaiha."*

Jewel touched his chest, a tight smile on her lips. "I see the burning scar just here. You've not forgiven me. Please, let this pain go."

"You could've done...anything else but forfeit your life...and hers."

"It's done, Da. Please don't carry a wound I cannot cure any longer."

Jedediah looked down. "All right. I'll try."

"Good enough," Jewel said.

"Is Lanea here?" Jedediah asked.

"Who?" Jewel said.

"Your half-sister," Jedediah scowled at Marc. "The one he murdered."

"Plenty of relatives have parted the curtain, but none named Lanea."

"That's not possible," Jedediah said. "She died in my arms."

"I am sorry, Da."

Jedediah frowned, brows pressing together. "Plenty? Your Ma and sister, but who else?"

Jewel swept a hand. "All these are your blood." Her expression darkened. "And all have cause against you for their deaths."

Jedediah's eyes swept the crowd. *Not pigmies, children...starved children, but how am I to blame? They're neither my offspring nor my victims.*

Jedediah's vanquished foes urged the children forward, increasing his unease. He'd never turned away a child—certainly not one of his blood. He'd never been casual with his seed, but his gut and the mirrored anger he'd seen cemented a dread that proclaimed them his kin.

A small girl, a round-eared echo of Lanea, stepped closer and patted his thigh. Jedediah squatted down and met her eye to eye. "What's your name?"

"Girl."

"Don't you have a real name?"

She shook her head.

Jedediah turned his attention toward Jewel.

"Jedediah, look out." Kane leapt forward. He grabbed the girl as she clawed a hand through Jedediah's chest. Agony shot through him as if she'd raked him with Drake's talons.

She scurried from Kane's grip, cradling a tiny wisp of power in her little hand. Others surged toward her, but she shoved the mote into her mouth. The effect lasted only a moment, but the power seemed to fuse her afterimage to the beautiful apparition on the surface. An eerie giggle escaped her lips, her face transported like a drug addict getting a long overdue fix.

"What the hell just happened? Mama? Jewel?"

The pigmies charged, bowling him over. Small hands slashed through him, stuffing mouths with glowing motes. He lurched up, trying to make his feet under the weightless horde. Vertigo stole his balance, and strength fled his limbs. He'd felt the same at least once before, lying in a Vietnamese jungle bleeding to death.

Jewel hurried to his side, crying and begging. "Stop. Please! He can't help if you kill him."

Threat of death summoned ingrained instincts. He summoned his staff, but the pygmies gobbled the magic before he could collect enough for even such a simple spell. More bodies crowded him. They pressed closer than should've been possible, apparitions overlapping to rake his soul with their greedy claws.

Vengeful laughter roared from Marc O'Steele.

"That be enough." Mama stomped a foot.

The pigmy piranha ignored her, continuing the feast of tiny, torturous bites with no intention of stopping.

"Stop." Kane's voice reverberated. A cold, glowing mist curled around his spirit body "Harm him no more."

Spectral blood stained young faces, most with the barest edge of after-shadow peeled away from their whole. They scattered, wrinkles and shrunken appearance gradually fading back into their second natures.

Jedediah writhed and gasped. Pain lanced through him from countless claw and bite wounds. "What just happened? Why did they do that?"

"They were trying to eat you," Kane said.

"Mama thinks they wanted to be eating your magic."

"What? Why?" Jedediah asked.

Girl stepped from the crowd. "Because you stole ours."

"I never took from a child," Jedediah struggled back to his feet. "Barring taking a toy as punishment. How is it you say these are my blood?"

"You never dallied carelessly in your youth?" Jewel asked.

"I've never laid with a woman that weren't my wife saving Lirelaeli and that weren't by choice."

"You're certain?" Jewel asked.

Jedediah folded his arms. "I ain't in the habit of discussing intimates with my daughter, but yes, I am as sure as Mother's love and Father's rising."

"Well," Kane cleared his throat. "You probably wouldn't have been present to make grandchildren."

He glared at the boy. "Ain't none of my get still living. Those without magic are long dead and those with, taken by tragedy. I kept a close eye on each wither they wandered until the day the Reaper took them."

"I don't know what to tell you, Da, but blood kin they are to the last."

Old foes slid through the children, whispering in ears.

"Y'all leave those children alone. Mama? Kane? What perverted their spirits like this?"

"You did." An angry seven-year-old boy pointed imperiously. "You came to our homes, murdered our mothers and stole our lives."

"I did no such thing," Jedediah said.

"Lies," Marc said.

"You stay out of this, or so help me—"

"Get him," the boy screamed. They swarmed him. Jedediah maintained his feet only moments. Vertigo and exhaustion stole his strength in tiny fistfuls.

"Stop," Kane ordered.

The dead ignored him.

Kane's voice rose to a shriek, cracking as he yelled. "Stop."

Jewel and Mama tried to stop them, but only a few of the children ceased their attack.

"Get off me," Jedediah shouted with waning strength. "I'm warning—hells, screw warnings."

He reached out into the earth to wrench it around him as a shield. Magic coursed into him, dying before it became so much as a dust storm. He called lightning, but it crackled like ineffectual static before it could surge to a full charge. Fire failed to come at his call.

Darkness pressed close on his vision. Pain ripped through his every inch. He struggled through murky thoughts and blinding agony for any defense.

A mousy little fellow in the back of his mind offered up a solution on a silver platter. Jedediah ripped power from the nearest children. They screamed, but he pushed guilt to the side. He used the twice-stolen power to draw more and more. Soul-knotting screams shook the spirit world around him. He shaped the power into a flimsy shield that did nothing against accusing glares.

The seven-year-old spat at Jewel. "Told you he won't help us."

Jewel's expression darkened. "How could you? I told them they could trust you and you hurt them."

"I have the right to defend myself," Jedediah said.

"Even if it means hurting children who've already been injured?" Jewel hitched Pearl up on her hip. "That's the same thinking that murdered them."

Jewel fled into the surrounding darkness without a backward glance. Children followed her. A few enemies lingered but departed after testing his shield. Only one spirit remained—Jewel's husband.

"For what it's worth, I'm sorry. You were right to do it."

His strength faltered. He awoke crumpled upon soft ground in absolute darkness. Cold permeated his bones and pain his flesh. Agony consumed even his soul and left his years heavy with their accumulation.

"You dead?" Mama Yamai asked.

"Well, I'm starving to death," Kane said.

"Not you, boy, *Jedaiha*."

"Guess not," Jedediah said. "I'm blind again. Kane, do you see my eye?"

Something heavy dropped into his lap. "Release O'Steele, *Jedaiha*. It is my wish. Let it clear the debt you owe for your life."

"No," Jedediah whispered. "He killed my daughter."

"I do not think he did," Mama Yamai said.

&

Jordan woke high in Lynelaen surrounded by gorgeous men and women, their beauty lessened by the bend of concerned expressions. Silver gilt verdant foliage high above, elegant dwellings blended almost seamlessly with the trees. A single dark spot marred the surrounding beauty—Lirelaeli's frown.

"You are a troublesome child."

"Lirelaeli," a woman scolded, her concern accentuating the faintest wrinkles beneath silvery hair. "Your child is injured."

How old is this elf?

"She's always injured, Haliathu. She's always mixed up in mischief."

"Children will be children," Haliathu said. "What happened?"

"Fauns," Jordan croaked. "They attacked in the forest. I sent Nip here for help, but the elves that came shot me."

"Preposterous," Lirelaeli said.

"The arrows we pulled from her were elven make," Haliathu said.

Jordan shook her head. "I don't even know how they penetrated the stone shield I erected."

Haliathu turned a bloody arrow over in her hands. Her wrinkles deepened and her expression darkened. "Your shield was magical?"

"Earth, but I used magic to build it," Jordan said.

"Dragonsteel." Haliathu lifted the arrow's tip for the others. A murmur ran the crowd. "What elf shot you with this?"

"We did," Treevoran said. "She attacked, murdering two of our number."

The Arctic Ocean poured down Jordan's throat into her gut. *Murdered? As in dead? As in I killed them?*

"I welcome you into my house, and you'd slay your cousins?" Lirelaeli's glower softened toward Treevoran. "Are you well, my love?"

"Bloodied and heartbroken at this horrifying crime," Treevoran said.

Jordan's heart wrenched. She'd hurt Treevoran. She'd broken his heart. She struggled upright to beg his forgiveness. A darker voice rose its head. *Good. He attacked me. He more than deserves it.*

Haliathu held up a hand. "Why are you carrying Dragonsteel when you know it's forbidden to keep such artifacts?"

Treevoran shrugged. "It isn't forbidden to carry those."

The scent of impending rain filled Jordan's nostrils. Her heart twisted at the familiar scent. Water licked the arrows clean, displaying gleaming metallic tips.

"This is fresh forged," Haliathu said. "How did you come by it?"

"What does it matter how he came by them?" Lirelaeli asked. "My daughter has murdered two of our kin."

Jordan followed Lirelaeli's gesture. Chalet and an elven male she didn't know lay on the wooden platform, their blood staining wood smoothed by countless doeskin boots and silken slippers. Stone shards left torn silks blood-soaked around impaled flesh.

I killed them. Oh, God. I'm a murderer. Tears fled her, too disgusted to remain in her eyes. *I am an ogre, a monster that killed those beautiful elves....*

Jordan's attention returned to the present. The elves squared off over her, anger leaving a burned tang in the air. Haliathu demanded punishment for Treevoran, but Lirelaeli protected her apparent lover at the expense of Jordan herself. Her adopted mother decried her for disgrace brought upon them by her kin killing, but the old matron seemed uninterested in blaming Jordan without her side of the story.

A young elven woman knelt and tilted her head, golden silk tresses cascading over her shoulders. "Tell me."

Her high-pitched voice felt strange in Jordan's ears. The magical tone wasn't bespelled. It didn't carry with it glamour or coercion. Jordan whispered the day's troubles, finding words pouring out of her about the tiniest detail and related explanation.

"Nip could tell...," Horror widened Jordan's eyes. *Oh, God, Nip! Where are Nip and Beryl? Did I kill them too?*

❦

Drake plunged into a world painted deep greens and browns. Muddied and mottled, the water offered an aquatic woodland panorama. The sharp, citrusy tang of algae teamed up with a metallic bite of polluted water.

Now I really I wish I'd saved that last Cherry Coke.

A push of shapeshifting magic grew membranes over his eyes and cleared his vision. The brackish water resisted his enhanced sight, limiting its useful distance. Pain sliced across his throat. He opened his mouth, trusting the Spring knew its business as he sucked water in over new gills. Cramped lungs relaxed. He pushed the magic into his limbs. Frills sprouted and extended until Drake sliced through the water with shark-like grace.

A flick of tail turned him back toward shore. Rocks piled up against the manmade coast. Small holes dotted the embankment hiding little creatures unwilling to welcome the reddish-brown dragon into their homes. Sparse schools darted away from him at first glimpse.

Drake turned his attention to the lake bottom. Old tires and lost wallets, discarded guns and a few human bones rotted with the fishes. What he didn't find among the detritus was an entrance to a dragon's lair.

Drake growled, sending bubbles skyward.

It's here somewhere. I can feel him, almost hear his heartbeat—a long slow thump timed with the crash of waves.

He shifted through various versions of sight, trying to find a seam.

Nothing.

Drake swam methodical circuits. When still nothing came to eye, he drew upon his aeromancy. It struggled against his draw, preferring to rise up and out of the lake rather than sink deep into it at Drake's call. He relented before his magic did. He pulled on the water, memories of Lanea's taught tricks and cheats helped him draw more water from his eyes. Aquamancy wasn't the preferred element for the senses he sharpened, but it warped his sight, smell and hearing in a fashion that improved them in the watery world.

He scented the water first. He got nothing new—nothing in so dynamic an environment as a lake.

Glamour.

Jedediah had harangued and cajoled Drake throughout the early years of his apprenticeship, always challenging him to do more and more with glamour until it served whatever need arose. Glamour gravitated to the Fey, especially powerful Fey like dragons, but unlike the lesser Fey, he'd been content to muscle through with simple but overwhelming illusions.

The kind of huge muscling that wipes all scent, all sight, all hearing. I'm surprised I can even taste the pollution considering how thick this must be. Lanea's musical laughter echoed in his memory. She'd laughed at his early attempts, but taken the time to explain the elven perspective on it. Elves didn't let the glamour act on its own accord to protect them. They shaped it like master sculptors. *If it hadn't been for Lanea, this is all I'd have been able to manage too.*

Drake took in his surroundings once more. He focused, narrowing his attention from the broad to the specific. Willpower and disbelief leveraged correctly had penetrated glamours for him in the past. *All I need is one small thing out of place to use as a fulcrum to get beyond all this.*

He slowed, scanning for inconsistencies Jedediah taught existed in every illusion. He searched for the flaw, the edge of the blanket. His thoughts shifted to Lanea. Pain lanced him, sharp and dull like a melody with a staccato backbeat. Days lazing with her at pond's edge slid a smile onto his beak.

No. Focus. That's the glamour distracting you. Salyse needs your help.

Lanea and Salyse, beautiful aquamancers both. Lanea had been beautiful in more than the elven way. To her cousins, she wasn't beautiful—especially not to Lanea herself. Her humanity hadn't robbed her in Drake's mind. She'd glowed with a beauty so deep down even a blind, stupid dragonling couldn't help but notice it in the first blink of his eye.

Regardless of personal risk, her mischievous nature turned nurturing with regard to him—well, mostly. She taught him, helped him, got him out of trouble so many times. She'd really cared, perhaps not in the ways he wanted, but he understood. They were different species. It separated them even if a hopeful little voice insisted it didn't matter.

Jedediah would probably throw me out if he knew I'd fallen for Lanea. Drake cursed. *It did it to me again. Every time I pass a particular area I get distracted.*

Gilrender had proved himself craftier than Drake'd thought at first blush. There seemed no way an untrained dragonling like Salyse could've broken the glamour unless Gilrender had come out to meet her. If he lingered long enough, the water-kin dragon might come out to Drake.

Or he might let me rot out here while he's content to lay low and wait.

Drake chuckled, once again releasing bubbles to rise from the corners of his beak. The defense offered by the strong if simple glamour provided him something of a challenge he intended not to forget anytime soon. It's potency, however, offered Drake a seam. He altered his search pattern by inches and degrees, careful not to change either drastically or too quickly lest it expose his awareness of the spell's nexus. He extended his senses in all directions, keeping his attention on the side nearest the lair's spell. Pass after pass, he gnawed at the edges of the seam he'd uncovered. He found other seams. Silt near the entrance shifted stiffly. Plants swayed too perfectly. Water dipped to colder temperatures typical of deeper depths.

Might as well be blinking neon.

The glamour lay across the lair's opening like a gossamer veil. He circled it, eyeing edges he'd missed before and ensuring he knew the crevice's dimensions.

Large enough to hold me twice over. If he's as big as all this, barging in might not be the best choice. Drake squared his metaphysical shoulders. *Salyse needs help. I need to find her Dame. If he's her friend, he'll understand.*

Drake shot upward with all the speed he could manage. He launched from the water, snapping open his water-adapted wings. Changes to their shape hampered his flight. He beat upward and upward in a slow spiral. He eyed the water below, finding the entrance through blurry vision.

He dove like a shrike, wings pressed hard against his body. His beak slammed into the lake surface, stinging as it cut him a line through the water too fast for the glamour to turn him away with its distractions. Adjusting course with tiny shifts of wing, he plunged through the glamour and into darkness.

33

DARK OMENS & HIDDEN PLACES

Myn'Glent Ah Elirymn knelt beside a pool gazing at her reflection behind Mythela'Raemyn's great ziggurat pyramid. A soft dappling of silver turned her original chestnut into a silver-crimson. The ever-spreading silver discomforted her teacher and her mother, but she delighted in the new color.

Kind of makes me look older, not that they'll treat me like anything more than a child until I've grown into my hooves.

She trailed fingertips through to pool, upsetting the reflection. Naiads gambled beneath the water, chasing fingertips and the ripples they left behind. Her smile broadened. Water was the best element ever, not that all the other yearlings agreed—particularly not the colts adamantly opposed to bathing. She loved the feel of it on her skin, the sound of its motion and especially its calm, soothing nature.

Being in the water is like being whole.

A tug stabbed her scalp with pain. "Ow, be careful."

"Sorry, sorry," tiny piccolo-like voices apologized over and over. The little dew drops—cousins to the other pixies though made entirely of water—argued softly with the one who'd pulled her hair.

"It's okay," Myn'Glent said. "Are you done with the braids?"

They couldn't seem to agree.

Pain seemed part of her life, her sleeping life if nothing else. It plagued her nightmares. They came every night, like horrifying specters somehow chained to her soul. Sleeping partially in water eased them, though sometimes she dreamed she too was made all of water just like the dew drops. Her dream self was better. It was beautiful and graceful like the hand-inked lithographs of elves in the archives. Her dream self possessed the same perfection. It was all the things Myn'Glent wasn't. It wasn't a disappointment.

Myn'Glent turned her head much to the complaint of the dew drops. She examined the small round things peaking from the intricate braids.

I wish my ears were pointed. They just look wrong.

"Myn'Glent!"

The far off call of her teacher broke her out of wishful thinking. A moment later, her mother's call joined Midall E'Cru's.

Myn'Glent cringed. *What didn't I do properly this time?*

The voices neared. She didn't want to see them. She didn't want to see the disappointment in their faces, particularly MidCru—the great granddaughter of the previous High Shamaness. They wanted so much from her, expected her to learn so many things as an Acolyte of the Path. All she seemed able to learn was new ways to screw up.

"Are you done *yet?*" Myn'Glent whispered.

They still couldn't agree.

"Then find me later." She hurried from the pool and away from summons. She kept her head and torso bent low, wishing she could slip in and out of shadows like the elves were reputed as she raced to the jagged mountain edging the Dragon Spring gate. Few came near the sheer rocks unless a dragon wished passage beyond to the source of all magic.

I want to go so bad, but if I don't finish the Path, I'll never even get close.

Midall E'Cru's voice continued to chase her, though her mother's fell behind. The shamaness no doubt had some sort of tracking spell for her pupil. Myn'Glent smirked. She drew upon herself, a scent of impending rain refreshing her as magic flowed to her fingertips. It cascaded over her skin, washing off the trace like prey losing dogs in a river.

She rushed along the rocks, too hurried to delight over the fascinating things living among the rocks: families of lizards, insects and small rodents to name a few. There was only one of the rock's treasures she desired—the cleft. She wove through pines, following the thin game trail she'd first followed to discover the entrance.

She squeezed inside with no time to spare, scraping against the rock. *It's getting tighter. How much longer will I be able to use it for escape?*

Once inside she slowed, setting each hoof down with care to prevent echoes betraying her hiding spot. Veins of gold and glittering quartz shone in a glow cast by phosphorescent mushrooms scalloped up the cave walls. Myn'Glent slowed more, enjoying rock formation and small cave insects competing with the mushrooms for most dazzling glow. A shaft of sunlight beaconed from the far end of the passage.

How did I come so far without realizing it?

Stepping into the sunlight washed away the last vestiges of the protective barrier defending the valley. Outside, MidCru's spells wouldn't be able to find her. She hurried out, wishing she had more time for the formations and cave life.

She emerged onto a grassy precipice. A spring serenaded her from the small groove it'd cut down the rock face near a pair of old pines. Its glistening stream cascaded off the precipice to places Myn'Glent sorely wished to visit. Another pine bent sideways off the opposite end, turning upward as if it'd changed its mind in early youth and chosen another path.

Maybe I should follow its example.

She paced the edge. The precipice would hold three adult centaur, but she'd never shared her discovery. The others knew she was different, even the others studying *Lah'Phriel*. Her mother insisted the others suffered jealousy unbefitting an acolyte, but she wasn't so sure.

I am different, and I was too free with my opinions when I was younger. I know better now that I'm grown, but they still remember. And in lessons...well, they won't forget the plants.

They'd been brought together to help encourage some of the new plants. It was supposed to be a simple spell—transfer life energy into them like healing small wounds. They were only expected to help the seedling stretch their roots a little.

I was so careful. I even used only shaman magic.

Myn'Glent cringed. Her plant had exploded upward, growing a year's worth in a moment, but worse every plant in the nearest three rows had grown too. They shot upward, outstripped the soil's nutrients and more than half died.

Tears collected at her eyes but she refused to let them fall. She could do that because of the water magic that came so easily—a magic her teachers said she wasn't supposed to have at all.

Though I'm not sure they're right. The archives suggest the old followers of Lah'Phriel had powers my teachers disdain as wizard magicks.

There wasn't anything wrong with shamanistic magic. It did wonderful things, but the lessons were so grave and tedious, and the power seemed somehow limited. They scowled when she tried something new with it, usually punishing her for using wizard powers even when she insisted otherwise.

I could've done it with water magic or earth—not that I know how I know. It just feels like water on my coat, like it's part of who I am. She stomped a hoof, heat bubbling up inside her. *They are jealous. They can't do it, and they don't understand it, and anything they don't understand is bad somehow. How can supposedly wise people think that way?*

"Of course you found this place," Midall E'Cru shook her head. "I should've remembered it before now."

Myn'Glent Ah Elirymn spun toward her mentor. *How'd she squeeze through the entrance?*

"You shed my tracking spell somehow," MidCru said. "I thought you wanted to learn how to be a shaman. Shaman do not shirk their responsibilities."

Myn'Glent weighed lying, telling her mentor the barrier had rid her of the trace. *No, she'll know. She always knows.*

"What am I going to do with you?" MidCru asked. "How long do you expect to be able to hide who you are?"

What? Myn'Glent met her mentor's gaze. "I don't understand."

Midall E'Cru folded her arms. "You've more potential than any other yearling, but you're obstinate. You refuse to learn, somehow relying on wizard magic when you're supposed to be learning what we're trying to show you."

"I wouldn't presume to correct you, Mistress."

"Really? That'd be a first."

"I'm trying to learn. I try to use the magic you've shown me not any other. I'm not trying to disappoint you, really, I'm not. I believe you when you tell me I'm not using the right magic, but I don't understand how that's possible. You've never taught me anything but shaman magic."

"Understand it or not—and I'm don't think you're so ignorant of the difference as you claim. You know things none in the valley know, and I suspect my grandmother is partly to blame."

Myn'Glent's hand went to the little tickle at the small of her back.

"Show me."

Myn'Glent lifted her shift.

"It's moved and grown more pronounced."

"It's not just a rash, is it, Mistress?" Myn'Glent lowered her eyes. "Is it the reason I'm a useless freak?"

"You're not a freak," MidCru gazed off the precipice into the distance, her eyes sliding out of focus. "Beautiful here, isn't it. I'd forgotten. Times seemed much simpler when I was only a yearling dodging lessons to hide out here. Not that my teachers would've shared omens with me any more than we share them with you."

Cold washed through Myn'Glent. Dizziness robbed her balance, and she stumbled a step closer to the precipice.

MidCru took her arm. "You're pale as a ghost, child. Are you all right?"

"Am I going to die? Is that why you won't share the omens with me?"

"We're all going to die," MidCru said.

"Mistress, please," she begged.

"I'm not sure even the former High Shamaness could indeed see the future, but the omens are of greater things than one acolyte's fate."

Myn'Glent exhaled. "Then the mark doesn't mean I'm going to die."

"No, I'm pretty sure it means you've already died—twice."

Jedediah stepped from the hearth into the welcoming swelter of a typical Georgia day. He turned his wizard eye to ensure Kane came through behind him rather than tamper with something in the library best left alone—again. Motion caught his eye as Kane exited the hearth with a disgusted expression.

Billie Jo bound into his arms. "Jedediah!"

"Um," Jedediah extricated himself. "Hello, Billie Jo."

"I'm so sorry for everything I said. It was just…it doesn't matter. I love you." She sprang down the stair, opened the rear of her minivan and drew out a stack of cupcake carriers. "I made cupcakes, oh and pies. Would you rather have pie?"

"Jesus, lady, you opening a bakery?" Kane asked.

Jedediah cuffed him.

"Oh, you must be one of Jedediah's apprentices," Billie Jo raced up the stairs, arms wide with a cupcake in one hand and a pie in the other.

"Don't touch me." Kane stepped back. "I don't want to see you die."

Billie Jo's smile flickered. It lit brighter a moment later. "How about some cobbler? Baked chicken?"

"I'm happy to see you," Jedediah said slowly. He invoked his Sight but didn't see any enchantments or lingering Fey glamours. "Are you all right?"

"I love you. I miss you. Please forgive me," Billie Jo said.

Sarah bound up the stairs and placed a paw on his foot.

<Jordan is in trouble.>

Jedediah tensed, drawing his staff from the air and hunting the horizon for Stormfall.

<Not the dragon, elves. Fauns attacked. Nip fetched elves to help, but they too attacked.>

"Why didn't he help her?"

"What?" Kane asked.

"Not you," Jedediah said.

"He's on the phone," Billie Jo whispered.

"No, he's not," Kane said. "The mudpuppy is talking to him tele-pathically."

<She escaped injured toward Lynelaen. Her stone impaled Beryl. Nip brought her home for help.>

Billie Jo frowned at the dog. "They're magic too?"

Kane rolled his eyes.

"Is she all right?" Jedediah asked. "Does she need healing?"

"Who's hurt? Mistress? Jordan?" Kane asked.

"You know, I bet I can find a recipe for dog biscuits."

Sarah cocked her head at Billie Jo. *<I have healed her. We must now wait to see if she survives. Is your woman in need of healing?>*

"Not sure," Jedediah said.

"Hey, tell me something already," Kane said. "I went into the nudie hut."

Jedediah narrowed his gaze. "Is there something you're not telling me?"

<The elf Treevoran shot her with Dragonsteel. Nip scented it.>

Lightning shot through Jedediah, every inch of him alive with burning anger. He froze, eyes judging the sun's position. He raced over to the nearest vehicle.

"Hey, where are you going?" Kane asked.

"We'll be right here," Billie Jo said.

"Great," Kane waved to match Billie Jo. "Leave the necromancer with Betty Crocker. We'll have loads in common."

"Are you hungry?" Billie Jo asked. "I could make Macaroni and Cheese, maybe baked potatoes?"

The engine roared, tires kicking gravel at the piled building materials. They squealed as they bit highway. He fought the wind into a glamour, uncertain why it chose to fight his control when he needed it so badly. It kept him hidden all the way to the park. Jedediah threw off his seat belt and bolted out of the door before the truck came to a full stop. He heard its bumper knock into something he'd worry about later as he settled a mist walk over himself.

Every careful step through the wood added kindling and coal to his temper. Treevoran—twice warned and once ass-whooped—should've known better than to do anything with one of his daughters beyond politely staying as far away as possible. He blew by a colony of oakmites, the wind of his passage tossing them from their branches. He ignored the angry chitters and threats at his back.

Lynelaen appeared nowhere near soon enough. He raced up the spiral stair, trading mist walk for a full on sprint. Treevoran stood with his back to the entry arch in a large group of arguing elves, one hand on Lirelaeli's butt. A sudden gut punch stole Jedediah's breath. He regained it and drew upon his power to seize the elf.

Magical energy rushed into Jedediah, a floodgate opened to the Dragon Spring. It drained away almost as fast. Jedediah called again, drawing on potential energy in the wind around him and the life energy incumbent in Lynelaen. He threw the spell forward.

A ghostly hand seized Treevoran, spell's repulsive edge knocking Lirelaeli sideways. Elves reacted at once, but before they could address him the power of the hand fizzled. The construct holding Treevoran disintegrated.

What the hell?

Jedediah drew power to reassemble it, but the harder he drew the less he seemed able to maintain.

Has this got something to do with those restless children?

The creak of a bowstring brought Jedediah's attention back to the moment. A matronly elf shouted objections, but Treevoran sighted down his arrow and let it fly. A shield spell wouldn't stop Dragonsteel, especially not with whatever menaced his magic. He sank into his element and slid around the arrow sidestepping past it and correcting his stance. He slipped around another and another.

Treevoran noched three at once, forcing Jedediah into a base slide to avoid the assault. Jedediah's staff jumped to his hand in time to slam it into Treevoran much the same as Jordan attacked Arthur. Crossed rapiers stopped his blow.

"I've been assaulted by this wizard before," Treevoran said. "I call upon the Elven Council for judgment and punishment for his crimes."

Jedediah spun his staff, swept it in a fancy one-handed spin assault and slammed his other fist into Treevoran's face. "I told you we weren't done, boy. Today is the last day you threaten one of my girls."

"Jedediah, please stop," Haliathu said.

Treevoran's blades jabbed and slashed, glancing off silver-steel rings and finials decorating the lightning-struck black walnut. Jedediah drove a series of assaults at him, forcing Treevoran back through the crowd. Jordan lay at its center, puffy red eyes wide with shock. Blood stained her clothes, so dark compared to her pale skin that the color seemed to tint the world.

Jedediah's staff leapt from hand to hand—deflect and feint, swing and riposte. Short arc's flashed from his hands, their light burning in his eyes. Treevoran's bladesmanship proved itself beyond gainsaying. His speed matched Jedediah's as both sunk into the Zephyr to match the other.

Jedediah's wizard eye flicked invisibly to and fro, desperately trying to keep up with his attention. Slow responses and narrower vision cost Jedediah blood. A Shawnee warcry split Jedediah's lips. He surged forward, letting Treevoran's blade bloody him as he rushed the elf. A heavy work boot slammed into Treevoran's shin. The elf went down, and Jedediah's staff followed him with a two-handed blow.

Treevoran rolled out of the way. The black walnut struck the elven platform. Splinters exploded, and broken shards of the thick ancient board tumbled to the forest floor below. Rapiers slid upward under Jedediah's guard. One stabbed into his gut, the other left a bloody line along one forearm. Jedediah yanked his staff back to bind their weapons, but Treevoran slid his blades out of the trap.

Jedediah's staff whirled. He stepped forward in a dance of quick strikes, long sweeping blows, and scorpion tail thrusts. Years of life as both hunter and brave showed in every move. The Maykujay warrior who'd slaughtered entire forts full of European soldiers pursued Treevoran with all the furious skill he could summon.

Somewhere in the background elves argued. Some tried to stop them. Some cheered one or both combatants on. Jedediah didn't care about anyone but the pale girl watching him. He was not about to let her down after she'd come so far, done so well. She was his daughter, blood or no blood, and no jumped up pointy-eared pervert was going to steal her honor or shed her blood.

Jedediah swept his staff in a wide arc, power roaring out of him. A shockwave of electrified wind slammed into Treevoran. The elf braced crossed rapiers against it, a magical shield layered between them. It knocked the elf backward anyway. Treevoran tumbled onto the suspended catwalk, an anchor post knocking one blade from his grip.

A spike of kinetic force slid from Jedediah's staff. He hurled the spear. Treevoran rolled to escape, colliding with bridge support ropes.

The spear appeared in Jedediah's hand again only long enough for him to hurl it once more. Treevoran launched himself over the high bridge's side, swinging rope to rope around the catwalk and back onto it from the other side.

Jedediah charged. Fists slammed into Treevoran. They drove into body and face with all the strength Jedediah could put behind them. A rapier slid into Jedediah's gut. Treevoran jerked it downward, pitching its tip to thrust upward under Jedediah's ribcage.

A blast of lightning almost weakened to apprentice level knocked Treevoran backward. Jedediah wrenched the rapier from him and tossed it over the side. His staff appeared. He swept Treevoran's legs as the elf struggled back to his feet. Jedediah seized a handful of the arrows from Treevoran's quiver and slammed them wholesale into the elf's back.

Treevoran screamed.

A dark smile grew across Jedediah's face. He reared back to drive his spear home. Sparks played along its edges, dancing from rune to rune. "*Now*, it's over, boy."

"Jedediah!" Jordan screamed.

Thestle and another of Treevoran's elves tackled Jedediah. The impact threw him forward and over the railing. Jedediah twisted painfully, catching a handful of twined rose vines.

Thestle knelt, knife's blade lowering to cut wrist and vines.

"That is enough." Haliathu stomped a foot. Ice snowflaked outward from her boot.

"He attacked Treevoran," Lirelaeli said. "We all saw it. Sad as it is, my daughter's murderer must pay for his crimes."

Haliathu stepped into Lirelaeli, icy blue eyes piercing upward into Lirelaeli's face. "You are not a council elder, girl. I said stop, and they—"

Lirelaeli shoved a finger into Haliathu chest. "I'm not some spring maiden. I am Lirelaeli Ermy—"

"You will be silent, or you will be silenced," Haliathu said.

Elves erupted into fierce objections.

"You wouldn't dare," Lirelaeli said.

"I'll try not to enjoy this." Haliathu flicked her fingers, ice shooting across Lirelaeli's mouth.

Jedediah struggled onto the bridge. "I'll be damned."

Haliathu glared at him. "You will if you disobey me again."

Uproar turned to shoving. Tempers flared. Weapons appeared. Jordan cowered in the midst. Jedediah's spear appeared in his hand. His eyes strayed to Treevoran's back.

Haliathu's voice dropped to a dangerous level. "Jedaiha Two-Hawks, elf friend, centaur brother and Guardian. Don't even think about it."

Her tone brought all eyes to her. She assessed the crowd a moment, straightening to her full, glorious if imperious height. "Elani?"

The young blonde looked up from her position next to Jordan. "She speaks true. They attacked her, in league with the rogue centaurs."

Jedediah froze. *Elani? As in Elani U'Dora Wysinara?*

Elani smiled. "Yes, Guardian. Pleased to meet you, too."

"Take your child home and care for her, *Jedaiha*," Haliathu said. "We will deal with those who've broken our laws."

"We broke no law," Thestle said.

Haliathu pointed. "You attacked your cousin without slight or provocation."

"That she'd even call her polluted blood elven is provocation enough," another elf said.

"I said enough," Haliathu said.

"Want I should knock some heads together for you?" Jedediah said.

Lirelaeli glared, her lips still blue from the melted gag. "So primitive. So unworthy."

Jedediah's gut knotted. He fought the lingering compulsion and the guilt it slathered over his consciousness.

"*Jedaiha*, go. You've no place in this."

"Besides," Elani said. "You must go now if you're to find what you seek before others steal it."

Jordan sat beside Jedediah, the old blind man driving them sedately back toward the farm. He'd explained both blindness and the spell employed for vision. She didn't offer to drive. He'd take care of it. It felt good to let him take care of everything.

"You're going to have to go back for your car," Jedediah said.

She nodded at the opposite window, fighting tears. Jedediah was back. He'd fought for her, but he wouldn't have had to if she hadn't killed two elves.

I'm a murderer.

"I can have Al tow it back to the farm if you like," Jedediah said.

"Uh huh."

The sight of bloody elves dead on Lynelaen's platform surrounded by the living beauty sculpted by its populace burned its way indelibly into her mind. She'd killed them. They'd forced her hand, attacked her without provocation, but she'd killed them.

Jedediah seemed to know her mind. "You defended yourself, girl, nothing more."

The tears won. "They were so beautiful. I destroyed that. I killed them. How many years did I steal?"

"Rotten fish wrapped in gold still ain't edible."

Lanea's words. Tears turned to sobs. "I *murdered* them. They'd be alive if I was any good at magic. I could've stopped them. I could have escaped. Something."

She tensed at Jedediah's hand laid upon her knee. "You're coming along well. You've only been working about a year. Spellcraft takes time, don't you ever forget that."

She turned away again, fighting to stop the tears. *If I could do aquamancy, they'd do what I told them. I'm no good at this magic stuff. I'm just no good.*

"It's my fault really."

She caught pain in his blind eyes a moment before he turned away.

"I should've been here teaching you. If we'd had time to work you through basic aeromancy, you could've called me for help instead of Lirelaeli and her people."

"It wouldn't matter," Jordan snapped. "I suck at magic."

"That ain't true."

"Fine. I suck at any magic outside my body."

"Girl," Jedediah's exasperation turned the one word into an indictment.

"I can't do it, Jedediah. You're at war, and what good am I? None. I can't take care of myself. I can't protect myself. I'm a liability." Her voice trailed off as her fear tiptoed out of her mouth in a whisper. "Maybe you should just leave me at Mae's."

Jedediah's palm knocked her head forward. "Don't you utter that kind of horseshit in my presence again, young lady. You're family, and we don't ever give up on family. Do you understand me?"

"Yessir."

"You're an apprentice, Jordan. You're not supposed to fight wars. You're expected to study under a teacher, but your teacher went off mewling like a wounded kit."

"Your daughter died. It's natural—"

"I should've spent less time wallowing like an idiot and more time taking care of the daughter I've still got." His face turned toward her. Milky eyes seemed to bore into her. "You *can* do magic outside yourself. You've done it before. It's in you when you want it badly enough."

She shook her head.

"You need to get over yourself and get out of your own gorram way."

She snorted.

A smile flickered at the edges of his lips. He'd invoked the curse from her favorite show to make her laugh. Warmth kindled in her chest, slowly thawing the ice left behind by elven deaths. He believed in her. He loved her.

"I told you before, I'm proud of you, girl. You did well in my absence, took care of stuff that really wasn't yours to do. That don't mean you still don't have to get over the doubt shackling your magic."

The fight flashed back into her thoughts. "Speaking of, what happened in Lynelaen? Why'd you fight Treevoran hand to hand? An elven duel thing?"

"Elves don't have anything like the centaur's Right of Long Knives."

They pulled into farm drive. Jedediah parked next to Billie Jo's van. He scowled at it.

"Jedediah?"

"Something went wrong with my magic. I need to find out what."

"Does that mean you won't be able to repair the farmhouse?"

Jedediah snorted, climbing out of the truck. "I'll rebuild the farm in due time, but hammer and nail rather than magic. Some things are worth toiling by hand to ensure they're done right."

Billie Jo rushed up to them, a worrisome smile on her lips. "Cupcake?"

"Thank the Reaper you're back," Kane said. "If I'd had to listen to one more recipe, I'd have sent her off to Him myself."

Jordan shared a look with Jedediah.

"Billie Jo, we should sit down and talk," Jedediah said.

"No, please, I told you I was sorry. Don't send me away. I love you. I want to be with you. I'll do anything."

"I'm not sending you away, but a lot is going on right now." Jedediah smacked his lips. "It might be best if you went home for right now."

"I don't have a home," Billie Jo said.

"What the hell did you do with the one I bou—the one you won?"

"Stormfall smashed it," Jordan said.

Jedediah cursed. Billie Jo mumbled something about meatloaf.

"We could sit down at Cheraw," Jordan said.

"It's out of food," Kane said.

Jordan scowled at him. "What is it with you?"

"*Children.* Come with me." Jedediah led the way over to the old well. He cranked on a spicket at its base, ejecting water onto the ground through a haphazardly coiled hose. He stepped up onto the well's wall. Jordan rushed forward to stop him. Two strides brought him to the center of the ten-foot mouth. He stood on the emptiness, ignoring gravity and the long drop.

I don't feel any extra wind to support him. Jordan folded her arms. "You're wasting water."

Jedediah smirked. "Come on up, it's solid so long as the water's running."

Kane leapt up first, jumping up and down to test nothing. Billie Jo muttered something about leaving an oven on, but Jedediah extended a hand. Jordan helped her up and joined them in the center.

"Lower us," Jedediah said.

The transparent surface sped downward. Billie Jo's eyes widened. She cried out as their feet rushed toward the water below and passed straight through it.

"I'm dry," Jordan said.

"Let out your breath if you're holding it," Jedediah said. "Lift's in a different plane than the well water. Actually, it's the other way around."

"Okay," Kane said. "Seriously cool, but how is it done?"

The lift settled into a dark circle of concrete block. Old mounted bulbs flickered reluctantly to life behind iron cages. A single oak door offered them an exit, an iron ring hung between thick iron bindings. Jedediah stepped forward and knocked the ring twice before pushing open the creaking door.

"How come I didn't know this was here?" Jordan asked.

He pushed a pinch of mint into his cheek. "Wasn't time to tell you."

"Why'd you knock?" Kane asked.

Jedediah gestured down a long, narrow hall lit by more caged bulbs. "Far end's trapped with crossbows loaded with fireiron."

"Fireiron?" Jordan asked.

The old man paused. "Self-igniting magnesium."

"Cool," Kane said.

"Ouch," Jordan said.

"Is there an oven down here?" Billie Jo asked.

Jedediah pulled a torch from the sconce just inside the door and led the way down. The hall ended in a switchback. A portcullis broke up the next series of halls every ten paces. They shifted one direction or another out of their way as Jedediah neared, never slowing them. The hall widened to accommodate a set of double doors half again as wide and three times as thick as the previous.

Jedediah slid the still unlit torch into an empty sconce. The portcullises crashed into place behind them.

"Ah," Jordan said. "I wondered why we needed a torch when the halls had electric lighting."

He pushed them open, grunting at their resistance. "Need to come down here with an oilcan."

Lights flickered to life, illuminating a massive open warehouse. Rune-carved pillars held up a ceiling lost in shadows. Jordan stepped forward, hesitating at the last moment. "Traps?"

"Safe enough if you don't do anything foolish." He focused on Kane.

"What?" Kane asked.

"Dear God," Billie Jo said. "Is this a bomb shelter or a museum?"

"Yup." Jedediah gestured. "There's plenty of food and stuff, and back there are a couple of RVs for privacy. The walls are all bespelled against earth magic."

Jordan cradled her face. *We're right below the greenhouses. No wonder.*

Ten-foot high box store shelves split the massive space into an elaborate maze. She rushed forward through the rows. Crates and boxes, chests and footlockers lined the shelves. Labels advertised clothing, MREs, tools and raw materials. Weapon racks edged the walls, arms hung from their hooks obscured by wrappings of oil-treated cloth. Further in display cases replaced the tall shelves composing the maze.

Something about this place just feels, I don't know, off.

Kane unwrapped an Egyptian lajatang. He spun it experimentally.

"Put that down, boy."

"Why?" Kane asked. "It's too long for me to poke out an eye."

"Because I'm bigger than you."

"Blind old fart," Kane mumbled.

"Arrogant young know-it-all." Jedediah stuck his tongue out at Kane.

Jordan snorted.

She passed a hand over a dusty glass countertop, revealing a wealth of jewels and precious metal ingots, firearms and crystalline decanters filled with colorful liquids. Jedediah led Billie Jo past her and off to one side. Industrial garage doors rose to expose alcove after alcove.

He led her to one of many sitting areas vaguely reminiscent of a furniture showroom. Wine racks filled others. Dressed armor dummies stood rank and file between even more weapons, seemingly organized by era. One alcove bore shelves thick with a countless number of the encased models—cars, planes, carriages, coaches and several military vehicles. The next bay held a full sized tank while the opposite contained a partially disassembled 1965 Mustang convertible. The license plate under its chin read: MasonS.

"Holy shit," Kane said. "What are those?"

Jordan turned to find Kane lifting plastic from a standup Ms. Pacman game. A shrouded army of arcade machines rivaled the armor dummies.

"Hey, how do I turn this on?" Kane asked

Jedediah gestured. The alcove exploded with light and electronic sound.

Kane cheered. "Wow, these are cheap. Only one quarter."

"Let me get you some sweet tea," Jedediah said.

Billie Jo nodded.

Jedediah gestured for Jordan to follow. He led her into a kitchen alcove and pointed her to a cabinet. "Tea maker's in there. That wall's dry goods. Get her some tea going."

"What are you going to do?"

"I've got some spell sensors down here a ways."

"What the hell is this place?" Jordan asked.

He smirked. "Call it my interpretation of the Boy Scout motto."

"You weren't a Boy Scout."

Jedediah shrugged, disappearing deeper into the warehouse.

She finished the tea and stirred in sugar before he returned. A freezer offered stale-smelling ice, but it didn't matter with the amount of sugar Jedediah always insisted went into the tea.

They returned to find Billie Jo standing at the alcove's edge searching the expanse for something. Jordan handed over the drink, and Jedediah walked around her holding out an old gold and crystal something.

She watched him, different shards lighting and dimming as he frowned over the artifact. He set it down and frowned at Billie Jo.

"What did you find?" Jordan asked.

"Nothing. Not an iota of magic in her body," Jedediah said.

"You figure her zeal to be with you is real then?"

"Yup, but something still ain't right."

"What now?" Jordan asked.

Kane looked up from Ms. Pacman. "Can we go to town for video games from this century?"

A wave of Jedediah's hands robbed the arcade alcove of power.

Kane groaned. "I just got to a new maze."

"Kane and I are going to see WaphRae," Jedediah said. "Billie Jo will take you into town so you can practice with your coach."

"I want to go with you," Jordan said. "You might need my help."

"Kane will do."

"Well, thanks. Way to make me feel wanted," Kane said.

"Boy, do you ever stop whining?"

"Only to empty a pantry," Jordan said.

Kane straightened his padre hat and glared at both of them.

CONFLICTING INTERESTS

"Are we *ever* going to save Mistress?" Kane asked.

"The curse afflicting me makes it unsafe to assault our enemies."

"That's a no, right?"

"A not right now." Jedediah pushed a pinch of mint into his cheek.

Kane sensed the ambush in the sudden quiet of insects. He slowed, and Jedediah slowed in response. Kane veiled his sight in the cold magic from his core. He used it to see heat and saw the fires of death all around peering down arrow shafts at them.

Jedediah raised a hand. "We seek Waphri Ah'Raemyn."

The shaman eldress stepped into view a few moments later. "We welcome *Feihtor Ah Mythela'Raemyn* once more into our camp."

"Warm welcome," Kane muttered.

WaphRae scowled. "You bemoan our caution? We have colts and fillies to protect, yearlings not yet grown into their hooves and the timeworn within our camp. Armed centaur have been spotted along the treelines, though none have penetrated the forest."

Warriors stepped from cover, lowering weapons to salute first Jedediah and then himself.

"I'll look into it," Jedediah said. "Beware also that elves have answered Velith'Seravin's rallying call."

"Surely not," ChiRie said.

"What brings you back to us so soon, Jedediah?" WaphRae asked.

"Unless I miss my guess, a curse," Jedediah said.

ChiRie covered her mouth. Something about Jedediah caught her attention, and she leaned closer. "Master Wizard, have you been blinded?"

"Mother's embrace, she's right. Is it this curse that's stolen your eyes?" WaphRae asked.

"Stolen my eyes, my years, maybe even my magic," Jedediah said. "I've come seeking a cure from the hands of *Lah'Phriel*."

"If it is within our power, we'll lift this blight," WaphRae said. "Do you know how you contracted this affliction?"

"Vengeance," Jedediah said.

She frowned. "Go ahead of me, ChiRie. Have our spirit walkers prepare."

Kane's stomach grumbled.

Jedediah scratched salt and paprika stubble. "Didn't Billie Jo just feed you?"

Kane shrugged.

WaphRae escorted them to a small tent, leaving them in the care of a brown filly and a young palomino barely old enough to be considered a mare. They served food and drink. Kane ate everything and insisted they bring more.

Bored and still hungry, Kane asked Jedediah what'd transpired with Jordan. The old man told him. Mention of the fauns drew a curse from Kane's lips. He fiddled with his hat. "That's my fault. They wouldn't be after Jordan if she hadn't defended me."

"They're Wizard's Bane, boy, and she's a wizard."

"If you say so," Kane said.

WaphRae entered. "We are ready. Please come with me."

She led them into a huge tent nearly as big as the main pavilion. Shaman and their acolytes formed a four-pointed circle. Furs covered the floor and ceiling at their center, painted with symbols and runes to represent divine and infernal magicks.

Jedediah was seated on the rug. He floated off of it a moment later. Centaur walked the circle, acolytes handing them components and instruments as the spell built.

Power pushed against Kane's skin. It swirled the wind within the tent and called out to his own, chilling Kane's body to the bone. The fires painted on the rug flickered. The stars on the suspended fur sparkled. Shaman and shamaness swirled elements, drawing a kaleidoscope of glowing color.

Kane sidled up to ChiRie. "What's going on?"

She shushed him.

"I'm just trying—"

"ChiRie," WaphRae snapped. "Take the boy outside. I don't need him interrupting a great working."

"I want to help." ChiRie said.

"Go," WaphRae said.

ChiRie's shoulders hunched and her frown seemed to drag her face out. She grabbed Kane's arm and frog-marched him out of the tent.

Kane snatched his arm back. "Wasn't my fault."

"Was too."

They folded their arms and pointedly ignored one another. Boredom crept up on Kane. He relaxed his stance. "Why do the centaur have names for Jedediah?"

"You don't know?" ChiRie asked.

Kane shook his head.

"Your master is a great wizard. He's done so many services for the centaur people above and beyond sheltering us from normals."

"He's not my master."

ChiRie frowned. "Even before Jedediah was a Guardian, he served the High Tribe. A clan of miners claimed the mountains around Mythela'Raemyn intent to mine it for gold rumored to be hidden there."

Kane shrugged. "He kill them all?"

"No," ChiRie laughed. "Being the only two-legger available, the

High Shamaness sent him to treat with the clan. It's said they were exceptionally stubborn for normals."

"So then he killed them," Kane said.

"No. While he was there he fell in love with the clan leader's daughter and she with him. They ran away together."

"How the hell did that solve anything?"

"Her dowry included the disputed land."

"What's a dowry?"

ChiRie rolled her eyes. "You're hopeless. Want to tour the village?"

Kane shrugged. "Does sleeping with some guy's daughter cover all the names you guys have for him?"

"No, only the title *Feihtor Ah Mythela'Raemyn*. He's also known as *Lyanthen Ah Lah'Phriel* for his help during your revolutionary and civil wars. He's given time and of himself, even curing plagues our shaman couldn't conquer."

"He's a wizard not some kind of cleric."

"He is very resourceful and has many allies. It was foolish of Velith'Seravin to call him an enemy."

"Foolish or not, it seems like Wizard's Bane is attracting all kinds of followers," Kane said.

ChiRie sighed. "Younger centaur don't remember his deeds. They want to run and lord over normals like texts say we used to do."

Kane snorted. "You're not exactly old."

She smiled. "No, but the Path of *Lah'Phriel* delves deeper into our histories. I came to Fleet Hoof after the High Tribe censured it for Velith'Seravin's crimes."

"Why?"

"I wanted to be part of its redemption. I wanted to meet the wizard who'd saved my tribe from slaughter centuries ago," ChiRie shrugged, a giggle escaping her. "I guess I'm just a romantic looking for an adventure."

"Why not join up with Wizard's Bane then?"

ChiRie looked surreptitiously around. A moment later her image shimmered, resolving into a cute girl in jeans, a concert t-shirt and hair to match Jordan's—if orange. "I'm *really* good at glamour."

"So?"

"So my tribe was near a city. I went there, explored…learned about modern normal life. The Guardians have good reasons for keeping us hidden."

"Jordan has that shirt," Kane said.

ChiRie beamed. "I copied it. I want to go to a Djinn Storm concert *so* bad."

She dropped the glamour, and they strolled through the camp. She explained the layout—security wise as well as tribal stature. Foals and yearlings raced up to her with questions and play requests. They shied away from Kane, noses wrinkled and hooves stomping.

Kane sulked. "They seem to like you."

"I'm a tree fallen over a stream…you know, for crossing."

"A bridge?"

"Right. I only just crossed over from yearling to filly, so for a shaman, I am young enough they don't really respect me yet." ChiRie laughed. "I should probably be upset by that, but it's good they come to me for knowledge rather than the alternative. Besides, I learn faster answering their questions."

Kane shoved his hands deeper into his pockets.

"You're bothered by the way they treat you?" ChiRie asked.

"Nah, I don't care what children think."

"You do care."

"Do not."

"I think you do. It upset you that they react as they do, so you objectify them, call them children when you're barely a man as I am barely a filly."

He shrugged.

"It's your smell."

"It doesn't bother you."

"It does, but those on the Path can't step away from things they dislike. We have a duty to look beyond the ick—or in your case the smell of death. Besides, you're occasionally very sweet."

Kane fought the smile, but it emerged from his frown anyway. They continued on in companionable silence.

Kane cleared his throat. "Can I ask a question? I don't want to offend you."

"You may ask," ChiRie said.

"I don't know much about centaur except their habit of trying to kill me, but my father bought and sold thoroughbreds. You used the word yearling, does it mean the same as it does with horses?"

ChiRie peered deep into his eyes. He met her warm, golden brown—a lighter version of Drake's—as she chewed her words. "That's an offensive question—like asking you your age in terms of monkeys—but I don't think you meant offense.

"Many centaur dislike horses. To be so compared is the height of affront probably because we are so similar save our intelligence. For one sweep of seasons we are a foal, and for the next, we're named yearling. Two more we live as colt or filly, finally becoming stallion and mare beyond."

"So you're only just older than two years old?"

"Don't you know better than to ask a lady her age?" ChiRie asked.

Kane stammered.

She laughed. "Just teasing you. Yes, I just turned two."

"If you age like horses, how can Jedediah have known some of you for decades? Father says his horses aren't worth more than glue after about fourteen."

ChiRie scowled. "I don't think I like your father."

Kane shrugged. "Who does?"

"We live for many decades—assuming no misfortunes. Some centaur see the dawning of their third century. I've heard of only one who saw its sunset."

"Wow." Kane shook his head. "I can't imagine living so long."

"You jest. Wizards live hundreds of decades."

Kane shrugged. "Maybe, but I'm thirteen. I can't imagine being so old."

A shift in the air turned his attention toward the shaman tent.

ChiRie turned too, probably feeling something similar. "Come on, let's see if they've cured your master."

"He's not my master."

❧

Jordan parked Jedediah's old Charger around the corner from the Bridgeport house. Her limbs hummed a warm, happy tune that didn't quite equal Marnie's expression at the end of practice. The woman had offered Jordan lunch, droning on and on about the opportunities ahead. Her enthusiasm had been contagious, but the day's events had also been exhausting. All Jordan wanted was a warm shower and fresh clothes.

Crystal met her at the door in a lovely dress.

Jordan pressed her lips together. "What's up? Why're you dressed up?"

"We're having a party to celebrate Arthur's release."

Jordan groaned.

"You have a few hours yet. I've got everything set up but the food."

Jordan climbed the stairs to their bedroom. "Still under lock and key?"

"Yeah. Good practice?"

Jordan frowned at the frilly pink dress draped across her bed. "What the gorram hell is that?"

"Mae picked it out," Crystal said.

"Doesn't she get that I don't do pink?" Jordan peeled away her sweaty shirt.

Crystal assumed a falsetto. "Ladies should wear color-appropriate clothing."

A blaring horn interrupted their laughter. Jordan glanced out the window. Mae stood imperiously next to the car, glaring up at them. She pointed emphatically at her feet.

Jordan sighed. "All I wanted was a shower. What else can go wrong today?"

Crystal shrugged.

Jordan pulled the shirt back on and hurried down the stairs, if only to make the blaring horn stop. A sedan pulled up as she reached the car.

"Get the wheelchair from the trunk and help Arthur into the house." Mae turned her attention to the two men getting out of the new car. A brittle smile rose into place. "Agent Ridley, I didn't expect to see you so soon."

"Help me out of the car already," Arthur whined.

Jordan pulled the wheelchair out, struggling to get it opened up and braced. She flashed Ridley an exasperated smile and wheeled the chair around.

"My new boss wanted to meet Jordan," Ridley said.

"Faye," Mae corrected.

Jordan's attention shifted to them. Arthur cursed, falling back into the car. Crystal snickered.

"Sorry, Arthur," Jordan said.

A handsome older man stepped between them, ignoring Mae entirely. Unlike Ridley's rumpled suit, the new fed's attire was immaculate and expensive. Short, dark brown hair glinted red in the sun, and mahogany eyes pierced all the way to her core.

"Jordan, this is Director Laru," Ridley said.

"It is a pleasure to meet you, Miss." He extended a hand.

Jordan took it. Heat shot up her arm like he'd injected fire into her veins. His grip kept her from jerking away, and his head cocked to one side.

Pyromancer? Jordan swallowed. "Uh, it's a pleasure to meet you too, sir."

A smile spread across his face that Jordan could only call predatory. "Oh, I like you, Jordan."

"Faye, and as her guar—"

Director Laru's glower cut the words from Mae's throat. For a moment, Jordan thought his eyes glowed. When he turned them back to her, they held only warmth. "I've heard quite a bit about you, but I'm confused to find you here. I understood your relocation from New Jersey found you a much more suitable guardian."

"The filthy, murdering clod farmer abandoned her," Mae said.

Director Laru shifted his attention to her. "Are you still talking, woman?"

"Don't speak to my wife like that," Louis said.

Ridley's boss stepped around the car to him. "So you are the man of this house? You are responsible for all that happens in your domain?"

Mae opened her mouth, but Jordan cut across her. "It was nice of you to make the trip, Director. You wanted to ask me something?"

He smiled at her. "Yes, it's about the request made to Agent Ridley. Do you honestly wish it to be fulfilled?"

"Um, what request?" Jordan said.

"Regarding your status in the foster system," Ridley said.

"Oh." The ramifications of the question swam through her mind. They were asking whether or not she wanted free of the foster system. If she agreed, she'd be free of Mae and able to return to Jedediah. "The foster system or the whole system?"

Laru smiled. "There are some systems you cannot escape."

"Foster," Ridley said.

"Yes, please."

The federal agents shared a look, thanked her, and drove off.

"Well, I never," Mae said.

Jordan rolled her eyes.

Mae's slap hit her without warning. "Get in the house this moment. You stink to holy heavens. People will mistake you for homeless with a reek like that."

Anger flared, heating her fingers much as Laru's touch had. *Not soon enough.*

Mae seized her by the hair, hand raised for another blow.

"What? I didn't say anything."

"Don't try lying to me, Faye. You may not have opened your mouth, but I can see the disrespect behind your eyes."

Jordan opened her mouth. A gigantic roar shook the world.

"Whoa," Arthur said. "How'd you do that?"

Jordan's eyes shot skyward. The whole world seemed to smash

down on her at once. Stormfall circled not nearly far enough above. "Shit."

Mae slapped her.

Jordan's gaze flashed around, panic and fear pummeled her in preparation for the paralyzing dragon fear she felt edging its way toward her.

Crystal's voice sounded like she felt. "Jordan?"

Mae slapped her. "Do not call her that."

Anger surged into Jordan, but she didn't have time for it. She whipped around to Louis. "Get Arthur back into the car. Crystal, go with them."

"You don't give orders here," Mae said.

Stormfall slammed down into the street, talons shattering asphalt in all directions. *<Bow down, morsels, and worship me with your last breathes.>*

Arthur slapped hands over his ears, one cast knocking him hard in the head. Louis whirled, mouth moving soundlessly. Mae turned toward the dragon with matching fury on her face. Jordan yanked Mae toward the house before she could make things worse.

"She's blocking the car," Crystal said.

Crap, what do I do? I can't just let her eat them no matter how much they might deserve it. Jordan shoved Mae and gestured Crystal forward. "Forget the car. Get them to the cellar, hurry."

"The farm?" Crystal said.

"Yeah," Jordan squeaked, drawing on Mother with all she had as she turned to face Stormfall. "I...I'll hold her off somehow."

I'm going to die.

<Yes.> Relish poured off of the word. *<You're all going to suffer for the indignities paid me by that little girl.>*

The sedan pulled up in a rush, sliding sideways to a stop against the curb. Two of its wheels lifted off the ground, crashing back down with a wild jounce. Ridley and Laru leapt from it, the former raising a pistol.

<Cower mortals.>

The compulsion shoved Jordan to her knees. The Bridgeports

hit the ground too, only Mae hesitating. At the car, Ridley hid, but Laru stood his ground.

"Get them to safety," Laru said.

"Director?" Ridley asked.

Stormfall stomped the sedan's hood, lowering her massive maw toward the two men. *<I said cower.>*

Jordan took advantage of the distraction to yank Crystal up and shove her toward the house. She had Louis pushing Arthur and Mae in motion before Stormfall's head turned back their way. The dragon reared back her head. Her chest swelled.

Jordan tackled the fleeing group. Driveway arched upward in a concrete barrier. Heat slammed into her.

"My house," Mae said. "My things!"

Jordan glanced upward. The edges of the concrete melted down its surface, several dollops threatening to drip atop them. Jordan grabbed Arthur and wheelchair up in her arms and raced for the backyard.

Ridley appeared at her side, Crystal over one shoulder and his other arm dragging Mae. "Where are we going?"

Crystal's reply broke with each bounce of Ridley's shoulder in her gut. "There's a portal inside the cellar where she sends us for punishment."

"A what?" Mae snapped.

"Shut up and run," Jordan said. "Is he going to be okay?"

"He seems to think so," Ridley said.

Stormfall roared. More fire turned the sky red.

Pyromancer, he might be okay...right up until the moment she eats him.

They reached the cellar. Jordan set Arthur down, ripped the hatch off its hinges, snatched the ladder off the wall and shoved it into place. "Down, now. Crystal first so she can activate the portal."

"What kind of nonsense is this?" Mae asked.

"Do you speak English?" Jordan snarled. "There is a *dragon* here to eat you. Follow Crystal. She'll save your life."

Mae slapped Jordan. "Do not ta—"

Jordan slapped Mae, sending the woman flying. *Gorram it, I forgot about strengthening myself. If I'm not careful, I'm going to hurt someone...or kill them...again.*

Ridley helped Mae up, leading her to the cellar entrance. "Go down. Do as Crystal instructs. That's an order from a federal officer."

"I will not be ordered around on my property," Mae said. "I am in charge."

Arthur made a disgusted sound from within the cellar. Ridley shoved her into the hole. A deafening roar rent the air. Stormfall crashed through the burning house toward them.

Jordan set herself, shouting over the ring in her ears. "Get them through, Agent. I'll help your boss."

Director Laru's voice boomed out as he strode into view around the house's side. "Oh no you don't. I'm not through with you. You know, you're the most insufferable female I've ever encountered."

Louis yelped as Crystal shoved him out of sight. Mae raised a hand to strike. Crystal stuck her tongue out and dove through the portal. Mae pursued in a huff.

Smart girl. Jordan turned back to the fight as Stormfall bathed Laru in flame. The fire dissipated to reveal his glower. Stormfall's tail slammed into a still-standing section of house, sending walls and furniture flying toward the Director.

Ridley grabbed Jordan. "We have to go too."

"What about him?"

"I have my orders."

Jordan dropped down. She touched the screw to reactivate the portal. She raced through to find Mae's fist holding Crystal's hair inside a circle of snarling mudpuppies. She turned around, searching for Ridley. He studied the door frame on the other side of the portal.

"Just come through."

Ridley shook his head. "Keep them safe."

Jordan lurched forward. Ridley kicked one of the doorframes. The back of the fridge appeared. She swore.

Mae released Crystal and rounded on Jordan. "You brought that...that thing, didn't you? It destroyed my house."

"Technically it was after me," Crystal said. "Mason and I kind of pissed her off a little."

Mae's shocked expression fixed on the smaller girl.

Crystal smirked over folded arms. "I have to say, when I envisioned getting my revenge on you, it wasn't fire breathing. So, without a house you can't foster anymore, can you?"

Kane stopped short at the expression on Jedediah's face. He'd seen the old wizard thin as spiderweb and frail as spun sugar. He'd never seen him defeated. Sensing the audience, Jedediah raised a smile to his face—a delicate glamour easily penetrated.

"We failed," WaphRae said. "Whatever seeded this curse did so too cunningly for our skills."

"What now?" Kane asked.

Jedediah shook his head.

"You can't give up, you just can't. I need your help to save my mistress."

"The High Tribe has magicks beyond us," ChiRie said.

"Yes. We'll go there," Kane said.

"Too dangerous, particularly to you," Jedediah said. "Last time we travelled there, others were injured, and I spent three weeks in intensive care. Velith'Seravin has an army now, sorceresses. Journeying outside the barrier with only my staff and the hatchets I picked up from storage isn't wise."

"Then…I'll stay behind," Kane said.

The earth shook. Kimberlite slid upward from the soil. "Little Mother set me to watch you, so I will go by your side as shield and warrior."

"Like hell you are. I can take care of myself."

"Obviously." Kimberlite's withering glare shifted to ChiRie. They shared a knowing look typical to women down through the ages. "Nonetheless, it's my mistress's command that I protect old and grumpy here."

Jedediah frowned at her. "When did she do that?"

"I was set to ward Crystal, but the dragon destroyed the house I guarded," Kimberlite said. "When I caught up, she sent me to watch you."

"That's exactly why we can't risk it," Jedediah said. "Stormfall's rampaging. Fauns and elves are attacking on all sides. I can't run off to Mythela'Raemyn."

"You're giving up?" Kane asked. "I can't believe you're just going to roll over and let fear steal any chance of regaining your magic."

Jedediah stiffened.

Panic shot through Kane. "I'm sorry, Master. I shouldn't have spoken to you like that."

Jedediah closed the distance. Kane backed away from him but found a wall of feminine rock in his way. Jedediah's hand came down. Kane flinched. The hand rested on Kane's shoulder. "You're annoying, boy, but you're not wrong this time. I'm going to Mythela'Raemyn, but you'll have to stay behind."

"Wait, what?"

"You said you'd stay," ChiRie said.

"I know I *said* that, but just to get him to go. I didn't expect he'd make me stay once he decided to go."

"Careful what you wish for," Jedediah said.

"Can I come?" ChiRie asked.

"Yes," WaphRae said. "I'll assemble a hunting party to escort us."

"You two do know this ain't some cross-country hootenanny, right?" Jedediah shook his head. "Kimberlite, take Mauve's boy—"

The stone elemental shook her head. "Nope, staying with you."

Jedediah growled. "The boy needs protection."

"I do have a name, *Master*."

"I've been ordered to protect you, not him."

"By an apprentice."

Kimberlite shrugged. "She outranks you, *aeromancer*."

ILLUSIONS OF GRANDEUR

Drake swam downward through a rough-hewn tunnel reminiscent of something dug by gigantic worms in a late night movie Lanea'd shown him. Talon lines overlapped on the rock. Layered scars indicated multiple passes or possible later expansion.

How would I build a lair? He laughed. *It'd have a Cherry Coke fountain for one.*

The tunnel turned toward the shoreline. It meandered, rising ever so gently through earth and stone. Smoother rock encircled protruding nubs.

Places he scratches his scales or strips shedding skin.

The tunnel dumped into a hollow a few lengths past a newer passage. It seemed an earlier nest, but one big enough for Drake's own use for some time to come. Unease itched the scales between his wings. The new tunnel shot a nearly straight line, going under the sleepy town.

How far under? Does it intersect sewers? Will buildings fall into it if I crash it down?

The pathway climbed suddenly, emptying into the subbasement of an old, collapsed cannery. Drake rose from the surface beneath old beams and charred debris which held up a mud-patched rubble ceiling. Earth and sand formed a soft island littered with old bones, chunks of fallen basement and the murderous glare of a mottled-green dragon.

Gilrender uncoiled from around his treasures, flared his wings and hissed.

Best not to project thought, lest he thinks I'm claiming him inferior—or thinks I'm just outright insulting him. Draconic growls, hisses and snarls relayed Drake's mind. "I'm here for neither treasure nor combat challenge. I stake no claim upon this lair, but seek the help of Gilrender, renowned friend of Salyse."

<*For what then do you disturb my rest, dragonling?*>

Drake shielded his own thoughts to keep his demonstrative responses to himself. "Salyse spoke long of your greatness, your friendship and your generosity."

<*I'll not give you treasures.*>

"I seek no treasure. Salyse was captured by Wizard's Bane. I hoped you might know where to find her Dame."

<*What is Wizard's Bane?*>

"May I show you mind to mind?"

Gilrender's lip curled. After a moment, it smoothed. <*I do not like to be touched.*>

Drake smiled. *I needn't touch you.*

Gilrender's eyes widened. <*How old are you?*>

Much younger than you, but very well trained. Drake projected all he knew of Velith'Seravin, Wizard's Bane and what had become of Salyse.

Gilrender snarled. His tail thrashed. Chunks of rubble dropped into the water, and the ceiling shuddered.

Yes, they deserve punishment. I seek blood price for harm to mate and clutch mate, but for now, I must put aside my fury to seek Salyse's Dame and her safety.

<*You have no mate. No dragon would accept such a puny thing to sire her clutch.*>

Drake kneaded the ground beneath his talons. *Though it matters not, she and I were fostered together. Will you grant me what I seek? I know not what Wizard's Bane will do to Salyse while we tarry.*

<They'll do nothing. We are dragon, and they wouldn't dare.>

Drake rolled his eyes. It wasn't exactly a surprising attitude—precisely the perspective Velith'Seravin might count upon to preserve his people long term. He waited, hoping Gilrender had the information and would share it. The ceiling shifted. More debris fell. Drake tensed.

<I see no gift, no bribe, no reasons to grant you anything. Its gift beyond value I've not yet enjoyed your flesh.>

Heat flashed through Drake. His scales bristled, and his talons itched. *I am Rydari Phriel, sired by Lailos Prielaru and Stormfall, and I would not be so easy to devour as you suggest. I came in honor to help a mutual friend, but if Gilrender desires to try his might, I'll happily strip his scales, break his wings and leave his half-eaten carcass beneath the ruins of his rat hole.*

Mocking laughter filled the lair.

Drake reached into himself, sinking into the magic stored within and stretching out toward the Spring for more. He pushed the power out his talons, whispering to the earth and willing it to obey. Mother responded to his power. She told him of the lair. She murmured its flaws and boasted of its strengths. She spoke of brick and concrete of how it endured and how to bring it all crashing down.

Salyse called Gilrender water-kin, and his lair confirmed it. The much larger dragon was all strength and all but crippled where it came to terramancy.

I seriously doubt he can earthswim.

He pushed power into his limbs, reshaping into his human form —though not bothering with clothes.

Gilrender's laughter increased. *<You mean to frighten me as one of the kine?>*

Razor talons became nimble, sharp-nailed fingers. Electricity sparked from one hand, and crackling ice trailed arctic fog from the other. He sent his will out through bare feet, thanking Jedediah for all the stubborn insistence that Drake practiced every element. The lair shook.

Gilrender stopped laughing.

I can freeze your escape and collapse this lair with a mere thought. Perhaps the great Gilrender has heart enough to share where Salyse claimed her Dame laired that such knowledge might help save her.

<You wouldn't dare, dragonling.>

Are you sure? Have you ever lost a mate?

Longing filled Gilrender's reply. *<No.>*

What would you dare for a mate that loved you like a bird loves flight? For a mate whose touch exceeded the thrill of your fiercest kill? For a mate whose beauty made sunset drab and glorious scales soft and dull?

Gilrender lowered his head. *<A foe ten times my size.>*

Drake met Gilrender's gaze, his own fierce expression reflected in sorrowful dragon eyes. *With nothing to lose and no fear of death, you might win. So choose. Try me or help me rescue Salyse.*

<Can you teach me to speak with stone and ice?>

I can try, but such is neither easy nor quick. Why didn't you study terramancy during your fosterage?

<My Dame was killed before I was of age, so I was never fostered. I can glamour and work a little water, that's all.>

Your glamour is incredibly strong.

Gilrender smiled. *<Grant me the knowledge I ask, and I shall give you mine.>*

On my wings, I'll return once Salyse is rescued. You learn in three moons, or your lessons are over, agreed?

<Agreed.>

Kane returned to the farm at a slow sulk. He'd wanted to go with Jedediah rather than stay within the farm's borders. A sacred valley didn't sound like the kind of place he could rustle up a cheeseburger, but it did sound better than sitting around doing nothing.

I've done basically nothing since I got here.

He strode out of the forest to see an angry group surrounded by mudpuppies. Hurried steps brought him into range of an argument.

"We're going back," a woman said.

"Then you're an idiot, Mae." Jordan snapped. "We're staying here where it's safe, well, relatively safe."

Mae? Oh, Jordan's foster mom.

"I'm in charge. You do what I say," Mae said.

"Not anymore. Director Laru is going to remove me from the foster system, so you and your orders can go dumpster diving for all I care," Jordan said.

"What about me?" Crystal asked.

Kane joined the tableau.

"She's got no home, so you stay here," Jordan said.

"Here?" Mae asked. "Where, in that pile of rubble?"

"There are beds available in the refrigerators," Kane said. "Inside the well too."

Arthur spluttered. "You want to camp out in appliances?"

Kane opened his mouth but hesitated. *How am I going to explain what I meant to a normal?*

"You children are not in charge here. You two are coming with me, and you," Mae wrinkled her nose. "Take a bath you filthy heathen."

"Make me, shriveled old crone," Kane said.

Mae stormed up to him, grabbing a handful of hair. Kane screamed. Visions of her death swam through his mind's eye. Her hand slammed into his face. He didn't think. He threw power into her. Darkness swelled as power washed out of him in a dizzying wave. She fell away, tangled fingers dragging him forward.

"Love!" Louis shouted.

Sound went fuzzy to match the world. Kane's vision tunneled. Everything went black.

Kimberlite's heavy footfalls led their way down the corridor. Jedediah followed but didn't like it. It chaffed that the walking rock refused to obey him, deferring to Jordan who wasn't even present, all over a matter of elemental affinity. WaphRae and ChiRie walked behind him, their whispers almost soft enough not to reach his sensitive hearing.

The others stayed eerily silent in the magical corridor. He'd thought at first the hunting party had returned to the Fleet Hoof encampment, but other indicators had informed him otherwise.

The first gateway dissipated his wizard eye. He hadn't been able to bring it back. He felt the magic radiating from the corridor's edges and used it to traverse near its center. He couldn't see what they could, but he knew the Path, its arched gates, and the sometimes disturbing revelations that came from looking too hard through the boundary.

"Jedediah has an interesting theory about the mechanics of the corridor," WaphRae said. "He told me he thinks it passes through time, space and possibly other planes to provide an inviolable passage from entrance to exit."

"How could our elders have built it through time?" ChiRie asked.

"Chronomancy," Jedediah croaked. "Dangerous to experiment with, even worse in anything as complicated as this."

"I thought those clocks you told me about employed chronomancy," WaphRae said.

"Yes, but in a limited fashion worked out by other, smarter wizards than I."

ChiRie snorted. "Who's smarter than *Feihtor Ah Mythela'Raemyn?*"

"The wizard that cursed me for one," Jedediah said.

"Whatever," ChiRie said. "So if I forced my way through the boundary, would I end up in a different time?"

"I think so," Jedediah said. "Assuming you survived. Why's the hunting party so quiet? Parties without hope of game were always roudy in my day."

"You cannot see *Lyanthen Ah Lah'Phriel.* There are things beyond the corridor and danger knots my gut."

Jedediah glanced toward the warrior's voice. His beard itched a little, but not to a degree that instigated unease. "I've seen many things that ghosted beyond the barrier, not few that later haunted my nightmares. They can't get through."

"You're sure."

"Absolutely positive," Jedediah said.

They made camp when WaphRae called a stop. Hunters set watch, but soon fire's warmth and contents of their skins eased them into a joyful mood. Notes floated out of the darkness, a jolly rhythm swirling around the blind old mage.

They set off again the next morning, quiet but no longer silent. WaphRae prepared ChiRie quietly, but no one seemed to have any particular use for him.

ChiRie broke off mid-question, sucking in breath. "What in the Creator's world is that?"

Jedediah smirked. "I don't see anything."

The huntsmen muttered, their unease carrying far more weight than that of a green child on her first big adventure.

"What do you see?" Jedediah asked.

"There's a two-legger of some kind beyond the barrier. It's gaunt, and its skin's a sickly, almost waxy grey."

"It doesn't look like the poor thing's eaten in weeks," WaphRae said.

"Could it be undead?" ChiRie asked.

"Not by the way it moves," WaphRae said. "Though its clothes are horribly torn."

Frustration ate at Jedediah. All around him voices told him about the creature, but crippled and blind he was impotent. *Useless as teats on a gator.*

"It's looking at us, too," ChiRie said. "Its eyes are sunken and so dilated and bloodshot its thin sclera's almost pink."

"You're imaging it," Jedediah said. "It can't see through the barrier. It's probably hunting some rabbit in its own timeline."

Hesitation laced ChiRie's typically optimistic tone. "It looks starved and half mad."

Jedediah growled and grabbed the nearest centaur. He closed

his eyes and pushed power into the other person. ChiRie gasped. Jedediah's vision came into focus staring at himself. As it had been when he'd worn a centaur body, everything had a greenish tinge.

"Look at the creature please," Jedediah said.

The sight shifted. Wispy red hair tangled atop its head like knotted spider silk. It passed a purpled tongue over broken teeth and thin lips.

"Jedediah! Step back," WaphRae said.

ChiRie's eyes shifted to WaphRae first and then back to the creature, leaving Jedediah disoriented.

"Move slower," Jedediah said.

"Jedediah, get back," WaphRae repeated.

He crossed his arms, ChiRie's sight settling on him. "Where's the sense in all that? Nothing can breach the corridor in the middle?"

A muffled shriek rent the air. It jumped in volume. Nausea pummeled Jedediah, knocking his mind end over end in a tsunami of dizziness. His legs buckled, and he watched himself fall. Two icy claws wrapped around his neck. He saw the creature atop him. He struggled against it but fighting it in person while seeing it from someone else's point of view threw off his reactions.

He struggled to evoke a magical defense, but even the limited power he'd managed before refused his bidding. Flecks of stinking saliva dripped on his face. Teeth sunk into Jedediah's shoulder.

Pandemonium erupted around them. A throng of swirling limbs and lashing tails did all it could to induce vomiting. Jedediah threw off the spell as heavy footfalls announced Kimberlite and creaking strings foretold raining arrows. The claws and teeth tightened. Energy drained from him. He struggled to form words.

Sustained effort freed a raspy croak. "Stop, don't hurt her."

"Kimberlite, hold it still, and I'll work a bind," WaphRae said.

"I'm trying, shaman. Work your magic already."

WaphRae cursed. "ChiRie combine our power."

Purple spots swelled and shrank in the darkness. Jedediah's lungs burned. ChiRie's voice rose in a birdsong. He felt the shamanistic magic brush him. It vanished.

"That's not possible," ChiRie said.

Jedediah's heart thundered, and he opened his mouth, but no suction drew in breath.

"Get her off of him," WaphRae said.

"She'll tear his throat," Kimberlite said.

"I'll heal it," WaphRae shouted. "She's not letting him breathe."

Pain tore his throat. Warmth flooded his neck as air burned its way into his lungs. Jedediah gasped two breaths. He managed a third. Hands grasped his throat. He struggled to get away.

"Stop," WaphRae said. "I'm trying to heal you."

Power trickled into him—weak but heady like the afterglow of guzzling a case of portable ley line potions. Pain eased. He heard scuffling, curses, calls for rope.

"Jedediah?" WaphRae said. "Still with us?"

"Yup." Jedediah nodded.

"You carrying any of that red punch by any chance?" WaphRae asked.

"Afraid not."

"It sucked my spell power away," ChiRie said. "The bind was almost fully formed, and then something just absorbed it."

"Like parched soil drinks a rainstorm," Jedediah said.

"Should it have been able to do that?" a hunter asked.

Jedediah struggled to his feet. "No."

"How'd it get through the barrier?" a hunter asked. "You said it was impossible."

"No idea. Is she restrained?" Jedediah asked.

"Yeah, but it's beastly strong. Doesn't make any sense."

"Dear Creator, what is that thing?" ChiRie asked.

"We should kill it," the hunter said. "Put it from its misery."

"We can't." Jedediah sucked in another breath. It burned, both with the passage of air and the medicine which soured his stomach. "This mystery must stay with us."

"Do you know what it is, Jedediah?" WaphRae asked.

Part of him wanted to hitchhike on someone's eyes again, another part dreaded the sight of the thing which did the impossible just to throttle him. "I fear that—one way or another—it's my sin."

Jordan endured four days near constant bickering with Louis and Arthur in Jedediah's storage hideout. She cursed Kane once more and whatever magic he'd used on Mae. She'd have asked, but whatever he'd done had either taken too much out of him or backfired horribly. Louis had complicated caring for both by repeatedly trying to leave and bring back an ambulance, while Arthur tried to kill himself by repeatedly getting into Jedediah's treasures.

Billie Jo arrived on the second day having been kicked out of her hotel for repeatedly sneaking into the room service kitchen. Mason helped care for Kane with Crystal his constant companion. Louis drove Billie Jo into emptying the warehouse kitchen stores by constantly complaining or comparing everyone to Mae's lofty standard.

Jordan relocated Mason, Crystal and Billie Jo to the Cheraw farmhouse. Crystal showed them how to contact the caretakers and have groceries delivered. Crystal and Mason came and went with meals and other baked goods deliveries.

Mason grabbed his bag and snuck out through the portal. He crossed the boneyard to the Weems portal, but the refrigerator offered him no passage. Crystal appeared, tousled hair draped over pink pajamas. "Leaving for the tournament?"

"Yeah."

"You weren't going to say goodbye?" She fidgeted.

"I didn't want to wake Mom."

"Right."

"Wish you could come."

"Really?" Her cheeks darkened.

"Yeah, but they'd miss both of us."

She studied her hands.

"Um, well, goodbye," he said.

Crystal closed the distance in three quick steps. She grabbed his shoulders and pressed her lips against his. Warm and soft, but held stiffly against his own, they sent his mind into a whirlwind tumble. She eased her lips from him, her cheeks even darker as she whispered. "Good luck, Mason. Bring back a trophy."

His brain froze, unable to speak or do anything about the goofy expression chiseled to his face.

She giggled, squeezed his hand and disappeared into the night.

When his body resumed function, he cut across the farmland toward a country store a mile or so down the road. He'd have taken one of Jedediah's trucks, but he didn't want the noise to alert anyone. The distance didn't bother him. His feet barely even touched the ground.

He waited outside the convenience store, chewing on a cheap breakfast dog. He mulled over his original plan. It'd been so simple —ride out to Crystal's, use the portal, take one of Jedediah's trucks and go to the dojo. That was before Stormfall destroyed his house and his bike with it. It was before his mom had gone all strange and told him he could practice magic. It was before her weird baking obsession had gotten them kicked out of their hotel.

He liked being back on the farm. He'd even considered asking her for a ride to the dojo. She'd probably have given him permission to go on the three-day tournament trip to Atlanta, but he didn't want to chance it. She'd just as likely come to her senses.

The taxi driver pulled up outside the dojo. Cars filled the dark parking lot dropping off the others headed to compete. The fare on the meter almost made him choke. He pulled his wallet and counted out all the money he'd scrounged for the trip, paying it to the driver and still coming up short. Terry spotted Mason and called him over. Mason set his wallet on the seat and dug through pockets, finishing up the fare with coins.

Mason's sensei emerged from the dojo as he jogged over to the group. A large figure moved through the building, shutting off lights and disappearing deeper inside.

"Mount up," Truth said. "We'll pick up donuts on the way."

"And coffee?" one of the boys asked.

"Sure." Truth smiled. "And coffee."

Flash glanced around. None of the students climbing into the van with Zero and Bianca could see into the darkened hall. He activated the passage and descended into the basement. He made a thorough sweep and took several minutes to reassure himself that he was alone.

Mo Sha and Falcor will be here once they've completed their mission.

He took up position within the circle, closed his eyes and stretched out with his senses. Glowing runes colored his eyelids.

Heady energy swirled into him. He exhaled and shuddered, an addict long overdue for a fix. He felt a night breeze ruffle fur he no longer wore. Absent claws kneaded fresh soil. A far away forest sang a chorus of life. Memory or imagination, he felt once more as one with the wild—the grown bear he'd been born to become before Zero abducted his destiny.

Before Mo Sha erupted from her cocoon, he'd been Bianca's guard. A silent sentinel along the wall, he'd witnessed her training. She too had taken to the magic like an addict. She too had selfish intentions for the power Zero offered. The difference was one of ego. She wanted to rule. He wanted to go home.

Few chances allowed him private use of the crystals. His moments of true self came few and far between, the draw of it growing each time he stole a few minutes.

What would it be like to do this with a class overhead now that I've come so far?

He wouldn't find out. Bianca hadn't allowed him such a chance. She wasn't one to share. Mo Sha had kept him from the circle whenever Bianca taught a class overhead.

Marc didn't know about the magic. Bianca believes she's the only one Zero's taught. She figures on getting rid of him and using her newfound power to replace the board. A chuckle escaped him. *Boy is she in for a rude awakening.*

Zero had a purpose to her amassing power. It wasn't to make her a rival, and it certainly wasn't because of her bedroom charms. In the end, Flash doubted she'd like whatever Zero had in mind.

Flash inhaled more power. He could almost feel the breaking of limbs in his teeth, the taste of blood luxurious in his mouth. The feeling faded, lessening as the stored power left behind by Bianca dwindled.

Tears ran down the Samoan's face.

He wiped them clear, growling at himself. He had to prepare. Zero would be displeased if their meeting with the dwarves went poorly. Flash rose, unsteady at first, and headed for the parking lot.

What is she up to that she drained so much power out of the crystals?

Zero glanced in the rear view mirror at the boys bouncing off their seats on caffeine and sugar. A dark smile played across his lips. His time pretending to be Mason's kindly teacher neared its end. The oldest kids supplied dirty songs for the drive, and young Mason seemed only too happy to learn. He sang with them, listened to boastful adventures and laughed at filthy jokes. He looked as if he belonged.

He doesn't, and if they knew he was a cheat using magic to improve his fighting, they'd probably shun him—not that I'll tell them. That would jeopardize the plan.

None of the boys paid much attention to either traffic or the city around them. Many had visited Atlanta, been stuck in its morning traffic a time or two, but driving was someone else's problem. They'd arrive at the tournament somewhere at city's center sooner or later.

A militant soccer mom cut them off. Zero hit the brakes, throwing his passengers forward.

"Sorry." He flicked an angry hand. Four tires exploded. She lost control, careened off to one side and into a small sedan. The boys twisted around to watch the accident. None of them saw his smirk.

They arrived at the convention center without further incident.

"Get your things together while I fetch our passes. Stay by the van."

A metal chair propped a door open, a sign taped to its face directing him into fluorescent gloom. He strode down a long line of competitors and coaches. Bianca emerged from a side hall, displayed a handful of passes and slipped back out of sight. He followed. She grabbed him, slammed him against a wall and kissed him hard.

The thought of the boy's death excites her? I wonder how she'd view her own. Zero smiled. "What is our status?"

"Plenty of solid competitors. He'll be knocked out of the competition before ten o'clock," she said.

"Good. Once eliminated, boredom will lead the boy's feet to wander."

A feral smiled parted her lips. "And then I get to kill him."

"No, Bianca. It must look as if he's vanished off the face of the Earth, but with just enough evidence to send Shine after Velith'Seravin."

"You're sure Shine cares enough about the boy to come looking?"

"Yes."

"Can't I kill him and just lay a false trail?" Bianca's hands traipsed down Zero's chest. "Pretty please?"

"No. Tip off the centaurs. Track the boy. If they leave a mess behind, clean it up. We want Shine to believe they took him away—hurt but alive."

Zero took the passes and left her in the hall. He found the boys milling around the van and horsing around. He put on his coach face and cleared his throat.

"Settle down. Why are we here?"

"To kick butt," one of the boys said.

The others laughed in agreement.

"Winning would be nice, but we're here to test ourselves,

sharpen our skills through competition and fair play. Have fun, but stay out of trouble. Stay focused, win or lose graciously. Don't start any fights off the mats."

He passed out the badges and maps.

"Now, get inside, get changed and I'll see you on the tournament floor."

Roughhousing and laughing, they rushed the building.

He smiled, dropping his voice too low for them to catch. "Oh, and no wandering off."

3 6

ACID, DEATH & TUMBLEWEEDS

Bianca paced the tournament floor like a tiger with a toothache. Zero's own smile lingered only through sheer force of will.

Mason bounced up to him, grinning ear to ear. "Did you see that?"

"Don't get cocky."

"Three straight wins already today, Sensei. I haven't lost a single match in two days. Talk about ninja-wizard, I'm half way to the semifinals."

"Pardon?" Zero's brows rose.

"Nothing," Mason beamed. "Can you believe how well I'm doing?"

"Still a long way to go."

Mason joined the others. High fives and back pats welcomed him back to their number.

Zero hid an inner scowl. *Damn boy's faster than before. Despite a weak talent, he's glowing.*

"What the hell is going on?" Bianca asked. "His fighting technique is barely better than the others, but he's wiping the mat with them."

"Combine that with his speed and they're just outclassed." Zero

431

shook his head. "He should be spent by now using that much speed."

Bianca frowned. "What if the problem is the way we trained him?"

"How do you mean?"

"The crystals beneath the dojo drained him while he practiced, right?"

"Of course, they drained all life energy."

"What if it amounted to body building for his magic? Is that possible?"

Zero considered it. *Could constant draining have deepened his reserves? I've never exposed a talent to them over a prolonged period.*

Mason should've exhausted his reserves after using that much speed for three bouts, but he bounced around like a superball. He watched Mason's next match with a singular focus. Right before he stepped onto the mat, Mason took a drink from his sports bottle. He slapped the top back down, a tiny bead of silver-mint liquid dribbling down the outside.

Portable Ley Line. Zero grinned. *Two can use magic to alter the rules.*

Zero timed the force lance with exacting precision. Mason launched into a spin kick. His foot came out from under him. He dodged around his opponent's desperate blow, forcing Zero to slip a frictionless layer of magic beneath one foot as Mason's weight shifted. He went down. The other boy tried again for the match point. Mason slipped away. The third accident allowed the boy the point by so narrow a margin Zero cursed.

He glanced at the other boys. "I thought he'd pull it off."

Mason shook hands with his opponent. He rejoined the group deflated.

"Good effort, Mason," Zero said.

Others consoled and congratulated Mason as he joined those already out of the tournament. He frowned at his hands, but when the next match started, he brightened, cheering his teammates with the others. The event broke for lunch.

Mason scowled while the others ate. A few broke off chunks of food and shared with him, but Mason didn't buy anything himself. When the tournament resumed, he didn't wander off. He kept with his teammates, cheering those still fighting.

You're a tiresome young man.

Zero bought drinks, thanking the Creator for Mason's gender. Separating Mason would've proven more difficult if he visited the bathroom in a group.

Mason threw another bottle into the trash. Growing discomfort suggested a bathroom break, but Terry was on the mat in a heated contest. Mason shifted position, trying not to visibly squirm while still resisting nature's call.

Terry fouled his opponent, bringing the tied match to a halt.

Come on, Terry. Mason squirmed. *Quick point, you can do it.*

Discomfort grew teeth.

Terry slid beneath his opponent in a runner's slide that cinched him a spot in the semifinals—not quite Mason's move, but close. Mason congratulated Terry on the run, hurrying off the main floor and down one hall. He slid on linoleum, whipped open the bathroom door to find an Asian woman blocking the bathroom.

"Can I get by?" Mason asked. "Are you done?"

She shook her head. "The other one's open."

He glanced at the ladies room.

"Not that one, small fool. Go down this hall, take a left then a right. Can't miss it."

Mason frowned. "Yeah, thanks."

He raced down the hall. The janitor dropped her mop, the stick clattering loudly, but whether or not she picked it up was last on his list of priorities. He took a corner, sliding into one wall on the highly waxed floor. He made it half way down the corridor before he realized he'd taken a wrong turn somehow. The hall ahead of him had no bathrooms, no side doors or hallways. A palette of boxes blocked the emergency exit of an otherwise dead end.

"What's the matter, little boy?" Bianca asked in a babyish voice. "Got to go potty?"

"Sensei?"

"I told you I was going to kill you."

Mason chuckled. "You know where I can find a bathroom?"

She ignored the question. "Zero told me not to do it, but I can't lie, thanks to that worthless farmer. Do you know how frustrating it is running a criminal organization with no ability to lie?"

Zero? Criminal organization? Cold filled him. *The Namhaid. Crap, what do I do?*

She opened a hand. Swirling green magic blossomed above her palm. "Give Shine's daughter our regards."

Crystal arrived alone with a heavy tray heaped with shepherd's pie, pot pie and peach cobbler. Louis and Arthur had disappeared somewhere in the warehouse to sulk over Nip and his siblings preventing them from leaving. Jordan set out plates. "Get Mason to help you set the table, all right?"

"He's busy."

Jordan sighed. "I guess I can't tell Billie Jo she can't give her son things to do. Get things set up, go back and give her my thanks."

"Okay," Crystal said.

Kane wandered into the room looking like death reheated. "What smells good?"

Exhilaration sent Jordan rushing to embrace him only to be repulsed by his stench. "Not you. Go shower in one of the RVs. Then you can tell me what you did to Mae."

Kane further tousled his hair. "It worked?"

"If by worked you mean she's been comatose for days, yeah, it worked."

Kane smirked. "Living death."

"Like a sleeping curse on that show?" Crystal asked.

Kane shrugged. His stomach grumbled as he stalked behind Jordan's back toward the food. She pointed. "Shower first, Mister."

Crystal laughed.

"Finish setting up then go tell Mason that Kane's awake."

Jordan left her to it and headed toward the bedroom alcove where she'd stashed Mae. The other woman slept on, unmoved from the last time Jordan'd checked on her.

Got to get Kane to snap her out of it...after dinner. I'll enjoy one more peaceful meal. Neither Mason nor Crystal showed up for the evening movie. *Guess they've got their hands full with Billie Jo.*

Mason stared at the swirling green power gliding gently toward him at fastball speeds. The play of light was beautiful, inky green whirls forming an amorphous missile like an old science fiction movie.

Hope she threw a fastball and not a curveball. Mason dove sideways, power coursing through his limbs.

Her second pitch hurdled toward the endpoint of his slide. He flipped, scrambling backward in the fastest crabwalk he'd ever managed. He tumbled into a hole that shouldn't have been in the linoleum, skin burnt by acidic spell residue. He frantically wiped his hands on his jeans. The denim ate away, spilling his phone into the hole. Acrid melting plastic declared the phone's fate.

"I just got that phone."

She answered with a third acid sphere.

Adrenaline rushed through him, anger a close pursuer. He leapt out of the way, charged in closer and swept her leg.

Bianca's laughter joined twin plumes of flame bombarding him. Her casual derision sent an ice age down his spine in a conga line. A wind jet shot him sideways a hair's breadth ahead of the fire.

He shifted the jet, shooting past her as bolts of fire peppered the hall behind him. He slammed into an invisible wall. Pain shot through his head. The world swam. Alarm bells joined the ones ringing inside his skull. Sprinklers deluged him in foul smelling water.

The alarms fell silent, and the sprinklers stopped before fully extinguishing the flames. Mason rolled to put out his gi. He leapt up and charged Bianca. She threw a pair of bolts. He dodged, wind shoving him along atop the slick tile. He leapt over a fireball onto the wall, ran three steps and pounced atop her.

She was gone by the time he hit. Her laughter filled the hall. He hit the floor. Twin firebolts shot over him.

He spun. Wind pushed the water from around his feet. He arced an electrical charge toward her through the water. She threw out her hands. The lightning jumped from the ground back at him like a boomerang.

Mason jerked and convulsed. His limbs felt aflame, though probably not literally despite the smell of burned skin and hair.

Footfalls hurried toward them in the distance.

Please let it be help.

Sensei Truth stormed into view. Dark tendrils of power shot out of his hands, wrapping and writhing around her.

He has magic too? Mason squeaked. "Sensei?"

"I told you to have the centaur kill him," Truth snarled. "I will be obeyed, Bianca. Look at the mess you've made."

Mason uncurled, every limb in agonizing pain.

The Asian janitor appeared. "Master, Mistress, Falcor cannot hold off the authorities much longer without slaying them. May I slay the whelp for you?"

Holy shit, is everyone trying to kill me?

"Go back there and help him, Mo Sha," Sensei Truth said.

Mo Sha turned her back on them and headed up the hall.

Mason didn't know what to say. He stared at his teacher, trying to understand what was happening. Sensei Truth's inattention left Bianca to break her bonds. She leapt at Mason, both hands aflame. A tentacle slammed her through a wall, aluminum frames breaking with the drywall.

Mason'd always been a small kid. For years, he'd had too big a mouth and often had to slip by or away from bullies. Every muscle in Mason's body hurt, but he knew an opportunity when he saw one. He thought little thoughts, focused whatever he had left of his magic into being small, unobtrusive, invisible and snuck toward the fire door.

Neither of the adults trying to kill him noticed until he slammed through the fire door setting off another alarm. Mason shifted focus from invisibility to speed. He downed the rest of the portable ley line potion and ran like Stormfall herself dogged his heels.

Mason ran and ran and ran, turning at random. He pushed the last of his strength into a sprint down an alley. He collapsed between a dumpster and brick wall. His arms and legs shook. His breath refused to catch up. Each breath hurt almost as much as his burns. He'd forgotten all about the bathroom, but his bladder reminded him. He relieved himself in the small shadows behind the dumpster. The alley slanted the wrong way, soaking the knees of his burned and ripped gi.

Mason collapsed where he knelt, body shaking. He thought about crying, but exhaustion took him first.

Billie Jo woke Jordan with a plate full of steaming peach muffins. Jordan rubbed her eyes. "What time is it?"

"Five," Billie Jo said.

"Can't breakfast wait?"

"Mason's missing."

Jordan's gut knotted. "What do you mean?"

"I thought he was helping you until Kane woke me rummaging in the kitchen," Billie Jo said. "I asked if he and Mason were ready for breakfast."

"Mason's not over here," Jordan said. "I thought he was doing stuff for you."

Billie Jo shook her head. "Crystal told me he was busy, so I assumed you had him over here."

"Is Crystal over there?"

"Yes."

Unease spread a cold dread through Jordan's body. "Can you get her over here please?"

Billie Jo pressed her lips together, offering a single firm nod. She returned with Crystal, Kane and a larger load of muffins. Jordan filled another mug with tea and put it in front of Billie Jo.

"Do either one of you know where Mason is?" Jordan asked.

Kane shook his head, mouth too full to answer.

Crystal refused to look at her.

"Crystal?" Jordan asked.

Crystal offered an apologetic shrug. "He went to Atlanta day before yesterday for a mixed martial arts tournament."

Billie Jo fell out of her chair, spilling tea all over. She wrapped her arms around her knees. A manic grin filled her face as she rocked. "I'm going to need more flour."

Kane choked on his muffin, forcing Jordan to slap his back and shove her tea into his hands. "Damn it, Crystal. You knew he was gone when you brought dinner two days ago."

Crystal retracted into herself, once more an image of the mouse Jordan met her first days at Mae's.

Jordan shoved down heat and worry, softening her tone. "I'm sorry I snapped, Billie Jo's worried, and well, we've got a lot of enemies right now. Something could happen to him."

The words which escaped Kane's mouth fell like hammer blows against a tomb door. "He could die."

Something about the tone of his pronouncement released a stampede of icy spiders to skitter along Jordan's skin. "Do you know something? You've seen Mason's death, haven't you?"

Billie Jo's rocking worsened.

Kane wouldn't look at her either. "It probably meant nothing."

"What meant nothing? What did you see?"

Kane shrugged. "A place I've never been. A wizard and a centaur fighting. Mason in the way or maybe the prize."

"Have you ever been wrong?" Crystal squeaked.

"Maybe?" Kane said.

Billie Jo wailed.

"I'll go get him," Jordan said.

"I'll come," Kane said.

"No, you have to stay inside the barrier, particularly if there are Wizard's Bane involved," Jordan said. "Stay here, look after everything and bring Mae out of whatever you did to her."

Kane's eyes rolled into his head. He hit the ground. Crystal yelped. Both rushed to Kane's side. His eyes returned to normal, swung left and right before fixing on Jordan. "You have to hurry. Something huge and metal is about to crush him into a brick wall."

"Where?"

Kane's color drained away, tears gathered in his eyes. "I don't know. Hurry, please. He's my only friend."

Jordan tore off without a backward glance. She raced up the well, into the yard, slid across the Charger's hood and gunned the engine. It peeled out, gravel flying up in her wake.

Something tiny nudged Mason's face. He brushed it away. A pungent reek wrinkled his nose.

"Wake up, little master."

The willowy little voice felt like a whisper. It'd nudged him before. It'd bid him wake before. It seemed a kindly voice, but Mason just wanted to sleep. Pain seeped into his consciousness. His muscles ached. His skin burned. His head pounded.

Mason opened an eye, realizing the stench was him. There was brick and metal and a grey, cloud-swarmed early morning sky.

"Wake, little master, please. They'll be here soon."

They? My sensei's? Mason lurched up. His head caught the dumpster's edge. Pain exploded. He seized his head and screwed up his face. "Gorram it to hell!"

"If you say so, little master, just so long as you move, sir."

"Sir?" Mason said. *Why's someone calling me 'sir?'*

Mason searched around him for the voice. Trash blew through the alley, a random detritus to tumble over the heavier debris which stubbornly held its place. There was no one there.

"Hello?"

Worry intensified the little voice. It came from behind him, back where he had lain a moment before. "Rise, little master, you must move. Death is coming."

Mason searched behind. He couldn't find the speaker. "Death? *The* Death or my teachers or—"

"The Trash Masters are coming. The Trash Masters, little master."

Mason frowned. The engine of a large vehicle rumbled in to fill the alley. Mason tilted his head, peeking around the dumpster. A garbage truck trundled down the trash-strewn alley. It lowered its forks, driving them straight for the dumpster. Gouges in the brick behind him offered testimony to the amount of force a garbage truck might use to drive the huge garbage receptacle *through* the space he occupied.

Mason scuttled out from behind the dumpster. The truck's tines speared it, driving it against the wall with a clang. It dumped and dropped onto the ground with an uneven bounce.

A large woman leaned out the driver's window. "Go home, kid. Whatever made you run, it wasn't the end of the world."

"Okay."

The truck drove off, leaving Mason alone in the alley—maybe. "Hello?"

"We're honored to have served, little master."

"We?"

Motion drew Mason's eye. He bent down to examine the little creature. It resembled a cross between a maple leaf with a head where the stem would be, a pixie and flying squirrels he'd seen on the Discovery channel. Mason's gut tightened.

Lanea'd left it on Discovery and glamoured the remote so I had to get off the couch to change it. Wasn't worth the effort. He chuckled. A second with dandelion fluff hair hid behind the first. "What are you? That was rude, wasn't it? I meant who are you?"

"Tinsel," he said. "And to answer your other question, I'm a tumblebee."

Mason's brow rose. "A what?"

"Tumblebee, little master. Surely you've heard of us."

Mason shook his head. "No, sorry."

"Your scent marks you as a wizard of air. Didn't your Master teach you your allies?" Tinsel said.

Mason looked down at his burned and soiled clothes. He sniffed and coughed. *How can he smell that under this stench?*

"You saved my life."

The fairy bowed at the waist. "My pleasure."

"You're air sprites?" Mason asked.

"Pixies."

"How'd you end up with a name like tumblebees?"

"You've heard of tumbleweeds, yes?" Tinsel asked.

Mason nodded. "Like out in the desert?"

"Yes," the other pixie squeaked. Her face turned down. "We lived in the wilds of the west before normals forced us to abandon our rolling homes."

Tinsel bowed his head. He extended his arms, stretching the membranes out to catch a breeze. He floated upward, flipping over himself much as the fluttering papers rustled by the wind until he lit upon Mason's shoulder.

"Just as with our forest kin, our wild lands were endangered by man's expansion. We've learned to live in cities." He gestured at the trash. "Plenty of wind chariots here."

The second tumblebee flitted onto Mason's opposite shoulder.

"There are other fairies in the city?" Mason asked.

Tinsel laughed. It reminded Mason vaguely of the whistle you heard in old western movies right before a showdown. "Of course, little master."

"Call me Mason."

Tinsel bowed again. "I am honored, Master Mason. Do you seek other Fey?"

Mason glanced around. "I'm lost. I need to get home, and I need help."

"You haven't a pocket talking box?" Tinsel asked.

"No," Mason said.

"There's a talking box on the next corner," Tinsel said.

"A pay phone?" Mason said. "I thought they tore all those down, except in airports."

Tinsel smiled. "Much like the trash here in the alley, this part of the city is forgotten. Why remove something you forgot was there?"

Mason scowled. He'd lost his wallet. Sensei Yves destroyed his phone. He had nothing. "I don't have any money to use it. Do you know any Fey that might take a message for me? Maybe earth Fey?"

Tinsel frowned. "Why talk to mud when we can serve you better?"

"I didn't mean any offense, Tinsel. Jordan's closest. She's a terramancer."

Tinsel screwed up his face in concentration. "Is she incapable of normal speech?"

Mason laughed. "Sometimes I have to wonder. She's from New Jersey."

Mason's stomach rumbled. He looked down at the tattered sandals given him for use on the tournament mats. "Do you have any food? Maybe some clothes and a place to clean up?"

Tinsel glanced at the dumpster. "The Trash Masters have emptied the receiving place."

Mason frowned. "You eat out of the dumpster?"

The second tumbleweed tilted her head. "There is a reason we should reject the donations given us by the normals?"

Mason pressed his lips together, shaking his head.

"We will do better for our new little master," Tinsel announced to the alley. "Ribbon and I shall take him to the train station for washing. Bring him food and fresh garb."

Two sheets of old newspaper, a burger wrapper and torn Doritos bag tumbled down the alley opposite the wind. Mason could just see the tumblebees attached to them now that he knew where to look.

PERILOUS JOURNEY

Atalon drove Drake into the cold rock wall. Jagged edges cut into his scales, blood making the floor slick as he scrambled out of the way of a follow up blow.

I meant no disrespect, Matron.

<*You invade my territory, tell me my daughter was taken by lowly horses, and you expect me to follow you blindly? Leaving my hoard unprotected?*>

Drake dove low over a tail lash, the glistening blue scales clipping one wing. *I do not crave your magnificent hoard. Salyse needs rescue, and I cannot do it alone.*

Salyse's mother reared back. Drake wrenched rock from her lair floor. Flame washed around it, melting the edges. He shifted a tundra in from the outside, cooling the rock to keep it in place.

<*You are unworthy of my daughter, Stormfall's whelp. You'll not manufacture lies and heroics to earn a mating.*>

Drake fought off a blush. *That's not my desire either.*

<*My daughter's not sufficient for the child of glorious Stormfall?*>

Drake snarled frustration, flame licking from his nostrils. *I would be grateful if you would listen to me, Matron. I desire nothing that is yours. Wizard's Bane abducted her on her way home.*

<*Lies. I entrusted her to a powerful wizard. She'd suffer no danger,*>

and the kine wouldn't dare eject Salyse before her training had been completed.> Salyse's mother smashed the hot rocks from her way, a second talon gouging rock where he'd launched himself upward only moments before. Drake flipped at the ceiling, digging shapeshifted talons into the roof and running along it like a lowly rock lizard.

I swear on both Sire and Dame that Wizard's Bane slew Salyse's foster family, tracked, attacked and abducted Salyse. I've Fey witnesses.

Tail spikes slammed him into the ceiling, several piercing wings and scales. Drake drew on the Dragon Spring, pushing the gathered power into his body. She yanked her tail from him. Shaping magic agonizingly attacked the wounds as he launched himself onto her back. She danced and thrashed, but he dug talons shaped to pierce rock into her shoulder wing joints.

Please, Matron, if you will not help me rescue your daughter then at least let me remove myself from your august presence.

<You will stay away from my daughter, Stormfall's get.> She hunched, slamming her tail against her back as her wings slapped together.

Drake leapt clear and dove. A talon batted him from the air. *Well someone has to rescue her, don't you think? I'd have expected my mother to abandon her child, but I figured a dragon as honorable and righteous as you would rescue her child from Wizard's Bane.*

Salyse's mother slowed. She cocked her head, gaze narrowing like a hawk eyeing a rabbit. *<If lesser Fey have taken her, they will deliver her to my lair to stop the rivers of blood.>*

If Drake had possessed a hand, he'd have drawn its fingers over his face. *Wizard's Bane, Great Lady, they and they alone have trespassed against you.*

<If one has raised limb against an Elder Fey all are complicit.>

The other Fey want to help us. They'll tell us where to find Salyse.

<They'll tell me, or I'll feast on their children.> Her talon slammed him into the floor, a second slapping him into a wall on the bounce. *<You will flee my sight lest I start my feast with you.>*

Drake closed off his mind. He wanted to scream. It'd taken days of searching through northern tundra to match Salyse's memories up enough to find her mother's lair. He had no idea what nefarious plans Velith'Seravin intended or how many other dragonlings they'd captured, killed or tortured. *At best she's going to slaughter every tribe and Fey settlement between here and Velith'Seravin's door. Worst case, she'll just rampage the countryside killing Fey and normal alike until one delivers Salyse. I've no choice but to do this myself.*

He fled, prickled though his pride felt. Salyse's mother's rants faded quickly, suggesting the Elder Fey either wasn't trying or had limited mental range. He paused to tabulate broken bones and lacerations. He summoned power and shifted broken to whole before hurrying back to his motorcycle.

A dwarf sat atop his bike, watching Drake approach. He spat dark liquid on the ground between them.

I'd appreciate it if you'd step away from my bike.

Dandelion fluff eyebrows rose. "Polite dragon, eh?"

Yeah, but I'm in a bit of a hurry.

The dwarf grinned his half melted mouth and stepped away with a sweeping gesture of invitation. "Don't let me get in your way."

Thanks, success and riches on your house.

The dwarf's dark eyes crinkled in mirth. "May it be so, from Elder's lips to the Creator's ear."

Drake shifted shape, hurriedly dressed in clothes drawn from his saddle bags, and drove southward away from Salyse's mother and the odd dwarf. The road stretched ahead leaving Drake once more to musings. Histories Jedediah insisted every pupil study taught that centaur and normals called Indians had been tied once far before the Europeans arrived dividing tribes and continent.

What relationships do normal and centaur share on other continents? Do Asian centaur revile humans? African? Do some live in harmony? Was it some particular incident that drove a wedge between them or is the hatred a specialized jealousy fanned by VelSera's rhetoric.

Drake pulled into a truck stop. A semi exited as he entered. Someone walked over Drake's grave. He shook off the shiver, hoping it no more than Salyse's mother's nasty thoughts. He fueled up the bike then went inside to grab fuel for himself. All the shifting had left him ravenous enough to eat the dwarf, not that he'd have done something as impolite—or so like his mother.

His last two twenties bought a half dozen bottles of Cherry Coke and twice that many heat lamp burgers. *I'll have to use a little more gold potion and hit a pawn shop again soon.*

Drake sat on the bike, scarfed down the dry, over-salty burgers and washed them down with the nectar of the gods. He tossed wrappers into the bin, belched, and tucked the last two bottles in a saddle bag. Drake resumed his southward journey toward more civilized temperatures.

Drake glanced at his mirrors. A large pickup truck—the kind with the extended wheel wells sheltering double tires—rocketed up his back trail. He squinted at its top, trying to tell deer rack from police lights. His speedometer read ninety-three. He'd kept the speed down, not figuring the forested highway as good a place to run full out like the open middle states where you could see highway patrol a long way before you entered gun range.

Truck's hauling ass. Drake shrugged it off. *Maybe he knows where the cops hide.*

Drake edged toward the shoulder, giving the truck plenty of space to pass. The road rose, curving right—the perfect kind of blind curve for a radar gun just beyond the trees. He backed off on the throttle. The truck slowed too, no doubt for the same reasons.

He came over the rise into teeth, but not bear teeth. Two heavy pickups parked with horse trailers blocking the road. He hit the brakes, hoping to avoid the accident.

But neither truck looks damaged.

Centaur piled out of both trailers. Options raced through his mind—none included stopping. He could try to earthswim him and the bike under the obstructions. If his swim proved less than perfect, he might do their job for them. He could unfurl his wings and fly them both over—though he couldn't see what more lay beyond the trailers.

I could ditch the bike and rip some centaur limb from limb.

His teeth put in an appearance, anticipation of centaur flesh and blood quickened his heart rate. A small thought bemoaned the damage to the bike, but vengeance and the whereabouts of Salyse more than paid for repairs.

Drake's wings snapped up, reappearing scales shredding clothes away. He slammed the bike into a centaur, launching airborne before the sword-lance threatened his hide. He met a cloud of arrows above the trailers. Drake snapped his wings tight against his body, diving teeth and talons into the archers responsible. Two arrows penetrated beneath his wing joints which would've made flight impossible. Luckily, he wasn't flying, but a shooting bullet of blood and horror.

Talons shredded through a centaur, separating horse from man in a spray of blood. He hit the asphalt beyond, dug claws in to slow himself, reversed directions and pounced on the next nearest centaur.

For Jordan and Nibble.

Drake shifted to a scale-armored human shape. Burning muscles and popping bones expelled arrows and repaired damaged flesh. "Where is Velith'Seravin? Send the coward out to meet me."

Two centaurs leveled barbed lances, each dragging a chain. Drake recognized the half-melted sorrel of Sinesh Ena'Donishe and his stooge palomino stallion, Hynar Ah'Klach. Three more centaur ran at their flanks, these armed with swords.

"I'd have thought you'd have learned, char-face," Drake snarled. His fingers flew through a spell, but a dark cloud of arrows forced him to finger a second on his off hand. Force blasted into the galloping centaur's teeth. A curved whirlwind threw descending arrows outward in all directions.

The force wave parted, split by the barbed lances. SinDon and Hynar charged untouched through the broken spell. The centaur behind them proved less fortunate, the wave leaving them a crumpled tangle of broken limbs.

Drake shifted the whirlwind to throw the spears off. They cut through it. Drake launched himself skyward, shifting back to his natural form. Lances pierced his lower body. Searing pain pushed everything else from his mind. He fell, wings forgotten. The barbed heads burned like acid in his writhing flesh.

"Shapeshift away from *that*, dragon," SinDon said.

Drake snapped and snarled like a wild beast. Lance shaft's splintered between his teeth. He pushed against the pain, shoving the lance heads from him with shapeshifting magicks. They burned and sliced, cutting opened new flesh he pushed at them with unending pain.

Jedediah insisted his pupils practice every school of magic. Drake blew off the lessons, knowing better than his Master what skills he needed most. Jedediah hadn't tolerated his attitude. He'd forced Drake to learn aquamancy enough for healing and aeromancy sufficient to attain a low glide, pyromancy and the stubborn terramancy he hated but Jordan loved.

Drake drew water from the bloody ground, wrapping centaur fluids around the lances. A pillar of rock thrust him upward out of the reach of their spears. It was crude work at best—guaranteed to earn him Jedediah's reproof.

And if I live long enough for him to yell at me, I'll admit how wrong I was.

Arrows followed him, but a jet from his flame lung left a hole in their assault significant enough to prevent harm. SinDon and Hynar grabbed the chains dangled from the barbed heads lodged in Drake's flesh. They yanked, nearly pulling him from his perch. Drake dug in his claws and ripped lances from his torso. The metal burned his talons like no fire ever had. He found the chains no easier to hold.

Drake sucked in breath and blew out his fire lung, intent to melt the horrid things to slag. The semi he'd passed at the truck stop blocked off easy escape. Its nearby trailer bubbled and melted, but the undamaged spearheads cooled instantly. A beak the size of a surfboard grabbed at the opening's lip and started ripping.

Ah, hell, it can't be.

"I hear your mother's the queen of the sky," the dwarf he'd met earlier grinned. "I know for a fact old Skyraker fears Mathilda here."

Skyraker? Queen of the Sky? My lazy mother?

The roc somehow squeezed inside the trailer ripped at its shell with violent snaps of her beak. Drake rushed his wings back into flight condition and leapt skyward. Archers filled the sky with arrows. He flipped, side-slipped and rolled, bathing them in a gout of flame before beating hard for open air.

"Chicory, get your pet masters moving," SinDon said.

The dwarf wrapped on another trailer. "Get on out here, girls. Prey's on the wing."

A shrill, hard cry split Drake's ears. "No, do you know whose child that is?"

"Get out here and do your job," Sinesh Ena'Donishe said.

"Your roc is loose," Chicory said. "Best get out here and give it orders if you don't want Rydari Phriel to escape and tell his papa what you've done."

Drake dive-bombed a troop of centaur, exhausting the last of his flame lung. The trailer holding Mathilda broke apart like a tin egg. The massive bird leapt skyward, casting a shadow over the whole tableaux. It circled once and then headed west.

"Hynar, if the worthless harpies won't come out, set off the explosives."

Four harpies bolted from within the trailer. Scaly legs flexed wicked talons. Dark molting wings carried them airborne. Glowing eyes promised SinDon death until they turned their gazes to Drake. They shrieked chorused birdsong. Mathilda banked a graceful arc, her gaze worse than her mistress'.

The roc cried out a challenge.

Mathilda dwarfed him. She was easily as big as Gilrender, and he didn't doubt a match for his mother despite their size difference. Its razor beak and massive talons might as well have been Dragonsteel. Were he Gilrender's size, his spellcraft might've turned the tide. Two of the harpies sang at Mathilda, adding vicious attacks to the arrows still flying. Beneath him centaur massed in numbers he'd hesitate to challenge with tooth, talon and fire.

They didn't hit anything vital with the spears because they meant to disable and take me alive. Where are the other harpies?

He spied them rising a lazy spiral in the distance, weighted chain nets hung from their grip. He searched for an escape. Rocs were big, deadly and expert flyers, but without the harpies controlling her, Mathilda was too dumb to do anything but head home—assuming he didn't piss her off.

On the ground, even his motorcycle would have a hard time staying ahead of a determined centaur—let alone a small army of them. If SinDon had spread them out in the forest, he'd be hard pressed to escape.

Earthswim? He wasn't great at it, managing by overwhelming power from the Dragon Spring to overcome his poor skills. It might prove his only escape. It might break every bone he had. Drake's gaze flit to the dwarf. *This trap is too good. SinDon's an idiot, the dwarf has to be running this show. No dwarf will figure an air-kindred able to earthswim. It's worth a try.*

Drake folded his wings, slipping out from under the nets cast about him. He pushed away everything else in the world, focusing on Lanea, Salyse and terramancy. He'd failed one, but he wouldn't fail the other. He wouldn't be captured. His beak slid into the ground with effortless grace. He followed, shallowing the dive in a random direction. Earth scraped his insides like sandpaper. He redoubled his focus, lessening the friction.

Something wrapped his beak in agony. He jerked backward. Pain burned lines across his tail. Drake thrashed back and forth as lines of pain wrapped him in torment. Earth slid downward. He emerged at the feet of a dozen centaur and one dwarf.

"Skyraker'd be proud, boy. You're hella hard prey to nail." The dwarf cast another net over him. It didn't burn Drake's scales. The lower net dipped just beneath the surface, ready to slide out and fill his mind with pain. "Shapeshift to human form if you please."

Drake shook his head. He had to resist. There had to be a way to escape.

Sinesh Ena'Donishe strode up to him. "Shift to human shape or die."

"Go mount a mule," Drake said.

The butts of spears jabbed at him from half a dozen angles.

"I get to kill you if you continue to disobey," SinDon smiled. "So, shift or grant my fondest wish."

Drake blew flame at him, but the net somehow kept the fire within its boundaries.

Chicory stepped up to Drake's beak. "You're beaten, boy, but life is hope."

"What do you care?" Drake snarled.

"You're bagged. I get paid either way," Chicory spat. "Better for you if you live, don't you think?"

Drake shifted toward human.

"Not the wings," SinDon said.

Once Drake looked the part of an incubus, SinDon shoved him down in the net and fitted a runed collar around Drake's neck. Two solid bars, manacles and fetters later, Drake had been trussed up like a pig for roasting.

"This Dragonsteel was forged by our finest Scalereaver Arcanists. It's coated. Too much friction will wear off the protection that keeps you from burning right this moment. It'll absorb any magic you try to use. It'll convert magic to heat, melting off the coating." Chicory spat. "Do we understand each other?"

"What now?" Drake asked.

SinDon nodded to Hynar. The large palomino drew a curved blade colored much the same as the lance heads. Drake tensed. The blade sliced off Drake's wing, leaving burning agony behind in its wake.

Drake screamed.

Hynar feinted several practice swings where Drake could see them. The second slice proved far worse for the anticipation. Drake howled. Tears streamed down his cheeks.

Sinesh Ena'Donishe bent down until his face was as close to Drake's as he could manage. "Burns, doesn't it?"

Drake glared at the smirking centaur. "When I escape, you're my first celebratory meal."

"Victory!" SinDon raised his hands. A wicked smile filled his face. "Now, beat him unconscious. Don't leave any bones unbroken."

The eldest harpy landed atop a truck, fixing SinDon with matronly disapproval. Her harsh rasp rose above Drake's screams.

"Why in the Creator's name? Do you have any idea what Elder Lords will do when they learn of this?"

"What makes you think anyone will ever learn of this?" SinDon asked. "Dead dragons tell no tales."

❧

Jordan pulled up in front of the dojo. The lights weren't on, but she pounded on the door. Text on a flyer, its back to her in the door, bled through enough for her to make out the word tournament.

She sucked in strength. It welled into her with almost no effort. She hardened her fist, smashed the glass and ripped the flyer from its jagged edges. She turned to go, eager to leave before police arrived and doubly so to find Mason and bring him home.

Something stopped her. Her hands itched. She needed to go inside. She drew in earth like she did in the forest, masking her face in a layer of stone against possible video surveillance.

The dojo smelled of sweat and disinfectants. Power throbbed beneath her feet. *That doesn't make any sense.*

Jordan layered her vision with magical energy. Auras eased into view like fading specters. A strong one emerged from down the hall, exiting through a rear door. She hurried down the corridor, all too aware a silent alarm might be bringing the law. If they caught her, no one was available to save Mason.

She tracked the aura to a solid wall. Bones of a spell mechanism offered her access. Stairs led downward. A palpable air of sorcery filled the basement. She followed it to a room beneath the dojo floor. Lines and runes otherwise invisible to untrained eyes painted a carpet. They reached out to crystals at four points. Weak light throbbed in their heart, somehow drawing in ambient energy—the dimmest of which a crystal radiating earth energy.

Oh, frak. Oh frak, oh frak, oh frelling frak.

Jordan sprinted out of the dojo. She leapt into the Charger, rocketed out of the parking lot and onto the interstate ramp wishing she could glamour the car to keep away the police.

Mason checked his reflection in the mirror. The shoes felt too tight. The sweatshirt hung to mid-thigh. The replacement clothes weren't the height of fashion, but they were warm, clean and dry. Flame left him with a bald swath, but Tinsel's girlfriend Ribbon provided him a Braves ball cap.

"You and Ribbon have a nice place here?" Mason asked.

"We're happy," Tinsel said.

"Oh," Mason's hopes fell.

"Have we done something to displease you?"

"You've been so helpful, I just wanted to reward you. Jedediah's got all this land. He lets Fey live on it, and...it'd be nice to have Fey friends like Jordan has."

Tinsel brightened. "Master Mason would call us friends and invite us to live on his land?"

Mason shrugged. "Guess it's not a good idea. I mean the farm doesn't have any trash or tumbleweeds."

Tinsel clapped his hands together. "It is indeed a fortuitous day that brought Master Mason to Tinsel's alley. I shall propose to Ribbon today, and we will come with you to where you dwell."

"First we have to figure out how to get me home," Mason said.

"Come, I shall take you to an earth Fey city. They will reach your Jordan."

They exited the bathroom. Tinsel tumbled off his shoulder to a waiting Ribbon. Mason turned his back, glancing around Underground Atlanta. It didn't look like a train station. Restaurants and curio shops, bracketed by freestanding stalls and the occasional musician or beggar lined the dim corridors. A model train engine stood freshly painted on one side of the passage, still and unable to take him home.

Ribbon's delighted squeal proceeded her impact against Mason's check. She kissed it over and over. "Thank you, Master Mason, thank you so much."

"Please, just call me Mason. So, how do we find this earth Fey city?"

"By train." Tinsel pointed to the painted locomotive.

"That train doesn't work," Mason said. "It's just for show."

"Not just for show." Ribbon giggled. "It's the way to go."

Tinsel rolled across the pavement like a wayward leaf. He stopped, seemly caught on a step up to the train's engineer compartment.

Mason checked the area, glancing side to side. He didn't see either sensei, *Namhaid* gunman or centaur, but something had his nerves on edge. He'd trained under the people trying to kill him. She'd even told him so.

"Come, little master, while the coast is clear."

He checked their surroundings once more before hurrying across to the train and into the engineer's compartment.

A police officer snapped an order. "Hey, kid, get down from there."

Where did he come from? Mason tensed. "Can you do a glamour to make it look like I got down?"

"Not from him," Tinsel grabbed onto the edge of the furnace door and heaved. Ribbon tumbled down, joining her strength to his. It cracked open, revealing a ladder leading down.

"I'm warning you," the officer said. "If you don't get down I'm going to arrest you."

"Okay," Mason eyed the small furnace door. "I'll get down."

He rushed forward, snagging the door to bring it closed behind him. Like with the refrigerators in Jedediah's boneyard, the entrance seemed to admit him regardless of apparent size. He hurried down the ladder, waiting for the telltale shout of his impending arrest. The furnace door opened again with a squeal of metal. The officer glanced down the tunnel. Mason tensed. The bearded face broke into a wide grin. He winked and ducked back out. The door above closed, stealing what little light the dim area offered.

Mason descended the cramped access tunnel. Its walls seemed to squeeze tighter, loosen and narrow once more—a long stone throat swallowing him. The ladder went on forever. Mason's foot came down onto hard rock with a surprising suddenness. Tinsel and Ribbon pushed on the wall, revealing a door he couldn't have seen.

How many other doors did I pass unnoticed?

They stepped onto a crowded platform around multiple tracks.

Mason gaped.

Centaur stood head and torso above the crowd dressed in tribal leathers and modern clothes—though Mason had no idea how they'd have managed the tunnel he'd entered. Dwarves chatted amicably with varied Fey, some sipping designer coffee and others gulping from pewter flagons. They were and weren't the dwarves of fantasy movies. Small axes and wide-bladed swords hung from leather belts or thongs draped over the shoulders of suit jackets. Facial hair varied from trim executive styles to the unruly food-riddled beards portrayed by movies.

A train pulled into the station. Gangplanks extended from the platform to passenger compartments, allowing egress for a tide of Feymanity. The train itself defied any expectation offered by the old steam engine far above. Sleek lines, glass and metal gave the apparently floating vehicle a science fiction aspect. Glowing lines flowed over its surface, defining angles on the otherwise smooth, rounded train—a river of light flowing from nose to tail again and again making it almost look like it was already speeding away.

Ribbon nudged Mason. "Ticket, little master."

"Um, thanks?" Mason eyed the centaur nervously. "How did you get this?"

She blushed but didn't answer. Mason turned it over in his hands. The writing reached off its surface, constricting his throat with shock and excitement. He read it three times, unable to believe the words across its surface: Single Round Trip Transit – Atlanta to Atlantis.

REALIZED DREAMS &
NIGHTMARES

Kane slammed a fist against the arcade machine. "Damn ghosts cheat."

Crystal chuckled.

He turned toward her. "What?"

"Um," Crystal chewed her lip.

"What?!"

She shifted from one foot to another. "We might have a problem."

He scanned the rest of the warehouse. "Can't whatever it is wait? Jordan's only been gone a few hours. What could possibly have gone wrong?"

"Billie Jo is baking."

"She's always baking."

Crystal shook her head. "Something's wrong."

"A lot wrong's with her." He checked his phone. "Like dinner's late."

Her expression hardened. "Look, Kane, you're normally kind of funny, but I think something's wrong and you're the only mage I've got right now."

Kane rolled his eyes, but he followed her up the lift and across the boneyard to the Cheraw portal. He hesitated. "This isn't a trap is it?"

Crystal frowned. "What are you talking about?"

"You're not being forced to take me outside the barrier, are you?"

She planted hands on her hips. "Now you worry about that? After you blew up Jordan's home?"

He rushed through the refrigerator. The aftertaste turned his stomach, but it complained about emptiness. The heady scent of bread, sugar, cinnamon and other spices filled the farmhouse. He followed his nose to the kitchen.

Kane stopped dead at its entrance. Piles of precariously balanced plates stacked cookies and cakes, baked chicken and breads, sweets and savories in every flavor of the rainbow. He glanced at Crystal. "What the hell?"

She pointed.

He stepped further into the kitchen. Billie Jo sat on the floor. Tears ran streaks through flour-powdered cheeks. She raised an anguished gaze to him. "Help me...please."

The pitiful words chilled him. Pain nearly radiated from her worrisome, manic smile. "H-how do I help?"

"Make it stop." Fingers kneaded dough. "Please, make me stop."

"What are we going to do?" Crystal asked.

Kane shook his head. *I've got no idea. Jedediah couldn't figure out what was wrong. How am I supposed to help her?*

"Please." Billie Jo rocked back and floor, Barbie-doll smile cemented into place.

"Just stop," Kane said. "You don't have to cook."

Billie Jo shook her head back and forth. Giggles bubbled out of her lips, mad and gut-wrenching.

"It's okay," Crystal said. "We have enough food."

Billie Jo sobbed and laughed in a strange hybrid convulsion.

"Why are you baking?" Kane asked.

"I have to bake. Baking makes things better. Baking replaces...worry."

"It does?" Crystal asked. "Does baking make you feel better?"

Billie Jo nodded. "No."

"You bake to distract yourself from what's bothering you?" Crystal asked.

Billie Jo shook her head. "Would you like some cookies?"

Kane's brows furrowed. Whatever was wrong with her seemed to be getting worse. He didn't know what triggered it.

"Don't just stand there." Crystal whispered. "Do something."

"I'm open to suggestions."

"Kane, you have to figure something out. She doesn't sleep. She just bakes."

"Sleeping pills?" Kane asked. "Chloroform?"

"Do you have either?" Crystal asked.

"No." Kane examined his hands. He wasn't sure what was wrong. He wasn't sure when anyone else would return to help. A shadow of insanity ghosted across Billie Jo's crooked smile. He'd put Mae into an enchanted sleep. He had no idea how to get her out of it, but it kept her quiet. The same might offer Billie Jo escape from whatever plagued her.

There's no one else to do anything. I have to do something.

Kane drew upon his power. Cold spread out through his limbs. He'd worked the spell in a panicked rush on Mae, but this time he thought through every element his mistress taught him of the enchantment. He was about to lock his friend's mother in an endless sleep he wasn't sure how to reverse.

It's this or a padded room. I think Mason would prefer his mother sleeping but sane, at least until Mistress has been rescued.

Kane's hands swirled through motions, tracing the curves of her aura with lines of his own. Indigo power swept her aura, leaving frosted blue behind each gesture. Her muscles loosened. The smile slid from her face as Kane's power slid her as close to death as he was able. The magic formed as he desired, every line as Mauve had described.

Something went wrong.

Indigo power swirled around Billie Jo. It raised a wind that didn't blow, sending icy fingers across the chalkboard of his soul.

"Get out," Kane shouted.

Crystal hesitated.

"Now!"

She bolted as the tornado of power whipped outward separate from the physical world and not disturbing a single sprinkle. The power slammed into him. The grave reached out for him, trusted companion turned rabid dog by some force he didn't understand.

His gaze shot to the woman locked an eyelash away from death. Indigo swallowed his sight leaving an after-specter of an ancient and tortured soul on the kitchen floor. His Sight wavered. It faded. Everything else followed.

* * *

Myn'Glent released the magic. The crying foal quieted.

"Well done," MidCru said.

Pride swelled in her chest. MidCru was young compared to many of the Path teachers, but her reticent praise carried more weight—at least to Myn'Glent. "That spell seemed more efficient."

MidCru gasped, pressing a hand to her breast. "More effective than wizard magic?"

Myn'Glent chewed her lip.

Her mentor sighed. She shooed the foal into her mother's arms and turned back to Myn'Glent. "What is it?"

"Promise you won't get mad?" Myn'Glent's gut tightened. She'd considered the things she'd found in the archives, going over them and over them and then debating the words perched on her lips.

"You know I'm not going to promise that without more information."

"What if...what if it *is* wizard magic?"

MidCru blinked. "What?"

Words poured from Myn'Glent in a rapid fire succession. "I've been reading up in the archives, and I am pretty sure, no I am convinced, that the things I've been reading indicate that shaman magic is essentially wizard magic."

She gasped breath.

"If that were true more of us would be able to do what wizard's do."

Myn'Glent cringed. "What if we can and just don't know it?"

Stubbornness filled MidCru's expression.

Myn'Glent cut her mentor off before the shaman had a chance to shut down her argument. "The Path teaches that the Creator gave us a world in balance."

"Right. Wizards use arcane magic. Shaman and druids work life magic. Clerics channel divine or…," MidCru scowled. "…infernal powers. Witches and mystics dabble in all three."

"*Lah'Phriel* refers to the spirit, but literally it means wind." Myn'-Glent knelt, drawing the complex diagram she'd seen in the archives. Lines and circles composed the various disciplines. She'd barely finished the drawing when another centaur galloped up to them.

"MidCru, *Feihtor Ah Mythela'Raemyn* has been spotted climbing the grand stair. He's accompanied by a large escort."

Myn'Glent's mentor scowled. "He can't have heard the news while in the corridor. What other calamity is on our doorstep?"

Myn'Glent's heart raced. *Feihtor Ah Mythela'Raemyn* was a great wizard with vast knowledge and power. He could help her prove her theory. With his backing the centaur shaman might embrace expanded abilities, giving them an advantage in the conflicts brewing outside the valley. *I have to meet him.*

"Maybe he just wants to visit?" Myn'Glent ventured. "I could greet him and find out."

"No!" MidCru almost shouted. She softened her voice. "Acolytes do not welcome so great a centaur to Mythela'Raemyn. We'll discuss this lesson later. Return to the healing enclave and help tend those in need."

"But, MidCru…"

"I told you no, and I meant it." MidCru turned to the other centaur. "I'll dress and attend to the gateway arch as soon as I can.

Jedediah crested the top of the grand stair, stepped across the threshold from corridor to valley and summoned a wizard eye. ChiRie rushed up to the entry arch, hands caressing the intricate designs carved into the pillars supporting it—just as WaphRae had on their last visit. He glanced at the older shamaness to find a warm, indulgent expression.

A welcoming party of centaur galloped up to them. Midall E'Cru led them, the attractive young centaur out of breath. They performed the elaborate bow and greeting, while he chaffed at the protocol delaying his business. They greeted WaphRae then each centaur and Kimberlite in turn.

"What brings *Feihtor Ah Mythela'Raemyn* back to us once more?" MidCru asked. "Jedediah, what's wrong with your eyes?"

"Jedediah's been cursed," WaphRae said. "We were unable to lift it."

"Stolen, along with my magic." He squared his shoulders. "I need your help, and we need someplace to lodge this girl."

"She penetrated the corridor somehow," ChiRie said. "And she seems to absorb magic—though that has nothing to do with Jedediah's problem."

Unease flitted through the reception party. An undercurrent of tension caught his gut, wringing it inside out. Tension built as silence dragged on.

"What are you holding back?" Jedediah said.

"The elders and the new High Shaman will want your news," a centaur said. "He'll want to fill you in on our other troubles."

Jedediah gestured. "Lead on."

"Should we lodge the girl first?" MidCru asked.

He shook his head. "Bring her some food, but otherwise we travel with our troubles on our backs."

MidCru led the way deeper into the valley. ChiRie gawked and asked questions until WaphRae shushed her. Mixed emotions further abused Jedediah's stomach as they parted a circle of cherry blossom trees. White blossoms tinged palest pink perfumed the air, and wide branches shaded the council area. Battle-garbed centaur statuary supported a stone ring, leaving twelve gaps into its open-sky amphitheater. Age discolored the rearing stone pillars, but their intricate carvings remained sharp.

Lelai Muen'Myn is gone. It's only natural they elected a new High Shaman.

The centaur in their center made a large contrast to his seemingly frail predecessor. He had a warrior's build, aged muscles still carving hard enough lines into his dark skin that they might've been made by a chisel. His robes covered much of his light-swallowing black coat. His tail lashed back and forth—the only sign of impatience or displeasure.

"The Mother has sent *Feihtor Ah Mythela'Raemyn* to us in our time of need. Thank the Creator."

"Not to be rude, but misfortune brought me. Have we met before?"

"No. Unlike…my predecessor, I travelled among the tribes getting to know our people, their hearts and their troubles. I returned when I heard of her passing and was honored to receive election to her empty mantle."

"Great. You got a name?"

The High Shaman scowled. "Lailar E'Seradi."

"Go by LaiSer?" Jedediah asked.

ChiRie giggled. "Laser?"

Lailar's voice hardened. "No."

"All right then," Jedediah said. "I've been cursed. I got with me a girl what's been attacked by an unknown party. She somehow managed to step through a corridor wall from about two centuries back guessing by her rags. What've you got?"

"I have a dragon rampaging through the northern continent, slaughtering tribes and demanding the return of her daughter."

Jedediah glanced sideways.

"Elithori E'Kyraia," MidCru said. "We don't know where her daughter is, but she's claiming Rydari Phriel told her we have her."

"If Drake said the centaur have her, he'll mean Wizard's Bane." Jedediah scowled, shaking his head. "Ain't no way even Velith'Seravin's dumb enough to kidnap dragonlings."

"She seems unconvinced by that argument," Lailar said. "We need you to go stop her."

"Nope, not happening."

"Are you not *Feihtor Ah Mythela'Raemyn*, great Guardian of the centaur tribes?" Lailar asked.

Heat built up beneath Jedediah's skin. "Yup. Ain't you High Shaman, responsible for the safety and well-being of the tribes?"

"As High Shaman I am calling upon you to resolve this."

"Sorry, this curse has me down for the count. Remove it, and we'll talk."

An eerily familiar aura caressed his, drawing his attention to a shift of movement. The pompous ass that'd replaced Lelai Muen'Myn faded into the background. He was snarling, probably at Jedediah. He couldn't have responded if he wanted. Despite all his experience with aeromancy, Jedediah couldn't find his breath.

Jedediah's heart stopped.

A topless girl, yearling based upon her physical development, peeked into the open air amphitheater. She stepped more fully into view. From the waist down, the silver-crimson centaur was horse. Above that was the young girl that'd played at his feet, filling his life with mischief and laughter.

Lelai Muen'Myn's words seemed to whisper through the amphitheater, lingering in the place they'd been spoken so long ago. "There will be darkness, dear Jedediah, and great pain. You'll not understand what I invoke here, perhaps ever, but it's a gift for love I couldn't return before."

"Dear Creator." Jedediah gasped. "Lanea."

Mason, Tinsel and Ribbon boarded the train. He wove across the plush carpets, between large comfortable leather chairs to an unoccupied corner. The seat had its own computer—more advanced than the one he wanted for Christmas.

A young dwarf attendant came along before the train pulled from the station. She—at least he thought the beardless dwarf was female—approached him. "Care for some breakfast? Something to drink?"

Mason's stomach grumbled. "I lost my wallet."

"Meals are included in your fare."

"I thought companies were cutting that sort of thing."

She smiled again. "Possible, but we always run at a profit —always."

She brought him an enormous hearty breakfast suited for a miner's or in Mason's case a minor's appetite. He stuffed himself, dozing in the pleasure of a sated appetite and comfortable chair while Tinsel and Ribbon watched for danger.

Tinsel nudged him awake. "Master Mason, lunch has arrived."

A heavenly aroma awoke his appetite. An attendant slid him a steaming plate of Mount Cheesesteak and the Potato Wedge Foothills. Mason dug in with unrestrained gusto. He noticed Tinsel watching him.

Mason struggled through a stuffed mouth. "Wha?"

"Dwarves have always liked rat, but I didn't know your people did as well," Tinsel said.

"Most of your people treat them like a plague," Ribbon said.

"I'm eating rat?"

Tinsel and Ribbon nodded.

Mason shrugged and took another large bite. The dwarf replaced his empty plate with a full one. He saved the last half for later.

"Please tell us about your home," Ribbon said.

Mason nodded through a yawn. He told them about everything: Jedediah and Jordan, Drake, Kane and his mom. He described the farm, the forest and the Fey he'd met there. Ribbon asked the same questions his mom had when they'd won their house. He answered what he could, his responses satisfying both tumblebees.

Jordan pushed her luck to the breaking point. She pulled up to the tournament only to be barred entry. She cursed inwardly and considered breaking the poor security guard in half. She circled the compound, looking for a stealthy way in and wishing not for the first time that she'd managed to learn earthswimming.

Workers filed in and out of a propped open fire door. She followed one in, pretending she belonged. The hallway underwent heavy repair. A deep hole gaped in the floor. Scorch marks marred walls. Pieces of ripped up tile and damaged drywall piled in one corner, a melted cellphone half hidden in the debris.

Dread welled up. She drew magic over her eyes. A battleground of residual sorcery painted the scars and burns around her.

"Hey, girl. What are you doing here?"

"What happened in this hall?" Jordan asked.

"Someone screwing around with fireworks."

"Did they get hurt?" Jordan forced the question out. "Did anyone die?"

"No. What are you doing here?"

Jordan found air again. "Um, sorry, got turned around. I'll just return to the tournament."

They let her penetrate the convention center. Banners designated the various competing dojos. A woman scowled beneath the one matching Mason's. Jewelry and various items on her body pulsed dimly with magic, but the woman herself generated none. Jordan searched the crowd of boys. None had magic. None were Mason.

She committed the woman to memory. Her hands itched. She wanted more than anything to march across the tournament floor and wring the answers out of the woman's neck. She waited, cursing every moment until one of the boys slipped off toward the bathroom.

"Hey, can you tell me where Mason is?"

He blinked at her. "What?"

"Mason Bartlett?"

The handsome teen closed the distance between them. Jordan tensed for attack. "He's missing. Sensei Truth is trying to figure out where he went."

"When did he go missing?"

"Sometime yesterday."

"When was the last time you saw this Sensei Truth?"

"The same."

Jordan wanted to scream, but the boy hadn't done anything wrong. She sucked in Mother's stolid strength. "Thanks."

"Are you like Mason's sister? I've seen you sitting with him at school."

"Something like that."

"Want to go out sometime?"

Jordan smiled at the irony. Life and death on the line and her social life decides to make an appearance. "Thanks, but I have to find Mason."

She left him to his business, unsure what to do next. She weighed assaulting the woman but starting a fight that might get her arrested could cost Mason his life. She returned to the damaged hall, studying the fire door from the outside. Faded magic stretched out in two directions, but she couldn't tell which trail Mason had left behind.

Follow blindly and hope for luck or return to the farm for Nip?

She tried following. Overlapping auras fouled the trail. She struggled through, pumping magic into her senses until pain pressed the space behind her eyes. She cursed every lost moment, wrong turn and time backtracking. She wound through the city until she came upon a concentration partially hidden by a dumpster. Deep grooved scarred the bricks behind it. She bent close. Stench clung to the concrete, but no evidence of blood painted the alley.

A Doritos bag tumbled down the alley, other random trash flipping end over end in a soft wind. She cursed again, and backtracked out of the alley and along another faint track she hoped would lead her to Mason.

His trail dead ended at an antique train engine.

Jordan shook her head. *What the hedrin does this mean? Where is he?*

"I'd appreciate it if you stepped away from the engine, young lady."

She turned to the policeman addressing her. Thick bodied but shorter than her, his bearded smile felt good natured. "I don't mean to bother you, but I'm looking for a boy whose gone missing."

The officer offered Mason's description as a question.

"Yes, oh, thank Mother. Where'd he go?" Jordan asked.

"He and a couple of tumblebees descended to the station. I didn't see him come out."

Her brow wrinkled. She glanced around for a sign that might fill in the gaps. "What station?"

"The Atlanta Underground Dwarfrail Terminal."

"Underground Atlanta Dwarf...rail?"

"Other way around. Look, just take the ladder inside the engine's furnace."

Jordan drew out the word. "Okay. Uh, thanks for your help."

She descended the tunnel to the train terminal. The presence of centaur unnerved her, but she trusted the armed dwarves working security to keep the peace. She questioned several uniformed dwarves, quickly learning that Mason had boarded a train bound for Atlantis.

She bought a ticket and boarded the next train. That Atlantis still existed pushed her weird-o-meter back to the level it'd been when she first learned about magic, but she didn't care where the train went as long as she could catch Mason and get him home safe.

Mason stopped short, exiting passengers jostling the awed youth. Trains populated a partially transparent tower of platforms rising out of sight, many making his recent transport seem old and ugly. The platform above him spun. It's train launched into open air, arching forward into a transparent funnel-shaped tunnel which slipped beneath the ocean.

He stepped to the edge of his platform, gazing downward at circling gulls and gorgeous blue water. Tinsel directed him to an elevator. A pungent sea smell less prevalent higher in the train station met him on the ground. A mosaic of marble tiles spread out a map beneath his feet, fantastical creatures he recognized as real rather than mythology marked its unraveled globe.

Mason marveled at the sunken city-continent of Atlantis, awed by its apparent unconcern that it wasn't supposed to be sunbathing in open sight. The city rose around him, a wonder of artistry, science and function. Lynelaen paled in a comparison, if only because Atlantis's construction was all craft and no glamour.

Tinsel said he'd take me to earth Fey. I thought brownies, maybe a stone elemental like Kimberlite. His gaze wandered the crowds and building. *I never imagined a high-tech metropolis filled with cosmopolitan dwarves and Japanese tourists.*

Though few normals populated the train station, those he did see suggested Atlantis wasn't a very closely guarded secret. Fey—some new and strange, others familiar—filled the amazing city. Several centaur disembarked an elevator. He slid behind a support pillar, but they either didn't notice him or didn't care.

Mason relaxed. He turned his back on them running dead into a dwarf with a push broom. "Excuse me, sir."

The solid-looking custodian wobbled but didn't fall down. He leaned against his broom. Its handle pointing to a badge declaring his name: Bartle. "You make a habit of knocking into people trying to do a job?"

"Not all the time." Mason grinned.

Bartle snorted. "Cheeky little mageling."

"Can I ask you a question?"

"Dare say you just did."

"What? Oh, ha-ha. Is the sky real?"

"You get a lot of fake skies where you come from, boy?"

"No."

"This ain't no elf warren, illusion and lies ambushing your senses with every step. We prefer real to lies and deceit."

"But if the sky's real, how come the world doesn't know Atlantis is here?

Bartle chuckled. His laughter stopped. Mason followed the dwarf's gaze to a discarded sports drink bottle dropped by an ill-tempered, two-headed troll arguing with itself.

"You'd think with two heads it'd have enough sense not to litter."

Mason forced an apologetic smile.

"Where were we? Oh, the world knows we're here. Calling us the Bermuda Triangle these days."

"You kill people that stumble upon this place?" Mason asked.

"Mad, violence-inundated children," Bartle grumbled. "Look around, mageling. If you were a normal and found this place, would you go back?"

"Guess not, but what about satellites?"

Bartle snorted. "Who do you think invented satellites, youngster? Humans?"

"The Japanese?" Mason ventured.

"Where'd you come in from, the sticks?" Bartle asked. "Everyone knows we funnel all new tech through Japan."

"What? Why?"

"Damned nukes destroyed one of the best mushroom suppliers we had. Only right and civil that we help them rebuild."

"Right," Mason chewed his lip. "Makes sense if you like mushrooms."

"You don't like mushrooms?" Bartle asked. "Mother drop you as a baby?"

"I don't think so, but I need to get back to her." Another group of centaur exited an elevator. He recognized the half-melted sorrel and another centaur barring a lightning scar Mason'd given him. His gut tightened. He shifted, keeping Bartle between him and the new arrivals.

I barely escape the Namhaid and run straight into Wizard's Bane. My luck can't possibly get any worse.

The dwarf glanced over his shoulder. "Friends of yours?"

"No, they're trying to kill me."

"Those are the ones you told us of?" Tinsel asked.

"Yes. Please, Bartle, is there any way you can help me? Maybe point me to the authorities?"

Bartle frowned at the centaur then back at Mason. "Unless

they've done something illegal on dwarf soil, there's nothing the authorities can do. Do you have any gold?"

"I lost my wallet and all my money."

Bartle scowled. "You seem like a nice kid, but dwarves aren't fond of mages. Without a way to pay for help, you're going to be hard pressed to find any."

"I just need to make a phone call for help."

"Atlantean phone networks don't overlap with that used by normal, y'all don't even have 6G yet. Maybe a magistrate could grant you protection, pretty sure old agreements with the centaur nations haven't been rewritten to exclude human descendants."

"Not to be dense, but which tribes are we talking about?"

"Cherokee, Eskimo, Zulu, Aztec," Bartle said.

"Aren't the Aztecs extinct?" Mason said.

"If you say so," Bartle said. "Look, boy, I've got to get back to work."

"Thank you, Mister Bartle."

"Good luck to you." Bartle pushed his broom away, mumbling to himself. "Kid had good manners for a mageling."

Ribbon slipped from inside the sweatshirt's hood. "What do we do now?"

"Um," Mason chewed his lip. He dug the round trip ticket from a pocket. He still had a full stomach and half a sandwich. The Wizard's Bane centaur hadn't seemed to notice him. A scan of the crowd showed him at least a visible police presence. "Chance things here. See if we can get in to see a magistrate. If we can't get things settled one way or another, we'll head back to Atlanta."

CURSED

ason expected a fortress, maybe a palace, but he found the magistrates housed in a big government high-rise in the upper city. Metal posts and velvet ropes formed a lengthy maze climbing a shallow ramp toward the entrance. Dwarves and other Fey filled the queue, awaiting audience with one of the magistrates.

For an underground race, Dwarves sure seem to love the outdoors.

Mason scanned the crowd, but he saw no sign of Wizard's Bane. He stepped into line, eyes checking and rechecking his surroundings. Security guards and lower level functionaries in marginally cheaper suits policed the queue. A level down and some short distance away, thousands of dwarves swarmed a parade ground moving in practiced formations.

He addressed a young dwarf woman Lanea's age. "Pardon me, ma'am."

She glanced up from the infant in her arms, fingers still tickling its first thin curls of a beard. "Yes?"

"What are those dwarves doing down there?"

She drew the baby closer to her chest. "That's a training ground. That formation is for close combat assault."

"Who are they planning to attack?" Mason asked.

Her face darkened. "I don't know. Maybe it's connected to the rumors of a coming war."

Mason swallowed. "Couldn't it be for something else? Like defense or something?"

"No, every dwarf serves in the National Defense Force. We all learn the formations. That one is definitely offensive and those uniforms aren't DNDF."

"You all serve? Why?"

"It's how we earn our rights and freedoms. By serving the nation, we earn a say in how we're governed.'."

An unsettling feeling filled Mason. *Does that have anything to do with Wizard's Bane war against wizards? Are the dwarves preparing to attack us?*

He fretted over the possibilities, moving slowly forward as the line progressed. A little more than an hour later, he'd advanced a quarter of the way through the line. A resounding gong thundered throughout the city. The lady that'd helped him sighed. She set the infant in a stroller and turned it around to exit the line.

"Ma'am? I'm sorry to bother you again, but why are you leaving? Where is everyone going?"

"It's drinking hour. No point in waiting anymore. The queue will reform in the morning."

"But you said it's an hour," Mason objected.

She smirked. "Ever try to keep an eye on your watch with a flagon tipped up to your lips? Besides, magistrates work hard. They seldom restrict their relaxation to only an hour."

"But...I need help today."

She gave him an apologetic smile and pushed the carriage back out of the maze. He watched her go.

Now what?

Mason shuffled forward through the maze, letting the ropes pay attention to where he went. A few of the slower crowd meandered from the line far ahead. He had no place to go. He could return to Atlanta, be stuck closer to home.

"Do you know him?" Ribbon asked.

Mason looked up.

Zero smiled. "Hello, Mason."

Mason backed away, ropes slowing his progress. "What do you want?"

"I wanted you to intensify the conflict between Velith'Seravin and Jedediah. Unfortunately, that requires you to vanish, preferably with a blood trail."

Cold washed through him. His teacher, the man who'd helped him with bullies, who'd taught and encouraged him talked about Mason's murder as if was less important than doing laundry.

"I don't want to die."

Zero offered him a sad smile. "It's for the best. Take it from me, Jedediah would've been a more disappointing father than your own. He'd have ignored you, given you enough training to get yourself killed—assuming he didn't sacrifice you to his enemies."

"How would you know?" Mason stumbled, scrambling under the ropes that had caught him.

"We share a mother, well, different bodies but the same soul," Zero said. "Elsabeth turned her back on her clan. Her death stole him from us—just like he disappeared after Lanea's death. It hasn't cost you a sibling...yet."

"Master," Tinsel said. "Enemies to your right."

SinDon and the other Wizard's Bane centaur rushed toward him.

Mason bolted through the dwindled crowd, jostling people in return for threats and barbed jibes. He had to reach the magistrates' protection.

A lingering functionary called after Mason. "Hey, boy. No cutting in line."

Mason ignored him, giving up the rat's maze as a death trap. He drew speed into his limbs and raced through the maze, leaping, sliding and knocking ropes from his way. He glanced back as he neared the safety of the front doors.

Zero strolled through the broken maze, seemingly unconcerned that Mason might escape. SinDon bulled through the queue, some of his fellows tangled in poles and ropes.

Mason exploded through the doors, onto a marble foyer and

ran bodily into a two-headed troll, this one with both a man's and a woman's head.

"Halt!" the troll-man said. "Where do you think you're going?"

"They're going to kill me," Mason said. "Please, I need to see a magistrate."

"It's drinking hour. They're busy."

Mason peered up into his face then hers. "Please, I'm alone and stranded. I'm being chased by a deranged wizard and a psychotic centaur tribe."

"Let him through, Lesh," As the troll woman spoke, the troll's body writhed. Its waist narrowed, muscles thinned, and breasts swelled on its chest.

"He's making it up," Lesh said, the body reverting to its masculine form.

Male became female once more. "What kid makes up lies to see a magistrate?"

"It doesn't matter, Nita," Transformation back to Lesh left Mason dizzy. "It's not the way it's done. He can come back tomorrow for a proper audience."

Swelling breasts told Mason the troll-woman disagreed. Her hands perched on her hips. "If you send him outside and he gets killed, who do you think's left to clean it up and take the blame?"

Muscular arms folded over a shrinking chest. "Ain't my fault."

Mason looked back and forth between the two arguing heads. "Please, I'll do anything."

Lesh scowled. Nita moved their arms out of the way of her expanding chest and planted them firmly on widened hips. For a moment Mason thought they'd change again, but Nita's voice softened. "The supreme magistrate's session hasn't ended. Through the metal detectors then up to the forty-second floor. He'll see you safe, dear."

"Thank you." Mason bolted through the detector and raced for the elevators. He prayed all the way up, managing the forty-second floor without cursing out loud. He rushed across a small foyer toward large double doors, some language he couldn't read declaring something in gigantic letters over it.

Mason stopped short. "There, the planter. Hide there and do the western whistle thing to warn me if he catches up."

"Yes, little master," Ribbon launched herself toward the ficus.

Tinsel followed. "We will alert you."

Mason shoved the heavy doors open.

A deep baritone boomed with an air of finality. A dwarf in steel-grey robes struck a jeweled hammer on the arm of his chair. "That's settled. Now, if there is nothing else, Velith'Seravin, its drinking hour."

Mason froze.

Eyes of a centaur entourage turned to meet his entrance. A delighted smile filled Velith'Seravin's face.

"What's the meaning of this interruption?" The magistrate demanded. "It's drinking hour. Courts are adjourned."

Mason cringed, walking forward through a crowd of would-be killers making every effort to keep his shoulders from hunching. "Please forgive me, your supreme magistratedness. The security troll said you'd be able to grant me protection."

"From what?"

"From him for one," Mason pointed at Velith'Seravin. "Also a mercenary wizard that chased me into the building."

"What would you have to fear from our honored friend, Velith'Seravin?"

"He's a wizard, Lord Gralkon," VelSera said. "He's also a dragon friend."

Lord Gralkon scowled. "We've nothing to offer a mageling who befriends dragons."

"Please, Lord. I'm no one's enemy. I'm not even a teenager yet. I just want help going home. Please just help me contact my mom and grant me sanctuary until she comes for me."

"I think the scars you left on Rhinlar E'Hynar's face spin a different story." Velith'Seravin said.

Mason considered lying. He considered defending his actions. "I did hurt him when he attacked us. I'm not proud of it."

Velith'Seravin grinned. "Great Lord Gralkon, grant me this mageling for crimes against my people."

Gralkon raised his hammer.

A weedy whistle split the air.

"Hold," Zero's voice boomed off the walls. "I oppose Velith'Seravin's claim. He is an oath breaker, and the boy is mine by kin right."

Velith'Seravin darkened. "I don't know you, wizard, but I warn you not to make an enemy of me. The boy will die."

A malicious grin filled Zero's face. "Yes, he will, but not by your action *warlock*. Did you or did you not betray and assault Master Remi, a satyr in good standing with the dwarven nation?"

Velith'Seravin darkened.

"Take care with your words, lest Gralkon's hammer reveal spoken lies."

The hammer can detect lies? I'm so glad I told the truth. Mason tensed. "Wait, if the hammer tells truth from lies, then you know I told the truth."

Lord Gralkon inclined his head. "It is so."

"Both of them want to kill me. I just want to go home in peace."

"You're a mageling, boy. You might speak true when it serves your purpose, but I fear both these are well known to court and Thane."

"You're going to let them kill me for how I was born?" Mason's heart sank. "Magic is evil, and since I was born with it, I'm an evil thing that must die?"

"Well spoken, boy," Velith'Seravin fixed his gaze on Zero. "Every mage should be put to death to protect the Fey from their evils."

"Tribal Elder Two-Hawks is well-known to this body. He has proved his friendship to the dwarves many times over," Gralkon said. "If the boy is kin, then he's protected under the same articles that allowed you to negotiate the alliance we just finalized."

"He wants the kid dead, I want him dead," Velith'Seravin said. "Give him to me, and we both get what we want."

"Insufficient," Zero said. "I must first question him."

"He's not yours to question," Velith'Seravin said.

Zero raised an eyebrow. "Lord Gralkon, you know the depths of my mines. They speak in favor of my rights as kin and Tribal Elder."

"No!" Velith'Seravin charged Zero, front hooves flailing.

Mason's pulse skyrocketed. *If he defends himself with magic, the magistrate might help me...or he might surrender me to Velith'Seravin. I'm not chancing it.*

He slunk toward the door as Zero responded to Velith'Seravin's attack with a blur of martial arts. Velith'Seravin's companions joined the fight at once, leaving their leader to step back from the assault.

Mason whispered. "Tinsel, call the elevator."

Arrows flew.

Hooves struck.

Mason bolted for the door, but the fight forced him to double back and circle around.

Zero rolled between two centaur, striking them at pressure points and immobilizing them. He slid around another attack, seizing an axe and wide-bladed dwarf sword from their wall mount. He flourished them with expert skill.

"Lord Gralkon," Zero gasped. "Bear witness that I didn't attack these deceitful centaur, and that I didn't insult you by spilling blood on your floor."

"Do what you will in defense of your honor," Gralkon said.

Three centaurs charged Zero. He scattered their chunks across the floor.

"Together," Velith'Seravin said. "Slay the wizard."

A clear path opened before Mason. He sprinted for the exit. Velith'Seravin leapt his compatriots. Zero snatched a hoof, using the other centaur grappling him as an anchor to pull VelSera down. He rushed toward Mason.

Velith'Seravin leapt Zero. His hand seized Mason's neck and lifted him from the floor. Panic flooded through Mason. He drew all the power he could, preparing to deliver all the lightning his body could manage.

Zero's voice reverberated with compulsion. "Put him down."

Mason slammed into the floor. The tiles drove from him what

breath was left. Before he could inhale his face was pushed into the stone floor by a hoof the size of a soup-plate.

"I assure you," Zero said. "Should you surrender him, he'll die just as you wish."

"Why would a wizard kill another wizard," Velith'Seravin said.

"Speaking to the spirits of my people does not make me a wizard."

"Answer my question," Velith'Seravin said.

"He is ward to my enemy."

"I'm no one's—"

Another hoof slammed into Mason's back. It drove the wind from his lungs, ribs audibly snapping. The shift of weight that had allowed the stomp had applied excruciating pressure on Mason's head. Breath wheezed and gurgled in his chest. Tears soaked his face. All Mason wanted was to go home.

If he raises that hoof to strike, I have to move like I've never moved before.

"Give him to me," Zero said.

Jordan shoved past the other passengers onto the platform. Hours wasted in luxury had felt like torturous years. The shock of finding blue sky over Atlantis instead of water lasted only moments. She dragged magic over her eyes, shoving strength into her limbs as she bolted for the platform edge. A dwarf in security uniform shouted at her to slow down. She leapt at a support pole along the raised platform's edge, swinging over the side and down to the next level. She repeated the move, shooting down to ground level with a knee rattling impact.

Mason's trail caught her eye at once. She hadn't known she'd recognize it or him until she'd seen it, but somehow tracking him through Atlanta had identified something about him to her subconscious.

Jordan put her head down and ran like she'd never ran before.

The trail meandered a bit, but she cut off the corners and apologized to anyone her haste knocked over.

High-tech buildings built with old world flavor blurred by her. Ramps and stairways climbed up and down to varying levels, but she followed Mason's path upward toward the large towering buildings at city center.

She caught sight of him. She sucked in breath to call his name, but what little she managed into her lungs fled at the unmistakable sight of Sinesh Ena'Donishe and other Wizard's Bane centaurs chasing him down.

They're going to kill him. I have to stop them. Jordan sucked in power instead of air and threw it with all her might. *Please work.*

A pillar of stone launched centaur pursuers skyward. One after one like a series of whack-a-moles, rock shot out of the ground beneath them. Sinesh Ena'Donishe jogged backward at the last moment, the stone pillar cutting him off from Mason and a large redheaded man. For the blink of an eye, she thought the man Jedediah. Her spirits rocketed. They crashed in even less time.

Sinesh Ena'Donishe turned toward her. Fury filled his melted features. He drew two hafts from behind his back, constructing the sword-lance as he charged past his fallen tribesmen.

Her staff shot into her hand. She ran toward the centaur. Both hands gripped the petrified wood like a long baseball bat. Runes blazed magma orange up and down its length.

She slid beneath his lance, concrete ripping pants but not armored skin. She swung upward into his gut. SinDon reared, lessening the impact that sent him over backward. She leapt up. The staff slammed down. SinDon rolled, shoving the blade into her ribs.

Fear screamed at her that Dragonsteel would pierce her armor.

The tip embedded itself a few inches, but it clearly wasn't Dragonsteel. Jordan yanked it out of her flesh and jerked it from SinDon's grip. Hooves flashed at her face. She rolled out of the way, discarding the sword lance. He charged again. Her staff cracked across a flailing leg with a sickly sound.

SinDon didn't cry out. He ripped a metal pole off the ground, swinging it and its velvet ropes. The base slammed into her, sending her careening into more. SinDon charged, good leg lashing out. He kicked the staff from her hand.

Black spots swam into her eyes. Vertigo swelled.

Jordan gouged a chunk of concrete from the ground and slapped it across her wound. Twin SinDon's slammed hooves into her, nailing breasts and shoulder but narrowly missing her head.

She thrust a hand toward his face. He dodged backward, but her staff shot out of the ground into his jaw. She leapt at him. Arms seized her mid-leap, lifting her from contact with Mother. The softened concrete fell away from her wound, ripping with it what clotting it'd managed.

She flailed and swore. The arms gripped her in a way that neutralized her enhanced strength. Somewhere in the background, someone was calling on them to stop. She couldn't stop. Mason needed her. She had to save him.

She swung her feet forward with all her might as if the centaur's arms were nothing more than a playground swing. She kicked them back again, shattering lower ribs. Her captor crumpled with a cry. He fell partly atop her. She struggled to free herself. SinDon charged her, recovered sword-lance pointed at her head.

She summoned her staff. It rocketed at him, dragging metal poles and ropes in its wake. Jordan shoved the dead or dying centaur off of her, refusing to think about its death or her part in it.

Mason needs me.

She grabbed a long dagger from the fallen centaur's belt, slashing the blade across his throat to be sure. She charged SinDon. He tore the last of the ropes from him and set his lance for her charge.

Jordan sprang with all her might.

SinDon's blade slammed her sideways midair. The force of the blow bit into her side. She hit the ground, rolled to lessen the damage and drew concrete into her body to patch both bloody wounds.

A sword-lance struck from nowhere. She grabbed it behind the head, summoned her staff into her other hand and cracked it across SinDon's face. He reeled, releasing his weapon. Jordan kicked him, sending her huge opponent careening a dozen yards through the maze. Jordan slammed it across her knee, discarded the elongated staff and lunged sword point toward the centaur.

Another Wizard's Bane young enough that he resembled Mason charged her. She sidestepped his assault and cut the torso from his body. A second swing lopped his head off to complete the set.

She turned back to SinDon, bloody sword dripping and lungs heaving. She drew more power. She doubled it, tripled it. She drew until every inch of her felt as if it might explode from the pressure.

Two centaur helped SinDon back to his feet. They turned as one to attack her. Rage thundered in her ears. She hurled the sword with a primal scream to deafen the world. "Just die!"

The sword rocketed across the distance. Poles launched up in its wake. They flew at the centaur from every direction. A double dozen weighty missiles streaming velvet slammed into the centaur trio, smashing them together and impaling them with blood-spraying force.

She summoned her staff on the run, pushing away the bloody carnage and the dark pleasure of their deaths. Arms grabbed her. It took her a moment's struggling to realize the arms too short to be a centaur.

"Stand down. You're under arrest for murder in the Dwarf Nation of Atlantis."

Jordan fought them. "No. Let me go. Mason's going to die."

"Don't make us hurt you," a dwarf woman cautioned.

Jordan summoned her staff into the dwarf's face. It slammed the woman off her feet. Jordan called it again. It drove her captor's head forward. She grabbed the head and hurled him over her body. Her staff filled her hands once more. She turned to face a dozen armored dwarves. They spread out, encircling her.

She swept her staff at them, a wave of stone shooting out of the ground in a jagged, spiky arch. A hand yanked her backward by her hair. Another hand impaled her with something blunt. She heard a crackle of electricity, but she didn't feel its bite. She elbowed her attacker, followed it up with a staff to the face and leapt over the next dwarf toward the government tower.

She raced across the intervening distance. Mason needed her. She had to save him. She bound up the stairs as fast as she could manage and wrenched open the doors.

A massive green-tinged fist slammed into her face. She somersaulted backward as a security troll glowered down at her hand. "I broke a nail."

Dwarves leapt atop Jordan. Manacles snapped around her wrists and ankles, but she kept fighting to reach the building.

They dragged her past what remained of the three centaur. Sinesh Ena'Donishe struggled away from pooling blood and the mutilated bodies that had shielded him from the worst of her assault. The half burnt centaur glowered at her through its one good eye. He gurgled a curse she couldn't understand. His chest heaved and fell still.

"No!" Velith'Seravin raised his hoof to strike. He bellowed. Burning flesh filled every nostril. He seized his glowing chest.

Do or die. Mason acted.

EPILOGUE

Silent Revenge

They dragged Drake into some sort of oil field. Metal birds bobbed heads up and down, pumping oil from the depths. Huge modified tanks dotted the scrub, all guarded, but chanting centaur surrounded one. Runes glowed along its outside and metal shook beneath an onslaught of sound.

A door opened in its side, reverberating sound exploding in volume. A centaur yearling exited the tank with a food tray. Within the opening, he glimpsed Mauve, strung up by arms and legs. She resembled a skeleton. Limp, once-lustrous hair curtained her face. As if she felt his regard, she raised her eyes to meet his. Hell blazed in the sunken sockets just waiting to be unleashed.

Drake thought fast. He was too broken to fight. The Dragon-steel restraints kept him from shapeshifting to heal his wounds, but Mauve was a power like Jedediah. Using magic to help her would heat his bonds, melt the coating and subject him to unendurable pain.

But provide her a single chance and every centaur here burns.

Drake drew his power. The manacles, fetters and collar heated almost at once. He focused against the pain, drew on his element and sucked all the air from the closing tank.

A moment before agony blinded him, he could've sworn he saw the corner of Mauve's lip curl.

"We warned you against trying to escape." Hynar Ah'Klach kicked him. The impact worsened the already unrelenting pain. "We were going to take you out of those before we caged you, but I guess now we won't."

Another centaur opened a huge tank, muscling Drake onto a raised platform. "We're a little full up right now. I hope your new roommate isn't hungry enough to eat you."

They threw him off the platform. Broken bones and burning flesh slammed into the tank's bottom far below. Something moved in the shadows. Soft blue-silver eyes slid into view, surrounded by oil-fouled silvery scales.

Drake's expression mimicked Mauve's. *You're all going to die.*

THE STORY CONTINUES...

Keep reading for a sneak peek from
Bittergate 3:
Forge of War

Thank you for reading *The Wizard's Bane.*

Word of mouth recommendations and book reviews are insanely helpful, not just to other readers, but to an author's success. More-over, we use these reviews to know what *you* want to read more of. Please consider leaving a short, honest review—nothing special required, just a sentence or two about how you felt about this book. I can't thank you enough.

If you loved this story and would like to stay up to date on the latest book releases, promotions, giveaways, and a free story, please be sure to become a member of the Delirious Scribbles Readers Group. [Your email address will never be shared, and you can opt out at any time.]

Begin your journey, just scan this image with your phone camera!

Keep reading for a sneak peak....

GRAVEYARD OF THE AGES

Sound bombarded Mauve in deafening pulses that threatened to make her stomach disgorge what little of the foul gruel she'd barely managed to swallow. The yearling centaur gave up feeding Mauve as a bad job or maybe some kind of punishment to vent his misguided anger. He pushed through the sphere of life magic walling Mauve away from her greatest ally: Death.

Velith'Seravin—leader of the so-called Wizard's Bane tribe—thought himself clever. He'd bragged often of the genius behind his shaman cutting her off with a life magic barrier.

What an idiot.

As a necromancer, she had an affinity for death magic, but only a clod-headed fool thought life and death magic were enemies.

They're old friends constantly walking one with the other.

The sound was the only reason she hadn't ripped the life from his body and made him her thrall. The constant bombardment made concentration impossible. Extended sleep deprivation distanced her further from the ready supply of life magic and the elemental sources kindred to her talents.

She let herself hang from her chains, pain and agony in her limbs long numb. Once honey brown locks hung limp and dirty, shielding her from hopeful glimpses of the outside world.

Where are you, Jedediah? Did they kill my precious Kane before he reached you? She snorted. *Precious might be a bit much, starvation must be getting to me. Maybe I'll saddle Jedediah with him for a decade as payback for making me wait. It'll be good for the boy to learn other aspects of magic.*

Sunlight overwhelmed the small electric lights, making thinner clumps of hair glow. Little hairs too long unshaven rose along her skin. She raised her chin, *knowing* someone was looking straight at her.

Bruises and bones poking out firm muscles colored the handsome young man dressed only in chains. His eyes met hers, filled with anger, will and hope. *The sight of me brings him hope?*

He screwed up his expression. Smoke plumed off his chains, an odd skin sloughing off the metal. Pain wracked his body as glowing metal burned him. *What are you doing, boy?*

Wind whipped around her in a sudden rush for the door. She gasped a moment before the last of it left her in airless silence. A corner of her mouth curled upward.

I don't know who you are, boy, but you'll have my thanks when all is done.

Mauve drew in a metaphysical breath, sucking the life energy caging her into her body. The emaciated state of her muscles couldn't be fully restored with life energy alone, but it was a start. She drew more energy, earth and death, air and life—the elements of a necromancer.

Velith'Seravin had left her with plenty of time to plan. She knew that if an opportunity to free herself arose, she needed to be ready in advance.

Mauve stretched her power downward into the black sludge filling half the tank. Oil. Black Gold. The remains of dinosaurs left under pressure for years...dead dinosaurs.

Serve me, my pretties...

Look for more great books like these at a book reailer near
you and learn more at www.deliriousscribbles.com

ACKNOWLEDGMENTS

Wow. We survived another Bittergate adventure. Thank you for joining me on this journey. It was dark and heart wrenching—for me at least—and filled with surprises. It left a lot up in the air. I hope you enjoyed The Wizard's Bane anyway. I only feel a little guilty about this ending. It isn't as if we won't suffer together between now and when I write the next one. What little I know about Bittergate 3 guarantees it's going to be a doozy.

This one had a very sparse team, though I know they worked hard to keep me and the story on the straight and narrow. My proofreaders, editors, fellow writers—and especially my readers— all help me strive for the best stories I can offer you. I love them for it, and you for reading them.

Special thanks go out to Scott R. Jason, Justin, Bryan, Trint and of course B, B, & J. Also thanks to Sarah's little Joslyn for bringing a some pixyish giggling into my world—hers, not mine. I don't giggle.

Drake and Jordan, wow, guys, just wow. Glad to have you back Jedediah, you had me worried there a while. Mason…well, I hope you've got some trick up your sleeves boy. I'll see you all in a few months once Scion 3 is done.

ABOUT THE AUTHOR

Photo credit: Jim Cawthorne

Michael J. Allen is a star-lord, goofball, and USA Today bestselling author of character-driven, multi-layer, full-spectrum science fiction and fantasy novels - pretty much whatever madness sprouts from his head... (Learn more at www.deliriousscribbles.com)

LET'S CONNECT

I love chatting with my readers, and hope you'll join my reader groups. If you'd rather stay up to date without joining in on the fun, there are plenty of ways to follow along.

— MICHAEL J ALLEN

READER GROUPS:

Discord : https://discord.gg/WeM4bwq
Facebook: https://www.facebook.com/groups/dsreaders
MeWe: https://www.mewe.com/join/dsreaders

FOLLOW THE SCRIBBLER:

www.deliriousscribbles.com

amazon.com/-/e/B0096GEILG
bookbub.com/authors/michael-j-allen
facebook.com/deliriousscribbler
goodreads.com/deliriousscribbler
instagram.com/thedscribbler
x.com/Thedscribbler